THE DARKEST SEASON

by Bruce T. Jones

ISBN 978-1-63393-398-9

Published by

The Twisted Pen

310 30th Street

Virginia Beach, VA 23451

TwistedPenPub@gmail.com

In association with

köehlerstudios™

This book is dedicated to the dreamers,
who aspire and create,
those who suffer and battle afflictions every day
and refuse to surrender, and my loyal fans,
steadfast friends, and loving family.

You continue to inspire me beyond measure.

The Darkest Season

Bruce T. Jones

CHAPTER ONE

ALL MEN LIVE for the hunt. It's instinctive, embedded in their DNA. For Alex Tepes, the hunt was unquenchable. It was the very reason he journeyed to the desolate highlands of Cape Breton, Nova Scotia.

The game was large and dangerous for the unskilled, the climate and terrain intense. When the hunt was done, another began. In the quaint villages that speckle the coast, Alex sought the one woman that would surpass all expectations. The elusive traits of the perfect partner: confidant, friend, playmate, and lover.

Preferring isolated villages and towns to the metropolises, Alex watched, listened, and waited. Exposure to big city life can sour any person's disposition, creating cynics, skeptics, and general pessimism. After decades, he discovered most women's desires didn't coincide with his own. Their aspirations for the material world exceeded the life he'd chosen. *Who could ever be satisfied by the simplicity of his life in Saint Andrews?* he had often thought.

Throughout his forty years, Alex had witnessed the pitfalls of the seven deadly sins. His solution to avoid it was simple: seek out nothing and usually nothing will find you. Living in a small town removed temptation—but not all. Alex's biological yearnings were grinding down his philosophical zeal to the point of collapse. A senseless night of unadulterated sex with a tavern wench in Ingonish proved to be the exclamation point to a rather shallow, unfulfilling week away from home.

Returning home to New Brunswick offered no comfort. Having lived in Saint Andrews for nearly ten years he was all too familiar with the local fare, outside of a promising tourist or two. Knowing if there were to be any salvation to his abysmal blues, a road trip south was in order. It would only take a month or so back in the uncivilized world to once again send him racing for the serenity of his Canadian solitude.

Alex stared at the blank screen of his laptop; for far too long it had blankly stared back. The poetry that once flowed from his mind like a ravaging tide had receded. Inspiration would have to be rekindled through a vagabond expedition. But where?

Alex tapped Google Maps. *Yes, the coastal roads, perhaps all the way to Miami,* he thought with a grin. The trip promised numerous tacky beach communities, but it also offered smaller coastal towns such as Portsmouth, New Hampshire and Pawley's Island, South Carolina.

Looking over the route, Alex's sense of adventure erupted into a frantic assembly of the required travel elements. He packed a few pair of denims, mostly white dress shirts, and one-shoe-fits-all-occasions crocodile loafers. In less time than it took to choose a route, he was headed for the door.

The Tepes Motor Vultur purred to life, its 791-horsepower engine yearning for the open road. The weather had been dry and the roads were mostly clear. The challenge would be spotting black ice and eluding the ever-present highway patrol. The Vultur was manufactured with the latter precisely in mind.

Throwing his bag in the trunk, he marveled at the beauty of the high-gloss carbon fiber finish compared to that of his twenty-six-year-old rusted red Dodge pickup. The car had been a family gift, an indulgence Alex would have never considered. Truly, the Dodge was his heart and soul. Its four-wheel drive was better suited for a mid-winter trip, but with over 200,000 miles already clocked, a 5,000-mile road trip was not in his or the truck's best interest.

That being said, the Vultur was made for the hunt—attacking the asphalt, passing cars like they were slalom gates, and avoiding moose, elk, and whatever else dare cross the frozen pavement.

Undoubtedly this missile turned heads with every car it passed, but that had nothing to do with Alex's begrudging love for this machine. Slipping into the cockpit, the car embraced the driver, its intuition one with its pilot. The designers at Tepes Motor Works must have possessed some magical power, for no other sports car on the planet could connect with the driver's heart like this beast.

For Alex, night was the only time to drive. On these roads, traffic was practically non-existent. Running at speeds up to 170 mph, the Vultur gripped the road like a runaway rollercoaster, shredding US1 as if it were a turbo-charged wood chipper. It was just outside Bath, Maine when Alex had his first encounter with a rookie trooper with something to prove.

Alex slowed to a 75 mph pace, knowing in the next quarter mile the trooper's vapor lock would detect the Vultur's speed. He killed the headlights, running solely by the illumination of the three-quarter moon. One hundred yards away, the trooper's blue flashing lights glared to life. Alex checked up on the brakes, giving the trooper a false hope of easy submission. It wasn't until Alex was practically beside the trooper that he yanked the gearshift into second and exploded up the highway. The hunt was on, the roles reversed, and Alex loved every testosterone-fueled orgasmic second.

Toying with the trooper briefly, Alex allowed him to close the distance. As he neared, the Vultur's very illegal auto-kill detector alerted Alex of the trooper's failed efforts to electronically stall his engine. Failing to power down Alex's car, the trooper frantically attempted to close the gap once more. When he was almost in range for tire darts, Alex downshifted and nailed the accelerator. By the time the trooper reacted, the Vultur was in fourth gear at 200 mph; a fading memory of a summons he would never write. Alex knew, in a weakened moment of shame, the trooper would resort to the radio for backup. At that hour, in this neck of the woods, most of his backup would be in bed. Not being one for playing the odds, especially on his first night out, Alex bailed off the highway at the New Meadows River exit and headed south.

Alex had intended to make it to Portsmouth, New Hampshire on the first leg of his journey. However, the rural routes forced Alex to zigzag across Maine's narrow back roads until he was south of Brunswick. This was an inconvenience, but well worth the price to pay, even if only for fifteen seconds of ball-busting fun.

It was somewhere on the darkened, twisted roads, where the frozen fields blazed white by the light of the moon, that Alex realized he had been stolen away much too long. It was in these solitary miles where the purr of the Vultur and the rushing winds were the only sounds that he began to think of his parents and the amazing love they had shared.

Alex realized his emotional void had widened. He knew an exceptional woman would help fill that hole in his life, a woman who would challenge his intellect, push his physical boundaries, and basically rock the foundations of his existence. The only problem: from the day he was old enough to begin refining his desires, he had yet to find her.

CHAPTER TWO

THE WARM TRADE winds blew steadily from the distant Caribbean, up the slopes of the densely forested mountains. A thousand feet below the summit, a campfire flickered among the trees, creating shadows of a mystical dance. On a stony cliff, Ştefan stood vigil, a hundred feet above the commotion, hidden deep in the heart of the John Crow Mountains. Proudly, he watched in silence, observing his personally chosen followers gathered below in a euphoric celebration.

Fresh blood—human blood—was on the menu tonight. Too long had they abstained from the vital substance that gave life and strength to his race. He had raised each man from the throws of death and, guided by his rules, they remained a secret cult. Regulations were laid down to maintain their growing numbers in the shadows of the mountains, mandates to conceal the creation of an invincible army.

He purposely trained them to survive for long stretches without blood, knowing the day would come when it might not be readily available. For weeks at a time his army, now 162 strong, had survived on small animals' blood, or none at all. The instinct to kill and feed was strong amongst Ştefan's race. This was a test of strength, endurance, and discipline. The underlying beauty of this vast land was an endless supply of peasants, whose random disappearances would scarcely raise an eyebrow. Tonight, he too would feed, but not just on any ordinary victim. Ştefan's taste was more refined. He would travel to Kingston and find himself a beautiful young black girl. The seduction would be short lived and the sex mutually satisfying. And then the *coup de grâce*; Ştefan would drain every last drop of blood from her body. The vivid images began to stir an erection.

"Ştefan, it is almost time," Morgan called, approaching from the trail below.

"They are yours tonight, Morgan. I believe a trip into Kingston is in order for me."

"Not feeling in the mood to share?"

Ştefan smiled slyly, unable to conceal his dishonest intentions. "No. I believe it may be time for me to find another new recruit."

Morgan knew the drill, but felt compelled to ask. "Then I should come with you?"

"No, Morgan. It is time for you to achieve a position of higher authority. I made you first, but *they* all consider you their equal." Ştefan fanned his hand in the direction of the fires below. "They must learn to follow someone other than me, should something ever happen."

"If you honestly fear something might happen, then it would be wise to stop these trips into Kingston, especially alone. Take me with you."

Ştefan turned aside, as if to embrace the gust of wind that suddenly arrived. His long blonde hair answered the call, flowing like a great stallion's mane.

"The time has come to create proper rank and order. The day will soon be upon us, the battle for all ages. Not all of us will survive. And if there is no rank and order, our cause will fail along with my demise. If we fail, you may be certain of this, our race will be driven into the depths of extinction."

"Wasn't that your father's—"

"Don't speak of him or my family," Ştefan interrupted sharply. "Although they have proven to be a great disappointment, they are my family. Once we have won absolute power, they will *finally* understand the necessity of my grand designs."

Morgan recoiled. "We are so many. How will you decide who is to lead?"

"You already know those amongst your brethren cut out for leadership, and those to follow. Sadly, there are a few who must be destroyed. Their lack of discipline has already threatened our security, and they will do so again if given the opportunity."

"I was curious as to when you were going to address their insolence."

"Everything I have done, and *will* do, is according to a plan. Timing is a key component. Our growth as an army was the first step. *Our* future as leaders of the new era will follow, all in due time."

Ştefan peered at Morgan sternly. "I have changed my mind. Let's go down to the ceremony together. But tonight I will observe, and at my command, you will take charge of the ceremony."

Morgan's expression of pride could not be restrained. "Thank you, Ştefan, I will not let you down."

"Come then. Let's go down to the basin and feast on the flesh of these weak mortals."

"Ştefan, I have always wanted to ask, and if you truly wish me to be a leader then I think there are some details I believe you should share. What happens if a vampire consumes too much blood? If he were to drain the blood of a human to the thralls of death?"

Ştefan knew the answer; he had done so 162 times. But he was unsure if the time was right to share his knowledge. His vampires were still infants by immortal standards. It was counterintuitive to all of his teachings to share the ecstatic bliss of taking another's life. Ştefan grabbed Morgan's shoulder and turned him.

"You must not repeat this, not yet. A time will arrive, very soon, when many will know the experience."

Ştefan sighed, his steely gray eyes briefly tracking a passing bat. "It is a pure orgasmic bliss, intoxicating to the point of temporary madness. Once we are miles from Jamaica, I will instruct the brethren. But it must never happen on this island. An army this size could kill half the population in a month. Our secrecy is maintained by control of information. Because of that, there is not one among us who has yet suffered the unquenchable thirst."

After a quiet and reflective trek down the mountain, Ştefan and Morgan approached the massive assembly gathered by the campfire. Working his way through his followers, Ştefan studied the ten victims, bound to stakes, just outside the glow of the crackling fire. Stripped of their clothing, most of the women appeared to be around age thirty. The majority appeared to be native, although two were clearly Caucasian. One was a peasant, the other most likely European, young and beautiful. Ştefan approached Thomas, who flanked the intended sacrifices.

"This one," he said pointing to the European woman. "Where did she come from?"

"The albino?" Thomas replied. "I think Tyrell and Jim found her outside of Manchester, in a village."

"Look at her. She is no albino! If she was in a village she is some type of missionary."

Lacking any resistance, Ştefan turned her cheek forcefully. He pried her mouth open and looked inside. "This is not some random islander," he snapped. "Have Tyrell and Jim take her back before the elixir wears off."

"They'll miss the feast," Morgan objected.

"As they should. If this is some college student her people, and the local law, will be combing the entire island. I haven't invested the last two years of my life to have two buffoons screw up everything."

"I'll find them now," Thomas snapped respectfully.

Ştefan grabbed Morgan by the elbow. "Make sure Tyrell understands how crucial it is she is returned unharmed and unaware."

Morgan nodded. "Of course, Ştefan."

Ştefan began untying the girl as several of his brethren looked on with great curiosity. One of Ştefan's followers, an oversized, chiseled, black-skinned native, the one known as Apollo, watched bewildered before he began to approach. Because of his size and strength, Apollo was considered the most dangerous of Ştefan's acolytes. If there were to be one who would ever challenge Ştefan, it was whispered Apollo would be the man.

"Wut are ya doin,' brotha?"

"This woman is no commoner. She must be returned," Ştefan growled, annoyed with his troops reckless selection.

"Return, mon? There won' be enough for da feast." Apollo crossed his arms in a defiant manner.

"We will have to make do, *mon*. Apollo, you *do* understand why we have the laws I set down?"

"Yea, mon. But it like you don' wan' us to share in no pretty lit'l white girls."

"Trust me, Apollo. You find a pretty little white girl that can disappear without half the island searching for her, and I will let you stand first in line. Understand?"

Apollo shook his head and walked away without a reply. Ştefan knew that one day he might have to harshly deal with Apollo, but for now, he needed him to help control his ever-growing population of vampires. He looked back over his shoulder and observed his clan had begun to close in. He raised his hand and signaled for them to cease their advance.

Moving down the line of nine women, he breathed in the scent of each one deeply. All were barely conscious of the fate about to befall them. Ştefan returned to the one possessing the most beauty. He whispered into her ear, "Wake up, my dear."

Her emerald eyes rolled open, and she gazed upon the hungry mob, yet no fear was apparent. Her light-brown skin was flawlessly smooth, like a marble Madonna. As Ştefan inspected the details of her face, he allowed his lips to caress the flesh of her neck. "Do you know who we are," he asked softly.

"Yes."

"Do you know our purpose for you?"

"Yes."

"And do you give yourself freely?" Ştefan watched as her glistening full lips parted.

"Yes."

Ştefan turned to the assembly. "Tonight, brothers, we begin preparations for our journey. In giving their lives for our great cause, these women will live on beyond tonight through our deeds and accomplishments. As their blood courses through your veins, you must honor their sacrifice. As their spirit departs, your body will grow strong, nurtured by their ultimate gift. It is through this process we receive our power and our eternal life. It is through this gift we will come to conquer the world."

Cheers erupted. Ştefan motioned for Morgan to come forward. "See that you drink of this girl last when the others are gone. Bring her into our family. Tonight, it is time for you to create."

"But a *woman*?" Morgan was genuinely surprised. Ştefan had only taken men into his army thus far.

"The time may come when we will need a woman to help serve our cause. It is best to create her now, and make certain of her training before we embark for Europe. Tonight belongs to you, my friend."

Ştefan turned and headed back up the path that led to the cliff. His appetite for the kill no longer beckoned him to Kingston. Upon returning to the stone ledge, he set his gaze toward the distant ocean and far beyond to Romania. The breeze stiffened, its voice played amongst the leaves of the trees, intertwined with the sounds of the feast that echoed up the ravine from below.

His vision of a new world order would soon be realized. His army was concise and lethal, yet trained to refrain from the very nature of the curse that created fear in the mortal race. Armed with the knowledge of his predecessor's failures, Ştefan was poised to conquer a nation and, ultimately, the world.

CHAPTER THREE

"FORTY YEARS, COUNT Tepes. Why on earth did it take you that long to bring me here?" Samantha dramatized, feigning displeasure.

"First off, after the convent fiasco, it has taken me forty years to tolerate French accents." Nicholas returned his attention to the book in his hands.

"Bullshit, you've never had issues with Gabby, Angelique, or Sabine's accents."

"Well, you never did ask me to bring you here until now, did you? Secondly, any time you wanted, this could have been a girl's trip," Nicholas huffed. "Besides, I have never had a burning desire to return. I'm sure somewhere in a stack of dust-covered warrants there is one with my name on it. I was a bad boy in France back in my CIA days."

"Of that there is no doubt," Samantha scoffed, before taking a sip of her wine. "You know," Sam said as she swirled the glass of chardonnay, "it's a shame I will never know the true taste of this wine, or at least what it would have tasted like as a human."

"A true curse." Nicholas sighed as he closed the book with a thump. Placing it heavily on the table, he knew reading time was over. "I did warn you."

"And I would be seventy-five, all wrinkled, and completely

unable to do the things we just did in our bedroom." Concealed by the white linen tablecloth, Samantha's hand moved to his thigh.

Nicholas smiled. "Touché, although your sister looks pretty damn good for her age."

Samantha cut a suspicious glare at her husband. "You always did have a thing for Dee."

"She was always my back-up plan. You know, if things didn't go right for us."

Samantha pulled her hand away quickly, propped them both under her chin, and smiled sweetly. "Well, Nick, do you think things have gone well for us?"

"Lord, Sam, it has only been forty years. Ask me in another century or so."

Samantha and Nicholas chuckled at his joke, and then Sam slipped into a solemn mood. "I miss Mom and Dad. And I worry about Dee, all alone."

Nicholas reflected on his departed best friend. If it had not been for Phillip, Dee's late husband, Samantha would have never come into his life—and most certainly he would not be a vampire, and most likely would have died years ago.

"It is a shame Phillip had to die so young. But they made their decision. You know I would have done it for them, if they wanted it."

Samantha looked at the passing traffic from their roadside table. Blindly she reached for her glass and took another sip. "I miss getting drunk and suntanned."

"I miss your suntan too." Nicholas's hand slid under the tablecloth until he found Samantha's leg. He smiled devilishly. "But I must admit, outside of the tan, your legs don't look bad for seventy five."

Samantha's body tensed as she objected in her well-rehearsed French dialect. "Count Tepes, if you continue to touch me in such an inappropriate manner I shall be forced to summon the gendarmerie."

"You mean like this?" Nicholas slid his hand directly between Samantha's legs. She closed her eyes and groaned softly. "Too bad that dress I just purchased is still in the bag." As Samantha's head rolled back, Nichols caught the scent of her arousal.

"Count, if you do not stop, we will have to go back to the hotel."

Nicholas was now on a mission. It was dark and the tablecloth sufficiently concealed his intentions. As his caresses intensified, Samantha parted her legs. With fingers fast and nimble, he unfastened her jeans and worked the zipper down. Samantha looked at Nicholas with dreamy eyes. "Are you seriously going to do this right here?"

Nicholas plunged his fingers deep inside Samantha's pants. "Does that answer your question?"

"God," Samantha purred. "I love being a vampire."

"We should eat," Nicholas suggested as they strolled down Rue Lord Byron. "I can tell you are in need."

"I wouldn't have been, if you had kept your hands to yourself." Samantha prodded Nicholas for his hand as she studied the Parisian architecture on the car-lined, narrow street. "I know there's so much more to see in Paris, but right now I miss New Orleans. Not that I'm ready to go back, I just miss our neighborhood and the familiarity of our home."

"Well this street is certainly not the best Paris has to offer," Nicholas explained. They walked another block in silence, studying the unique features of every building, each pointing out the intricacies that the buildings possessed before Nicholas returned to the previous subject. "If we find a couple, we could seduce them back to our hotel. Then there would be more than enough for the both of us."

"Are you feeling the need to bond with our dinner again? You know I have never particularly cared to mingle with our victims before I sink my teeth into their necks. The small talk is so superficial. 'Oh I love your hair, and wherever did you get those cute shoes, and oh, by the way, I hope you don't mind if I to drink two pints of your blood. I am so sorry about the teeth marks I will leave behind.'"

Nicholas smiled at the notion. "I don't know. It seems as though over time I have begun to appreciate the interactions with the humans who provide our sustenance."

"I don't think your father would agree."

"You are right about that. He would still have us drinking the blood of goats and pigs. But I find French blood exquisite, and as we are in France, it would be such a shame not to indulge, at least once. Besides, how long did we abstain? Twelve years of drinking the blood from animals and donor bags. You know how I detest that tainted plastic taste. And what salvation did all of that misery bring us?"

"Darling, you know it's also about preserving secrecy. Sooner or later, somebody will discover our handiwork on a person, and then where would we be?"

"Twenty-eight years. Not one red flag reported," Nicholas boasted. "And if it ever happens, it would be such an isolated incident that nobody would suspect that a pair of sinister vampires were roaming the streets of their community."

Samantha stopped in her tracks and let go of Nicholas's hand. She waited for him to turn around and return to her. With her hands on her hips, she quipped, "Did you just call me a sinister vampire?"

Nicholas squirmed. "No."

"That's funny. It sure sounded like you did." Samantha extended her index finger and jabbed it into his chest. "Everything your father has achieved has been accomplished by following the strictest of disciplines, something you used to understand. If the day should arrive that our secret is discovered, *everything* could be ruined. And I *think* you are smart enough to realize how much is actually at stake."

"So what you are saying is that you are willing to go back to blood bags and furry creatures?"

"No, I *am not*." Samantha mocked Nicholas's habitual lack of contractions, which was particularly irritating during his occasional bouts of stubbornness. "But I think that cavalier attitude you wear, like a coat of honor, needs to be checked at the door. When *you* convinced me to drink—you called it *blood off the tap*. It was never the blood of socialites. Now it can't be anything but."

"Their blood tastes better," Nicholas insisted.

"So this selfish indulgence, what if our sons were to do the same and foolishly get discovered and then be executed? You'd be okay with it because *it* tastes better?"

"Sam—"

"Don't *Sam* me. I've never liked this hypocritical standard. It's not the way of our family. I know you feel as though you've lived a full lifetime already, but I would like us to share another hundred years, or more. Maybe it's time we re-examine our feeding habits."

"You know we are careful, Sam. And all this other bullshit about salvation and redemption? I don't buy in, not anymore. We've had this discussion—more than once."

Samantha dropped her hands and took up Nicholas's. "I know, baby, but it just seems like an unnecessary risk. It's like you're doing this to replace the thrills of the life you left behind."

Nicholas cracked a smile. "Listen to you, *baby*. The years in

New Orleans have certainly rubbed off on your dialect." Nicholas stiffened as Samantha cut a glare. "Okay, I get it. I do not necessarily agree, but your viewpoint has some merit."

"*Viewpoint? Merit?*"

"Alright, I get it. You are probably onto something."

"*Probably?*"

"Okay, you win. But how about a compromise?" Nicholas searched Samantha's eyes for an opening. "Blood from a latex bag is worst than diet sodas. You know it is."

Samantha rolled her eyes. "A compromise, just for tonight. No couples, no personal interactions, and rest assured, we are not going spend half the night looking for that perfect meal. We are going to feed and then leave."

"Deal!" Nicholas laughed. "Perhaps we could find a drive-through serving Frenchies." He grabbed Samantha's hand and tugged playfully. "Come on, *baby*, all of this negotiating has left me famished."

CHAPTER FOUR

ALEX WAS DRIVING one of only seven Vulturs in the country. If caught, it was not a stretch to assume he would be judged guilty by mere association. Simply owning the same car as last night's *perpetrator of recklessness* was a sure bet to get him detained. Not wanting to spoil the trip before it had a chance to get started, he decided to avoid the interstates completely.

Creeping along at the posted speed limits down the coastal roads, Alex began to regret his smart-ass antics. After three nights on the road, he had only gone as far south as Cape May, New Jersey, a full day behind schedule. Making reservations from Internet searches while on the road, Alex booked a room at a rather large Victorian cottage just off the beach, the Angel of the Sea. Standing in front of the cottage, he marveled at the intricate latticework, high pitch rooflines with dormers, and all of its spindle railing. Compared to the simplistic lines of his home, the two-hundred-year-old inn's construction and maintenance boggled his mind.

A rather attractive brunette answered the bell—Alex fancied her shoulder-length, curled-like-spiraled-pasta, and burnt-sienna hair and especially the way she filled out her skinny jeans. Her flirtatious smile emblazoned her average lips and abnormally pale face. Alex's large chestnut eyes swelled. A voice in his head whispered, *Not now.*

The next evening, after crossing the Delaware Bay, Alex

zipped past Rehoboth Beach, heading south on US 1. His thoughts occasionally drifted to the night clerk in Cape May. Ninety-eight percent of his brain had regrets about what could have been.

Cruising at a faster pace down the ocean highway, he felt relatively safe from the BOLO that was most likely issued in Maine. No longer desiring to taunt local law enforcement, he cruised down the Eastern Shore at more moderate speeds and eventually crossed the Chesapeake Bay Bridge into Virginia Beach.

As sunrise loomed several hours away, Alex once again opted for a historical hotel. The Cavalier was perched on top of a hill, rising majestically above all its crammed surroundings. He discovered the hotel possessed some spiritual aura, conversations and memories of life and love long forgotten, drifting aimlessly down the narrow halls. The Grand Old Lady had been refurbished some thirty-five years ago, and unlike The Angel of the Sea in Cape May, some of her original charm had been extinguished by the modern-day makeover.

Alex checked into his room and then crossed the street to walk on the beach. The December night air had a refreshing bite to it, so what was to be a quick stroll turned into a full night of overdue reflection. After several years in New Brunswick, Alex discovered his love for the frigid temperatures over the melting pot of his Louisiana roots. He liked how the cold put a blush on a woman's cheeks and nose and, especially, her lips. How he loved kissing those lips, so cold, only to discover the warmth of her inviting mouth.

Stirring just before dusk, his thoughts turned to Charleston. Back in his car, and eager to resume his journey, he grumbled at the excessive number of stoplights. Catching yet another cursed light, Alex spotted a Java Hut and decided a strong cup of espresso was in order. Caffeine, like alcohol, offered virtually none of the human benefits, but Alex did enjoy the savory flavor. Once inside, he perused the patrons for that unique face, ones whose eyes begged for conversation and, so often, a source of inspiration. Finding none, he ordered a Black Eye and moved to the end of the walnut counter and awaited delivery.

As the door of fate blew open, complimented by a blustery chill, Alex spied the object of his desire. Her wavy, dark-brown hair spiraled down to her shoulder blades. Her skin was pale, as though it had never felt the warmth of summer, and the chill had flushed her sharply defined cheekbones. Her gentle dark eyes caught Alex's intent as they connected. She smiled that familiar smile of, *"Do I know you?"*

Alex's heart skipped as her ruby lips parted. She turned her head down shyly and suppressed a smile. The sapphire-blue knit dress and boots contoured her curves so completely. Her shape reminded Alex of the curves of the Cabot Trail. And oh, how he loved to drive that road.

She peeked again to find him transfixed, then quickly turned back to the baristas. Alex *knew*. If this encounter was forsaken, ill consequences awaited. *But for who*? He moved in quickly before the moment faded. "Excuse me. Will you allow me the privilege of buying your drink?"

As she looked up, it was evident some force of awkwardness played upon her.

Her rosy blush quickly covered her face. "Do I know you?"

"No, not yet." Alex's smile was gentle, his tone softer than usual.

"Then, no thank you." She ordered her drink and paid. Traveling to the end of the counter to await her beverage, she purposely avoided any further eye contact.

"Alex," the barista called.

As Alex collected his drink, he intentionally turned into her. Again, she turned her face nervously away. "I'm sorry if I'm making you feel uncomfortable, it's not my intent."

"It's alright," she said without looking up.

Alex sat his cup on an open table and returned to her. "I know you must get hit on all the time, but I'd really appreciate it if you would join me, for just a few minutes."

Turning her face slowly, their eyes met. "I'm on my way to meet my fiancé."

"Five minutes, it's just a cup of coffee."

She checked her watch. "Five minutes, that's all."

Alex couldn't help but smile. "Five minutes could change your life." The smile she returned was guarded. *But at least she smiled,* Alex thought. "You know, actually, there's no way you could know this, but *this* almost never happened."

"You don't know how right you are."

"My name is Brian Alexander, but everyone calls me Alex. And you are?"

"Sarah," she replied cautiously.

"Is the clock running already?" Alex checked his watch. Sarah nodded her head. "Who are you?" he asked.

"I already told you."

"No, not your name, but *who* are you?"

"Like, what do I do?"

"Yes, what do you do? What do you like? What makes Sarah wake up smiling in the morning?"

Sarah looked at her watch. "There's only four minutes left. Are you sure you want to waste it on that?"

"Absolutely."

Sarah rolled her eyes skyward and sighed. *If he weren't so damnably cute.* "I graduate in the spring, and I'm going to be a biologist. I want to work in medical research. I love to dance and workout."

Sarah glanced up at the ceiling as if more answers were written above. "Let's see. I'm an only child. My dad is General Phillips, whom you might have heard of. Life growing up was rather . . . difficult. My mom died when I was four, and dad was rather protective as you might imagine." She paused again, perhaps to review her checklist. "I like to go out, but I'm not much of a party girl. I like to people watch, like now, watching a guy try to pick up a girl."

Alex smiled. "How am I doing?"

"So far, your time's almost up."

Alex studied her relaxing expression. For the first time she did not look away. "Are you happy?"

Without an immediate reply, he knew something was amiss. Not wanting to leave her hanging in discomfort for too long, Alex changed the subject. "You said you were engaged?"

"Kind of. More like we're talking about it. Brad is studying for the bar exam. Once he passes and I graduate we will probably set a date."

Alex noticed in her descriptive analysis she was lacking any visual or audible cues of bliss. "And you've got a date tonight with him?"

"Yes, we're meeting downtown."

"Usually, this is where people say *I don't mean to pry*, when in fact they do. Why isn't he picking you up?"

Sarah's eyes trolled to the parking lot outside the frosty window. "He's with his friends. I usually meet him later."

"Usually? Whose idea was that? If you were my fiancé, or just a first date, I'd be *usually* picking you up all the time. I already don't like Bradley."

An odd expression transformed Sarah's radiant face, which

prompted Alex to repeat his question. "Are you happy, Sarah?"

She looked in his eyes and could not hide the truth. "Are you?"

It was Alex's turn on the hot seat. "I live most of my days in isolation, by choice. *I* am a bitter disappointment to my family. All of their aspirations for my life, I had no desire to fulfill. I have not seen them in years, which is probably a good thing. I've never been married, not even close, probably because of my . . . let's just call it my complex personality." Alex sipped his coffee. "So all things considered, I'd say yes. I am happy."

Sarah studied his rugged, but very attractive, physique. "No serious girlfriend? Outside of being some kind of sociopath, your story doesn't strike me as that of a happy guy."

"I've got a great house, I hike, sail, bicycle, eat whatever and whenever I want, and mingle with friends when the urge strikes."

"Like now?"

"No. Nothing like now. This is different."

Sarah began to spiral her hair nervously as she contemplated where her next question might lead. "Do I dare ask *how* this is different?"

Alex surveyed the cafe briefly before thumbing in the direction of two attractive women. "If it were either one of them, I'd have been out the door five minutes ago and on my way south."

"That quickly? I'm surprised, or maybe honored. Where are you going in such a hurry?"

For having just met a complete stranger, her ease of conversation surprised him. From a near-hostile beginning, she settled in quickly and was at ease with personal issues. "I'm headed south along the coast, eventually all the way to Florida."

"Just passing through?"

"Yes, something like that." Alex was trying his best to be coy.

"Then it would appear that we were doomed from the beginning."

"I *wouldn't* go that far. Sooner or later I'll have to head back north. I'm sure, given even the slightest motivation, you might find me in your neighborhood again."

"And what motivation would it take?"

Alex sat quiet for a few seconds thinking about his father's dire warning years ago, *One day this could happen to you.* He was referring to his love-at-first-sight encounter with Alex's stepmother, Samantha. Alex snapped back to the present.

Realizing Sarah had yet to answer his pivotal question, Alex pressed, "I'll ask you again, are you happy?"

"No," Sarah replied softly as she shook her head, her eyes becoming glassy. Sarah looked at her watch in a near panic. "It's been *ten* minutes. I have to go." Catching her balance with the table, she looked to the safety of the parking lot. "Thank you."

Rising with her, Alex placed his hand on top of hers. "I'll walk you out."

"No, please." Snatching her hand away, Sarah darted for the door, absentmindedly leaving her purse behind.

Alex scooped it up and followed in hot pursuit. Sarah was out the door of the cafe before he could stop her. "Sarah, your purse," Alex called as he chased her out. From behind, he watched her hand swipe across her cheek. She sniffled and shrugged her shoulders before she turned. Her expression nearly knocked the wind from Alex. "You might want this," he said gently.

"Thank you." No longer wanting to look into his eyes, she held out her hand but looked over his shoulder at the cars passing by.

"I'm sorry," Alex said. "I didn't mean to upset you." As Sarah attempted to retrieve her purse, Alex's grip held fast.

Sniffing back a tear, she replied, "It's alright."

"One last thing," Alex said before releasing his grip on her purse. "Before all life and love fades into a distant memory, kiss me."

"I can't, I am in—"

Not permitting her to finish, Alex's lips went to Sarah's. Delicately at first, and as her resistance melted he held her head and kissed her deeply, with a passion from an unfulfilled void in his soul. Noticeably trembling, Sarah wrapped her arms desperately around him.

Time lost its boundaries and agendas wasted away, as the two explored destiny's intentional collision of souls. Eventually, their lips painstakingly parted, Sarah's tears dried by passion's flame. Alex's hands remained, his fingers gently caressing her face.

"Who are you? Your kiss . . . I felt you . . . deep inside, in a place I feel you've always belonged."

Alex did not answer, and Sarah honestly had no explanation for the sensation, so the pair lingered in a delicate silence. Finally Sarah took the initiative. "I have to go, can I give you my number?"

"No. When you are ready, and you need me, I will be there." In parting, Alex kissed Sarah again, finding her lips now invitingly soft. Sarah blushed, her spirit warmed from an unexpected encounter; trespassed by this thief in the night.

CHAPTER FIVE

EVEN THOUGH IT had been six months, Ştefan navigated the river as if its features were branded in his brain. As the river narrowed, he steered the many twists and turns, avoiding submerged stumps as if he had a built-in sonar. It had been over a mile since he passed the last ramshackle bayou shack. Between the distance, underbrush, tupelo, and cypress trees the view from the surrounding swamplands was now sufficiently obscured.

Ştefan had leased this branch of the river and surrounding lands twenty years ago as a hunting and fishing refuge. The winding, skinny offshoot smack in the middle of Bayou Sorrel had little purpose to Louisiana, so the state was more than happy to write a long-term lease.

In an effort to guarantee his privacy, Ştefan employed an overseer, Lemar, who lived on a small houseboat just inside the mouth of the shallow waterway. His intimidating physique and reputation for lunacy was well known across the bayous, enough to keep most of the curious on the far side of the river, even when just passing by. Ştefan waved to Lemar as he idled past the pontoon boathouse.

Ten minutes up the river, his getaway emerged from between the thick layer of Spanish moss-covered trees. From the exterior, Ştefan's place appeared rather dilapidated and run down to the point that any would-be looter would not bother to give the structure a second glance.

Killing the motor and drifting to the dock, Ştefan scanned the front of his bayou hideout. The barred and smudgy windows were so filthy only a vague perception of light shown through. As his footfalls creaked across the battered timbers of the porch announcing his arrival, he heard a faint commotion.

The rustling of fallen leaves and underbrush interrupted the momentary stillness of the swamp. Ştefan dropped to a knee as the disturbance grew closer. Within seconds, a steamy breath expelled from the cover of the undergrowth that surrounded the shack. A deep guttural growl warned; this creature did not care for intruders.

Imitating the warning, Ştefan growled back.

The beast burst from the shrubbery and knocked Ştefan to his back. Pinned by the massive two hundred pound wolfhound, Ştefan stared at the fang-like set of canines just inches from his throat. Saliva dripped onto his face as the beast snarled.

Ştefan sneered and rumbled a growl in an effort to intimidate the creature. Not frightened by his antics, the beast clamped its teeth around Ştefan's neck.

"I give, I give," Ştefan pleaded.

The beast withdrew its mouth and dropped its buttocks down on Ştefan's legs, its tail flopping side to side. Then came the tongue; wet and disgusting, the beast had its way with Ştefan's face. "Romjin, get off you big fur ball."

Romjin obeyed promptly. He backed off Ştefan and then waited eagerly for a round of praise. Ştefan grabbed a handful of thick gray fur and tugged back and forth. Romjin's hair was too thick for his skin to be reached, but the tugging motion seemed to please the wolfhound. "I have to go see her now, boy. Any suggestions as to what I can say or do to ever make it right?"

Romjin's ears perked and he let out a whimper, as if he understood. "Go find your brother," Ştefan ordered playfully. Romjin took off into the bayou in a full sprint and within seconds all traces of the hound was gone. Ştefan sighed and turned his attention to the rusted padlock. Forcing the key, he jiggled and twisted until the lock popped open.

The door creaked loudly as he stepped in; a shadowed figure crouched deeply in the furthest corner, fear blanketing her pale, green-eyed face. Her wiry, once wavy, blond hair had grown unruly and now draped halfway down her back. "Is it time?"

"Reese," Ştefan said with compassion.

"Is—it—time?"

"No."

"Then why have you come?" Reese asked defiantly.

"I'm sorry it's been so long, but I have been preparing an army—an army that will give you the freedom I've promised."

"You don't need an army. Just let me go," Reese pleaded. "I promise I'll keep your secret." Reese took two measured steps from the corner. "Ştefan, I know you still care for me, otherwise I would be dead. Please, let me go."

"You know I can't. We've discussed it a hundred times. There's too much at stake." Ştefan walked midway into the single-room shack leaving the door enticingly open.

Although the exterior of the shack appeared as if a strong wind would blow it into the swamp, the interior was just short of lavish. The cypress hardwood floors were immaculate, its low-luster sheen hiding any dust. The contemporary furniture looked as if it had just been delivered. Cypress cabinets, stained just dark enough to give contrast to the floors, hovered just above the dark granite countertops. Ştefan glanced just beyond the brushed silver faucets to the knife block. Everything was in order.

"I don't care that you're a vampire, or your family. I just want to go home."

Ştefan raked his hands through his hair. "Reese, I'm so sorry this ever happened."

Reese had continued her cautious advance, until she was only a step away. "Then make me like you, or let me go . . . or just fucking kill me!"

Ştefan eyes darted to Reese's hands. It was almost a year ago when she tried to stab him with a makeshift stake from a broken bed slat.

"In less than sixty days you will have your freedom and not have to suffer my fate to gain it. And from that day, I will make the world yours, if you want it, or simply your freedom."

"Damn it, Ştefan, I just want to go home—now. I've lived in this isolated hell hole long enough." Reese clenched her empty hands before thumping them on Ştefan's chest. "If you ever loved me, please."

Reese's touch made him grimace, as if her hands burned his chest. Her torment forced him to turn away. "I am so sorry I fucked this all up, Reese."

Reese became preoccupied with the open door. *Can I make a run for it?* It was night and the bayou appeared as black and void as a starless galaxy. She knew the odds of survival, particularly at night, were bleak. In her mind, she watched the door close with a resounding thud as she tried to devise another strategy. Instead of escape, she chose to follow Ştefan. From behind him, she reached her hands to his shoulders. "I promise I'll keep your secret."

Ştefan turned, his angst apparent. If his coup should fail, Lemar could set her free. But if he failed and she was set free, she could expose what remained of his family. *No*, he had to succeed, or Reese had to die. Those were the only options. Without an acceptable answer for Reese, he switched subjects.

"Has Lemar been good to you?"

"Not good enough." Her ambiguous reply was laced with cynicism. "I tried to fuck him for my freedom, and then I just tried to because I wanted to. But either he finds me completely unattractive or he's gay."

"Lemar is a loyal friend. As such, he would never lay a hand on any part of your body."

Reese's hand stroked Ştefan's face. "How about you. If I love you, like it used to be, would you take me with you?"

Exasperated, Ştefan pulled her hands away. "You do understand why you are here?"

"Yes."

"And if I take you with me, the danger ahead is just as bad, if not worse."

Reese worked her hands free and into Ştefan's hair. "I don't care anymore. I'm ready to die if that's what it takes."

"What it will take is for you to give me a few more weeks." Ştefan's face was close to Reese's, closer than it had been in months. Ever since the day he shared his dark secret, the physical and emotional distance between them had grown unbearable. "If it's true that you would honestly choose death, then when I return the choice will be yours. Freedom, death, or if you could ever find forgiveness—you will know more love than you could ever imagine. I will lay the world at your feet and all will bow down before you."

Reese trembled as she leaned forward and kissed Ştefan, innocently at first, but as the flame of passion ignited she became wildly uninhibited. Her hands pulled at his hair as her sexuality erupted. Two years of deprivation had left her near crazed for any man's touch. She had loved Ştefan once and then learned to hate him. Pity, anger, and so many other raw emotions all exploded in an instant. "I hate you," she uttered as she kissed Ştefan frantically.

"I know," he replied as he hastily shed Reese of her clothes.

It had been two years for Ştefan as well. His love for Reese was the root of his celibacy. At this point he no longer cared whether her actions were deceitful, a grudge fuck or maybe, by some slim chance, an opportunity, a crack in the door, to earn her forgiveness. Naked, and completely enthralled in passion, neither seemed to notice that Romjin had found his brother. The wolfhounds watched intently from the porch; the dance of broken hearts unfurling before them in the depths of the bayou.

CHAPTER SIX

STROLLING WITHOUT PURPOSE hand in hand, down Avenue Gabriel, Samantha and Nicholas passed the green and gold ornate rear gates of Élysée Palace. The midnight December air was crisp and chilled, causing the streets to be mostly deserted.

Samantha pulled Nicholas close and nuzzled her head into his shoulder. "This might sound confusing, considering what I said earlier, but part of me wouldn't mind living in a place like this."

"Are you referring to Paris, or this palace?"

"Both."

Unfazed, Nicholas did not break his stride. "Mmm, I see. Romania and my father's palace a bit too gothic for you?"

"Well, it isn't the coziest home on the planet."

"So I guess Poenari is definitely off the list of future homes?"

"I don't know why your father had those damn ruins rebuilt. I'm a vampire—and that place still gives me the creeps."

"That's because my ancestors still haunt the old castle." Nicholas made his best evil-eyed expression. "But you know how he feels about it. I think he and Angelique would rather live there than the palace."

"They can have them both." Nicholas finally stopped and looked into Samantha's eyes. "I'll take our home in New Orleans any day over those dark places," she said.

"Sam, I'm feeling a little hostility towards my family here. What's the real issue?"

"You already know, Nick." Samantha tensed.

"I bring you to Paris for two weeks so you can experience Christmas here, and you want to discuss that now? Right here?"

"I'm sorry, but all of these Christmas decorations remind me of all those great years back home with the boys. I know Angelique is beside herself. We don't even know if Alex is alive. It's been ten years. And now Ştefan has been gone for almost two years."

"At least we know *he's* alright."

"Nick, he's not alright."

"You know I've tried talking with Father. But his mind seems to be as thick and hard as the granite walls of Poenari. He grew up in a different age—where defiant sons were put to the sword. Everything he has done to create a legacy, we have all turned our back on him."

"It's not like the time clock is ticking. We all have centuries to change our minds. Sooner or later, New Orleans will be like Atlantis. And then who knows, the high grounds of Romania might look pretty good." Samantha's forced smile was anything but reassuring of her mood.

Nicholas took Samantha's hand and resumed the stroll. "They're both alright you know. Maybe not entirely happy with our family dynamics, but in time they'll come around." As they continued down Rue de Rivoli in silence, Nicholas and Samantha reflected on how the bonds with their sons might be repaired.

Turning into Place du Carrousel, Samantha exclaimed, "Oh my. Isn't this right out of a movie?"

"Which one?"

"*The Da Vinci Code*."

"That old classic? I probably haven't seen it in thirty years or more. Who was the actor?"

"Tom Hanks," Samantha recalled.

"You sure it wasn't Tom Cruise?" Nicholas asked, as he intently studied the timeless buildings.

"No, he's the one that played a vampire in Anne Rice's book."

Nicholas turned unhurried, taking in the illuminated spectacle of the Arc de Triomphe du Carrousel and then the Louvre. "What's it been? Seventy years?" he mumbled to himself.

"What did you say?" Confounded by her husband's musings, Samantha tried to get in his line of sight.

Nicholas snapped back into the moment. "Tom Cruise, what I

would have given to meet him."

"I didn't know you were such a fan," Samantha replied.

"I'm not. I just would have liked to watch him shit his pants when he met a real life vampire."

Samantha chuckled and took Nicholas's hand. "There's my happy husband."

Nicholas grimaced. "It is much easier when we talk about things I can fix."

Crossing the Seine River, Samantha and Nicholas continued their meanderings up Rue des Saints-Pères until they arrived at the corner of Rue de Verneuil. On the corner, a woman stood smoking a cigarette.

"Her." Nicholas indicated.

"Why her? She looks a little sleazy."

"Because our last two snacks have been *hims*," Nick stated, thrusting his hands on his hips. "I'm starting to feel that this pattern developing in your appetite will lead you astray, or eventually change my sexual preferences."

"Hah! I seriously doubt that, Nick."

"Besides, I find *her* acceptably attractive, and if I'm not mistaken, I think she will be open to my proposal."

"Nick, with your power of persuasion, every woman is potentially open to your proposals. Let's see how you fare without them."

"Oh, you do not think I can pick up a woman with human talent and charm alone?"

Samantha scoffed. "She's what, twenty something? You're one hundred and five, give or take. You're old enough to be her great grandfather." Sam's attitude was playfully cocky and antagonistic.

"Do I look one hundred and five?" Nicholas raised his chin and thrust out his chest.

"Go for it, Romeo, but absolutely no vampire mind games. Remember, I'll know if you cheat."

"And when I prove you wrong?"

"One of us will owe the other some *just desserts*." Samantha's expression changed instantly. *That* expression always preceded extraordinary earth-shaking sex. Win or lose, the end result was going to be *une nuit de la victoire*.

"A kiss for luck." Nicholas plunged into Samantha's mouth, kissing her like the very first night they met.

"Whoa, lover boy." Samantha forced him back. "First we feed.

Save that mess for later."

"Just warming your engines, *baby*." Nicholas smiled devilishly and then crossed the street. Having witnessed his passion, the young woman watched Nicholas approach.

Wearing a rabbit fur vest, red silk blouse, and a short black skirt, Nicholas was sure the victory was his. Her black leather platform pumps gave a pronounced hump to her calves. Nicholas studied her long, trim legs, his one true Achilles' heel, and mused, *Perhaps those are thigh highs, or maybe even a garter and stockings*. Before Samantha could hone in on his delight, he focused his attention northward. Her hair was cast-iron black and her lipstick the same hue, her skin pale, almost . . . *undead*.

"Do you speak English? My French is not so good."

"Yes," she replied, her accent transporting Nicholas back to his New Orleans nightmare, back to the third floor of the Old Ursuline Convent. He had already heard hundreds of women speaking French, but for some reason this woman's voice resurrected visions of Monique. His first thought was to turn and leave. But the bet was on and he needed to feed, as did Sam.

"My wife and I, we are looking for a little excitement. Something different. Perhaps you can help."

"Do you like to dance?" Her tone was snarky and, unbeknownst to her, motivated Nicholas all the more.

"No."

"If you are looking for drugs, I cannot help."

Nicholas knew she was lying; her eyes were unable to conceal her habit. Nicholas looked down her body. "Are you going to make me specifically ask?"

"Are you *gendarmerie*?" She looked over at Samantha, and then looked around the block suspiciously.

"No."

The woman nodded in Samantha's direction. "Is she watching, or participating?"

Nicholas smiled ever so slightly. "She will most definitely be participating."

"For the two of you, one thousand Euros." When Nicholas did not flinch, she reached between his legs. "Your pretty wife, this is what she wants to see, yes?"

Nicholas grabbed her hand, which had already begun to generate a response. "I think what she wants will come as quite a surprise. Do you have a room nearby?"

"No, but the Verneuil Saint Germain is just up the street." She knew the hotel was expensive but judging by the way the couple was dressed, they could afford it. Perhaps tonight she could earn an entire week's wage, or more.

Nicholas motioned for Samantha to cross the street. "Baby, this is—I'm sorry, I did not get your name."

"Tori," she replied with a wink intended for Samantha.

"Ladies, I will go ahead and see if a room is available. If so, I will call with the room number."

As Nicholas walked away, Tori gave Samantha the once over. "You have done this before, yes?"

Samantha looked down to Tori. Even in platform heels, she was a good two inches shorter than Samantha. Sadly, Samantha realized, this young woman was a prostitute. "No, never."

Tori slowly brought her hands to Samantha's waist while gauging her reaction. Sliding one hand up her stomach and one up her side, Tori continued until she reached Samantha's breast. "They are real, very nice."

Samantha pulled Tori's hand away. "I am new to this, and out in public—this makes me very nervous."

"I understand." With Samantha's hand holding her own, Tori couldn't help but notice Samantha's diamond ring. "You have been married long?"

"Longer than you might guess."

Samantha's uneasy tremble in her voice was wasted on Tori, who was busy scheming how to siphon as much money out of this couple as possible. "Your husband, he is a good lover?"

"Very good, quite skilled you might say."

"I guess we shall see." Tori smiled at the thought as they begin to follow in Nicholas's path. "Have you ever, as they say, gone down on another woman?" Tori smiled coyly.

"No." Samantha answered quickly.

Tori took Samantha's hand. In the cold night air Tori's hand, even gloved, offered no warmth, much like Samantha's. Anticipating the warm touch of a mortal's hand, Samantha showed no sign of her disappointment. A warm bath might be in order to enhance Tori's most unexpected, and imminent, interlude.

"So tonight, I will show you how it is done, and then *you* will pleasure me. And we will make your husband watch. And if he is a good boy, maybe we will let him fuck us after we have finished."

Samantha chuckled; that was a far cry from her husband's intended scenario. As they neared the hotel, a simple message scrolled across Samantha's phone, *407*. Within minutes they had joined Nicholas, who had already uncorked a bottle of merlot.

Samantha was surprised by the close quarters. "Wow, this is so—"

"European. As there were no suites remaining, I made the executive decision. It will do."

"It is nice," Tori exclaimed as she tested the mattress with her hand. While Samantha and Nicholas exchanged glances, Tori wasted no time; her vest and skirt were already on the floor.

"Slow down, Tori, there is no need to hurry," Samantha said.

"No, I am just getting comfortable." Tori raised her leg upon the bed, her enticement directed at Nicholas. Starting at her ankle, her hands stroked pleasurably slowly up her leg. Stopping briefly, she stretched and then popped the elastic lace band of her thigh highs. Her hands meticulously made their way to her lace thong. Taunting Nicholas with a sultry expression, she purred, "Do you like?"

"Samantha, dear, please show our new friend *just* how much I like."

Samantha stepped around Nicholas and pulled Tori to her body. "You are cold," she whispered, although her thoughts of warming Tori in a hot bath were off the table. She saw the way Tori was looking at Nick. And though he tried his best, Samantha knew Tori's seduction was taking its toll on her husband. *There is no way this girl is taking off any more clothes*, Samantha thought.

Samantha stroked Tori's hair as she inhaled her scent. "*Spiritul de întuneric,*

Te implore," Samantha whispered seductively."*Posedă această* ființă indisciplinat

Forja cuvintele mele asupra sufletului lor Viața lor să fie a mea sângele nostru să fie una." Samantha gently laid Tori's unconscious body on the bed and pulled her hair from her face. "Such a beautiful girl, before life got in the way."

Nicholas stepped in closer and studied her physique. "Yes, I can see that."

Without a scintilla of anger, Samantha spoke softly, "You wanted her, and not just her blood. I could sense it."

Nicholas knew there was no reason to deny it, nor did he want to. "For the short time we have known her, she sparked something.

Even you have to admit it."

Samantha looked back to Tori with hunger and an unfamiliar desire. "I have to admit, she intrigued me."

"Unlike you, I did not pry in your personal space when we shared those last two boys. Tell me, Sam, was it more than just their blood you desired?"

Samantha exhaled forcefully. "I'm sorry. I wasn't trying to spy on your thoughts. I think Tori rattled something loose. And those boys?" Samantha reminisced briefly about their last two victims. "I did find them attractive, but to be honest, sexually, they were just boys."

Nicholas placed his arm around Samantha's shoulder. "So what is it about this one?"

Samantha stroked the silky texture of Tori's nylons and grinned. "I don't know, maybe we're just hungrier than we realized."

"*Hungrier*, hmm. Hungry for what, I wonder?"

Samantha turned her head sharply and stared into Nicholas's eyes. "Hungry is not a metaphor. Forty years is more than a sexual lifetime for mortal couples. Is there something you need, Nick?"

"Outside of the blood of this woman, absolutely not. And you?"

"Not since the day I met you."

"Well, as we agree and I am famished, in a non-sexual manner mind you, I suggest we get started." Nicholas pulled Tori's arm to Samantha's mouth. "Ladies first."

Samantha produced a silver thimble-like puncture tool and plunged it into Tori's wrist. Nicholas held his wife's hair as she drew Tori's wrist to her mouth. Samantha's eyes rolled back in euphoric satisfaction as Tori's blood filled her mouth.

As Samantha's indulgence ended, she slipped a finger over the wound. "This one, her blood is different. It's not succulent like the other French." Samantha offered Tori's wrist to Nicholas.

As Nicholas began to partake in the vital nourishment, a strange expression came over his face. He continued to drink, past the point where Samantha knew he should have stopped.

"Nick? What are you doing? You've had too much," Samantha warned. "Nick, you'll kill her."

Nicholas stopped and slipped his finger over her wound. A tiny stream of blood ran down his chin. "She is very sick. She is already dying a most painful death."

Samantha grabbed Nicholas's arm. "So let her die. You can't do it for her. What would we do with her body?"

"She will suffer such a horrible death." With her wrist in one hand, Nicholas lightly brushed her face with the other. "This is far more humane."

"Wipe your mouth, heathen." Samantha snickered as she nudged Nicholas out of her way. Studying Tori's near-lifeless form, Samantha leaned in close to her ashen face. "She reminds me of Gabrielle, just a little." The bonds created by the taking of blood had endeared Samantha to all of her victims. Never had she experienced an actual kill, especially of the savage nature, such as Nicholas had in his waking days as a vampire. Samantha blew her breath lightly into the girl's face. "Tori, wake up, my dear."

Tori's eyes opened weakly.

"You are very sick, baby. Did you know this?"

Tori nodded in affirmation.

"Then you know the horrible death that awaits you?"

Again she confirmed.

"We can take your pain, right now, and end it for you. Would you like that?"

Tori's eyes revealed the true nature of her illness. The pills that controlled her pain had lost their effectiveness. She was scared—of pain, of death, of whatever waited on the other side. But how much more could she tolerate? Up until now, she lacked the courage to end her life. But in the presence of the vampire, a strange serenity wrapped its arms around her. "Please."

Samantha turned to Nicholas with a tear in her eye and whispered, "We will have to find a way to clean up. You do it, Nick."

Nicholas took Tori's chilled hand and brought it to his mouth.

Just as Nicholas began to draw the last ounces of Tori's blood, Samantha firmly grabbed his shoulder. "Make her one of us."

Nicholas turned to find a gleam in his wife's eye. "*Excusez-moi, ma chère?*"

"Take her. If she decides, or we decide, we've made a mistake, you can kill her later."

"*Kill her*, just like that? This is not Louisiana, Sam."

"Nick, we can figure it out later. Her life, it's been too hard for someone so young."

Nicholas looked down to discover precious drops of Tori's blood trickling down her forearm. Adjusting his thumb over her wound, he licked the trail of blood clean. "Sam, she's not the only one. We can't save them all."

Samantha sighed heavily. She knew Tori's fate had been written long before tonight. "I don't want to play God, but do it, for me."

"Then we are playing God. This was to be her fate." In Samantha's eyes, Nicholas discovered an uncharacteristic desperation.

"No less than you ending her suffering. Her fate *was* for us to cross paths tonight. Maybe her fate *is* to become one of us."

"Forty years of Samantha logic . . . can I ever be right when it matters?"

"It matters now."

Nicholas turned his attention back to Tori's wrist. No longer concerned about leaving a pair of incriminating fang punctures on her body, he raised her limp torso and lovingly tilted her neck aside. It had been almost forty years since he had attempted to make another. His mouth began to salivate as he inhaled her fragrance. The instinct to create, a force he had denied for so long, now compelled him. He had buried, and then all but forgotten, this primeval calling. He paused, his lips grazing the flesh of Tori's neck. He turned to Samantha.

"She is yours. You must do this."

Samantha looked first at Tori's fading eyes and then squawked. "Me? I can't."

"This binds her through all eternity to the one who makes her. You know this. I do not desire the responsibility for one more soul. You must do this. Come." Nicholas took Samantha's hand and drew her close. "When you feel her heart surrender, it is time to stop."

"How will I—"

"Trust me, you will know."

Samantha trembled nervously as she moved to Tori's neck. Tori's eyes seized with fear; the specter of Samantha's fangs was a horrific reality. As Samantha's teeth pierced her neck, Tori's body arched, and then relaxed as the remnants of her lifeblood was drained. As her senses faded, Tori spiraled into a world of darkness, and her pain mercifully vanquished.

Sleeping side-by-side and exhausted from the experience, Samantha cradled Tori in her arms. Nicholas had moved the teal leather desk chair beside the bed, where he sat quietly, admiring his wife's naked beauty.

Only an hour earlier, life hadn't been so beautiful. Tori's violent transformation took place in the shower; the expulsion of her toxic life, far worse than Nicholas had ever witnessed, or expected. Thankful for the slate, walk-in shower, Nicholas's clean up duty was relatively painless. Unfortunately, neither Samantha nor Tori would be wearing what remained of their clothes. Shredded and covered in vomit, nothing was salvageable.

Samantha woke and looked at her husband adoringly.

"Thank you," she whispered. Nicholas acknowledged with a smile. "I'll bet when the night started out, you never expected to have two naked women in your bed."

"Unfortunately, I'm in the chair, not in the bed."

Samantha smiled back. "I finally understand, about you and Gabby. I thought this bond that happened after I became a vampire by your blood was magnified by the fact I already loved you. I see the truth now. Tori, she is like . . . a part of me."

"And you are with her. And she will love you just as you love her. She will look to you." The vibration of Nicholas's phone interrupted his thoughts.

"It's home," Nicholas said. "It's nearly eleven. What are they still doing up?"

"What is it?" Samantha asked.

Nicholas read the text message. "Last night the Maine State Police put out a BOLO for a black Vultur. Of the seven registered Vultur's in the US, it appears as if this is the one with the disabled tracking device."

Samantha's eyes popped open wide. "Alex's car?"

"Possibly." Nick studied the phone as another message crossed his screen. "It would seem that the driver eluded the police and has vanished."

"Dear Lord, Nick. What do you want to do?"

Nickolas shook the phone several times then held it to his head. "Fortunately, we are stuck here until tomorrow night."

"Fortunately?"

"Yes, very fortunately. You and Tori need clean clothes, and besides, I'd like to remain in Paris for a bit longer. It would be a shame to cut our trip short over nothing. After all, it's entirely possible that his car was simply stolen.

"Are you sure?"

"If there is any real news, I'll reconsider." Nicholas pulled the drapes and looked down on the deserted street. "It will be dawn soon. I suggest you get some rest." Nicholas pulled the duvet from the bed and tucked it over the curtain rod. "You are going to have your hands full soon." He chuckled softly.

"How so?"

"Sometime today she is going to wake up. And you, my dear, are naked and in bed with a horny, French prostitute vampire." Nicholas could not contain his amusement.

"And pray tell where, exactly, do you think you will be, Count Tepes?"

"In the closet, baby, just like old times."

CHAPTER SEVEN

DECIDING TO NOT tempt fate for perhaps the first time in his life, Alex sprinted to his car like a flash of lightning. Gunning the Vultur, the tires churned the asphalt, leaving a cloud of burnt rubber in his wake; the hunt was on.

Sarah had already vanished. Alex gauged the surrounding streets and intersections and gambled she had gone straight. Alex drilled the accelerator and blew through yet another annoying stoplight.

Not bothering to check the mirror for law enforcement pursuit, Alex guessed Sarah's direction, dicing his way through traffic. At the next traffic signal he spotted her car.

Am I actually stalking this woman? he thought.

After several miles, Sarah pulled into a parking garage, slung her purse over her shoulder, and headed to the elevator. Alex quickly parked and followed.

No matter what I say going forward, it can't possibly come out right, he thought.

The elevator closed and Alex sprinted for the stairs.

"This is bullshit," he grumbled as he wheeled around and headed back. "Is this honestly how the romance of a lifetime is supposed to start? Quite the auspicious beginning, Douche, stalking your future lover?" Alex began to pace relentlessly. "What would Father say?"

Deciding his father's opinion didn't matter, Alex raced down the stairs and then continued to pace the sidewalk outside the parking garage, deliberating his choices. Minutes later, Sarah emerged holding hands with a guy.

"Seriously, that one, Sarah?" Alex grumbled.

From a distance, she appeared unsettled, forcing smiles that should have been natural. Entering a bar, the fiancé gave her a kiss on the cheek as he and his buddies headed to order drinks. Sarah and one of the other boys took a seat at a table and waited. Following the fiancé, careful not to be spotted by Sarah, Alex remembered one of his father's many lessons, *Keep your friends close and your enemies close enough to kill.*

The Ivy League prepster had his back to the bar with his congregation of two facing him. *The king and his court,* Alex thought as he cozied up two barstools down.

"How much longer are you going to play this one?" asked the dark-haired boy in the cardigan sweater. "Isn't it time you should cut your losses?"

"She'll go home soon enough, then it's party time. Besides, I have never invested this much time and money without getting laid. It's going to happen."

The boy with the curly red hair chuckled. "She really believes you want to get married?"

"Oh yeah, Pete. Hook, line, and sinker."

"So let's do the math, Brad," Pete rambled on. "Three months worth of dinner, movies, and slowing us down almost every weekend and nothing. Not even a blowjob? And think of all the pussy you've missed out on." He leaned in and spoke softly, "Just give her the pill, hit it hard, and be done."

"I don't need her unconscious to get what I want."

"It doesn't do that. This is that new pill, it just makes them wanna fuck like rabbits."

"Yeah, Brad," the other insisted. "Just give her one and get it over with already."

Alex was seething. To him these guys were the worst kind of pricks. And to top it off, Sarah was clueless.

"Do you have any on you?" Brad asked as he flipped his hair.

This is why I shouldn't have left Saint Andrews, Alex fumed. Brad's cliché hair flip infuriated Alex all the more. As he edged off his barstool, he glanced back at Sarah.

Walt produced a tablet from a small pillbox. "Don't leave home without it. Just drop one in her drink and your blue balls will be singing alleluia. She's going be so horny you'll probably need to call us in for back up."

Alex watched in absolute disgust as Brad dropped the pill into Sarah's drink without hesitation. Fantasizing where he'd like to shove Brad's beer bottle, Alex mused, *I hope you didn't spend all your allowance on that pill, you little prick.* For twenty minutes, Alex watched from the bar as Sarah nursed her drink. Eventually, with much coaxing, Brad led Sarah to the dance floor while his friends shared derogatory fantasies of what they would do with Sarah.

In the crowded space of the dance floor, Brad's hands begin to explore the curves of Sarah's body. Even without any evidence of reciprocity from Sarah, Alex knew the pill was beginning to take its toll. Initially, Sarah restrained Brad's hands from her more intimate regions, but within a short time span, her resistance ended. As she began to appear unsteady, Brad led her back to the table.

"Sarah's not feeling well," Brad announced with a wink. "I think I'm going to take her home."

"That's too bad," said the one who had initially sat with Sarah. "I hope you feel better."

Alex waited for Sarah and her friends to head for the exit before jumping from his barstool. Plotting a course outside to intercept Brad, Alex stopped in his path.

"Excuse us," Brad said with a tone of superiority.

Without warning, Alex thrust his open palm into Brad's chest. "I know what you did. She's not going anywhere with you, you piece of shit."

Brad threw his arms out as if to surrender. "Mister, I don't know what you think you know, but I assure you, you don't want to get in my way, not tonight."

"Alex?" Bewildered and drugged, Sarah rocked unsteadily as she tried to assimilate his sudden appearance.

Without any warning, Brad threw a full roundhouse punch but missed, as Alex ducked and delivered his elbow savagely into Brad's nose. The sound of bone on bone echoed under the patio awning. Blood hemorrhaged from Brad's face as Alex shoved him back to his friends.

"Anyone want a matching nose job?" Alex thundered.

Collectively, the three stared at their injured leader, awaiting his cue.

In a fit of rage and bad judgment, Brad screamed, "Mother fucker," and lunged head first toward Alex.

Alex simply thrust the butt of his palm into Brad's forehead, took a small side step, and watched as Brad did a face plant on the pavers.

"Next idiot?" With no takers, Alex reached for Sarah as two massive security guards were already heading towards the commotion.

"Easy, guys, this is over," Alex announced to the approaching bouncers. Once they recognized Brad on the deck, they smiled at one other.

The first bouncer nudged Brad's face with his shoe. "I'd buy you a drink, but it's probably better if you leave," he said.

"These pricks drugged her," Alex said as he took Sarah by the arm. "I'm taking her home. These guys are a liability. You might want to do something about them."

Sarah's legs wobbled, almost buckling, as Alex led her away. "Alex?" she asked in a semi-conscious state.

"Yes."

"You came back for me?"

"I told you I would."

Alex watched Sarah sleep that night and late into the next day. Each time she started to stir, he gently coaxed her back to sleep. Standing by the window, he occasionally gazed off to some long-forgotten horizon. Life had never been simple, and this new wrinkle would certainly complicate matters more.

Each time he focused on Sarah, he felt the crushing burden of his legacy and the expectations of his family. For nearly ten years his solitude had been the answer he sought. And now, as the day began its final surrender, the uncertainty of a new future began to stir. Ten years of owning every decision he made teetered on the brink of a collapse. Twenty-five hours had passed since he met Sarah, and Alex came to realize what had to be said, and done. The truth of it all, an unavoidable storm loomed dead ahead, and Alex's lies would never again afford him peace.

Sarah groaned in the darkness; Alex's silhouette by the window was barely discernable. "Where am I?" Unnerved by the silence, she called out, "Brad?"

Alex answered softly, "You are in my hotel room, Sarah." Alex watched, amused as Sarah pulled the covers tightly to her chin, as if they would shield her from the uncertainty of her predicament. "I had some toiletries sent up. They are in the bathroom. You should freshen up, maybe a shower might help clear your mind, and then we can talk."

"I can't see you," Sarah said with a tremble in her voice.

"No, you can't."

After a brief pause, she asked softly, "Alex?"

"As I said, freshen yourself, then we can talk. You've had one hell of a bad night."

Sarah slid from the bed, taking the comforter with her, unsure of her state of undress. Acclimated to the dark, Alex studied every detail of her frightened face. "Relax, Sarah, *you* are safe." Dragging the comforter, Sarah waddled into the bathroom and locked the door. Alex listened to the rushing water of the facet first and then the shower. Somewhere in between, he was sure he heard Sarah mutter, *Oh God.*

During the long night, Alex had already taken the opportunity to shower and change. Alex watched as Sarah timidly emerged from the bathroom. The nightstand table lamp was burning dimly and now Sarah could easily make out Alex's gently smiling face.

"We meet again," Alex said tenderly.

Sarah stood in the doorway, maintaining a safe distance with her hand gripping the doorknob firmly. "Why am I in your room? Did we—?"

"To answer the most important question first, no, we didn't."

"Then why was my underwear on your bathroom floor?"

Alex could not contain his sheepish smile. "You went to the bathroom last night before you passed out. I discovered them later, beside the toilet." Alex chuckled. "That would have been the icing on the cake . . . you wake up suddenly in a doped-up stupor and find me with my hands on your panties. Not to say that I would not have enjoyed your reaction, but no thank you. I left them right where you did."

Sarah blushed. "And exactly how is it I wound up in your room?"

Sitting in the desk chair, Alex rolled to the side of the bed. Patting the mattress, he invited her. "Please, I won't bite."

Sitting in front of her, Alex tried his best to hold Sarah's wandering eyes. "It seems your asshole boyfriend had grown impatient waiting for sex. His friend suggested he spike your drink with a drug to loosen you up, which he did."

Sarah's mouth parted as she absorbed the accusation. "Was there a fight last night?"

"Not much of one." Not wanting to come across as a brute, he didn't want to dwell on the fight. "You were so messed up, you couldn't even tell me where you lived. So I brought you back here."

"And how is it you just happened to be at the bar to not only save me but to also have intimate knowledge of what Brad was planning?"

"When you left the coffee shop, you took something without permission. I wanted it back."

"I took nothing from you, I promise."

"Yes, you did. So, I followed you."

"You followed me? That's creepy. Then you let me drink that drink. Then I wake up in your room, minus my underwear?"

"What would you have said if I had shown up at your table and started accusing Brad? I seriously doubt if you would have believed me. If I hadn't let you drink it, you would have never known what an asshole Bradley really was."

Sarah paused, her brain darting through scraps of memory. "Do you read poetry?"

"Odd question given everything that happened," Alex replied softly. "Not really, why?"

"Back at the coffee shop, you recited a line from my favorite poet."

Alex knew but wanted to hear the words spoken from her lips. "What was it?"

"You don't remember? You said, *One last thing. Before all life and love fades into a distant memory,* and then you said, *kiss me.*"

Alex closed his eyes as he relived the moment. "I seem to remember something similar to that. But I remember the kiss even more."

"How is it you recited a line from Dennison Bryant's poetry, word for word, if you don't read poetry? You had to have known me—from a lit class or some poetry workshop? Somehow you knew that was from my favorite poem."

Alex reached out and touched Sarah's hands. "You did kiss me."

"Alex, please. I'm trying to understand what's going on here. There's too much coincidence."

"Is Bryant really your favorite poet?"

"Please," Sarah implored.

"A very old, and wise friend preaches of absolute destiny. Me following you here, that wasn't destiny, but the reason I turned into the coffee shop? Damn, if Daniel wasn't onto something. I might have felt *it* in the coffee shop, but I didn't believe in it until just now. Until the coffee shop, I promise, we have never met.

"I'm not sure what you're saying."

"Sarah, I am Dennison Bryant. That's why I can recite the lines."

"Bullshit," she replied angrily, as she snatched her hands away. "I've met him. You look nothing alike. He's almost fifty years old. You are what, twenty-five?"

"Older." Alex grimaced. "Remember I told you I have some family issues?" Sarah's menacing glare illustrated just how badly Alex was failing. "Let me say my family does not approve of my career choice, so I use a pen name."

"Bryant's first book was published when he was thirty, twenty years ago. So I guess you wrote that when you were what, five?"

"I don't stand a chance of convincing you of anything in this room." Alex leaned forward to take Sarah's hand, but she pulled away. "Go with me. I promise I will prove every word I say."

"No."

"You didn't even ask where."

Sarah slid sideways in the bed, so Alex was no longer blocking her exit. "I don't need to ask where, Alex. You are psychotic, and I need to go home *now*."

Alex rolled his chair in front of Sarah. "How well do you know Bryant? Could you recognize his style? Even if it were something new?"

Defiantly, Sarah crossed her arms. "Of course."

"I wrote this last night, while you were unconscious." Alex cleared his throat and took a deep cleansing breath.

And she sleeps
As if she never felt the pain.
My eyes lay upon her flesh
And 'tween her dreams
I must reside, so fearful.
And she wakes,
Naked as truth, so fearful
The Dawn shall rise
And all that remains
Is the lonesome cry
The memory of love,
that never was.

Intoxicated by the words, Sarah was stunned. *How could this be?* The style was dead on, but there was no way Alex and Bryant were one in the same.

"Sarah, give me a day or two; I'll prove everything. Don't write me off just yet. I know this seems like some crazy movie plot, but you have to believe me. We would never have met if it wasn't meant to be."

Questions swirled in Sarah's groggy brain. "Alex, you'll have to forgive me if I don't call you Dennison, but my semester just ended. I'm going to go home to see my father for Christmas break next week. Beyond that, I don't know what to say. But if you'll walk me to my car, you'll have five or ten minutes to convince me that you are not some deranged lunatic."

There was so much more to tell, but the entire truth would only have her calling the police, or dying from hysterical laughter. Alex knew the rest would have to wait, for now. "Fair enough."

Heading back to the parking garage, both were reluctant to say much of anything. Alex knew with Sarah leaving town that one wrong word would destroy any chance he might have of seeing her after the trip.

As the elevator opened on the third floor, three rather large, ornery goons blocked their path. The spokesman for the trio, with the body of a heavyweight wrestler and a disproportionate sized pinhead, stepped right into Alex's face. "Say, bro, that's some fine poontanga you got there. Wanna share?"

Sizing up the three, he spotted a fourth man in a hoodie, lurking behind some cars. Stepping back, he reached in his pocket for some cash and offered up a few bills. "Let me buy you guys a few drinks, it looks like you need them."

"Look, bros, this pussy boy thinks his cash will buy him something," he bellowed.

As the three shared an obnoxious laugh, Alex focused on the shadowy figure across the garage, peering from behind a minivan. Alex's temper began to flare.

"You boys obviously need to get laid." He peeled a five-dollar bill off the roll and stuck the rest back in his pocket. "Go find yourself a nice hooker, boys. Be sure to share." Alex pulled out Pinhead's hand and slapped the money in.

Pinhead didn't bother to look but, instead, crumpled the bill and threw it on the ground. He reached out and stroked Sarah's hair. "No, I think dis *chica* will do us better."

Pinhead's arm did not break as easy as Alex expected, but when his elbow found the screaming man's nose he dropped to the concrete. Instantly, Alex's foot finished him off. Not giving the other two a chance to draw their guns, the second one received the heel of Alex's foot to his head, collapsing him faster than his amigo. A hammer punch to the third's one's throat had him gasping for air. Alex grabbed his greasy, black hair and yanked his head down to get acquainted with Alex's onrushing knee.

With all three on the ground, Alex collected their weapons and then took Sarah's hand. "Watch your step," he suggested casually, as if she were merely stepping over a puddle.

Alex walked to the minivan where he initially believed a cowardly, not-so-Good Samaritan was hiding. "Give me a second, please." He left Sarah in the middle of the garage and disappeared behind the van. The sound of a human body, or in this case a face, smashing into the metal of a car created a distinct sound; it echoed across the garage.

"No," a voice whimpered.

Dragging Brad by his hair, Alex returned to Sarah. With a swift kick to the backside of his knees, Brad dropped to the ground.

Sarah put her hands to her face. "Brad?"

"Tell her what you just did." Alex yanked Brad's hair back, forcing him to look up at Sarah. "Tell her you piece of shit or I will start breaking every bone in your body." Alex raised his fist, preparing to make good on the promise.

Brad threw his hands up in defense. "Okay, okay. I paid those guys to teach you a lesson."

"And tell her what you did last night."

Brad squinted at Sarah through swollen eyes. "I put a pill in your drink."

Alex yanked his hair harder. "Why?"

"To get you to sleep with me."

There was more for Brad to confess, but judging by Sarah's devastated expression, Alex knew she had heard enough. He released Brad's hair and leaned down to his ear. "You are fortunate she is with me. Usually, this is the time I would throw your ass from the garage, just to see if you bounce. Stay away from her, or the next time our paths cross *will* be the last."

"Let's get you home," Alex said as he took Sarah's hand.

Sarah jerked her hand back and looked down on Brad. The slap of flesh against flesh echoed across the garage as Sarah retaliated with all the strength she could muster. "Asshole!" With Brad at her knees, Sarah began to rummage for her keys. "I suppose in some bizarre way I should thank you."

"I'll settle for you not calling the police," Brad whined.

Sarah finally managed a smile as she walked away. Standing by her car's door, she sighed. "Who are you, really? I never pictured Dennison Bryant doing what you just did."

"I already told you. But if you're going to write poetry, you learn how to deal with a certain amount of mockery from the Neanderthals, especially where I'm from. My father was a mercenary. Everything you just saw, he taught me."

"Lucky for both of us, I guess." Sarah unlocked her car, tossed her purse in, and leaned against the open door.

The overwhelming sensation of last night's kiss rekindled in Alex's memory as he studied the details of her face. Did he dare? "I know this is a really shitty time for a first date, but we both need to eat. Have dinner with me, and I promise I won't follow you home."

"I should say no. But after seeing the results of your *persuasion*, I suppose I should agree."

"Trust me, when it comes to my power of persuasion, you have no clue."

Sarah drove to a small Mexican cantina a few miles away. In the ten minutes it took to get there Alex remained quiet, allowing Sarah to process all that had transpired. At dinner he could have filled the pages of a book from his relentless inquisition into her life. Her anecdotes about being the daughter of the most notoriously stern and intimidating army general amused Alex to no end. Once enrolled in college, her parental-induced social awkwardness played a role in creating this beautiful, but reclusive, biology bookworm. Then along came Brad, the asshole. Her first real boyfriend, and what a peach he was—until tonight.

After dinner, immensely relaxed, Sarah's driving no longer reflected the tension she had felt before dinner. As she drove up the ramp in the parking garage, Alex snickered. "Apparently, they picked up garbage while we were gone."

Sarah looked perplexed by Alex's observation.

"*Tres amigos*, they're gone. And a certain asshole as well." Alex could not tell if Sarah's smile was genuine. "I kind of feel bad about what I did with Brad."

"Why is that?"

"Well, I did put a pretty big dent in the back door of that minivan with Bradley's face.

Sarah rolled her eyes. "You shouldn't feel bad. He deserved it."

"Park over there," Alex interrupted, pointing to a spot away from Brad's blood pool.

Seeing through his intentions, Sarah's appreciation showed in her smile. "Where are you parked?"

"Close."

"Where? You don't want me to know what your car looks like, do you? Stalker."

In the last hour, Sarah's smile had blossomed, exhibiting a certain freedom, expressions that exceeded Alex's expectations. "Alright. I'll let you in on part of my little secret. Dennison Bryant, if you toss the name in a blender, it might come out loosely as Brian Denman Jr. But don't you dare call me Junior."

Alex saw the gleam in her eye and knew his warning was wasted. Before she had the opportunity to play the *Junior* card, he handed her his expired Louisiana driver's license.

After inspecting the well-worn card, she held it up and compared the picture with his face. "You were born in 2012?"

"Yes."

"You are really forty years old?"

"I'll take your tone as a compliment. Thirty-nine, if you want to be accurate." Alex watched as Sarah did the math in her head. "My first book published when I—"

"When you were a thirty-year-old freshman at Tulane," Sarah finished proudly. "*New York Times* best seller list. Quite the feat for a freshman. Why in the world did you use a pen name?"

"My family. There's a history there that I'm not quite ready to discuss."

Sarah handed back the license. "Hold on, *Junior*. I think I earned some juicy tidbits. I answered all of your questions, even details way beyond the bounds of first date knowledge."

"Yes, you did. But if I answer your questions, there may not be a second date."

Alex turned and looked out the window of Sarah's car. The

adjacent car's frosted windshields reminded him of home.

"I've got a proposition for you, Sarah, or better yet, an adventure. I want to take you to my home. The drive is only a few days, give or take. Along the journey, I will share . . . secrets."

"And where exactly are we going?"

"Canada. But anytime you feel like you're done with me, or the trip, I'll put you on a plane." Sarah's thoughtful hesitation stoked Alex's hope. "Call your father. Tell him you're going on a little trip and you'll be home in a week."

"When would we leave?"

"Right now."

Sarah giggled at the thought. "I might need my toothbrush and deodorant."

"Anything you need I'll buy on the way." Alex knew she was searching for either an explanation or an excuse. "It's time you do something completely illogical. Otherwise, you'll spend Christmas with your dad, come back and finish your semester, graduate, get a job, get married, have kids, and live out a perfectly well-scripted life."

Alex had just recited Sarah's hope chest list in condensed form. "You forgot my honeymoon in Maui." She pouted. "Besides, I have a bio project I need to work on. My laptop has—"

"We'll stop by your house and pick it up. But that's it. I'm serious."

"My project, I need time—"

"Oh for goodness sake, Sarah," Alex interrupted. "Here, I've got a project for you that will make you famous." Alex rummaged through the virtual trashcan of Sarah's backseat.

"I know it's a mess."

Alex found a blank scrap of paper. "Do you have a pen?"

She dug one out of her purse and watched as he began scribbling on the crinkled paper.

Alex turned the page to her. "I assume you know what this is?"

Sarah studied the symbols briefly. "Basically, it's a dead antigen. It can be used to create vaccines."

"Excellent." Alex scribbled a chemical element symbol next to it and handed it to Sarah. After reviewing the symbol briefly, she flung the paper back. "If you're trying to impress me with your knowledge of biology then try combining compatible elements."

Alex added a third symbol, handed it back, and smiled devilishly.

"What's that supposed to be, Einstein?"

"If you could fuse all three, without destroying the result, tell me, what would you have?"

Sarah studied the ingredients briefly and began to smile. "*If* you could combine them, you would have a super antigen, one that is regenerated and strengthened by the interaction of toxins. Hypothetically, with an injection of this, after a snakebite you would become immune to snake venoms and cancer would become the source of immunity to cancer. Alzheimer's patients would not only be cured but would possibly become more intelligent."

"You are good."

"We create formulas like this in our lab on a weekly basis. But in the real world, these elements cannot co-exist and survive."

"So they die?"

"Yes." Sarah chuckled. "And sometimes they explode."

"If I told you I have access to a living strain of this very antigen, would you want to see it?"

"That's like asking if you'd like to see me naked." Sarah blushed immediately, realizing her giddiness had seized control of her mouth. "No, I didn't mean that, but I did because I know you do, or at least I think you do, but I meant to just say yes, but we always say stuff like that in our lab. It's like a lab geek way of saying *no shit, Sherlock.*" For Sarah, the prospect of the antigen actually existing was mindboggling. "And they haven't, you know, seen me naked, but they would if this actually existed."

"It does, I promise you. And after watching you plop your bare derrière in bed last night, I wouldn't mind seeing it again." Alex opened his door and climbed out. "So, are you coming?"

"If you are bullshitting me, my father—"

"Yes, I know," Alex said as he rounded the car, opened Sarah's door, and extended his hand. "I used to say the same thing about mine."

Sarah locked her car and followed Alex. "Oh my, is this your car?"

"Yes, ma'am."

"I know you've sold a lot of books, but I never realized poetry paid this well."

Alex opened her door and slowly extended his hand. Without an objection from Sarah, he lightly touched her cheek. "As I told you before, I've got family issues."

Sarah suddenly planted her feet. "Hey, earlier tonight you said I took something from you at the coffee shop."

Alex smiled. "Yes, indeed I did."

CHAPTER EIGHT

ŞTEFAN STROLLED THE mostly empty streets of the French Quarter. At three in the morning and nearly freezing, only the hardiest of drunks or hookers found reason to roam. He liked these nights; it was easier to contemplate his logic versus the views of others, which usually meant his family. In the shadows of homes, abstractions drifted like long-forgotten haunts. Were the dead watching, standing vigil for some unseen cause?

One might think the living dead should be able to communicate with all sorts of spirits. His father insisted they spoke to him, guiding his path in the days of his turning. Ştefan frowned. *They never offered me jack shit.*

As he walked, occasionally he would bark out at the shadows, "What? If you have something to say, say it."

"What would you have me say?" the sultry voice whispered.

Not the voice he was expecting and, honestly, one he would have preferred to avoid. He scrunched his shoulders, not only out of guilt of his prolonged absence but also disgusted at her lifelong ease of sneaking up on him. "Isabelle."

"Ştefan."

Turning slowly, Ştefan knew the scorned expression that awaited him. Isabelle did not disappoint. Her beauty was remarkable and only served to remind him of his lifelong, unfulfilled infatuation.

"Isabelle, you look absolutely amazing. What are you now, almost three hundred?"

"Close enough." Isabelle flashed a curt smile. "Tell me, Ştefan, how long have you been back?"

"Four days," he groaned.

"Four days? Am I not the closest person you know in this town that you are still talking to? Or have you now estranged yourself from me as well? I suppose you are staying in a hotel?"

"Yes."

Ştefan's sullen demeanor gave Isabelle cause to hug him. She was all too familiar with his struggles, and his brother's, between the two worlds. "Let's walk." Isabelle hooked his arm and led him away, leaving only shadows behind. "It's been almost two years. How have you been?"

Ştefan had never been able to successfully lie to Isabelle for reasons he did not comprehend. So his choices were limited, which was the primary reason he had avoided her for almost two years. "You know, I'm dealing with life as best as I can."

"I'm sorry about Reese. Did anything ever turn up on her disappearance?"

How to answer truthfully? Ştefan turned away to conceal his facial expression. "No, the police found nothing."

"And you still blame your father?"

"Is there anyone more deserving, except perhaps my mother? She did nothing to sway his opinion. Oh, and let's not forget *grandfather*." Ştefan sounded agitated.

"We have both shared this affliction. To love a mortal, it is quite an impossible relationship."

"It doesn't have to be."

Sensing his growing anger, Isabelle pulled Ştefan closer as they walked. "We have all agreed, including yourself, relationships of this nature would inevitably expose our race. We would be hunted into extinction. You can't deny this overwhelming belief."

"I never have, but you *know* there is an alternative," Ştefan said, thrusting his arms out in frustration. "I'm tired of this life in the shadows."

"To make one, or a thousand, we will forever be labeled predators. And the world will justify the genocide of our entire race, peaceful or not."

"The secret society of Tepes. A family fucked for all eternity,"

Ştefan complained.

As they neared Chartres Street, Isabelle looked back up Saint Phillip. "You know, I'm not sure why, but I think this has always been my favorite street in the Quarter."

"Well, you have enough money, why don't just you buy a place?"

"My mother doesn't even know the source of my attraction to this street, but even so, I find it is a good habit to leave some desires unfulfilled. I wish I could help you understand, but you are still so young, not even forty years have you lived." Isabelle gazed upon all that surrounded them. "We are creatures of infinite possibility. Time does not work against us. We can travel the world, gain unlimited knowledge, fear no disease, and love as we please."

"No Izzy, *you* are free to love as you please, because *you* are a day-walker. If my mother had only remained mortal, like your father did, we wouldn't even be having this discussion." Ştefan kicked a loose stone. "You and Alex had it all, immortality, a regular diet, and a great tan."

"I don't have a great tan." Isabelle smiled, trying to soften Ştefan's ire.

"That's because you *choose* not to. But you do not crave the blood of the living as we do, so for you, love has only the limitation of a mortal's lifespan—or your boredom with them. I do not share your luxuries. If I were like you, I would still have Reese."

"But only for a time. Then she would pass, and you would find another love, the same as I have done. So if it is only a month or seventy years, there must be an end and, eventually, a new beginning."

"Argh," Ştefan moaned. He turned left onto Chartres Street, shuffling his shoes over the broken slate sidewalk. Isabelle walked briskly, catching up in the middle of the block. The pair strolled along for another block in silence. With its white walls looming prominently against the glow of the moon, The Old Ursuline Convent seized the pair's attention. "Have you ever seen it?"

"The third floor?" Isabelle guessed.

"Weren't you curious?" Ştefan stared at the convent as he rubbed the back of his neck. "Your mother was imprisoned there for over two hundred years."

"My mother. She could not bring herself to ever return to New Orleans. The thought of this place, of the convent guard who was my father, the life she lost to Monique, it has always proven more of a burden than she cared to face."

"Monique, talk about a true vampire from hell. I'm sure my father rues the day he crossed that bitch's path."

Isabelle reflected briefly. "Had Monique not committed her treason, she and Angelique would not have been banished to New Orleans almost three centuries ago. Your father would have never had reason to travel here and, therefore, never met your mother."

"But my father would still be a day-walker," Ştefan protested.

"Perhaps. *My* mother would have remained mortal and died two centuries ago." And although she never spoke a word of it, I think my mother would have preferred to remain mortal and experience the beauty of growing old and eventually heaven."

"Do you really believe that?"

"I do. One day some malady will inflict me and I too will go before God."

Ştefan scoffed. "And what will your creator say to you?"

Aggravated by Ştefan's snicker, Isabelle wheeled in front and cut him off. "Do you believe the spirit within your body was the result of some genetic accident? Man cannot create anything without using elements that have existed from the beginning of time. Look around you. Everything we make comes from things God put on this planet, not some ridiculous explosion in space."

Tongue-tied by Isabelle's harshness, Ştefan had no reply.

"When you have lived three hundred years, you might begin to understand."

"I want to see it."

"Heaven?" Isabelle feared Ştefan's desire might be more than a sarcastic opportunity to be disagreeable.

Ştefan's smile quickly returned. "No, the legendary third floor, you silly woman. Think about it. That's where this all started." Ştefan raised his hands, as if he were some type of monster. Stalking Isabelle, he recounted in a sinister voice, "Your mother and her friends, all mortal, feasted upon by Angelique and Monique until they were all made vampires. Prisoners of the evil, Catholic empire, locked away on the third floor of the convent for two hundred years. Enter my father, Brian Denman, the fearless mercenary and his flunkies." Ştefan forced a guttural diabolical laugh. "The epic battle, good versus evil, with the entire fate of the planet hanging in the balance. Come on, how can you resist?"

"And how do you propose we gain access?"

"Well, we could go knock on the front door and ask for

permission." Ştefan pulled his jacket up to cover the lower half of his face, as if it were a cape. "Or put them under the dark and creepy Transylvanian enchantment if they are not agreeable."

Isabelle stuck her index finger into Ştefan's chest. "Do not mock the ways of your ancestors."

"Oh, I would never be so bold as to mock Vlad the Impaler. But who's got time to remember all of that spell nonsense?" Ştefan jumped on top of the garden wall of the Beauregard Keyes House. "Me, I plan on exploring this the old-school way, the Brian Denman way. I'm going to climb through the tunnel, come up under the convent, and scale the escape trunk."

"What if it's been sealed?"

"Has it? I'm surprised your BFF, Daniel, didn't share that info with you. I heard the two of you spent so many hours reminiscing about the ancient days, you know, before I was born."

"You're funny, Ştefan. And don't poke fun at Daniel. He was a wonderful man."

"A wonderful jailor, don't you mean? How many years did he imprison your mother and the others?"

Isabelle rolled her eyes. "You are quite impossible tonight. Come down off that wall and we'll go collect your things. You can stay with me for as long as you're in town—or until you decide to make up with your parents."

"No, I'm not here to make up, and I'm not coming down. Come with me. Let's go see what remains on the third floor. Let's find out why it's been resealed." Ştefan held out his hand to Isabelle.

"It's dark in there and my eyes do not function like yours. And besides, I'm not going in any filthy, cobweb infested, damp tunnel dressed like this."

Ştefan cocked his head to the side, inspecting the body his eyes had already trolled over. "You do look mighty fine in those jeans, ma'am," Ştefan praised in his best over-the-top Southern drawl. "I do declare, that Japanese denim hugs your derriere so fine. Does your momma know you're out dressed like that?" Isabelle attempted to give Ştefan a scornful eye, but failed. "Now don't go get'n so high and mighty on me, missy. Father told me how you used to dress up, all sexy and Victorian Goth, seducing all those prairie boys into your lair. Why, I even heard you seduced the mighty Brian Denman."

"Ştefan, that's enough memory lane for tonight."

Ştefan jumped down from the wall and closed in on Isabelle. "I'll be damned. You still have feelings for him, don't you?" Ştefan's hand gently cupped Isabelle's cheek. "That is why you've never married." His eyes were unrelenting, seeking her hidden secret. "That is why I was never good enough for you?"

"No." Again, her voice revealed her weakness.

"I could have loved you, if you had only allowed me." Like a sorrowful ballet, the breath of Ştefan's words danced upon Isabelle's face. "I still can."

"What about Reese? You loved her." Isabelle tried to back away but Ştefan's hand slid behind her head.

"Reese never would have happened had you not driven me away."

With Ştefan's lips brushing against hers, Isabelle pleaded unconvincingly, "No."

"But we could be so perfect. I can give you the love you have denied for so long. And time would never play the villain for either of us."

As the tears welled in her eyes, Isabelle turned her face away. Ştefan gently guided her face back, forcing her gaze to his. Wiping her tears with his thumbs, gently he said, "He can never be yours, but I can."

In those bitter shadows of the convent, two solitary, love-lost creatures of the night embraced as the forlorn ghosts of the past watched in jealous sorrow.

CHAPTER NINE

IT WAS THE caress of a gentle hand, a sensation that beckoned her to stir. As the satin and flesh remained, an awareness of cool had intensified. Her eyes rolled open and discovered a room filled with light, only it wasn't light. It was merely a perception of images, brilliant new colors and hues, and a man.

From adolescent fairy tales, she knew the man standing before her. "You are the ferryman?"

"No, Tori. I am not," Nicholas said gently and then smiled. "Well, now that I think about it, maybe I am."

Their conversation stirred Samantha. She propped up on an elbow and gazed down at this new creation of her own blood. Tori looked back at her and sensed an overwhelming calmness envelope her body.

"It is you?"

With a sense of amazement and pride, Samantha nodded. It had been nearly forty years since she had given birth to Ştefan, and Tori's rebirth nearly overwhelmed her.

"Tori," Nicholas began, "Samantha has taken your disease. But it did not come without a cost. Do you remember anything from last night?"

Tori's mind was ablaze with new sensations. Trying to focus on details from the previous night did not come easily. "I remember undressing, for you"—Tori looked back again at Samantha—"and your wife."

"I want you to understand, this new life we have offered, it has limitations, and it has rules. You will live a great number of years and never know sickness again. Your body will age, but so slowly you will never see its effects. You will have power and dominion over all who cross your path."

"How is this so? I was sick and dying."

Tori sat up, the white sheets falling loosely around her waist. Nicholas attempted to hide his interest in her firm white breasts as her erect nipples taunted his manhood. With his best effort failing miserably, Samantha sat up, gently pulled Tori to her side, and pulled the sheets to cover her. "She is family now," Samantha justified, as she raised one brow and gave Nicholas the evil eye.

"Before I explain, you must know what has been done can only be undone by eternal death. Not like your sickness before, this death will come quickly and with minimal pain. If you choose this path, we will honor your wish."

With Samantha's body pressed tightly against her own, Tori felt the security of a nurturing soul that gave her courage. "Please, tell me."

"My wife and I are vampires. We chose to take you for sustenance, an event that you would not have remembered—or suffered ill effects from. But we discovered your disease, and after a debate, we chose to end your suffering and make you like us."

Tori weakly mumbled, "Vampires are not real."

"As I sit before you, I promise, we are real. And you, my love, are now one of us. Look at your skin—it is flawless. Feel the strength that builds from inside. And your pain, where once *it* was all there was, now you are free."

"I don't believe you," Tori murmured.

"It is true, Tori. You drank of my blood to become one of us," Samantha explained.

Riddled with despair, Tori clutched the sheets and pulled away from Samantha. "Can I leave now?"

"Not just yet. The sun has not fully set, and your clothes were rather ruined last night. I expect your new attire will be delivered shortly."

Uninhibited, Tori stood up, leaving her sheets behind. She scanned the room for any sign of her clothes. Once again, Nicholas's eyes could not help but inspect Tori's beautiful transformation.

Without a scrap of clothing in sight, Tori turned quickly and retreated into the bathroom. Samantha began to follow but paused just long enough to gain her husband's attention. As his eye's perused her curves, Samantha paused before closing the door. "Best not forget who waxes your coffin, Count Tepes."

Tori stood in front of the vanity mortified; only a blank mirror stared back. As Samantha touched her shoulder, she startled. "Where am I?"

"There are certain disadvantages to our race, mirrors being one. We learn to accommodate for these shortcomings." Samantha turned Tori toward her. "Look at me. Tell me, what do you see?"

Tori scrutinized every aspect of Samantha's body. "You are beautiful."

"As are you. I am seventy-four years old. My appearance has not changed since the day I was made a vampire." Samantha stroked her hands through Tori's hair, clearing her face. "I know you are scared, just as I was, but Nicholas and I will be with you on this journey. We will teach you all there is to know."

"Will I be able to see my family?"

"Yes, if you desire." Samantha took Tori's hand and guided her finger to her mouth. It had been forty years, but the memory of Angelique's ritual flashed brightly before her. Tori's finger explored her glistening, new fangs. Samantha pressed Tori's finger into the fang, causing a prick, startling Tori.

Samantha brought Tori's finger into her own mouth and tasted the succulent delicacy. She glided Tori's finger over her own fangs, remembering the exhilaration of Angelique's lesson. "You see, we are truly the same now."

Samantha surveyed Tori's body without envy. She fully understood her husband's fascination, for she felt it too. Was it a simple appreciation, or perhaps desire? Reaching for the bathrobe on the brass hook, Samantha handed it to Tori. "Nicholas has been a faithful husband for forty years, but like all men, he has his weaknesses. I think it best if you not force me to castrate him."

"And to think, I believed that was my purpose last night." For the first time, Tori allowed herself a genuine smile. "So, it would appear I have two choices. Live as a vampire or die. My options have doubled since last night. I choose to live."

Samantha opened the door and led Tori out. "Tori has decided to join our family."

Nicholas smiled genuinely. "I cannot wait to get out of this shoebox of a room. There is so much to show you."

Feeling apprehensive about her husband's enthusiasm, Samantha ushered Tori to sit on the edge of the bed. Nicholas had never given her pause for concern; his faithfulness had always been steadfast. But something was different, and not comprehending its origins troubled Samantha.

Samantha took Tori's hands in her own. "The most important things you may already know," she began. "The sunlight will sear, singe, and then incinerate your flesh. It is the worst way for a vampire to die. Always be mindful of dawn."

"I must return to a coffin?"

"No, just as there are no caskets in this room, you may choose to adapt similar sleeping habits. I can tell you, there is no greater rest and rejuvenation than the confines of a casket, but it is not a necessity. Garlic and holy water are—"

A knock at the door interrupted Samantha's instruction. Her eyes urged Nicholas to answer. "Dear, you are still naked," Nicholas reminded her. "I think for the sake of the man's blood pressure, perhaps you should cover yourself."

Nicholas tipped the room service valet and handed the packages to the women. "It's not that I don't enjoy the sight of your bodies but, please, for the sake of *my* blood pressure, get dressed." Another round of rapping sent Nicholas back to the door. "The valet must have forgotten something."

As Nicholas cracked the door, a gigantic, black Frenchman burst into the room pushing Nicholas back to the wall. With one hand around his throat and another gripping a gun he turned his eyes to Tori. "Where have you been, whore? I want my money."

Nicholas considered his defensive tactics; old school Brian Denman, or Nicholas Tepes, Prince of the Undead. With the pimp's hand firmly around his throat, Nicholas was unable to speak, and lacking the desire to get a bullet in his head, he chose to temporarily submit to the flesh bag's intrusion.

"Who is your whore friend, Tori?" he growled.

Samantha rose from the bed and as the pimp's eyes locked onto her perfectly sculpted curves and pale silky flesh, he mistakenly loosened his grip. Samantha approached, gliding her hands erotically over her flesh.

"Damn, bitch, I might have to try you out myself."

"First, let's see how you do with this. *Spiritul de întuneric, Te implore*," Samantha chanted. "*Posedă această ființă indisciplinat Forja cuvintele mele asupra sufletului lor Viața lor să fie a mea sângele nostru să fie una.*"

With his eyes rolling backward into his head, the pimp's gun tumbled onto the floor. Nicholas exchanged grips with the beast and hoisted him up by his throat. "Well done, darling. Now, would the two of you *please* put some clothes on before I'm forced, in earnest, to revisit last night's original proposal." Nicholas flung the unconscious trespasser onto the bed.

"Oh, is that so?" Samantha challenged, impervious to the unconscious pimp on their bed. She pulled Tori's robe off directly in front of Nicholas. While both stood naked, Samantha reached in the bag and pulled out two pairs of denims. "Size four. These *must* be yours," Samantha quipped. "Please allow me to help." Having perfected the art of erotic dressing for her husband, Samantha sadistically applied her craft, pulling and tugging until the denim mercifully stretched over Tori's naked ass.

The unbearable performance had Nicholas speechless and squirming in his loafers. Samantha pulled out the two shirts and brassieres.

"32 B, however did you guess that one, dear?" Samantha asked, as she inspected Tori's breast. Samantha continued to assist Tori, allowing her hands free range over her youthful counterparts flesh, until mercifully, her body was covered.

Now it was Samantha's turn, and tonight her husband would suffer for his not-entirely-innocent, smart-ass comments. Tantalizingly massaging her breasts, she took her sweet time slipping into the bra. Before she began the agonizing process of sliding her jeans on, she backed her naked buttocks against Nicholas's groin. Ever so slowly she worked the blue-washed fabric up her calves and then her thighs, grinding into her husband in the process. Feeling she had his full attention, she taunted.

"Are you alright, Nick? You feel so . . . tense." Before pulling the denim over her buttocks, Samantha bent down to her ankles, thrusting her ass directly in front of Nicholas, and then painstakingly stretched the skinny jeans up her legs. She then turned to Nicholas and made sure he had one last eyeful before pulling the pants around her waist.

"That was incredible," Tori observed.

Not finished with Nicholas yet, she put her heels on and dropped the shirt in his hands. "Could you please help me with this?"

Nicholas knew the difference between a demand and a request, so he obliged. As he pulled the shirt over her shoulders and began working up the buttons, he smiled as their eyes met. Her seduction had accomplished its intent, and her expression was a devilish reminder; Samantha rocked his world.

"Got any more smart-ass comments you'd like to share, Count Tepes?"

Nicholas strained to break from Samantha's tractor-beam gaze. After a brief struggle, he turned his attention back to the catatonic pimp. "*Non, Mademoiselle.* I have more than suffered through my lesson for tonight. But I do believe it is time for our Tori's first lesson—*le plat principal.*"

CHAPTER TEN

AS THEY CROSSED into New Jersey, it suddenly occurred to Alex that Sarah might not have her passport in her possession. With three hundred miles behind them, the last thing Alex wanted was to turn around and drive back to Virginia Beach.

"This might be a little late to ask, but I don't suppose you have your passport? You'll need it to cross into Canada."

"You didn't give me much chance to even think about it."

"I can fix it, if I can borrow your phone?" The only quick remedy to the problem involved a private conversation with an old friend.

"You know, anyone who can afford this type of car should be able to own a phone," Sarah said with a snicker. "Besides, isn't it a little late for a call?"

"Not for this friend."

Alex pulled the car to the side of the road. "This will just take a second," he said as he stepped out of the car. Grimacing, he dialed on the phone.

"It's me." Alex held the phone away from his ear for nearly thirty seconds while the voice raged on the other end. "I know, trust me, I know," he tried to explain. "I'll be in the city tonight. You can finish the lecture then. But right now I need a passport for a friend—by tomorrow."

The reply was somewhat tempered, allowing Alex to keep the

phone on his ear. "Yeah, well who taught me all of that?" Before the voice could ramp into another tirade, Alex intervened. "Do this for me, and I'll consider it."

Alex opened the door and pointed the phone at Sarah. "Smile." Before she had the opportunity to object about her makeup or hair, Alex snapped the picture and stepped back outside, closing the door. "You got that?" he asked into the phone. "Yes, I know she is . . . and please, not a word to the family." Alex hung up and climbed back in the car.

"I told you it was late. Whoever that was on the other end of the call didn't sound very happy, even from in here."

"Yes, my friend can be a little overbearing at times."

Alex pulled back onto the highway and Sarah feigned a yawn. "Where are we stopping tonight?"

"If you're okay, we will be in New York in a little over an hour. If you'd rather stop now, I'm sure I can find a hotel."

Find a hotel. The sudden thought of sleeping arrangements welled a knot in her stomach. Sarah felt confident Alex had no expectations, but what troubled her was that she might.

"I'm fine. But I'm going to have a hard time getting up early if you have plans. Thanks to Brad's antics, my sleeping schedule is upside down. Aren't you getting tired?"

"No. I've always been more of a night owl."

Sarah stared out the side window into the incandescence of the New Jersey Turnpike. "This is so unlike me," she said, her breath fogging the glass. "Last night I had some half-baked notion Brad might propose over Christmas break. Now, one day later, I despise the man I thought I would marry, and instead of crying my eyes out and scheduling six months of counseling, I'm heading to Canada with a virtual stranger without a clue of what's going to happen next."

"I would guess your orderly life is the by-product of being raised by your father. Order creates predictability. In that, there is a level of safety and peace of mind. But a life without thrills can dull the senses. I live in a healthy balance. Outside of you being victimized and hurt, I found last night rather exhilarating."

"I don't think I've come close to processing last night yet. And I'm not entirely sure I should even be here. I've got no clothes, not much money, and nobody knows where I am."

"Why don't you call somebody? Just hearing a familiar voice might help."

Sarah snickered. "None of *my* friends would still be up."

In her reply, Alex felt Sarah's mounting pain and anxiety. Easing the car off the road for a second time, he turned to her. Finding her gaze entrenched on the highway ahead, he spoke gently, "Look at me, Sarah." She turned but struggled to find the courage to look directly at him. "My eyes are just above my nose, not below my chin."

Alex reached over and took Sarah's hand.

"I know what you're going through. Part of it is fatigue, and the rest is something just short of shock. Most importantly, I want you to know that you are safe. Nothing bad will happen as long as I'm with you. If you want to go home, I'll take you straight to the airport in Newark. But if you choose to continue our little adventure, I promise, you'll have an experience of a lifetime."

Sarah was trembling. "I believe you. It's just . . . I've never done crazy, impulsive stuff like this before."

"I know. But you are in great hands because I have. I'm going to put on some soft music and shut up. Why don't you try to catch a nap for a while? You'll feel better, I promise."

"Instead of music, will you recite some of your poetry? Not that it will put me to sleep, but I know it will calm my nerves."

The gleam in her eye warned Alex he had no choice in the matter. "I can do that."

Sarah reclined her seat slightly. "I'll try not to focus on this whole Dennison Bryant thing. I've seen him you know, at lectures and a book signing, and I've already told you, you look nothing like him."

"Would you rather I do?"

Sarah turned on her left side and tucked her legs underneath. Studying Alex's face, she smiled freely. "He's pretty darn cute for an older man, but I guess you are too—for an older man."

"My father is not that different from yours, and my writings did not fit in with his expectations of grandeur. When my first two books were initially published, I refused to have my picture on the jackets and I used the pen name, Dennison Bryant, to protect my secret passion. After my second book, when I was twenty-five, with increasing demand for public appearances, I stole an idea from my family playbook, which I promise I *will* explain very soon. I decided I needed an alter identity to be my public image; the Dennison Bryant you know is actually Albert Wilson. I pay him to perform at public appearances. For almost fifteen years, he's been the face of my work. And as a result, Albert's done alright with the ladies."

"Oh, to think what I might have done with that imposter."

"Oh my, I've done it again," Sarah moaned as she walked into the kitchen. "What time is it?"

"Eight-ish." Delighted at her disappointment, Alex's motives would remain secret for just a while longer.

"How long have you been up?" Sarah asked as she moved closer to see what Alex was doing on his computer.

"A few hours. Did you sleep good?" Not wanting her to wake while he rested, Alex sat beside the bed, observing her, occasionally coaxing her back to sleep.

"I don't think I moved an inch. That bed was so comfortable, and the pajamas . . . I don't think I've ever felt any fabric so soft. Where did they come from?"

"A store here in the city. I'm glad you enjoyed them."

Sarah looked around the room; its beige walls were lined in copper and dark sienna cabinets, the walls speckled with wilderness photography. The walnut kitchen chairs were trimmed in rich burgundy suede. "I love this kitchen. Do you come here often?"

"Not so much anymore." Alex closed his laptop. "Come, you are really going to love this." Swinging open the French doors, he revealed the main living space.

Sarah's bare feet padded across the stone floor until she reached the Berber carpet. From there, she glided towards the picture window. "Oh my, Alex. This is amazing." The illuminated Brooklyn Bridge and the panoramic skyline filled her eyes with awe.

Alex silently glided behind her. "I used to sit here for hours and watch life pass by the window, wondering where on earth all these people were going or what their lives were like or if there was *someone* out there." Alex desperately yearned to wrap his arms around Sarah, for his lips to explore the essence of her neck and to feel her tremble in his arms, and to know it was his touch she craved.

Sarah leaned back and rested her head on his shoulder. "Can I ask you something?"

"Yes."

"You knew when you kissed me, didn't you?"

"Actually, I think I knew when you walked into the coffee shop."

Sarah exhaled softly. "Last night, the minute I put on the gown and laid in bed, I just knew you were going to come in the room. I was exhausted, but I kept waiting. I'm not sure when I fell asleep." Distracted by a passing ship in the East River, Sarah's thoughts strayed momentarily. "As I laid there *waiting*, I began to wonder if my being alone was all part of some elaborate seduction?"

"I'm not that devious." Alex chuckled as he combed Sarah's hair with his fingers, tucking it behind her shoulders. With one hand, he then stroked her temple softly while wrapping his other one around her waist, pulling her close. The caress of his sweet breath on her ear caused a tingle.

"When we kissed, did it feel like a simple seduction—or something more?" Alex asked.

"I think you already know the answer to that."

"So tell me, after having your life turned completely upside down, how am I doing?"

Sarah spun around, holding Alex's hand to her waist. "After last night, you are failing miserably," she said with a stern expression. "I was almost ready to sleep with you after that kiss in the parking lot, and that's before I found out who you were. And now I think I get it—all that longing and desire in your writing. This is where it comes from, right here."

Without warning, Sarah thrust her lips onto Alex's, unlocking all the passion she had forcibly contained for months. Alex knew where this was heading but could not bring himself to stop. Sarah's hands tugged at the sash of her robe and pulled it off her shoulders. With her firm, warm body pressed tightly to his, the scent of her arousal was dangerously overwhelming.

Alex pushed away and immediately pulled her robe up.

"Sarah. You don't know how much I want you right now. But I can't, not yet. Not until I've told you everything."

Dejected, Sarah stepped away and retied the sash. "Well don't I feel a little embarrassed." She studied the complexity wrought in Alex's expression. "Are you with someone else?"

Alex shook his head, indicating *no.*

Looking somewhat mischievous, Sarah chirped out, almost comically, "Is it an STD issue?"

"I wish it were that simple."

The December night had a refreshing bite. The air was dry and the brisk breeze added a punch, just as a reminder that in this city winter is king. Sarah pulled herself close to Alex as they walked.

Feeling her shiver, Alex offered, "We can always grab a cab, if you want."

"No, it feels good to walk." Sarah smiled, pushing aside the awkwardness of rejection in lieu of promised answers. "So how much is that apartment a night?"

Alex decided this was as good of a time as any to begin his confessions. "It's kind of free."

"Free?" Distracted by the aroma of stir-fried meats, veggies, ginger, and soy filling the air, Sarah turned her nose to the source.

"I haven't lived there for years but it's kind of my apartment."

"*Your* apartment?"

"Well technically the building belongs to my stepmother. My father gave it to her as a wedding present. When I turned twenty-one, they gave me the apartment."

"So you live with your parents?"

"No! Not really. The top floor is theirs. My brother and Aunt Dee have a place up there as well."

"So I'm guessing the Denman's are pretty well off? I didn't know mercenaries got paid that much."

"My father was an intricate cog in the South American drug trade. When opportunity knocked, he cashed in. When he worked in the Middle East he found organizations with agendas parallel to that of the CIA, and then sold his services for a job he was already there to do. When he retired, my uncle Phillip hooked him up with people who taught him how to invest, that building being one of those lessons."

Sarah eyed the campus buildings of NYU. "I would have liked to come here, but my father insisted I stay in Virginia."

"Well tonight you are about to become an honorary student." Alex bounded up several steps and swiped his ID badge. "After you."

As they entered the building, the echo of footsteps resonated down the hall. "What are we doing here, and why do you have an ID badge?" Sarah whispered.

"You don't have to whisper, it's alright we're in here."

Sarah's eyes were alert. "This is so cool. How is it you just happened to have access to the biology building?"

"Scott Walker is the dean of biology and a dear friend. When I told him I was bringing you over for an after-hours tour he sent the badge over to my place. He's already gone for the semester, otherwise he'd be giving the tour."

"I've read a lot of his research; he's brilliant."

"Not brilliant enough," Alex said with a frown as he swiped the badge and opened the lab's oak door. Flipping on the light switch, Alex said, "Impress me. Show me you know your way around a lab. We need a microscope, scapula, and three slides."

Sarah visually panned the lab before heading toward a supply cabinet across the room.

"Locked," she said as she flipped the padlock.

Alex jingled the keys before handing them over.

"I'm guessing you have something very specific in mind," she said.

Without replying, Alex pulled a stool up to the closest microscope. Smiling cordially, he silently took the blade from Sarah and pricked his finger, allowing a small drop of blood to drip on the slide. "Tell me what you see."

Sarah placed the slide under the microscope. Looking at Alex instead of the slide, she answered mockingly. "Blood!"

"Maybe you should take a closer look?" Alex prodded.

Sarah looked into the eyepiece and adjusted the focus. "What in the world?" Astonished, Sarah looked back at Alex. "What is this?"

Alex smiled mischievously as he took Sarah's hand and pricked her finger.

"Ouch."

Squeezing a drop of Sarah's blood onto a slide, Alex placed a tissue over the incision and asked, "Well?"

Sarah exchanged the slides and then studied the sample briefly. "Nothing remarkable, just my blood."

Alex took the last slide, squeezed a drop from her finger, and then added a drop of his. "And now?"

Sarah placed the slide under the scope and watched as Alex's irregular blood cells appeared to devour her own. "I don't understand this, I've never seen anything like it," Sarah exclaimed. "The incompatible cells should be dying, but yours appear to be thriving."

"Remember the formula I showed you? The one you said was impossible?"

Sarah stared at the slide and then at Alex, dumbfounded by the anomaly, which she believed could not exist. "Your blood, what have you done to it?"

"That's enough questions for now." Alex collected the slides and placed them in a Ziploc bag he had brought from the apartment. "I have more to show you, if you want to see."

"If I want to see? If you show me anything more remarkable than what I just saw, I might just kiss you again. You are going to explain this to me before the night's out?"

After locking up the lab, Alex led Sarah to the campus library. Latched onto his arm, her mind was racing. "I have a million questions, but I don't know where to begin. Is your blood some kind of fountain of youth? Did you do this to yourself?"

As they climbed the steps of the library, Alex asked, "How much do you know about Romania and its history?" Holding the door, he followed her in.

"I took Euro history my freshman semester. I know Romania is supposed to be a democracy, but its president has ruled for almost thirty-five years. He's referred to as King Tepes. I also know Romania is the most powerful nation in the Euro zone. That about sums it up."

As they strolled the isles of the library, Alex collected volumes from the shelves in the process. Once done, he pulled a chair from the table. "Please, have a seat."

Sarah sat down and gazed at the expansive collection of books that filled the great hall. Sitting beside her, Alex stacked the books neatly. Opening the first book, he flipped the pages until arriving at the desired photograph.

"These are the ruins of Poenari, home of the Tepes family. This picture was taken in the early 1900s." Alex flipped the page. "The castle was rebuilt around 2028."

"Quite an improvement." Sarah grinned.

Alex picked up the second volume and turned the pages, stopping on the exact picture needed.

"This is Vlad Tepes, the famed Prince of Wallachia, better known as Count Dracula, and the origin of all vampire lore. As you pointed out, the King of Romania's name is Levente Tepes. He is the grandson of Vlad. Somewhere around 1950, Levente and his wife were captured and entombed in the ruins of Poenari by the Communists."

Sarah studied the image intently, waiting for Alex to continue.

"Are you with me so far?"

"Yes." Sarah's casual grin had taken an uncomfortable turn. "Please go on."

"Before I do, I want you to think about what you just witnessed in the lab and the formula I showed you back in Virginia."

Sarah nodded, but could not hide her mounting uncertainty.

"Also, around 1950, before they were captured, Levente and his wife, Elisabeta, had a child, Neculai. To protect him from capture and certain death, he was sent to America for his safety."

Sarah was no longer looking at the pages, but instead staring at Alex. "Oh yeah, it gets better," he said as he blindly flipped to another page. "Exiled in America to avoid suffering his parent's fate, Neculai grew into adulthood. Over the years, *he* took on aliases to protect his identity, one being that of Brian Denman."

Sarah's lips parted but initially uttered not a sound. Tense seconds passed before she spoke. "I think you need to tell me, minus the family tree, what exactly are you saying?"

Alex cleared his throat. "My real name is Brian Alexander Tepes. I was named after my father's pseudo-identity, Brian Denman. The King of Romania is my grandfather, Vazul Dracula is my great grandfather, and Vlad Tepes—well you get the picture."

Stunned by the revelation, Sarah looked down to Vlad's picture. Suddenly, Vlad's similarities jumped right out of the pages at her.

"Oh my God." Sarah's fingers stroked the printed image as if her touch would reveal some hidden truth. "So, are you some kind of prince?"

Alex nodded. "If my family were to have their way, Brian Alexander Tepes would be the heir to the throne of Romania."

Sarah's voice became timidly soft. "And Vlad Tepes, *the* Dracula?"

"He is so much more than a myth or cinematic creature of Hollywood fascination."

"And your blood?"

Alex knew the train was about to derail, but he had to see this through. "It is the blood of my ancestors." The next question was unavoidable. If Sarah could not summon the courage to ask it, then he would be forced to confess his affliction.

"A *vampire*? Please don't tell me you're something that doesn't exist."

Alex nodded.

"Oh my God. Are you for real?" Sarah shrieked.

Sarah closed the book and stood up as tears welled in her eyes. "Can we leave now? I think I'm ready for that plane ticket," she said with a trembling voice.

"Yes, we can," Alex replied, hoping his composure might transfer to Sarah. "But first, let me ask, do you fear for your safety?"

Sarah looked around nervously, her hands visibly shaking. "I don't know . . . maybe. You do realize you've claimed to be two different guys in three days? Two lunatics. I thought I was falling in love with some wonderful guy."

"I am that guy."

"No, you're mental."

"No, I am not mental." Slow and steady, Alex appealed to the scientist rather than the nearly hysterical cynic. "Remember the blood work. What did *you* say about the formula?"

"I said it was impossible."

Alex held up the lanced finger. "Then I am impossible as well."

"I was in a horrific car accident, wasn't I? I'm really in a coma, in some hospital. If I wake up, you'll be gone, and life will be back to normal." Sarah's eyes darted around the library, taking rapid inventory of every detail. She sniffled and wiped her tears away, her voice broken, but softer. "This doesn't just happen in real life, a guy like you, the car, the romance—" Raising her index finger to her lips, she smiled at the ridiculous notion and then whispered, "Vampires."

Alex stood up. "I promise, you are not in a coma." As he reached out to caress Sarah's cheek, she turned her head. "The very moment I set my eyes upon you, I knew this had to happen. I wanted to tell you the truth before I fell in love with you, but it's too late for that."

"Oh God," Sarah's pleaded. "The vampire loves me?" Jumping up, she collected the books and began returning them. She turned quickly and managed a crooked smile. "I guess I should thank you—for not having sex with me."

Alex reached to touch her, but as she recoiled, he withdrew his hands. "If you leave, I will regret it for the rest of my life."

"I'm sorry, I think I have a few regrets already." Sarah stared and thought for a long minute. "You're not really a prince, are you?"

"Unfortunately, yes. And if you stick around just a little bit longer, I'll tell you the rest of the story, no strings attached."

Sarah snickered before returning to her housekeeping task. "I might as well, it's not like I'm going to get a plane at this hour anyhow."

Tailing Sarah like a lost puppy, Alex checked for unwanted ears. "I can get you a plane if you really want it, a perk of the family issues."

"I'm sure you can, Prince. I'm sure you can."

Alex grabbed Sarah's shoulder. "I'll make you a deal, Sarah. This is hard enough for me as it is, but if you will drop the defensive sarcasm, I'll give you a blood sample to take back home."

"You know I'll figure out how you did that trick, but sure, I'll play nice."

Alex took her by the arm and led her to a secluded corner. "Let me see your phone, please." Typing in a web search, he turned the result to Sarah. "This is the last photo taken of me with my family. I was about twenty-six when they tried to arrange a relationship with the lovely young Romanian woman you see in the picture. They wanted me to move to Romania, marry this woman, and assume a more regal position. It was their intention that by now I would be married and have succeeded my grandfather."

Sarah studied the image. "She's beautiful. But I can understand not wanting a betrothal, or the pressure of ruling a country, but that doesn't come close to explaining that vampire thing?" Alex's hands remained in Sarah's grip as she repeatedly stared at the phone and then at him.

The continuing conversation had lifted his hope. "Are you ready for the rest?"

Sarah nodded slowly, as if she was not completely sure.

"Take your phone and find my reflection in the glass." She did as instructed and began to angle it every which way imaginable. "It's not a hoax," Alex confessed. "We can go to the bathroom if you want, or any other mirror. The result will be the same." Sarah's mouth dropped open, as she mindlessly continued to angle the phone's screen. "This is why you have not seen me in the daylight."

"You are not mental," Sarah stammered. "This is all real?"

"If I didn't know *this* was real from the moment I met you, you would have never seen me again."

Sarah hesitated, distressed over the answer to follow. "Know what?"

"You already know the answer, because up until thirty minutes ago, and especially back in my apartment, you felt it too."

A partial blush washed over Sarah's face. "When you kissed me, I didn't see or feel any . . . weird teeth."

"If you decide to stay, there is much you will learn. But let's just say, my teeth get sizably larger when I'm aroused."

Sarah's expression was mischievously fearful as she considered her next question. "So, did they . . . around me?"

❧

"Thank you," Sarah said as Alex took her coat. "This has been the most incredibly illuminating night of my life." Sarah kissed Alex on the cheek and checked her watch. "It's early still," Sarah observed, her speech slurring ever so slightly. "The night's just getting started. What should we do next?"

The open-ended, suggestive question was courtesy of the bottle of wine Sarah had consumed with dinner. Her pheromones were broadcasting desire all over the apartment. Alex was simply delighted that Sarah appeared to accept the details of his affliction, even if it was temporarily contingent on her sobriety.

"Sarah, I want you to understand something." He took her by the hand and led her to the couch. "You and I, we both want the same thing right now. But you've had too much to drink. I want your head clear. I don't want excuses or regrets."

"I am almost perfectly fine, I'll have you know. But you should take advantage of me before I start overthinking this thing again. I was ready to make love, or fuck, or whatever vampires might call it, before you told me all that scary stuff. So we can forget you told me anything, forget the wine, and do what we both know I want to do."

Trying to get Sarah to understand, particularly in her current state, was going to be difficult. "Do you know what happens when we go in the bedroom?"

"You're going to drink my blood? Pffft." Sarah snickered happily. "Isn't that what you do?"

Alex rolled his eyes, regretting the wine by the minute. "Keep this up and it might be." Alex feigned a smile through his frustration. "If you had left tonight, it would take a while, but I'd eventually get over the hurt. But once we go in there, for me, there will be no turning back. What's in there," he said, pointing to the bedroom, "is so much more than just a fuck. It's my family, their expectations, and it's a fucking nation on my back. It is the game I fear, and it could destroy you." Alex stood, walked to the window, and stared out at Brooklyn. "Once we go in there, I promise, neither of us will ever be the same."

Transfixed, he stared out the window, wondering how in the hell to get his point across. Sarah silently approached and wrapped her arms around his chest. "The yearning in my poetry, don't you see it? It is you, it has always been you, and once we share that passion, I will be completely lost, in you."

Sarah pulled tightly, drawing Alex against the heat of her body. "Would that be so bad?"

An incessant rapping on the door interrupted Alex. He dropped his chin and shook his head. "We'll see how you feel after this. Better take a seat, please."

Alex inhaled deeply before opening the door.

"You sorry sack of shit," the voice bellowed before the door had hardly cracked open.

"Uncle Chuck. It's good to see you again."

The cordial greeting did not dissipate the fire in Chuck's eyes. He grabbed Alex by the collar, wrenching his shirt tightly. "You little shit, where do you get off disappearing for ten years."

"You know exactly why I did it. And it's your own damn fault I pulled it off. You taught me everything I know."

Chuck peeked over Alex's shoulder and caught a glimpse of Sarah's frightened expression as she watched the fiasco from the couch. "Is that her?" he asked as he dropped Alex to the floor. Walking over for an up-close inspection, Chuck cooed, "Damn, Alex, she's cute. Where'd you find her?"

Sarah snapped, "He didn't find me. We met in Virginia Beach, at a coffee shop."

"Feisty little tart." Chuck snickered. "Good luck with that." Chuck rounded the couch and gave Sarah a more thorough inspection. "So, you found her in Virginia Beach? I guess you were on the way there when you royally pissed them boys off back in Maine?"

"Maine was a momentary lack of judgment," Alex said with a smile. "Chuck, I'd like you to meet Sarah. Sarah, the big buffoon is my Uncle Chuck. He is my father's best friend and also in charge of family security, which is why he's acting like a gigantic ass right now."

Chuck sneered and was about to resume his ranting when another voice interrupted.

"Chuck, I told you to wait for me?"

"Damn, there goes the neighborhood," Chuck moaned.

"Alex!" Gabrielle shrieked as she bolted across the room and lunged into his arms, wrapping hers around him. Oblivious to Sarah's presence, Gabrielle planted multiple, rapid-fire kisses across his face.

Sarah coughed loudly as she inspected Gabrielle's model-like physique, lack of appropriate clothing, and her arms still locked around Alex.

With Gabrielle wrapped around his torso, Alex waddled to the couch. "Gabrielle, I want you to meet somebody."

Gabrielle loosened her grip and dropped to the floor. With a suspicious gaze, she asked in her *snippy* French accent, "And who is this?"

Alex knew the snippiness was merely Gabrielle's territorial nature. She had always been the gatekeeper when it came to his, and his brother's, dating selections. "*Gabrielle*, this is Sarah, my very good friend."

Gabrielle cut a glare to Chuck and punched his ribs. "Did you know he was bringing a guest and forget to inform me?" Chuck rolled his eyes as Gabrielle launched a short French tirade directed at him. She then shrugged her shoulders and smiled at Sarah. "I must apologize for my husband's ill manners. I was not expecting company. So stand up, let's have a look at you."

With an uncomfortable expression, Sarah rose slowly. Gabrielle's eyes traveled several passes over her body, every so often exclaiming, "Yes . . . yes." Gabrielle turned back to Alex. "Oh, Alex, she is most beautiful," she chirped. "So, the two of you, you are lovers?"

Sarah's eyes popped wide at the frankness of Gabrielle's question.

"Geez, Gabby," Alex objected. "Sarah, please forgive Gabrielle's complete lack of social skills. She's been married to the King of No Filter for over thirty years and some of his unique personality dysfunctions have rubbed off on her."

"It does not matter," Gabrielle chirped. "I am so happy the two of you are here. We will enjoy our time together. Tomorrow, I will take Sarah shopping and we will get to know each other, and you and the dog can go do what boys do. Until then, I will take Monsieur Chuck and work on his manners." Gabrielle took Chuck by the hand. "Besides, I sense we have interrupted something."

Gabrielle led Chuck out the door, leaving Sarah and Alex alone.

"Who was that, and what did she mean that she sensed they interrupted something?"

"Gabrielle is Chuck's wife, and they are vampires. Like me, their sense of smell is acute. And if you want to know, the scent of your desire, it's pretty strong."

"Oh no," Sarah exclaimed with a blush. "You can smell—every time?"

"Like a steak on the grill." Alex chuckled. "By the time you can feel it, your pheromones have already betrayed you." Alex's face illuminated at the thought.

"So every time I thought . . . "

"Yes, I did."

CHAPTER ELEVEN

ŞTEFAN PACED THROUGH the crowds of Bourbon Street. His anger drove his desire to feed. As he dodged the mindless drunks, he sized up each and every individual he passed. Isabelle's words had cut him deeply. *"You should never have done this to me."*

He continued to squeeze her cell phone to the point of crushing it. The more he dwelled on its purpose, the madder he got. *"Call your father,"* Isabelle had insisted, as she handed him the phone just before he left her apartment. For the vast majority of his life, Ştefan had done as he was told.

It was two years ago, eight years after his brother, Alex, had disappeared, too many long years of being the good son, trying so hard to atone for his crime, that Ştefan had learned that his lineage afforded him nothing more than a name, and a curse. Like his father and brother, Ştefan had no desire to rule Romania—until two years ago.

His love for Reese changed everything. From the throne of the most powerful European nation, Ştefan envisioned revealing the true nature of the Tepes family. No longer a secret culture living in fear of discovery, his race would multiply and become one of esteem and envy. *If* he had only been acceptable in his grandfather's eyes, Reese would have never been imprisoned, and his well-planned transgression about to transpire—only a dream soon to be forgotten.

Ştefan kicked a beer can in disgusted anguish. "Why are we so fucked?" he barked out.

At every pivotal junction in his life, Ştefan believed that fate turned his life to shit. His father had been born a half-breed, a *day-walker*, the unnatural offspring of a mortal parent and a vampire. While his father and Alex were born in the light, Ştefan was born into darkness. *Fucking cruel fate.* Samantha, Ştefan's mother, was a mortal at the time of his conception, and he should have been born a day-walker. But as Ştefan lay inside his dying mother's womb, Alex's mother, Angelique, saved Samantha's life with the kiss of Nosferatu. Thus, out of death, Ştefan and his mother both joined the legions of the accursed.

Alex remained a day-walker through his youth, and with his pure Romanian lineage, he was expected to rise to the throne. "The next King of Romania must walk in the light, and not rely on impostors to rule their homeland," his grandfather insisted. But Alex had no burning love for Romania, and certainly no desire to be its ruler. The curse that befell his father, through Monique's blood, would suffice for him. In secrecy, and with much coercing, Alex convinced Ştefan to share the curse of the Tepes family. Ingesting Ştefan's blood, Alex turned from the light, and then from his family.

Ştefan stood in shame and remorse the day his brother confronted their family, revealing his lost humanity. He helplessly witnessed the bonds of family love disintegrate, all destroyed by *his* hand. Alex's confession, claiming sole responsibility for his brother's deeds, did nothing to absolve Ştefan of his role. His self-induced guilt, and subsequent isolation, became Ştefan's constant companions.

Ştefan squeezed the phone even tighter, and then with all his supernatural strength hurled the phone far out of sight.

"So much anger from one so blessed," a voice called from behind.

Ştefan turned to find a haggard, pale old man with an unruly beard and eyes glazed by severe cataracts. "What did you say, old man?"

"For one so blessed with beauty, you have much anger."

Ştefan scoffed. "Apparently, you are the expert on the attributes of beauty?"

"I know what I see, for you have been in my dreams, boy."

Ştefan gazed about the passing crowds, looking to see if the old man had strayed from his family. With nobody paying any particular attention to the two of them, he looked back at the old man.

The old man leaned into Ştefan's ear and whispered sharply, "I know what you are."

Ştefan grabbed the old man by the elbow and tugged, leading him away from the crowds on Bourbon Street. Once a safe distance up Dumaine, he spun the old man around and peered into his eyes. "What am I?"

The shadows of the streets played across the old man's face, accentuating his cadaverous expression. "You are a vampire. The one who will deliver the dark into the light."

Ştefan stared at the old man, waiting for the *crazy as a loon* light to flash. Through the old man's opacities, Ştefan saw the truth buried deep in his eyes. "How do you know this?"

"I told you, you have been in my dreams, as has *he*, for many nights."

Ştefan pulled the old man close as a couple approached. "Who is *he*?"

"The Count Èdouard Barousse."

"And exactly who is this Count Barousse?"

"At one time he was a powerful, but cruel, plantation owner. He murdered, raped, and tortured anyone he pleased—until the day he met a young woman. I believe you may know of her, *Monique Beauvais*. It was this woman who sent Èdouard Barousse to his unnatural grave, an affliction I believe the two of you share."

"Monique, the one who turned my father into a vampire?" Ştefan awaited a confirmation that never arrived. "I have lived here many years. How is it I have never heard of his name?"

"A man of Barousse's disposition was missed but by few. Once his slaves learned of his unnatural circumstances, they removed his coffin by the light of day and entombed him in the bayous. They burned the mansion, the crops, and everything on that accursed plantation, even their own quarters. Some of those slaves were hung, the others were never found. But to this day, almost three centuries later, Barousse remains a prisoner of the bayou."

"Why do you tell me this? Who is this man to me?"

"You seek to change the world, yet you do not possess the, let us call it, *expertise* to accomplish such change. Without the aid of Count Barousse, you will fail." Although the old man's speech trembled, his message was resolute.

Ştefan studied the old man's features intently. In all his years growing up, there were only two people his father knew who possessed such foresight. This one would have to be past one hundred years of age. "Are you Daniel?"

The old man's dire expression softened as his head bobbed with nearly a smile. "I am but a humble messenger sent to set the Cairns before you." The old man pulled himself free from Ştefan's grip and turned away.

"How will I find him?"

"I can only offer you the advice I offered to another, many years ago. In faith, all that you seek can be found."

Ştefan had been beside himself, almost obsessed, to learn more of this Èdouard Barousse. Like the history of so many failed plantation owners, the Internet was void of accounts of these marginal landowners. Sending an old friend to city hall, Ştefan learned that Barousse owned a tract of land on the south side of the Mississippi, just beyond Westwego.

Just after sunset the very next night, Ştefan set out to explore the former site just off Bridge City Avenue. Passing by a multitude of unsightly industrial complexes lining the river, he couldn't help but wonder how beautiful it had been when plantation mansions and agriculture ruled the river.

Ştefan found it hard to imagine a mansion standing on the grounds before him. Guarded by a corroded metal gate, a cluster of rusty and dilapidated wooden sheds were the only structures to be found on the property. Still, according to records dating back to the early seventeen hundreds, this was the site of Barousse's plantation.

Ştefan left his car on the side of the road and hopped over the gate. The long grass waved in the breeze on the chilled, starry night as Ştefan moved decisively toward the ghostly structures. Appearing to be over one hundred years old, the shed felt as though it might collapse as Ştefan pulled on the door. Not wanting to assume these shacks were merely for storage, Ştefan inspected each one thoroughly. The first two sheds were filled with old rusted hand tools, shovels, picks, car parts, paint buckets, and a lawn mower that appeared unused for half a century.

With a firm kick, the padlock on the third shed door gave way without a fight. Inside, Ştefan found termite-eaten furniture, assorted pottery, filthy glassware, and several worn cardboard boxes filled with documents. Thumbing through the top layer, he found canceled checks, a Time magazine from 1961, and a few old plat surveys from about the same period. Although he found nothing of worth upon his hurried assessment, he thought it best to take the boxes for a more thorough inspection.

Ştefan returned to the illumination of the rising moon and studied the landscape. The back of the property was heavily wooded, but as there was nothing else to be found in the knee-deep weeds that surrounded the shacks, he ventured toward the dark confines of the forest. Pushing his way through the thick underbrush, the futility of his efforts began to grate on his nerves. "Isn't this great? I've got an army ready to conquer the world, and I'm off on some crazy man's scavenger hunt." Ştefan decided he had had enough. Making a broad turn, he headed back to the open field.

Mosaic patterns of moonlight filtered through the leafless oaks as Ştefan pushed his way back toward the field. At the edge of the tree line, he stubbed his toe on something hard. Bending down to inspect the object, he discovered several bricks buried beneath the leaves. As he continued to search, he found what appeared to be the remains of a fallen chimney. Judging by the age of the surrounding trees, the fireplace must have stood there hundreds of years ago.

"Èdouard Barousse, you son of a bitch, I'm on your trail." With renewed inspiration, Ştefan made his way back to the shed to collect the boxes of miscellaneous documents. As he carried the fourth box to the car, he heard the distinctive pump action of a shotgun.

"Where you goin' with those boxes, buddy?"

Ştefan stopped and set the box down.

"Slow now. It'd be a shame to shoot somethin' I don't wanna eat."

Ştefan turned slowly. "I'm from the law firm of Brown and Brown. There has been a claim on this property from a relative of the Barousse family."

"Shit, I ain' got use for no lawyers 'round here." The man spit in the direction of Ştefan's shoes.

Ştefan let the insult pass and continued calmly, "I'm sorry, sir. I was just going to take these documents back to my hotel to see if they contained any valuable information."

"I can tell you there ain' noth'n in dose boxes. So why don' you just put 'em back where you found 'em and git your pretty lawyer ass out of here." The man spit a second time, the glob of phlegm landing squarely on Ştefan's shoe.

Ştefan was losing his patience with the idiot before him. "Sir, if you will allow me to inspect these papers, I will gladly have them back tomorrow. Then there will be no need to involve any local law enforcement in the matter."

The Cajun thrust his gun in Ştefan's chest. "Put dem boxes back. An if I ever see your preddy ass roun' here agin, I ain' gonna bodder wit no warn'n."

"I tried," Ştefan announced. The Cajun never saw Ştefan's hand move or had time to comprehend what had happened. The shotgun had been tossed from sight, and with a constricting hand around his throat, he was being dragged toward the shed. Unable to scream out, he thrashed wildly at his attacker.

"Don't you worry now, son, this will only hurt a bit." Without any concern for this man's life, family, or purpose, Ştefan sunk his teeth deeply into his neck. The rich Cajun blood filled Ştefan with such a euphoric high, he did not even notice the man's death thralls battering and clawing at his body.

Ştefan dropped the carcass to the ground—the empty remains no longer a nuisance. With no imminent concern for the consequences of his feast, he returned to his task of securing the boxes. As Ştefan prepared to slam the trunk closed, he looked at his arm and saw the fast-healing scratches. "Shit, DNA," he muttered.

Begrudgingly, Ştefan moved the boxes from the trunk to the back seat. He then began his search for the shotgun, which would definitely reveal a nice set of his fingerprints. Once the gun was located, Ştefan returned and picked up the corpse. "Hey, dumbass, I hope you realize how much work you've created for me," he said to the dead Cajun.

Ştefan slammed the trunk closed. *Now, what to do with the rest of this mess?* Ştefan glared at the Cajun's truck. "Guess I can't leave you at the crime scene either." Ştefan knew the lecture his father would give if he ever found out about tonight. *What in the hell were you thinking? How could you risk our exposure so thoughtlessly?*

Back out on River Road, Ştefan had passed a dirt lot with several abandoned cars and, just beyond that, a dive bar. His plan was simple; drive his car to the bar and then return to the rusted pick-up truck and deposit it on the dirt lot with the other scrap cars, where it could go unnoticed for days or maybe longer.

On the drive back to the city, Ştefan reflected on the events of the night. His actions were completely irresponsible. He could have just as easily disarmed the Cajun and knocked him out. Perhaps an incantation would have worked even better. But what was done was done. The body had been deposited in the bayou and most likely would be devoured by the various species of wildlife before his truck would be discovered. Was the man's death born out of Ştefan's instinctive need to feed or, perhaps, frustration over his failed attempts at love? And after last night, how could he face Isabelle again, his sole remaining ally?

The absence of a wedding ring on the Cajun had relieved Ştefan, although the time had long passed to consider the morals of his actions. Often Ştefan had wrestled with the ethics of taking a life, but he knew the path he now traveled would require much death, perhaps even the death of those he loved.

It was just after midnight when he pulled up to his family home on Chestnut Street, in the Garden District of New Orleans. Ştefan had missed the home of so many great memories where he had grown up. His parents were the best he could have asked for, and he was as close with his half brother as any two brothers could be. Due to their nocturnal habits, their circle of friends was select, but with an abundance of French Quarter crazies, there was never a shortage of great friends to be made.

The white columns, green shutters, and landscaping were all pleasantly illuminated by accent lighting, hidden amongst the abundant variety of plants. Ştefan knew the minute he entered his home, his parents would know of his return. But he wanted access to his computer and possibly to some of the historical New Orleans books in his parents' extensive library.

As Ştefan entered the house, he immediately realized something was amiss; the alarm was always on. Isabelle had told him his parents were in France. At this hour there should have been no housekeepers or visitors. Ştefan began stepping softly as he advanced into the foyer. He checked the parlor and then the ballroom. As he entered the dining room, a scent grew familiar. Ştefan swung the kitchen door open.

"Somehow I knew you'd come here," Isabelle said, as she swirled her wine glass.

Wrought with guilt, Ştefan could not look her in the eye. "I have work, which I could not accomplish at the hotel. Why are you here?"

"Ştefan, I have known you all of your life. I held you as a baby. In so many ways you are like family." Isabelle held her glass high but peeked over the top. "Last night should have never happened."

"But it did . . . and we are not family. And it never would have happened if you had not wanted it as well."

"You love Reese." Isabelle replied sharply.

"Reese would have never happened if you had allowed yourself to love me . . . if my father would have allowed it."

Isabelle set her glass down, no longer hiding her face. "Your father had nothing to do with my feelings."

Ştefan closed the gap between them and finally looked into her eyes. "Who are you lying to?"

Isabelle rose from her stool. "Last night was weakness, and pity."

"Pity? Last night was amazing!" Ştefan exclaimed as he took Isabelle by the shoulders. "Look me in the eyes and tell me it was anything less."

Isabelle searched Ştefan's eyes and could not find a path to deny the pleasure she had experienced. "I will not tell you what you already know, but the pleasure does not justify the deed. I am sure every woman you have fucked finds you incredible. It is part of the allure of the being you are." Isabelle followed as Ştefan reeled away. "You rush to love like it will disappear completely if you do not conquer it. But it will always be there, when the time is right."

Ştefan turned again, his feelings uncharacteristically easy to read. "And apparently everyone but me gets to decide when that will be?"

"Love cannot be one sided, it doesn't work that way." Isabelle gave Ştefan a sympathetic kiss on the cheek. "Last night was a great fuck, but it was just that. I regret it."

"Yeah," Ştefan interrupted. "It seems everyone I cross paths with lately has regrets."

Isabelle studied Ştefan's face. "Don't forget I helped raise you. When I see that gleam in your eye, I know you're not telling me something."

"I killed a man tonight," Ştefan declared, with an exasperated sigh.

Trying to conceal her dire concern, Isabelle asked calmly, "Why?"

"He had a gun pointed at my chest. I was angry with him, with you, with Reese, with my family. I was just angry, and he paid for it."

"Where did this happen?"

"Westwego?"

"What on earth were you doing there? Please tell me. How did he die?"

"Old school vampire shit."

"And his body?"

"I dumped him in the bayou. By tomorrow, all of his soft tissue should be gone."

Ştefan's impassive explanation concerned her, not only because of his action, but if the body was discovered, the consequences could be disastrous. Isabelle looked at the watch on her wrist and then the phone on the wall.

"I know what you're thinking. Don't do it."

Defiantly, Isabelle went for the phone and dialed. "It's me. We have a problem." Isabelle waited only briefly. "No, it's not. It's Ştefan. There has been a feeding fatality." Again Isabelle listened. "No, he's here." Silently, with contempt in her eyes, Isabelle extended the phone to Ştefan.

"Chuck." Ştefan tried, unsuccessfully, to tame Chuck's anger, which could be heard across the room. "No, it's fine. I'm sure of it. Who was it that taught me about swamp dumps anyhow?" The lecture lasted a good two minutes before Ştefan could reply. Suddenly, Ştefan's demeanor changed. "Fine, I will call him, and I'll check tomorrow."

Isabelle caught the change immediately. "What is it?"

Ştefan raised his finger as he continued to talk. "I would like to speak with him, if you can arrange it. Yes, I'll keep a cell on me." Ştefan hung the phone up deliberately easily and turned to Isabelle. "Apparently, my brother has resurfaced in New York City—with a girlfriend."

Isabelle's emotions were swirling. "Where has he been? What's going on?"

"Chuck really didn't have much information other than Alex needed a passport for his girlfriend. Apparently, they are leaving the country. I'm guessing Romania."

Isabelle's hand covered her mouth. Like everyone in the family, she vividly remembered the rift created by the arranged marriage. Perhaps Alex had found a potential bride, one that might be acceptable in his grandfather's eyes. Ştefan too considered the ramifications.

Smiling ever so slightly, Isabelle retrieved her wine glass and topped it off. With a flat affect, Isabelle changed the subject. "I know he found you, for he found me as well."

Surprised by the revelation, Ştefan stuttered, "What did he ask of you?"

"It was not so much a question but more so information. I think.

I'm not sure what he expected of me. He told me there was another, Èdouard Barousse. He said my mother would know of him. Apparently, I am to contact my mother, but to what end, he did not elaborate."

"Was that Daniel?"

"Yes," Isabelle replied hauntingly. "I thought he had to have died years ago. It has been almost thirty years since I last laid eyes on him. I think Daniel believes he is out there, somewhere. Maybe we are to find him."

Ştefan did not believe that was Daniel's intended purpose, but he knew where Isabelle's loyalty would lie. "I have some documents in my car that may help us find him. I'll go get them. Why don't you call your mother and see if she knows anything about this man."

Isabelle was in the middle of the call when Ştefan brought the pair of boxes in. By the time he returned with the remainders, she was finishing the call.

"I'll see you soon, Mother. I love you." She turned to Ştefan who had already opened the box and begun flipping through papers. "My mother told me Monique had many lovers. Her favorite was a wealthy plantation owner by the name of Èdouard Barousse. When Monique and my mother were imprisoned in the convent, Monique swore Èdouard would come for them. Although Monique never confessed to turning Barousse, my mother always suspected her guilt."

"I was at the site of his plantation tonight," Ştefan confessed, without looking up from his task. "That's where I ran into the Cajun. Is it possible they guard Barousse's grave, like the Order of the Dragon guarded the convent and Poenari? Perhaps they are the ones that sent Daniel back to us." Ştefan continued to dig through the box. "Start with that one," he said, indicating the box on the kitchen table. "We're looking for anything that might be a plat of the original site or any document relating to the sale of the property."

Isabelle left the kitchen as Ştefan continued to rummage through the boxes. Moments later she returned with several weathered volumes. "Your father owns a copy of every book ever written about New Orleans. I have read most of them. Just guessing, Barousse must have died shortly after 1752. This book documents the plantations west of the Mississippi." Isabelle flipped thru the index and then thumbed through the pages. "Here it is, Èdouard Barousse's plantation."

Ştefan took the book and studied the delicate pages of the

historical diagram. With none of the modern landmarks present, he used the river as a reference point. "That's it. That's where I was earlier tonight," Ştefan exclaimed as he turned the book to Isabelle. "Damn, his property went all the way into the bayou. The Westbank Expressway cuts the property in half now."

Isabelle was busy ignoring Ştefan's trivial geographical discovery. Grabbing a second volume, she flipped to the index and then quickly found the page. "It appears they hung a slave by the name of Nathan Brown for the murder of Barousse and the burning of his plantation." She continued reading as she shooed Ştefan away. "Back to your flea market research boxes, I've got this covered." Isabelle scooped up the books. "I'll be in the library where the scholars belong."

Isabelle was busy typing search parameters when Ştefan entered the library with a fresh glass of wine.

"If you're thinking this will get me into that coffin of yours tonight . . . ," she said with wry a smile.

"No, but this might." Ştefan unfolded an extremely delicate and tattered parchment and laid it on the desk where she worked. "Look familiar?"

The drawing was crude, not even close to the professionally drafted documents of the time period. But the river was unmistakable, as was the wedge of land. Roughly sketched on the wedged parcel was a mansion, slave quarters, out parcels, indigo fields, and, on the furthest perimeter of the property adjacent to the bayou, a cross. "I think this might have been a cemetery or maybe, at a minimum, where the ol' bastard was buried."

Isabelle looked at her watch. "The sun will be up soon. I'll be back at dusk. We can ride out and see if there is anything left of this cemetery."

"Why don't you stay? You still have a bedroom here, don't you?"

Isabelle smiled. "If I thought you would keep your hands to yourself, I would consider it."

Ştefan placed his hand on top of Isabelle's. "You enjoyed yourself, so why not?"

"Because, Ştefan Tepes, you and I would never be more than a pleasure fuck in the night. You know this is true, and you know we both want so much more than that."

Ştefan rolled his eyes. Maybe she was right. His family would be dead set against it. But a few months from now, that might not matter. But he dared not risk sharing his plans with Isabelle. "You're right, but it was a good fuck, wasn't it?"

"Good?" Isabelle rose from the desk and placed a book under her arm. "I'll see you at dusk."

As customary, as Isabelle prepared to leave, they kissed by the door, the kiss lingering longer than either had anticipated. With mixed emotions, Ştefan locked the door and watched Isabelle drive away. He climbed the stairs to his bedroom, a place he had not slept in almost two years. Stripping off his shoes, T-shirt, and jeans he studied the poster bed with its down comforter and feather pillows. Undoubtedly, tonight his dreams would be filled with wild sexual fantasies, thanks to Isabelle, and, in part, a belly full of fresh blood. He looked upon his favorite works of erotic art from a deceased local artist, Peter O'Neill. To the right of the oil on canvas of a masked woman stretched across a piano was a solid oak door with a skeleton key lock. Ştefan pulled the key from behind his dresser and unlocked the door. Flipping on the light with great pleasure, he studied the row of seldom-used caskets.

Tonight he would sleep in complete peace. Tonight he would rest as his ancestors had for centuries. Tonight he would sleep with the dignity of a vampire. He pulled the oak door shut and slid the deadbolt closed. Raising the lid of the casket, he ran his fingers along the cream-colored satin lining. The intensity of the silky texture reminded him of Isabelle's skin. He stepped his naked feet into the casket and then slowly lay back while closing the lid. Ushering in absolute darkness, he drifted off, the warm, close confines bringing back childhood memories; cradled in his mother's arms, the world was good and he was safe.

CHAPTER TWELVE

IT HAD BEEN a restless day for Nicholas. Sleep typically came easy, but the thought of Alex's car being spotted had created anxiety, a feeling he generally hadn't dealt with for years. As he gazed around their room, the sight of Samantha and Tori sleeping in bed afforded a temporary reprieve.

Back safely in the confines of their own hotel, they were miles away from the choleric pimp they had left behind. Nicholas would have liked to kill him, but leaving a bloodless body at the Saint Germaine would not have been smart. Allowing Tori to drink more of his own blood than necessary, Nicholas knew it would be a day or two before he felt well enough to do much of anything.

With his wife and their newly made vampire sleeping peacefully, Nicholas sat in the dark, mulling over the turmoil that resulted in Alex's disappearance. Nicholas's father had been pushing Alex to assume the president's office of Romania. The prosperity Levente had brought to the nation would more than guarantee his son would easily win any election, if even an election were called for.

Levente had brought the impoverished nation to the forefront of European powers. In just two short years after their escape from the ruins of Poenari, Levente resurfaced as a legitimate descendent of the Tepes family and a major entrepreneur. Building relations with private investors, he quickly turned Romania into an energy and manufacturing powerhouse. With education reform the foundation of this new nation, he quickly became the people's champion. Within a few years he easily claimed the presidency. Every endeavor he championed, one question remained constant: How can we do it better?

Maintaining tight reigns over corruption and healthcare, the economy exploded. Humble and honest, but more importantly driven to perfection, every election became more a matter of protocol than necessity. Using a body double, Levente was able to meet the needs of public life while crushing all rumors of the family's dark past.

But time marched on, and the aging process of the presidential imposter was beginning to weigh not only on Levente, but his duped opponents as well. Levente's desire was for his son Nicholas to succeed him, but the power and public attention was nothing Nicholas desired. As a day-walker, Alex had been a much more suitable candidate to replace his grandfather. The family began crafting his image before Alex was twenty years old, parading him in the public eye, arranging dates with notable women worthy of one day becoming the future president's wife.

At such a young age, Alex complied with the perfectly scripted life. Quickly tiring of the prim and proper life, in his first open act of youthful defiance, he became a vampire by Ştefan's hand.

It was a devastating blow to the Tepes family, but one they knew they must overcome. Undaunted by Alex's rebellion, the family continued to forge ahead, seeking to modify their designs for his future. By the time Alex reached thirty, he'd had enough of his family's grand schemes.

How long had he planned this? Nicholas wondered. It was a monumental achievement to disappear without a trace from family so skilled in covert intelligence. Yet Alex had done so for ten years, or maybe longer should the lead on the car prove to be fruitless.

Night had come to the City of Lights and Nicholas ventured to the rooftop of the Hotel San Régis. Studying the lines of the Eiffel Tower from the terrace, Nicholas sighed, the burden of his missing sons and the absurdity of his family lineage weighing heavily on his mind.

Nicholas shook his head as he reflected on the night Angelique, now his father's wife, entranced him. Believing her true love, Levente, had perished many centuries before, she seduced the man she knew as Brian Denman, unaware of his true identity. Out of that unnatural union between a vampire and a day-walker, their son, Brian Alexander, was born a day-walker; his future would be one of obligations.

Only two years younger than Alex, Ştefan had been raised without the burden of expectation. While Levente had embraced Samantha, an American, as his son's wife, in his mind, Ştefan lacked the pure bloodlines to ever rule the homeland. Ştefan always appeared to know his place in the family order, and barring the death of the entire family bloodline, it was understood that he would never succeed his grandfather. Nicholas couldn't help but suspect that jealousy had played a part in Ştefan's role in Alex's conversion.

As fate would have it, Levente had survived and returned to rule his ancestors' homeland. He was often heard complaining that he married his true love, Angelique, two hundred years too late. However the twisted plot would eventually unfold, both his son and grandsons now all shared the curse of Vlad the Impaler, and Levente felt obligated to remain in power.

In a somber mood, perhaps tonight Nicholas would remain in his room and mindlessly lose himself in French television. But the images of Samantha and Tori alone on the streets of Paris did not offer much relief from his strife. Two beautiful women, one a former hooker and fledgling vampire, the other naïve and adventuresome, beyond reason at times, mixed in with nearly two million horny Frenchmen; this was a likely recipe for certain disaster.

In no better state of mind, Nicholas arrived back in the room to find both women dressed to kill and ready for action.

"If you were out looking for a hooker, I could perhaps give you a tip on where to find the best quality," Tori said with a smile.

The first reply that crossed Nicholas's mind, concerning their attire, would have surely put him right back in the doghouse. Lacking any humorous rebuttal, Nicholas decided to simply fess up. "I was on the terrace, waiting for you ladies to join me for a glass of wine. I couldn't stay in bed all day with the likes of you two deviants."

"Deviants?" Samantha cackled, obviously quite at home with her blood daughter. "Do you hear how my husband is referring to us? How should we respond to that?"

"If he were not your husband," Tori began, as she lifted a belt from the bed and ran her hand down its leathery length, "I have some friends that specialize in latex and whips. I think a few hours with them would teach him some proper respect."

Samantha laughed lightly at Nicholas's dismayed expression. "When it comes to teaching men respect, married or single, they all need to be taught their comeuppance," Samantha added. "Why don't we go have that wine on the terrace and discuss these friends of yours. Maybe they'll consent to loaning us some tools of the trade for the evening."

Nicholas rolled his eyes. Samantha's playful spirit had not diminished one bit over the years, but there was an underlying concern; she might be serious.

The trio sat on the terrace and enjoyed the skyline of Paris as Samantha and Nicholas further instructed Tori on the nuances of vampirism. With the temperatures hovering just above freezing, there were no other rooftop dwellers. Sharing the secrets of their family history, the good, the bad, and the butt ugly, they were all exposed with equal diligence.

Nicholas's jacket pocket vibrated, alerting him to an incoming message. As he read the message, he muttered, "What the hell?"

Samantha's eyebrows perked up. "What is it, Nick?"

"You would think after all these years, technology would have advanced enough that you get alerts when they occur, not a day later." Nicholas fingered through the app. "Our alarm in New Orleans was deactivated yesterday—by Isabelle?"

"So?"

"She has never gone in our house when we were away without asking first," Nicholas said.

"We are in Paris, honey." Not appearing overly concerned, Samantha refilled all three wine glasses.

"It's only a phone call." Nicholas tapped the app several times. "Aren't you at least curious?"

"Not to the extent that I would do what you're about to do."

"If that was Alex's car headed south, he might be at the house. You know how close Isabelle was to the boys." Nicholas studied the phone, sliding screens to view the various cameras. "He might have reached out to her."

"And if her plumbing in that old house is broken again and she just came over for a shower?"

"Then I guess we'd better hope she stays in the bathroom while she's naked." Nicholas began watching the video streams. "I hope you didn't want any more of that merlot you left by the toaster oven."

Samantha leaned in to watch, but Nicholas pulled the phone away. "Don't look. After drinking the rest of your wine, Izzy might be running naked through the house, or worse."

"Nicholas, let me see," Samantha demanded.

Samantha studied the images intently, rewound the feed, and played it again. "Something is wrong with her. Did you see her expression?"

"I did."

"We should call," Samantha insisted.

Tori watched the short debate in silent amusement. In her illness, she had given up all hope of ever having any relationship again. But now, not only was love possible, but apparently it could also transcend the ages.

"How about we finish the video first," Nicholas said as he playfully snatched his phone back.

"It looks personal. We should call."

"And if it's nothing? I'll finish watching first. Why open a can of worms if it's nothing?"

Samantha turned her attention to Tori. "Men. This is what you will have to put up with. It's enough to drive a woman to lesbianism."

Tori smiled. "I have been with both. Maybe he is worth the trouble."

"Son of a bitch!" Nicholas interrupted.

"What is it, Nick?"

"While you are busy discussing the finer aspects of turning lesbian on me, you might want to know that Isabelle's naked."

As Samantha reached for the phone, Nicholas turned his body away. "Bi-curious, you'll just have to wait your turn."

"Nick!" Samantha snapped.

"Sam, she's not really naked, but you might be interested to know, Ştefan is with her."

Samantha grabbed the back of Nicholas's neck. "Nicholas Tepes, hand me that phone right now."

"You can't call him, remember. This was yesterday. I think you're right though, they both appear like something might have happened." Nicholas turned his attention back to the phone, flipping between camera views as Samantha watched over his shoulder.

"Who's she calling? Do you think she tried to call us?" Samantha asked with a hint of desperation. As Nicholas continued flipping between cameras they observed Ştefan's arms loaded with boxes. "What do you think he has in the boxes?"

"Either that is the biggest Chinese carry out in New Orleans's history or they are definitely up to something," Nicholas said as they intently studied the phone screen.

"Books from the library? What in the hell are those two up to?"

Nicholas momentarily took his eyes off the screen and looked at his wife. "As long as they stay in view of the cameras, we will know soon enough."

After watching the pair continue their investigation, Nicholas replayed the video to see if he could decipher which books were removed from his library. "They are looking in my historical New Orleans collection." Nicholas fast-forwarded the video until Isabelle returned to the library. After burying herself in several other volumes, she moved to the computer. "Gotcha now, Izzy," Nicholas proclaimed.

Nicholas paused the video and logged into his home computer. "Èdouard Barousse? Who in the hell is that?" Again, they watched as Ştefan returned to the library and displayed an unrecognizable piece of paper. "Dammit, I want to know what those two are doing."

"Izzy should be up. We can call her." Samantha peeked back at the video, watching until the pair left the library. She then turned to Tori. "Please excuse our inattention. It is our son Ştefan, who we've told you a little about, and our friend Isabelle, who is, as far as we know, the last of the day-walkers. Whatever they are doing, their behavior is quite out of character."

"I'll say," Nicholas added. "Tell me what you think of this."

Samantha watched the video stream as the pair shared a kiss. "That was no friendly goodnight kiss. Something is going on between those two." Samantha reversed the video and watched again. "Whatever is going on, now I think a phone call is in order."

Nicholas took the phone back and scrolled through the cameras. "It would appear as though our wayward son is spending the night at home. I think instead of a phone call, we should fly home, tonight, and get to the bottom of this, whatever *this* is, and find out who this Èdouard Barousse is. If we leave no later than three, we can fly through the night and be at our home before sunrise."

"And what about Tori?"

"A passport for her will not be an issue. What do you say, Tori? Are you ready for your first trip to the Big Easy?"

Tori's delight was evident, and gauging by Samantha's gleaming smile, Nicholas knew his plan was well received.

"Two nights ago I was walking painfully to a most cruel and certain death. The two of you have rescued me, so wherever you lead, I will gladly follow."

Nicholas smiled ear to ear. "There you have it. New Orleans it is, baby."

CHAPTER THIRTEEN

ALEX WALKED TO the bedroom door, his heartbeat accelerated by uncertainty. He sighed relief, pleasantly surprised to find that Sarah had not lost her nerve and fled the state. Sitting in the living room, she was dressed in an oversized cashmere sweater reading on the suede sofa with her bare feet tucked beneath the ragged denim jeans. Her makeup was simple, scarlet lipstick contrasted by soft rouge and lavender eyeliner.

"Did you sleep well?"

Sarah tucked the book in her lap and smiled. "Very well, until about one. I found your note, and the envelope you left, and was pretty sure you wouldn't wake up for a while, so I went shopping . . . thank you very much."

"Money well spent, you look great," Alex said as he sat on the arm of the couch. "I have to admit, when I went to bed, I wasn't sure you would still be here when I woke up."

"I have to admit, I had my doubts as well, and still do. This is the craziest thing I have ever done by far." Sarah chuckled nervously. "But the more I thought about it, if you wanted to, you could have done pretty much anything you wanted to me already."

Alex's sly smile confirmed her suspicions. "What are you reading?"

Sarah's nerves returned and she blushed. "I . . . I . . . "

"If it's embarrassing you, you don't have to tell me."

"It's awkward," Sarah confessed.

Alex maneuvered to get a peek. "You can never go wrong with Anne Rice," he chortled.

"I've never read any vampire books, or Stephen King. I don't really like scary stuff, but I thought I should read something. I mean . . ."

"It's alright, Sarah." Alex slid down beside her and guided her hand holding the book back to her lap. Her perfume was light and clean and served its purpose well. Subconsciously, even the vampire was not immune to its captivating allure. "If you are worried I'm offended, I'm not. My father loves this book, but not the movie. It seems he had an issue with Tom Cruise for one reason or another."

"There are things I want to know, but I guess I'm a little uncomfortable asking."

Alex's face moved close to Sarah's. Reaching out, he slid his hand through Sarah's hair, to the top of her neck; her eyes rolled pleasurably at his touch. "First of all, ask what you want. I won't be offended by any question. Secondly, all the books on vampirism are fiction. You will read utterly preposterous claims, while others are spot on. But my family has worked diligently to ensure that there are no monsters amongst our people." As Alex explained, out of the corner of his eye he noticed a package on the foyer table. "I see Chuck had our passports delivered." Retrieving the parcel, Alex inspected its contents. "If you want to know more, there's a small suitcase in your bedroom closet. I'm ready to take you to my home."

"You don't want to stay here a few more days? There are a few things I'd love to see."

Alex glanced out the window at the Brooklyn Bridge; cars crossing below, like busy ants at a picnic. "The first thing I'll explain after we hit the road is why I want to leave now, and I promise, I'll bring you back, and then we'll do the city up right."

Sarah consented nervously, forcing herself once again from this *newly* discovered comfort zone. As she packed, Alex penned Gabrielle a quick apology for skipping out. In short order, they were out of the building and headed north up FDR Drive. Sticking to humorous, and sometimes awkward, tales of his New York experiences, Alex kept the conversation light until they were well into Connecticut.

Although Alex had no issues navigating without dash lights, the blackout interior of the Vultur was extraordinarily dark for Sarah. Only getting glimpses of his facial expressions in the passing headlights, it was hard for her to gauge his true disposition. Although through conversation Alex appeared at ease, his face occasionally appeared troubled. Finally gathering the nerve to breach her concern, Sarah asked, "Is everything alright?"

Alex turned to Sarah with a smile. "It is, but I keep thinking that Chuck has notified my father by now. It's going to be really awkward, but I've known for a while that after ten years, it's past time I do this. But I really don't want to get you involved until we see where this is headed."

"*This*?"

"Well yes, if you want a *this.* But there is no need to throw you under the bus until we see how long of a ride you stick around for."

"What about your mother? Is she still alive?"

"Angelique, the queen? Oh, she is very much alive."

Sarah twisted in her seat to allow a better view of Alex's face. "The queen?"

"Did I happen to mention I have family issues?"

Sarah listened intently as Alex squirmed in his seat, as if that would make his confession somehow less awkward.

"My mother, Angelique, and my grandfather, Levente, are both well over three hundred years old and were, and still are, very much in love. Remember how I told you about my family's plans to marry me off?"

Sarah nodded and replied with an air of uncertainty, "Yes."

"Well the same thing happened to my grandfather almost two hundred and fifty years ago. You see, the Tepes family has been vampires since the days of Vlad. But my grandfather, in seeking peace with the humans, endeavored to prove our race was more than just blood-craving savages. He had accomplished his mission, to a degree, after a marriage was arranged for him by the Order of the Dragon to a Hungarian princess. They believed a marriage between a mortal and a vampire would prove to the skeptics that our races could truly coexist. And while he did not love the princess, he submitted to the obligation, for the greater good of his country."

As Alex gathered his thoughts, Sarah became impatient. "Well?"

"Monique Beauvais, my mother's power-obsessed cousin, secretly plotted to murder the princess. Had she succeeded, my grandfather would have been free to marry my mother, placing Monique in a position within the royal family. But Monique's plot failed and my mother was unjustly judged guilty of the conspiracy.

She and Monique were banished to New Orleans, supposedly until the time my grandfather chose to end their exile."

Stretching against her seatbelt, Sarah sat on the edge of her seat. "When was that?"

"They were banished around 1750. Somewhere around 2010, while my father was on an assignment in New Orleans, he discovered my mother, Monique, and eight other vampires imprisoned in the Old Ursuline Convent. I know it sounds insane, but they were all well over two hundred years old."

"Oh, so that part of the age myth is true?" Sarah reacted as if hearing the results of a research project.

"Yes, it is true. So my mother had been imprisoned for nearly two hundred and fifty years. Along comes this good-looking guy, my dad, who inadvertently sets them free. But before fleeing, my mother spellbinds him and decides to end her two hundred and fifty years of celibacy."

Sarah's eyes enlarged to the size of ping-pong balls. "Oh my."

"Yes, you are staring at, *oh my*. In your literature, you will find it written that vampires cannot reproduce. But as it turns out, they can, as long as one partner is mortal. The end result is what we call a day-walker. Backing up the clock to around 1946, my grandfather eventually married another woman, Elisabeta. With her being mortal, it was not long after they married that my father was born. After World War II, as Communism spread, my grandfather's wife was murdered and my grandfather imprisoned in the ruins of the family castle."

"I am going to want the unabridged version one day soon," Sarah quipped.

"After I'm done, I'll open the floor for questions. So, just stay with me," Alex said. "Forty years ago, after my father set Angelique and her cousin free, Monique turns on my father, and in an attempt to kill him turns him into a vampire."

"So, your father was a . . . *day-walker*, but Monique turned him into a full-fledged vampire?"

"Exactly! So, after my father turned vampire, he goes to Romania, finds his father alive, entombed in the ruins of Poenari, and the rest is all boring history. Angelique marries my grandfather, my father marries Samantha, and here we sit."

"Holy crap! Your mother, Angelique, married *your* grandfather?" Sarah flopped back into her seat. "And your father was turned into a vampire by your mother's cousin—*Monique.* Who, if I've got this straight, was banished to New Orleans along with Angelique back in the 1700s? Two hundred years later, your father has sex with Angelique, not knowing her history with your grandfather, and you're born? Did I get that straight?" Sarah asked, her mind spinning from the complexities.

"It's a lot to absorb. And that's not even the full story. It's a good thing it's a long car ride to Canada."

"Can you repeat the whole thing again?" Sarah laughed nervously. "So, why are you a vampire? Did somebody bite you?"

"Well, not really."

Sarah mulled over the complexities of Alex's situation. "So, if your father was a day-walker and your mother was a vampire, wouldn't that make you a day-walker also?"

"God, this is going to get complicated," Alex moaned.

"Going to?"

"I was born a day-walker. I enjoyed the sun, ate anything I pleased, never feared a cross, and all that other stuff. The thought of drinking blood was . . . unpleasant, to say the least. Around age twenty, my aging process began to grind to a halt."

"That sounds pretty fantastic. What happened?"

"To explain how I was turned, I need to back track. As I already told you, Monique turned my father into a vampire. His wife, Samantha, who is my stepmother, became pregnant while she was still mortal. But a sniper bullet killed her with my half brother, Ştefan, in her womb. She was resurrected from the dead—you're going to love this next part—via Angelique, my mother."

"The queen?"

"Yes. So, Samantha and her unborn child, Ştefan, who would have been born a day-walker, both became vampires on that night."

Sarah shook her head slowly. "I'm confused. So you and Ştefan have the same father but different mothers?"

"Yes, Ştefan and I grew up together in Louisiana, raised by my father and Samantha. My biological mother, Angelique, moved to Romania and, as I said, married my grandfather."

"I think growing up, Ştefan and I were always jealous of each other's lives. My family decided, as day-walker, I was perfectly poised to succeed my grandfather. My grandfather, whose affliction remains unknown to the world, rules in secrecy behind the face of an imposter, kind of like Dennison and me. It was his obsession that

I, as his successor and a day-walker, could step out of the shadows and continue his legacy and free our race of the fear and persecution that has held us in bondage for centuries. So, I get to blaze this epic trail of glory, and Ştefan gets this great, carefree life to go and do as he pleases. As my family pushed harder to mold me into this little junior prince, I began to push back. I remember the very day I decided, *If I became a full-fledged vampire, just like my brother, they'd all leave me alone.*"

Alarmed and confused, Sarah tenderly placed her hand on Alex's shoulder. "So Ştefan bit you?"

"No. He didn't need to. We learned from my father's incursion with Monique, if a day-walker ingests the blood of a vampire, he will become a vampire as well."

"So what became of this Monique? She sounds quite ruthless."

"If you were to ingest a single drop of my blood, I could easily control your mind for hours, possibly days, without much effort. This was Monique's intention with my father. But unbeknownst to her, he was a day-walker, so instead of controlling him, she converted him."

"So what did he do then?"

Alex hesitated, knowing this was going to be a hard pill to swallow. "Are you sure you're ready for this one?"

Sarah nodded. "Can it get any more bizarre?"

"Oh yeah." Alex laughed devilishly. "Thinking she controlled him, and to a certain extent she did, her intention was to fuck my father's brains out, and then kill him. But, as it turned out, they fucked like a pair of deranged animals—and then he killed her."

"Ouch."

Sarah's reaction was impossible for Alex to gauge. Fascination, shock, confusion, repulsion, he could not get a read on her. "Can we talk about your life for a while now?"

"Oh no. This is way too fascinating. I hope you don't mind, but I have so many questions." Sarah's enthusiasm may have been born out of her scientific nature, or just desire to see if there was a bottom to Alex's dark past.

"I never actually considered the ramifications of telling anybody my family history. If the shoe were on the other foot, I certainly would have had an endless barrage of questions."

In a welcome moment of quiet, Alex was thankful Sarah had not asked to go to the nearest airport again. He turned to her, to find her smiling pleasantly at him. "As I said, it's a long trip. I'd much rather talk about you, but I understand your curiosity. Fire away."

"Why did your father want to kill Monique?"

"In the course of inadvertently setting them free, Monique and the others killed his best friend, Rob. So he and his crew, one of which was Chuck, whom you met last night, tried to capture the women and force them back to the convent. Needless to say, they refused. Most of them began murdering people, just like you'll read in that vampire book of yours. So, partly out of revenge and partly out of his duty to protect the city he had endangered, he set out to destroy them."

"If he wanted to kill them, why is it he had sex with two of them?"

Again Alex chuckled, this time harder. "Yeah, Samantha always wanted to know the same thing. But the truth of it is, vampires have a power to entrance mortals, making them subjective to our desires."

"Could you . . . did you do this to me?"

"No," Alex answered sharply. He turned his attention to Sarah's eyes. "I would never do it to you, but I easily could, if I wanted to. But we also possess this sexual allure that most mortals find nearly impossible to resist."

Sarah's expression changed. "Is this why I'm still in your car, or was halfway undressed last night?"

"As a vampire, I have learned many things in my ten years away. I have discovered how to mask my thoughts, and scents, even from my own kind. And I have learned to shield women from this supernatural attraction. Believe me, life gets rather mundane when every encounter has a predictable outcome. Seriously, the impulses I could plant in your brain would make a hooker blush."

Sounding suddenly frightened, timidly Sarah asked, "Did you?"

"From the very moment I set my eyes upon you, I knew what you were to me. At the coffee shop, when I asked you to kiss me, it wasn't a request that you could have easily denied. You might have tried, but you didn't. I know that. And that was the only time since. I didn't do it because I needed a kiss, I did it because if you did, I would know beyond all doubt, my intuition was right."

"And was it?"

At that moment, the anticipation in her eyes forced Alex to brake suddenly and pull off to the side of the highway. Gently grasping her face, he guided her to him and kissed her again. Magnetized by the warmth of her tongue and taste of her lips, Alex knew if he didn't stop, there would be no stopping. He pulled away. Her eyes were glistening, searching for something in his that he could not fathom. "As long as you stay, yes, my intuition was spot on."

"So how will I ever know the difference between who desires what?"

Alex hit the gas hard and pulled back onto the road. "If you want me, then it's all you, baby."

Sarah giggled. "Baby? Did I just get a promotion?"

"It's a *Nawlens* thing. You'll see one day. But in case you hadn't figured it out just yet, yeah, you got a promotion, baby."

The laughter was short lived before Sarah resumed her interrogation. "So, both women seduced your father, but why did he only kill Monique?"

"My father grew up in America, raised by his aunt, without knowledge of his true identity. He simply believed his family were commoners, killed in the war. During their brief *encounter*, Angelique had no idea of his heritage either. She explained her circumstances, how she followed the adamant laws of Levente Tepes. Levente believed vampires would one day peacefully and openly coexist with humans. Foolishly, my grandfather also believed this might be some mystical path to salvation that would free our family of the curse. Angelique abided by his theories, but Monique was hell bent on power and destruction, including my father's. Based on Angelique's confession, my father spared her life."

"So, have you ever killed anyone?"

"No."

"Do you drink human blood?"

"I drink the blood of mammals, including the occasional human variety."

"Would you drink mine?"

Alex checked the rearview mirror in an effort to delay his response. "I have no fervent desire to sink my teeth in your neck, if that is what you are asking."

Sarah's reaction was of genuine surprise. "Really? What about if we were married?"

"You need to understand, while certain aspects of our race appear desirable, vampirism is a curse. The very consumption of blood violates one of God's oldest holy ordinances. So, my simple answer is *no*, I would not ever want to see you cursed. And in retrospect, I should have never asked my brother to do what he did.

But even through evil, comes good. Point in case, here we are."

The cockpit again fell silent for a prolonged period. Sarah rubbed her fingers across the frosty glass. Although he desperately desired to know her thoughts, Alex steadily resisted the temptation to seek out her musings.

"You've become very quiet. Are you alright?"

"I've just been thinking. There's always this uncomfortable period—when two people meet and they try to guess the other's intentions. I think I know yours, or at least hope I know. But how does this ever work out?"

"My father and Samantha made it work very well for over a year. I believe if Samantha had not been shot, she'd still be a mortal."

"And she would be an old woman. But your father?"

"I know what you're getting at, but in the last forty years, there have only been four vampires made that I'm aware of. The infamous blood sucking ritual made Chuck and Samantha. Two were turned by the ingestion of blood, my father and yours truly."

"Gabrielle, did she make Chuck?"

"Chuck and Gabby were quite the odd couple, much like my father and Sam. Two mercenaries, a former prostitute and a feisty emotional train wreck, or you could call them a vampire, a day-walker, a jarhead, and a feisty emotional train wreck. By the time they reached Romania, Chuck was the odd human out. Shortly after finding my grandfather, the Order of the Dragon found them. Outnumbered and trapped in the catacombs of Poenari, Chuck was converted to aid in their escape. But you know, I've heard the tale a hundred times, and Chuck's conversion has always been the subject of comical anecdotes. I think everybody with the exception of Angelique has taken credit. Chuck likes to credit my grandfather, says it makes him royalty by default."

"So how many vampires exist?"

"My grandfather and mother, father and Samantha, Chuck and Gabby, Gabby's mother, Sabine, and my half brother Ştefan. Only one day-walker remains, which we know of, Isabelle. If there are more, we are unaware of their existence. So as you can see, we pose no threat for world domination."

"But if the world found out, it wouldn't take much effort to drive your family into extinction either."

Alex patted Sarah's thigh and then gave it a squeeze. "That's why we have kept our presence to a minimum, and secret."

"Maybe you shouldn't have told me. Won't your family be upset?"

"Oh, upset is probably just the tip of the iceberg. I've been missing for ten years, and now, there's us."

Sarah took Alex's hand from her leg and held it with both of hers. "You've known me for all of three days. There's still plenty of time for you to change your mind."

Alex took his eyes off the road and stared at Sarah long enough to make her swallow hard. "The chances of that happening are about as great as me taking a stroll to church in the daylight. I'll let you in on a little family secret. My father and Samantha met on an airplane and fell in love before they got off. Forty years of love-at-first-sight bliss."

Sarah frowned. "It must have been great growing up with parents in love. My father never even dated after my mother died. He never talked about it, but I think the heartbreak exposed vulnerabilities he'd rather not face."

"I know your father's reputation. What do you think he will do when he finds out about us, that is, if anything develops?"

"*If*? I wouldn't be sitting here, listening to the most incredulous story I've ever heard for *if*. Likewise, *if* did not nearly cause me to undress for you last night."

The vivid memory caused Alex to stir in his seat. "So?"

"If he gets to know you and likes you before he finds out the truth, then I'm sure he'll stop just short of a full military invasion."

CHAPTER FOURTEEN

"I DON'T THINK I've ever seen you in such unflattering jeans," Ştefan remarked.

Isabelle performed a quick self-inspection. "You didn't expect me to wear my good clothes to go traipsing through the bayous, did you?"

Ştefan looked at his own tailored clothes with regret. "To be honest, I didn't even think about what to wear, until now. I might be a little over dressed for our excursion." Ştefan's eyes followed Isabelle as she crossed his father's study. "You know, if you dressed like that more often, you wouldn't have to chase the suitors away."

Isabelle knew Ştefan's remarks were aimed at her greatest deficiency, her inability to have a meaningful relationship. "What a pity I wasn't dressed like this two nights ago."

Ştefan took the jab for its purpose. "Before you beat *that* dead horse, let's take some inventory. A. You are beautiful. B. Your body rocks. C. You don't hide it. I'm no different from any other man, other than I know your secrets. The seductress who craves desire, but won't be had."

Isabelle knew Ştefan had a point but wasn't about to admit it. She liked being the object of desire. It helped compensate for her unique abnormalities. "So, you are ready?" she asked, ignoring his observations.

Ştefan nodded, his eyes cut to acknowledge her slight. "I'm going to grab a quick pint, then we can go."

Following Ştefan into the kitchen, Isabelle trailed her fingers across the narrow cherry table in the hall. "Your parents keep the house so clean," she said as she inspected her index finger for dust. "Even when they are away. I am home every night and my house looks as if it has not been dusted in ten years."

"Samantha keeps it clean because she never knows who might show up. But it's not like anybody shows up unannounced. I'll bet it's been twenty-five years since my grandfather graced Louisiana with his regal presence."

"You sound bitter, Ştefan."

Paying no heed to Isabelle's observation, Ştefan unlocked the refrigerated wall cabinet and pulled out a bag. "Can I offer you some A positive?"

"No, thank you," Isabelle said with a scoffing laugh. "I'm not sure if you knew, but I used to drink blood, back before I understood who I was. Once I learned my past, I understood why I sometimes craved it. Once I understood my cravings served no purpose, it was rather easy to quit."

Ştefan held the bottle of scarlet blood to the light and inspected it. "I wish I could say the same for me . . . drinking blood, that is."

Isabelle smiled as she watched Ştefan drain the bottle completely. He rinsed the bottle before placing it in the dishwasher. "That was a lot to drink," Isabelle noted.

"I know," Ştefan replied with a guilty tone. "But I get tired of this family-induced rationing bullshit. We've been trained to drink blood like it's a rare commodity when, in fact, it's almost as abundant as oxygen."

"But if you are conditioned to . . . "

"Yeah, yeah, yeah, I know. If we ration our intake, then if the need ever arises, we can survive on a very limited supply." Ştefan forcefully closed the dishwasher. "More of the Tepes family propaganda. Anyway, if I wind up digging half the night, I'm going to need all the energy I can muster."

"That leads me to a question. What do you plan on doing if you find Barousse alive?"

"I haven't figured that one out yet," Ştefan said as he dried his hands. "If they didn't actually kill him then, just like my grandfather, he should still be alive."

"And then?"

"All I know is Daniel told me I had to find him. So maybe I'll take him to Daniel. Who knows, the old fart probably needs to make sure that all us vampire folk are accounted for, before he can finally kick the bucket."

Nicholas had been fixated on his wife's legs. Was it a mere coincidence she was wearing a similar skirt like the one from their first meeting on a plane, bound for New Orleans, forty some odd years ago? Or was it an effort to remind Nicholas who cleaned his casket? He felt his wife's eyes upon him every time his gaze happened to linger on Tori. Was it insecurity, the culmination of change, or the emergence of Ştefan and Alex driving his wife's erratic anxiety and mood swings? For Nicholas, basically nothing had changed, except Samantha's golden tan was sadly missing.

As Nicholas focused on the silky texture of Samantha's skin, her legs began to glow in a beautiful shade of brown. "Is that what you wanted to see?"

"Stay out of my head, woman."

"I didn't have to be in your head to know what you were thinking. You have always been painfully obvious. Maybe I should have just reminded you . . . I'm up here, Nick."

Nicholas gazed into Samantha's playful eyes. "If you are going to go *old school* on me, Sam, then perhaps you should call me Brian."

Samantha peeked back two rows to Tori, who had her nose pegged in a book. "If I wanted to go old school, then I would have done this." Samantha parted her legs and placed Nicholas's hand on her toned thigh. "Did you mean *old school*, like *this*?"

As vivid memories filled his mind, Nicholas turned and checked Tori's position, and then turned to Sam and whispered, "She is right there."

"And Tori hears everything you two are saying, or whispering," Tori called out. "Which would be entirely your own fault."

Nicholas and Samantha looked at each other and chuckled.

Samantha crossed her legs and adjusted her skirt back down. "Alright then, I guess we stick to business. Seriously, honey, I think you need to know what you are going to say." Samantha rolled her eyes toward Tori. "All of our justifications with the boys have now gone to hell in a handbasket."

First of all, Nicholas knew there were no acceptable validations for their actions. Debating internally, he had tried for two days. As far as his sons were concerned, he had made a hypocritical error converting Tori, even though Samantha had agreed with him.

"You're right. I broke the rules," Nicholas whispered.

"*We* broke the rules," Samantha said proudly. "She was worth saving. And you don't need to whisper. Tori already knows our situation, with our boys and your father."

"When you bit into her, you felt her suffering. But as her blood coursed with yours, you knew her soul was the one worth saving. I didn't understand that until I made her one of us. I've tasted the blood of so many, but in Tori, I experienced something unique. Unless our boys ever cross the path of such a soul, there is no way they will ever understand."

"That all makes perfect sense. But tell me, if that had been my explanation, what would you have said to the contrary?"

Samantha replied without consideration, "I'd say, our rules exist for our own protection. I'd also say, no matter how long we live, we will never possess the ultimate knowledge to make the right decision one hundred percent of the time."

"So perhaps I, or we, or better yet still my father, have not been right about our positions? What would you suggest, dear?"

"We need to talk with them, and see the world through their eyes first. You and your father were so hell bent on Alex succeeding him, you never really thought if it was right for him. And what does it matter, pure bloodlines anymore? We're all mutts. If Ştefan wants to take your father's place, why not? If he truly loved that girl, maybe it was wrong to stand in love's way. If he had a voice in it, what would Levente have said about me? You've known for years. It's time to deal with your father and the issues that have driven our sons away."

It was just past nine o'clock and although traffic was scarce on Lapalco Boulevard, there was enough to make her wait for the opportune time to pull off. Isabelle eased the car to a stop in the foot-tall roadside grass.

"According to the map, if it's remotely accurate, our turn should be just ahead, on the left," Ştefan reported as he compared the parchment with the modern map on his phone.

"And if it's not?"

"Then we will keep looking. Dressed like that, I'm guessing you don't have anywhere else to be tonight."

Isabelle backhanded Ştefan in the chest with as much force as she could muster in the limited space. "What!" Ştefan exclaimed as he shielded himself from another volley. "I'll bet you bought those jeans and jacket today, just for tonight. And I'll also wager, barring any similar excursion, it will be the last time that fabric has the pleasure of knowing your skin."

Isabelle delivered one last punch to Ştefan's shoulder. "You will rot in hell one day, Ştefan Tepes."

Ştefan snickered. "Was there ever any doubt?" He looked down the darkened road. "Keep on going, just ahead you can make a left. That should be Nicolle Boulevard."

Isabelle followed his instructions and turned off the four-lane highway. The road quickly merged down into two lanes, with the only illumination coming from the Volvo's headlights. "I must say this looks a little more like the kind of place I'd expect."

"It will be up ahead, about a half a mile on the left," Ştefan instructed. "Remember when I was a child how places like this used to scare the hell out of me?"

"I do. When you were little it was easy, and fun, to frighten you," Isabelle recounted. "Now look at yourself, getting ready to go traipsing through the dark and scary bayou."

"There it is." Ştefan pointed out readily. "Turn in and pull up to the gate." Ştefan jumped from the car, leaving his door open, and reached into the back seat for his shovel. In the brightness of the headlights, Isabelle watched as Ştefan made easy work of the rusted lock and chain on the gate. As he swung the gate open, he signaled for Isabelle to proceed.

Ştefan blew out a frosty puff of crisp December air. "Come on, Izzy. I'd like to get home in time for the *True Blood* re-runs." As she pulled forward, Ştefan jumped in and closed the door.

"Kill your headlights, please," he said, "and take it slow."

The trail was uneven, forcing the car to roll and pitch as if it were on Lake Pontchartrain in a heavy gale. Ştefan rolled his window down, deeply breathing in the night air. After they had traveled nearly a mile, Ştefan held his hand up. "Take your foot off the accelerator and coast to a stop, then turn the car off."

"Aye aye, Capitan."

Ştefan climbed from the car and retrieved his shovel and pick from the backseat. As he closed the door, he realized Isabelle appeared to be attached to the steering wheel. He rounded the car and opened her door. "Would you care to join me?"

"I can't see well enough to go hiking out there."

"I have a light for you." Ştefan extended his hand. Isabelle's hands remained planted on the steering wheel. "Is there a problem, Isabelle?"

"Aren't you afraid somebody will spot your flashlight?"

Ştefan snapped his fingers, expecting Isabelle to take his hand. Still, she did not budge. "What is it?" he asked impatiently.

"If you find this man's grave, what is it you plan to do with him again?"

Ştefan sighed. "*If* we find him, Daniel seems to have some purpose for him. Why else would he seek out both of us after all these years? So, *if* we find him, we'll take him to Daniel."

Isabelle's attention remained focused forward. "And you know how to find Daniel? Because I have no intention of taking a three-hundred-year-old vampire to *my* house. He's going to smell really bad after three hundred years, and Lord knows how much blood he'll consume."

"Oh, for goodness sake, Isabelle. If I can't find Daniel, we'll take Barousse to my house and I'll lock him in a casket until we figure out what to do with him. Okay?"

"There are a lot of woods. How do you know this is it? That is a very crude map."

Ştefan breathed in once more. "I can smell it. There is death, *old* death, in these woods."

"It could be a bear."

"Isabelle, will you please get out of the car. I would like to get this done and get back before sunrise."

"I don't think I can." Isabelle turned a nervous eye to Ştefan. "I don't want to go out there. The bayou scares me at night. It always has, and I just have a really bad feeling about this."

"Come on," Ştefan urged. "If you get too scared I'll bring you back."

Isabelle climbed from the car, took Ştefan's hand, and followed him to the tree line. "You know, if my car gets towed, you will be in a world of shit by sunrise."

Ştefan's smile returned. "Then I suggest we get going."

Clouds continuously obscured the moonlight, leaving the woods in darkness. Once safely inside the tree line, Isabelle turned on her flashlight. With her steamy breath playing in the mist of the cold night, shadows danced across the light beams, creating the illusion of moving trees.

"And where exactly are we headed?" Isabelle asked sharply, repeatedly fighting back the tree branches as they journeyed deeper into the woods.

Ştefan announced, "It's here, somewhere, right beneath us." Ştefan handed the shovel to Isabelle and began striking the ground with the pick in random locations.

"Wouldn't it make more sense to rent some kind of detector device? You could come back tomorrow night."

Pushing a rotted log out of his path, he swung again. The distinct clanging of iron on concrete sent an echo out that temporarily silenced the curious wildlife that had taken interest in the pair of foreigners.

Ştefan took the shovel and began clearing the soft sod. Roughly four to six inches beneath the surface, the distinct outline of a granite fixture began to take shape. Ştefan took the pick and pried at one end until a four-foot cross slowly emerged from the earth. "Uh oh," Ştefan cried. Closing his eyes and using his shovel, he flipped the stone monument away from the grave. "I think we have found him!" Ştefan exclaimed.

Dread had overcome Isabelle. What had started out as an amusing field trip was now a hellish reality. "Maybe we should call Chuck before you dig any deeper."

"Chuck is like my father. He would just as soon pile the dirt back on the site and walk away. No, Daniel put us on this task for a reason, and I will see it through."

Ştefan picked and then dug at a furious pace, tossing the majority of the dirt upon the offensive cross, which remained at his back. The night was growing short. Without checking, he knew the midnight hour had passed. The bayou had grown exceptionally still; the only sound to be heard was steel and muscle moving soil.

The hole on each side had grown to almost four feet deep when shovel struck a metal surface. Curiously, Isabelle moved slowly from the tree she had been leaning on to observe the object of Ştefan's labor. Again and again the shovel scraped steel, until all sides of the plate had been unearthed. Six corroded spikes secured the four-by-seven lid to the sides, still buried deep beneath.

Ştefan swung the pick swiftly and, one by one, unfastened the lid. "This is fascinating."

A chill ran up Isabelle's spine as she witnessed the unearthing of a tomb intended to remain lost for all eternity.

"What is it, Ştefan?"

"The plantation house and slave quarters were all the way up by the river. Do you realize what kind of effort it must have taken to get this steel all the way out here? To dig this hole? I'm guessing Barousse slept by day in a casket. They must have sealed the casket first then, knowing it would eventually decay in the soil, they built this metal sarcophagus to preserve the integrity of the wood."

Ştefan continued to labor until at last enough earth was moved to gain leverage on the steel cover. Applying all of his unnatural power, the lid stubbornly remained sealed. After several attempts, the seal finally cracked, and Ştefan pushed until the lid stood on its end.

"What in the hell?" Ştefan cried.

Sitting on a stump, Isabelle rose and returned to the hole to inspect Ştefan's newest discovery. "What is it now?"

"It would appear that they filled this box with something like tar or creosote, as a wood preservative. If there is a casket under all of this, it never would have rotted."

"If Barousse's slaves went to such deep measures to ensure he remained interred, then maybe we should rethink this," Isabelle warned.

"Slaves were extremely superstitious. If they believed Barousse was some kind of demon, then all of this would be an ordinary safeguard," Ştefan replied as he tested the sticky substance with his finger. "But it's getting late, and I have no intentions of putting everything back just the way I found it."

"Suit yourself. But don't say I didn't warn you if the sun comes up and scorches that pretty fair skin of yours."

Ştefan was too busy scrapping off the layers of tarry substance to pay much attention to Isabelle's fretting. Several inches down another obstacle greeted the shovel. Ştefan grabbed the pick and raked it across, exposing a metal-forged chain. Bypassing the chain, he raised the pick and struck the wooden surface near its bottom. The wood splintered. Again he struck, this time down the side, and repeated until he had sufficiently dislodged enough of the wood to remove it in large pieces.

Looking down curiously from the edge, Isabelle cried out, "Oh dear Lord." What appeared to be the mummified remains of a creature lay curled inside the coffin. "Is that him?"

Ştefan tossed his tools to the surface. "If you'll give me a hand, maybe we can find out."

"Please tell me you're kidding." Isabelle took three big steps back. "I have no intentions of touching whatever that is."

"Dammit, Isabelle. If I knew how worthless you were going to be tonight, I would have left you at home."

"I'm cold, I'm dirty, and I really don't like any of this. Trust me, I would have preferred to stay home."

Ştefan scooped up the lifeless carcass and lifted it up on the ground. He jumped out of the hole and dusted his hands.

"Can you at least carry my tools?"

"Aren't you going to fill in that awful hole? Somebody, or some animal, could fall in."

Ştefan shook his head in dumbfounded amazement. "The sun will be up in a few hours, and you're worried about somebody falling in a hole?"

Isabelle begrudgingly picked up the shovel and pick. "If your father finds out about this, he will have both of our hides."

"*If* he finds out about this it might be too late to realize just how wrong he has been about me."

Tori strolled leisurely up the sidewalk, mesmerized by the quaint subtleties of the garden district. Although the temperature was nearly identical to Paris, the chill in the air didn't seem as harsh. Climbing the steps, Tori remained transfixed by the landscaping and architecture of the neighborhood. Finding Nicholas and Samantha waiting patiently by the door, she smiled broadly.

"I always wanted a home with a big porch and a swing."

"Well, now you have one," Samantha said.

"I can't believe this. A few nights ago my life was shit, and now I am healthy, I have a new family, and I am in New Orleans."

Nicholas turned and opened the door. "Welcome home."

Tori stepped into the expansive foyer. What appeared to be thousands of crystals sparkled in the twinkling lights of at least fifty candles, immediately seizing Tori's attention. "However do you light them all?"

"Those are Romanian proton candles, and they last about twenty years," Nicholas explained proudly. "The lack of natural light causes them to spark and illuminate. You will learn in time, there is much energy hidden in the darkness."

"I have never heard of them." Tori circled underneath the

chandelier, inspecting the crystals' rainbow refractions. Curiously continuing down the foyer, Tori mindlessly admired the oil paintings adorning the walls. She turned first to the parlor and, after a few minutes, moved to the library. Samantha and Nicholas followed silently as Tori absorbed the amenities of her new home.

Nicholas stared at the disheveled appearance of his otherwise orderly desk. Having already witnessed the culprit's actions from the security videos, Nicholas thumbed through the paperwork that had been left behind.

"What is it, Nick?" Samantha asked.

"Either Ştefan has grown careless or he just doesn't care about this information."

"What information?"

Nicholas pressed the reprint button on his desktop printer and waited. Inspecting the document, he rubbed the back of his neck. "These maps all seem to point to the same tract of land, which appears to be the Barousse plantation, back in the 1700s. Apparently, Ştefan is on some scavenger hunt in Westwego. If anyone would know about this Èdouard Barousse, Angelique would." Nicholas tapped the black phone box on his desk. "Call Angelique."

"Nick, it's midmorning over there, she'll be resting."

"I have a bad feeling about this." Nicholas checked the time. "It's two hours until sunrise. I need to know what she knows about this man, right now."

"Alo?" a thickly accented voice answered.

"Costel, it is Nicholas. I know she is at rest, but I must speak with Angelique immediately."

"Yes, Sir Nicholas."

Nicholas turned his attention back to Samantha. "We know Barousse lived about the time of Angelique's imprisonment. It would appear, from all of this, for whatever reason Ştefan is looking for him, or something to do with him. I want to get out in front of this before it bites us in the ass."

"Who is biting who in the ass?" Angelique answered playfully.

"I hope nobody, but that might depend on your answer."

"I'm guessing by the hour, this is of an urgent nature. Is it about Alex?"

Nicholas looked to gauge Samantha's expression. Although Samantha and Angelique were close, Angelique's idiosyncratic relationship with Nicholas could sometimes create friction. "No, it's not." Although there was the potential sighting of Alex's car, without any confirmation he chose not to broach the subject. "A name has surfaced, I thought you might be able to lend some insight."

"He must be important to warrant such urgency."

"Èdouard Barousse," Nicholas answered firmly.

The light-hearted conversation ended abruptly, and a heavy sigh hissed across the speaker. "This is a very old name," Angelique said. "Why are you looking for him?"

"Apparently, Ştefan and Isabelle are researching the death of Barousse, and his plantation."

"Monique," Angelique replied.

The very mention of her name caused Nicholas and Samantha to cringe.

"Most of this history I believe you already know. When Monique and I arrived in New Orleans there was a period we were free, and it was *her* defiant killings that brought about our imprisonment. But prior to the imprisonment, Monique had sexually indulged in the aristocracy of New Orleans as well. Barousse was one of these men she took pleasure in.

"As you know, we were initially unaware that your father had sent his cousin, Victor Tepes, to oversee our exile. It did not take long for him to discover what Monique was doing, or for Monique to discover him. He warned that our secret had been discovered, and to protect us, he was placing us in the convent, under the pretense we had consumption. It was only to be a short-term solution. As Monique did not trust Victor, she sent word to Barousse, instructing him how to dispose of our ever-present watchdog. Promising our freedom was imminent, Monique's hopes soon began to fade as the days slowly passed; Barousse never arrived. And as the nuns learned what Monique was doing to the other quarantined women, measures were taken to ensure we never could leave. And so no one ever came, not for over two hundred years."

"We all know how that story ended," Samantha piped.

Ignoring his wife's sarcasm, Nicholas continued, "Is it possible Barousse was made a vampire?"

"Monique never confessed to such a deed, but knowing her as I did, I would say it was possible."

"Thank you, Angelique. Is my father doing well?"

"He is, but the unrest within the family troubles him. You and Samantha should come for a visit. It has been too long."

"We will, and soon. Thank you again, Angelique." As soon as the call disconnected Nicholas looked at Tori, then back to Samantha. "Yes, we have to go to Romania, as soon as this matter is cleared. He will find out about Tori sooner or later. Better he learn by willing proclamation than a forced confession."

"I'll make the arrangements next week," Samantha volunteered.

"I think, given the circumstances, and the evidence, unless Ştefan shows back up here tonight, I'll make a trip out to Westwego tomorrow to see if I can find what they were looking for. I think you should reach out to Isabelle and find out what she and Ştefan have been up to. And put Chuck on alert. I may want him here, as soon as tomorrow."

Samantha produced her cell phone. "How about I do that right now. You are too far removed from your career of playing cowboy. And the last few times you did, the results weren't that pretty."

"Whatever," Nicholas snapped as he began looking through the books on his desk. "Why don't you show Tori to her room, or maybe even a casket."

Tori stepped forward. "A casket?"

"We've already explained the benefits of rest versus sleep," Nicholas said as he looked up from his work. "You do not have to try a casket if you do not want, but one thing I will promise, the difference between a bed and a casket is like the blood of a rat versus the blood of a fine Frenchman."

"I would not know the blood of a fine Frenchman," Tori snickered. "I would say the blood of my pimp tasted more like the blood of a filthy sewer rat."

CHAPTER FIFTEEN

SARAH STRAINED IN the darkness, trying to catch a glimpse of anything besides the illuminated pavement. "So are you going to tell me where we're going, or is it going to stay a big mystery?"

"I could tell you, but you've never heard of it. Do you need to stop for a break?"

"Whew, for a minute I thought you were going to go cliché and say you'd have to kill me. And given your peculiar lifestyle, that joke would be in bad taste, unless you were seriously considering inviting me into Club V."

"Seriously, do you need a pit stop?"

"Are you kidding? It's freezing out there."

Alex glanced at the instrument cluster. "Technically, it's not freezing. It's thirty-three."

It was Sarah's turn to flash the *duuuh* expression. "Technically, I think you should go stand outside until you're ready to admit it's freezing."

"I can tolerate the cold a very long time, madam."

"That's good, because I think I see an arctic blast in your future."

"How about this, Queen of the Frozen Tundra? I'll admit you're right, if you'll tell me more about your life growing up as the general's daughter."

"Compared to your life, mine is such a snoozer," Sarah said.

"I find your life fascinating."

"Being the child of an army general is not as interesting as being the offspring of vampires and Romanian royalty, I can assure you. And speaking of fathers, why don't you make that call. I've pretty much heard it all, and I'm still here."

Alex said nothing but instead chose to silently study the road ahead. The Route 192 sign appeared out of the darkness, and he turned the Vultur aggressively, barely slowing.

Grabbing the door handle firmly, Sarah leaned into the turn. "Is this your way of saying you don't want to talk about it?"

Alex sighed heavily as he downshifted. "I'm sorry, but that is a touchy subject. Depending on how you are received, a hundred years may not be enough."

"I've got a splendid idea," Sarah said playfully. "Why don't you call them and ask?"

Alex gritted his teeth. "I've got a better idea. Why don't we call the general and tell him you are dating a vampire."

Sarah's smile evaporated. "You don't think I will?"

"Let me phrase it this way, *hell no*."

"That's not a lot of faith in the woman you profess to love."

Alex chuckled. "Apparently, we have a few hurdles to jump."

Sarah squeezed his shoulder. "We're going to stumble. I hope you've got lots of Band-Aids."

Rolling into Lubec, Maine an hour later, Sarah studied the rustic homes, buildings, and deserted streets in road-weary, mesmerized appreciation. Stretching her arms, she yawned. "Are we here?"

"Almost, but not quite. This is the last outpost of the US," Alex answered as he turned right onto Washington Street. Several blocks later, as they began crossing the Lubec Narrows, he joyfully proclaimed, "Welcome to Canada."

Sebastian, the customs agent, immediately recognized Alex's car as he rolled up to the checkpoint. "Welcome home, Mister Johnson," he said cheerfully. Stooping lower, he gave Sarah the once over, and with a surreptitious smile he asked, "I assume your lady friend has papers?"

"My sister," Alex explained as he handed over Sarah's newly minted passport. Without bothering to thoroughly inspect the document, Sebastian returned the booklet. "Welcome back,"

Sebastian replied before bending lower to address Sarah. "I trust you will find Campobello's beauty only surpassed by our hospitality."

"Thank you, Sebastian," Sarah replied.

"I'm sure I'll be seeing you around, Sebastian. Stay warm," Alex said with a double wink before pulling away.

"Sister, Mister Johnson?" Sarah complained. "Let me see that," she said as she took the passport and inspected her credentials. "Why not Smith or Jones? Why do I even have an alias?"

Alex replied with a smirk, "Nobody here knows my true identity. For arguments sake, let's say Sarah Phillips marries Alex Tepes. Sarah Phillips's passport has been scanned multiple times crossing the Canadian border, but just here. This is a small island. How long before our private hideaway is no longer private?"

"*Our private hideaway*? It would be nice if I knew where *our* hideaway is?"

"Campobello Island."

"So finally, this is where you live."

Alex's smile intensified. "Not really, but we're close."

Sarah sat back and crossed her arms. "Oh dear Lord," she crowed. "Sebastian didn't even scan my passport."

"So I noticed. If you had come through on your own, you'd probably have received the full cavity search. We take our security pretty seriously up here." Without skipping a beat, he asked, "You don't mind flying in a helicopter, do you?"

Sarah's anxiety remained unquenched. "We have to fly to get there?"

"Not all of the time. In the summer we'll take the boat."

"Alex, where are you taking me?" Sarah implored.

"Alright, alright. I own a little island, right off shore. It's called Casco Bay Island. It's just a short helicopter ride, not even five minutes."

"You own an island?"

"Technically, Dennison Bryant owns the island through a shell corporation. I just borrow it from time to time. But don't be too impressed, it's really small and it's really cold six months out of the year. In fact, it's probably *freezing* right now."

The land narrowed near Light House Point. Turning right, his headlights illuminated a small metal hanger and a helicopter sitting in the driveway, its motor already warming. Driving around the helicopter, Alex parked his car in the hanger.

"Are you ready?"

"I'm feeling a little woozy from the road. Are we really getting on that thing?"

"Yes." Alex began retrieving their few bags from the car.

"And we're flying in the dark? Where's our pilot?"

Alex took a deep bow. "Captain Tepes at your service ma'am. And don't you fret, I hear them vampire folk have excellent night vision."

"How far are we flying?"

"In the daylight, you can easily see the island from here. Hell, it's easy enough to swim the distance. If it makes you feel better, we can stay on this side until tomorrow night."

"No, I think I'll be fine," Sarah said, staring at the helicopter. "You just never told me you knew how to fly. It's just another surprise, that's all."

"Surely that pales in comparison to finding out your prospective boyfriend is a vampire?"

"Vampire I can deal with, this whole flying prince thing is another story."

"Well, unless you want to change your mind, we should get loaded. The night is growing short."

Alex closed the door of the two-seater after Sarah had buckled in. Handing her a headset for the short flight, he smirked. "By the way, you'll be happy to know it's not freezing, it's sub-freezing."

"As you are the first prince I've ever known, I have to ask. Are all princes such smart asses?"

"Nine degrees, if you care to know," Alex answered grinning broadly.

Sarah couldn't help but to smile at his charming humor. "So who do you know that will get up at three in the morning and arbitrarily warm up the helicopter?"

"Marcus, my caretaker. He lives in the cottage behind the hanger. He takes care of my house, the helicopter, and my boat. He keeps the fridge stocked as well." Alex twisted the throttle, and as the helicopter gently lifted, Sarah grabbed the door handle tightly. "Uh, don't pull on that, I'd hate for you to fall out."

Sarah jerked her hand back to her lap as her body tensed like a concrete pillar. "Sorry. I've never been in one of these. How can you even tell where we're going?"

Alex eased the cyclic back, sending them ahead at a slow pace.

"See the light just over there," he explained as he pointed to a solitary beacon against a sea of blackness. "That's home. It's a shame the moon is not full. The view is quite spectacular."

"You don't say."

Within a few minutes, Alex was setting the bird down on the retractable landing pad, about fifty yards from the house. Once the pad had pulled into the hanger, securing the helicopter from the brutal elements, Alex grabbed their bags. "Ready?"

Walking at an exceptionally brisk aerobic pace, Sarah huffed, "Exactly why do you choose to live in the North Pole?"

The front door swung open upon their approach, and as they entered, random lights began to turn on. "Well, isn't that nifty," Sarah chirped.

The door closed and bolted automatically. "I guess I'm your prisoner now," Sarah exclaimed. Before Alex could reply, Sarah was off on a self-guided tour. Her eyes were drawn first to the pale beech-wood floors covering the expansive lofted room. The walls were a pale sea green, which created a soft contrast with the off-white, Scandinavian furniture. Contemporary artwork canvasses adorned the walls; Chagall, Lorenzo, and O'Neill were all given their due respect with spacing and illumination. Across the room, the glass wall showcased the darkness of the night, giving no hint to the grandeur of sunrise less than two hours away.

"Alex, I'm almost speechless." Sarah walked deeper into the room, revealing the open-air kitchen. Wine glasses, copper pots, utensils, an espresso machine, and all sorts of gadgets appeared to have been precisely positioned on and above the black granite by an interior decorator and master chef combined. As Sarah studied the menagerie, she mumbled, "Too bad I don't cook."

Alex chuckled. "You'll learn."

"You weren't supposed to hear that."

Alex stepped behind Sarah and wrapped his arms around her. "Just so you know, I hear everything." As Sarah turned her head, he planted a soft kiss on her cheek. "I think I should pour you a glass of wine to help you settle . . . and sleep. Then I'll show you to your room."

"My bedroom?"

"You need sleep. The *last* thing you need is to have me in bed right next to you while you're trying to—"

"Or on top of me," Sarah purred as she turned into Alex's arms. Her lips softened, the wetness of her mouth inviting his lips to hers.

"Or maybe beneath—"

"I can think of a million worse things that could happen," Alex said. Sarah moaned as his hands gently tugged at her hair.

"Let me get that wine," Alex offered, needing to temper the flames.

"It's not wine that I need," she declared.

Sarah's hands strayed from Alex's shoulders and began exploring his chest. "I don't need any help relaxing."

Alex took her hands and tucked them behind her back. "Don't take this the wrong way, but after the day we've had I'd rather us both be rested before—"

"Before?" With her hands restrained, Sarah stepped forward, allowing her breasts to brush against his chest. Alex stepped back and allowed his thoughts into her mind. Looking into his eyes, but unaware of what had just transpired, she said, "Okay, I get it, kind of." With her eyes lacking believable conviction, she submitted. "I guess I'll take that wine now."

Sarah followed Alex to the kitchen with the wide-open eyes of a small child filled with amazement. "So, how many other women have been *here*?" Sarah asked as her hand drew circles on the countertop.

"Trust me, this is my home, not a sex playpen. I have entertained only a few friends over the years. And not once for the purpose of sexual gratification."

"Well, in that case, I will have no objections to this countertop or the table or the floor . . . should the occasion arise." Sarah smiled quaintly as she took the wine glass and walked away.

Sunset had long passed when Alex awoke. *Why do you live here?* Sarah had asked. This very night was the perfect example. The island's unique serenity enveloped the house and its inhabitants. Even the tranquility of Alex's casket back in New Orleans barely compared.

In the depths of quiet, Alex wondered if Sarah might still be sleeping. It had taken him years to master the ability to shut out the thoughts of others. Life had been too predictable before learning the skill; the hunt was no longer exhilarating. And Sarah Phillips was not a hunt.

Alex rose ready and titillated. Standing in the steaming downpour of his shower, the water rejuvenated him further. He wrestled his growing urge for Sarah, which grew stronger with each passing hour.

With only a solitary candle burning, the lights of Campobello Island intertwined with the star-filled night, filling the glass wall as if it were the door to another galaxy. Before the glass, Sarah's naked silhouette stood. Alex silently took inventory of her ivory flesh, beginning with her well-defined calves and exceptionally toned hamstrings that flowed precisely into the most perfectly curved buttocks. Sarah's waist narrowed at the small of her back and then gently contoured up until her back was obscured by waves of espresso hair.

Had Alexandros been resurrected and sculpted this manifestation of Venus to appease my longings? Alex mused. Mesmerized by Sarah's beauty, his yearning could no longer be restrained. In bare feet, the hunter's approach did not alert his prey.

As his hand touched her neck, Sarah startled. "You scared me."

"This view has never been more beautiful." Speaking softly into her ear, Alex sensed her fright dissipating.

"I'm sorry, this is somewhat awkward. I'm not accustomed to being naked in a stranger's home. Not that you're a stranger, it's just I wasn't sure how else to convince you . . . I know what I want."

Alex's hands slid around Sarah's waist, pulling her close. "Are you sure?"

"I have been up most of the day, thinking about us. You can make me a vampire, or not, or the wife of a prince or just live here on this frozen island in obscurity, it doesn't matter. There is nothing about any of this that scares me anymore. I will love you whatever we are, or wherever we go."

Alex breathed Sarah in deeply. Sliding his hands across her stomach, he paused briefly before caressing the sides of her breasts. Sarah shuddered as his fingertips explored her hardened nipples before continuing into the definition of her collarbone and shoulders. With a sudden tremble of anticipation, Sarah turned to Alex.

Sarah's eyes were searching, craving, as she pulled Alex's T-shirt over his head. From the moment their flesh connected, passion boiled.

With his hands exploring every detail of her face, their lips met with a surge of electricity that sent a sea of wetness between her legs. Sarah's breathing accelerated as she frantically worked the buttons on his jeans. Alex hoisted her against the chilled glass panels, while Sarah constricted her legs around him. Pressing her back forcefully, Alex entered her deeply with a sudden thrust. Bucking and groaning in wild ecstasy, Sarah discovered a euphoria unknown and the core essence of Alex's unearthly sexuality.

As the lovers lay on the white plush rug, their bodies glistened against the scintillating flames dancing across the oak logs. Patterns of playful fairies paraded across the white carpet, the flames fanning their bedazzling spell.

"I have to apologize," Alex confessed.

"For what?" Sarah asked as she rolled from atop.

"Some of this *experience* was not entirely natural. First off, I'm not normally this warm. I am because I have willed myself to be, thinking you would prefer a warm body to a cold one. Secondly, what you experienced, the sex, it was—"

"What was it? Did you put something in my wine?"

"No. But remember when I told you I could sense your emotions, your desires, even control your mind?"

"Yes?"

"I kind of lost control back there, and in doing so, I allowed you to experience all of my sensations, in addition to your own."

Sarah took a sip of wine. "So all of that, that incredible, electric-chair sex, that is what a vampire experiences each time?"

"On a smaller scale, yes," Alex confessed, as he began combing his fingers through Sarah's hair. "I knew it would be. I think I tried to warn you."

"So, if I was a vampire, the sex would be like that all of the time?" Alex affirmed with a nod. "Oh, I want some of that medicine," Sarah chirped.

Alex stretched his neck out and lightly kissed her forehead, nose, and then lips. "Would you like to try it again, without the special effects?"

Sarah frowned. "So you're willing to *fake it,* just to show me it doesn't always have to be that mind blowing?"

"Well, now that you put it like that, I'm guessing the answer should be *no*."

Sarah smiled broadly. "Good boy. I'm guessing you came up with that all on your own, without having to *sense* my answer."

Sarah stared at the shower, flabbergasted by its size and beauty. Jagged stones protruded from the walls creating nooks and crevices, which plants abundantly filled. Illuminated by what appeared to be natural light, the water streamed down like sheets of rain from the entire ceiling to the sounds of the Amazon.

"I've never seen anything like this before. I bet it's a bear to clean."

"Easier than you'd think," Alex replied as he pulled the robe off Sarah's shoulders, allowing it to fall to the floor. "I spent the rainy season in the Amazon, walking for hours, loving the sensation. This is the closest thing I could build to simulate it."

Sarah's body glistened in the warm water as she stepped in. "Oh my, this is different," she exclaimed as she brought her hands to her cheeks.

Raising his hand to the ceiling, the water above their heads slowed to a mist, while all around the water continued to cascade down. Alex lathered up a loofah. "Is it alright if I wash you?"

"I guess so. I've never had anybody bathe me before." Turning her back to Alex, she extended her hands into the rain. "Nice touch with the rain, Noah."

Alex tucked Sarah's hair over her shoulder and began scrubbing at her neck and back. "No miracle, just motion sensors," he confessed. Washing with his left hand, Alex's right kept busy massaging Sarah's shoulders and neck.

"Mmmm," Sarah moaned. "Keep that up and I may never get out."

"That's okay, there's a microwave and a fridge behind the rock wall," Alex said.

"If that weren't so absurd, I'd almost believe you." As the soapy loofah swirled and massaged Sarah's buttocks, she groaned with pleasure and parted her legs. Alex quickly worked his way down her legs.

"Have a seat," he instructed, as he guided Sarah to one of several specially designed shower seats. Once on the edge of the heated, stone bench, Alex began washing and kneading Sarah's feet. Reaching out, Sarah's hands began massaging Alex's head and tugging gently at his hair. Spreading her legs wide was all the coercing he needed. With the wave of his hand, the water began cascading down once more. Sarah arched back against the smooth reclined stones and allowed the warm water to rain down over her face and body. The loofah dropped to the floor as Alex's hands finished the washing process, sensuously and painstakingly lathering her stomach, breasts, and shoulders before working his way between her legs. As Sarah pulled Alex to her, his best intentions evaporated in the friction of their lathered flesh.

An hour later, and back in front of the fireplace, Sarah's hands explored the texture of Alex's chest. "So, what do we do tomorrow?"

"Tomorrow evening, I will take you to dinner and parade you around the island. This should put to rest the rumors of my sexual preferences."

Sarah's eyes perked up as she sprung up on her elbow, affording a better view of Alex. "There are rumors? Whatever would people say about you?" she teased in a Southern accent.

Alex looked Sarah in the eyes, his innocence abounding. "I've lived here a number of years now and have always been rather stand offish with the local shark tank."

"Why on earth? You don't expect me to believe that your rainforest shower was built for . . . *swimming solo*."

Sarah's words forced a chuckle from Alex. "I'll admit, it is an awesome shower, even when you only want to get clean. But this house is my sanctuary. The quickest way to destroy my refuge is to have some disgruntled lover banging on the door at all hours."

"So you've never brought a companion back here? Your bed—"

"Our bed," he proclaimed.

Sarah smiled. "Our bed, the shower, not even the kitchen countertop?"

"For the eight years I have lived here, this house has not witnessed a single night of passion."

"That sounds very lonely."

"Not here. I read and write, occasionally watch a movie, and on rainy days I'll watch the aquatic life and birds from my telescope."

"What about your more basic needs?" Sarah asked.

"I go to Halifax, or farther north."

"And when you're with someone, do they . . . you know?"

"Feed my need for blood? Never. Climax? Absolutely."

"They must be lined up for your return."

Alex had to laugh. "No. It's never been like you and me. And *that* was quite unintentional. Such an experience can taint a person's judgment."

"Thank God for accidents." Sarah's hand patted Alex's chest, feigning relief.

"I can see this conversation is going nowhere."

"No, seriously, I'm trying to understand. What you're telling me is if you had held back both times, like you do with other women, it would have felt like ordinary sex, but because you didn't I'm going to be ruined?"

"Maybe? I don't know for sure."

Sarah flopped to her back with an exaggerated sigh. "Great." She stared at a leaded crystal sculpture momentarily before turning her attention back to Alex.

"Can you use your mind control powers to cool things down a bit, you know, down there. I'm kind of feeling like a sex addict."

Alex rolled to his side, reached out, and began caressing Sarah's face. "Maybe."

"Show me."

"Try your best to stop me."

Sarah sat up, backed herself against the warm stones of the fireplace, and defiantly crossed her arms. "Give it your best shot."

Alex left the room and returned with a camera.

"What are you doing with that?" Sarah squealed as she attempted to cover her body with her hands.

Alex snapped a picture.

"Oh no, Alex Tepes. Don't you dare," Sarah objected stringently, unable to move. Studying Sarah's form, Alex telepathically forced her hands above her head, bunching her hair. "Alex!"

He took another picture. Unwillingly, Sarah stretched out on the hearth. Lying on the velvet pillows, her hands sensuously stroked her body. Again, the aperture snapped, capturing her raw beauty.

"You are such a natural, surely you have posed for Playboy," Alex jested in a French accent.

"Alex!"

"Try to stop me," he taunted. Rolling to her belly, Sarah's hips thrust upward, accentuating her already curvaceous derrière. Alex snapped off one last picture before setting the camera on the marble table. To punctuate the demonstration, he filled Sarah's mind with wild desire, enough to cease any camera shy objections. Gently massaging her back and buttocks, Alex slowly eased his mind control directives.

Succumbing to the seductive gyrations of his hands, Sarah made no effort to retaliate. "As soon as you're done, you *will* erase every one of those pictures, do you understand?"

"As soon as I'm done, my love, we'll see what develops."

CHAPTER SIXTEEN

"YOU TWO LOVE birds going to sleep the night away?"

Nicholas and Samantha opened their eyes to find Chuck's face uncomfortably close. Samantha grimaced.

"What time is it?" Nicholas asked.

"Just past sunset. Time to wipe the Sandman's turds from your eyes and let's get a move on. I'd like to hit Frenchmen Street by midnight."

"Sunset? How did you get here so quickly?"

"We came in just ahead of sunrise. Talk about cutting it uncomfortably close. My balls were sweating that one."

"Thanks for sharing, Chuck," Samantha groaned.

"You guys need to get dressed, especially you, Sammy," Chuck warned with a grin. "I can see your boobies."

Samantha tugged at the sheets until she was sufficiently covered. "Why on earth we agreed to make him a vampire I'll never know."

Chuck winked at Samantha. "Okay, so here's the plan. I'm going to take the old man with me," Chuck began as he grabbed Nicholas's pants and tossed them on the bed. "God, what kind of candy-ass trousers are these Nick? No doubt you bought them in France."

With a contemptuous stare, Nicholas pulled his pants on.

"Any how, I figured Sam and Gabby can go look for Ştefan and Izzy. Traipsing through the bayou is man's work anyways."

"Give me a few minutes and I'll meet you in the office," Nicholas said, as he pulled a T-shirt from the dresser. As Chuck was preparing to leave the room, the hidden door behind the bookcase swung open and Tori appeared, dressed only in a T-shirt.

"Hello," Chuck said as his eyes detailed Tori's physique. "Nick, did you and Sammy bring home a little *ménage à trois* action from Paris?"

Nicholas looked to Samantha first, who nodded, and then back to Chuck. "This is Tori, she is one of us."

"One of us?" Chuck asked as he stepped closer. "As in *vampire* one of us?"

Chuck cut his eyes to Samantha. "I didn't realize you were expecting, Sammy. I mean, I thought it looked like you might have added a few pounds, but I wasn't going to say anything, on account of I know how sensitive you get over that kind of stuff."

"Chuck," Nicholas said sternly. "We made her, Sam and I. She was dying and we decided to save her."

Tori held her ground at the edge of the bookcase, uncertain of Chuck's intimidating stature and tone.

"You decided? I'm curious, Nicky, how in the hell did you get the old man to agree to it?"

Again Nicholas and Samantha exchanged visual cues.

"Oh, I see. He doesn't know."

"Not yet," Samantha explained. "As soon as this business with Ştefan is concluded, we will go to Romania."

"Whoa, as your head of security, count me in for that one, buddy. Cuz you guys are gonna need a bodyguard."

"There will be no need for you to tag along, Chuck. I can deal with my father."

"Look out world." Chuck raised his hands high, as if he were preaching. "Brian Denman has been resurrected after all these years, and with a brand new set of brass balls, no less."

Samantha snapped the sheet off and rose from the bed, stopping with her hands on her hips directly in front of Chuck. "Do you have to be such a ball buster, Chuck?"

"Okay, Sammy, I apologize. You haven't gained a single pound," Chuck said. No longer able to hold back his amusement, he snickered. "Would I be Chuck if I weren't? Lighten up, Sammy. Besides, who's been saying for years the old man needs to change? Look what his policies have done to the family. You can't tell me Brian Denman wouldn't have set the old man straight years ago."

Samantha moved to Nicholas's side. "That entire fiasco sent Brian Denman to the grave."

"Yeah, and we *all* went there with him, Sammy. But none of us stayed there. Maybe it's time for Nick to step up. The old man's wanted it for years."

"Chuck, nothing will ever make me want that burden," Nicholas replied.

"Maybe this will change your mind." Chucked flipped on his phone and showed Nicholas and Samantha the picture.

"Pretty girl," Samantha remarked. "Who is she?"

"Her name is Sarah Phillips." Chucked flipped to the next picture. "Check out her ride."

"Is this the car you told me about?" Nicholas asked.

Chuck flipped to the map image. "The car is currently parked here."

Nicholas studied the map. "Is there any sign of Alex?"

"I would say if you happened to travel by way of Campobello Island, odds are damned good you might find him there."

"Chuck!" Samantha snapped. "Why are you being so vague? Have you found him or not?"

"I made certain promises. However, I did not promise not to use the latest in tracking technology or give disclosure on a certain hot brunette that was riding in the car that happened to match a black, four-wheeled family gift that was given to Alex."

"Chuck, are you in here?" Gabrielle called from outside the room.

Chuck cut a glance to Tori and replied, "We *all* are."

Gabrielle's smile was short lived as she discovered Tori, still partially concealed behind the bookcase. Instantly, she recognized the familiar scent of the undead. "Who is this?"

"This is Tori," Samantha injected, not giving Chuck the opportunity to stir the pot. "Tori, Gabrielle is Chuck's wife."

Gabrielle stood before Tori. "You are French?"

Tori nodded nervously, unsure of Gabrielle's intent.

Never forgetting Samantha's grace when they first met, Gabrielle quickly hugged Tori and remarked, "You are quite magnificent." Kissing her cheek, she continued, "I am sure we will have so much to talk about." Gabrielle looked at Samantha. "And Tori will be with us tonight?"

"I really don't think Tori is ready for a boys' night in the bayou," Samantha said with a smile.

Gabrielle gathered Samantha and Tori's hands and tugged. "Come with me, let's leave these two Neanderthals to their schemes."

Chuck and Nicholas watched the girls disappear down the hall. "Gawd, I thought they'd never leave," Chuck moaned. "So, what's the deal with Ştefan?"

"I am not sure. That's why we're going out to Westwego. Now tell me everything you know about Alex."

Chuck walked over to the bed and sat down. "He contacted me three nights ago, said he needed a passport for the girl. They were in the city two nights ago, and then they drove to Campobello. Once I knew he was in New York, I spent half the night locating his car. Little fucker thought he could hide it from me, but I found it and put the tracker on it, and now we know where he's hiding."

Nicholas scrolled back to the girl's image. "Who is she?"

"Name's Sarah Phillips. Apparently—are you ready for this?—she is the only child of General Stafford Phillips. What a fucking coincidence."

"Any idea how long they've been seeing each other?" Nicholas asked, ignoring the greater issue.

"The school is on Christmas break, so I couldn't find anybody to contact. But checking her credit card history, it's pretty consistent in location, until two or three days ago. I'm guessing dipshit was headed south and somewhere near Norfolk, Virginia they hooked up. She fell off the grid, and suddenly she's in New York with Dinglewad. I hacked her social media page and it would appear she was dating some almost-lawyer guy named Brad Stafford. I dug around through his network, and look at this douchebag."

"Jesus. What happened to him?"

"Yeah I know. Somebody kicked the living shit out of him. So I dug a little further and found Alex's squeeze used her plastic at a parking garage, not too long after buying coffee. Judging by the time she bought the coffee, the location of the garage, and the fact it was Friday, I figured she was headed out to party. So I started plugging the picture Alex sent me for her passport into facial recognition and the security camera files I hacked. I made you a little video."

Chuck handed his phone to Nicholas. Watching the clip, he learned quickly that Brad's injuries were the result of his son's skillful hands. Without knowing the nature of the altercation, Nicholas viewed Alex's precision handiwork with an air of pride. The next recorded clip was of Alex and Sarah in the parking garage elevator.

"This was the next night," Chuck explained. "You're gonna love this one."

As the elevator doors opened on the video, Nicholas observed the thugs waiting just outside the doors. Within a few seconds, after watching Alex methodically put them down, he boasted, "That's my boy."

"Yeah, I taught that punk pretty darn good," Chuck exclaimed as he sniffed at the air. "Say, dude, you might wanna get these sheets laundered, they got some strong sex funk going on."

"Alright, alright. Get your ass off my bed," Nicholas ordered as he pulled on Chuck's shirt.

"So tell me, bro," Chuck began, as he headed toward the door, "what's the deal with Tori?"

Nicholas shook his head. "Hell if I know, Chuck. It was not planned. Sam and I were just feeding when I discovered she had this lethal disease. Her death was going to be excruciatingly painful. I decided to take her life and end her suffering . . . but then, I just grew soft, man."

"And I'm right in assuming the old man don't know nothing about her?"

"Damn straight. After I take care of these boys of mine, we're going to fly over and tell him what we've done."

"Do you think he'll let her live?"

"Let's not discuss that right now. Tori is our blood and our family now. I will deal with my father." Nicholas appeared flustered at the thought as he randomly searched through drawers without removing any items. "Why don't you go downstairs and fix us all a drink. We'll have one with the girls before we head out."

"Roger that. But promise me you won't wear those candy-ass pants out anytime you're with me."

The girls were still getting dressed when Nicholas joined Chuck in the parlor. "You know, it's probably going to take them another hour. What's say we have our cocktail and hit the road?"

"Let's give them ten more minutes," Nicholas replied as he eyed the five crystal goblets of deep burgundy blood. "AB positive?"

"Can't slip one past you, can I? I figured Tori's first night here in Nawlens called for something a little special, you know?" Chuck pulled a folded piece of paper from his pocket. "While I was waiting

I went through the papers on your desk. I believe this is where we need to look."

"That's a big area," Nicholas said as he studied the drawing.

"Exactly, so I pulled Isabelle's GPS history and located exactly where she parked."

"You have GPS on Isabelle?"

Chuck grinned broadly. "I'm in charge of family security. I have GPS on everybody, including that little turd son of yours . . . again." Chuck made a fist and backhanded Nicholas in the chest. "Speaking of which, is Tori's disappearance gonna create problems?"

"The only one who may have been an issue was her pimp. Outside of that, I think everything is cool."

"Did you say, *her pimp*?" Bewildered, Chuck's jaw hung intentionally low. "Dude, you left a big juicy piece of pie out of the details."

"Her circumstances, Chuck, were much like Gabrielle's, only three hundred years later. So please, don't go busting anyone's balls over it."

"Did Sammy know she was a hooker?"

"Yes, Chuck, she did. And that *will* be the last hooker reference."

"So, the three of you, body fluids and blood everywhere?"

"No, there were no body fluids. Alright? Time to move on."

Chuck leaned in close. "So the girl's a professional, a pretty damn hot one, ya'll are in Paris, you and Sammy have been married forty years, and you're telling me you made her a vampire simply because y'all felt sorry for her?"

"God, you will never change," Nicholas moaned

Chuck put the Jeep in park. "This is the place. Party time."

Nicholas climbed from the Jeep and surveyed the double-track dirt road. "Are you sure?"

"Dude, dare you ask? Of course I'm fucking sure."

Nicholas rounded the SUV and studied the tall grass. "Somebody's been through here recently." They followed the bent grass until they arrived at the tree line. The few broken branches were all the indication the rusty, yet seasoned, trackers needed.

"You smell that?" Chuck asked, sniffing the air heavily. "Know what it reminds me of?"

"If you say my bed sheets, I swear I'll stake you right here and leave you to rot."

"Naw, man, it smells like the convent. That rotten vampire funk, remember?"

Nicholas sniffed the air. "Son of a bitch. I thought it was just bayou broth. But now that you mention it."

"Shit, man, how could you ever forget that stench?" Chuck inspected several more broken branches.

Nicholas didn't answer immediately but chose to follow Chuck in silent reflection of that fatal night. Forty odd years ago, they had broken into the convent and set free the curse of the *Nosferatu*. Daniel would call it, *Brian Denman's destiny*. And the cost of his destiny? The life of his best friend Rob at the hands of the vampires he set free.

"I guess I kind of blocked it out, the sensory memory. It reminds me of Rob, how we left his body in the convent. I drove that fucking stake through his heart. Looking at the two of us now, I have to say I really fucked up. Rob could still be with us."

The thought angered Chuck. "Shit, Nick, is that what really killed Brian Denman? Look, all we had to go on was what we knew at that instant. Those vampire bitches were evil, and for all we knew, Rob was going to be just like them. Shoe on the other foot, Rob would have done the same to you. And another thing, Phil and Jimmy had the choice to be like us, they didn't choose it, so there's a damn good chance Rob wouldn't want this life either. He died like a soldier. Back then wasn't that the way we wanted to go out? Fuck gettin' old and feeble."

Nicholas nodded as he absorbed Chuck's logic.

Continuing back on the trail, Chuck remarked, "Ol' Jimmy, I bet he's up there somewhere laughing his ass off at us two idiots trudging through the swamps on this miserable night." Chuck changed direction without warning, continuing to follow the fractured branches. "You know what Jimmy told me, back before he died? He said he believed choosing to live out his life as a mortal might be his one shot at salvation. You believe that shit? I told him, the only reason I chose it was because I was too big of a pussy to spend eternity in hell." Chuck snorted an obnoxious laugh at the memory.

As Chuck continued to forge ahead, Nicholas remained silent, mired in the memories of his passed friends.

"Don't this kinda remind you of the good old days down in Columbia. All we need are our guns and some coked up drug runners to kill. You know something, Nick? I think you and I *need* to get back to our roots. I mean think about it. It'd be a nice change of pace. Don't you get tired of reading books and bang'n Sammy and sipping blood from champagne glasses like some kind of fruitcake? With this equipment you and I are packing, we could really clean house on those dipshits down there. And think of all the money we could skim."

"No, Chuck, I really don't miss it. I think I've been carrying the burden of all the souls we extinguished over the years, and I just can't let them go. Maybe it was getting shot, or maybe it's the sum of all of it, that has just worn me thin."

"Shot?" Chuck exclaimed.

"How many times have you gotten your head blown open?"

"Well, none, now that I think about it. But you did break my fucking arm once." Chuck turned, walked backwards, and added, "Maybe you should see a shrink." As he was staring Nicholas down, he tripped on a board beneath his feet. "Oh shit," he cried, as he stumbled to the ground, falling onto a mound of freshly shoveled soil.

Nicholas helped Chuck to his feet, and the pair stared at the empty hole. "What the hell?" Chuck observed.

Alarmed, Nicholas replied, "A hole six feet deep, and three hundred years of missing trouble."

"It's strange—how little this place has changed in forty years," Samantha observed.

"It never does. Stores and bars come and go, but at the end of the day, it really isn't different. The people, different faces, but the same crazy attitudes," Gabrielle said.

"I think I understand the appeal of New Orleans now. I had heard stories, but being here brings it all to life," Tori added, as she absorbed the sensory smorgasbord of the French Quarter. "I find it peculiar. When we started out, I thought I was going to freeze in this dress. But I do not feel the cold at all."

"That is just another added benefit of our kind. We are far more temperature tolerant than our counterparts," Gabrielle explained.

The women lazily strolled, looking in the bars and the few shops that remained open. As they began their trek down Toulouse, Samantha's demeanor changed. Gabrielle immediately sensed it.

"What's wrong?"

"It's this street. This is where we met. Do you remember?"

"How could I forget? It was at the other end, in front of your hotel. I was with Celine," Gabrielle said.

"Not a very fun night, as I remember. And just up ahead, on the left, was that bar where they almost killed Dee."

"The Chamber. Nicholas told me the entire story. I never went in there, even after we returned to New Orleans. But we should check it out, if it's still there. Nicholas said Isabelle used to hang out there."

Samantha stared down Toulouse and a handful of memories she'd rather not relive. Since the days of her death and turning, Samantha frequently experienced the angst and visions of the dead, their souls bound to the halls and streets of the Vieux Carré. Staring at the manifestation of an isolated, sorrowful child in a passing window, Samantha understood the despair of spirits forever bound to a home no longer warmed by the love of family.

"Should we wait for your husbands?" Tori interjected.

"One thing that you must learn rather quickly, there is little for you to fear, and never wait for a man to do what a woman can do," Gabrielle said with a broad smile. "Come, Tori, it is time for your first lesson in Neanderthal management."

"Wait," Samantha implored. "If Barousse is in there, he mustn't know what we are. You're going to have to camouflage your scent and Tori's," Samantha said.

"If we do that, we won't be able to detect him," Gabrielle argued.

"If he is in there, he won't be alone. I don't want Ştefan or Barousse to sense our presence until we can get Chuck and Nick here."

"Dressed like you are, with your hair and makeup, Ştefan won't even recognize you. It would be funny to watch him hit on his own mother," Gabrielle said with a chuckle, as she took Tori by the hand and led her down Toulouse. It was just after twelve and a small crowd had gathered by the outer door of the Chamber. Gabrielle bypassed the line and went straight to the doorman.

"I have reservations."

"We don't take reservations, doll."

Gabrielle turned and winked at Samantha and Tori. She whispered insistently into the doorman's ear. "We have reservations," she repeated with a forceful tone.

"Of course you do," he replied as he opened the door without further deliberation.

Winding down the narrow alley, Samantha sensed an elevated

risk. She considered halting Gabrielle's charge into the pit of darkness. *Two minutes,* Samantha thought, *we can be in and out, and back on the street.* Passing through the inner door, a blast of ear-shattering, heavy metal music assaulted the trio.

Samantha studied the assortment of night crawlers inhabiting the bar, grabbed Tori and Gabrielle, and said anxiously, "Let's get this over with."

"It doesn't look like she's here," Gabrielle shouted over the music.

"There's a basement," Samantha replied loudly. "Nick told me about it."

Making her way down, Samantha couldn't imagine how Nick, or anyone, could navigate this dark and narrow abyss without the night vision of a vampire. At the bottom, Samantha stared in amazement at what appeared to be nearly a hundred people participating in some kind of ritualistic, orgy dance.

"Keep Tori close. I'll meet you back here shortly," Samantha instructed Gabrielle. Cutting through the heart of the crowd, for once Samantha was glad Nick was not with her. Having barely broken through the middle of the crowd, Samantha had already been groped a half a dozen times. Undoubtedly, her husband would have already smashed several faces.

Fully capable of defending herself, Samantha avoided the temptation that her husband would have succumbed to happily. As she worked her way out of the crowd on the opposite side of the stairs, she found the infamous cul-de-sac. Enhanced over the years with paint meant to replicate Monique's blown out brains, courtesy of *Brian Denman,* the shrine now appeared as an occult seat of honor.

At the table, four similarly attired men were seated. "Hello, Vixen," one of the men said, as he eyed Samantha top to bottom.

Samantha returned the gesture. The one that spoke was pale and gaunt; his long, black hair had an oily sheen. He was wearing a burgundy velvet jacket that appeared well worn. His scent was mortal, maybe.

The one seated at the end of the table, with streaks of grey through his hair and abnormally bloodshot eyes, placed his hand on Samantha's knee and began to work his way up. At mid-thigh, she slapped his hand away forcefully.

"Bitch, be gone," he ordered.

Samantha fantasized slamming his head into the table, a classic move she had witnessed Nick perform on several occasions. Not wanting to stir the hornet's nest, she played their game. "Not so quick, baby. You need to buy me a drink first."

"Get you own drink, bitch," the man replied, as he rubbed his hand.

"Nathan, don't be so rude," the first one ordered. "Go get our friend a drink."

"I have two friends with me."

"Nathan, get this sexy lady and her friends a round of drinks," he commanded.

Nathan cut a glare as he slid from the table. "Best be careful how you play, missy. You might just regret it."

"Nathan, enough!" The man snarled. "Please sit," he suggested, as Nathan disappeared. Just as Samantha sat down, Gabrielle and Tori appeared. "Are these your friends?"

Samantha turned, confirmed his observation, and then looked back to him. "Yes."

"And they are equally as beautiful. Ladies, please join us for a drink."

Tori was about to seat herself when Gabrielle restrained her. "We would love to, but we are looking for a friend."

"Have a seat. Maybe it is that I can provide some assistance."

"Tori, you sit," Gabrielle instructed. "I prefer to stand."

"I am Killian, and this is Dougan and Robert. Might I inquire as to whom you seek?"

Samantha leaned forward. "I'm looking for a friend. Maybe you know her." Samantha extended her phone with Isabelle's picture on the screen.

"This one looks familiar. I think perhaps Carthan might know her. But while we await his return, might I have the pleasure of your names."

Samantha deliberated momentarily. "I am Gwen, this is Sophia and Lexie."

"Lexie, did I discern a French accent, perhaps?" Killian asked Gabrielle.

After traversing the dancing masses and receiving a similar groping, Gabrielle was not in a particularly sociable mood. "Oui."

Unabashedly, Killian intently scrutinized both women's bodies. "Excellent, and what about you, Sophia?" he asked Tori.

"I am French."

Before he could continue with the interrogation, Nathan

returned with Carthan at his side. "Ah, Carthan, you have returned."

As Nathan dispersed the drinks, he nodded to Killian.

"Now, what should we toast to? Oh, I know, to finding your beautiful friend." Killian raised his glass and finished the burgundy beverage. He watched with anticipation as all three women drank. "Gwen, please show Carthan your friend's picture."

"I know this woman. She was upstairs earlier tonight. Perhaps, she may still be there."

"We should finish our drinks and see if your friend remains," Killian suggested. He continued to watch intently, as one by one, each woman finished their wine. "Come, let us see if we can find her."

Killian led the way, followed by Samantha, Tori, and Gabrielle. Carthan and the others followed closely. As they reached the second floor, Killian rapped loudly on the metal barrier. As the door swung open, an eerie, seductive wave of music escaped, enveloping the women. Once inside the spacious, dusky room, the unseen doorman closed and bolted the door.

Amidst the sparse flickering votives, Samantha searched the room for Isabelle. Her stomach churned instantly upon recognizing the table used to restrain Dee almost forty years ago. Nick's description of her sister's near fatal encounter filled her mind with images of sex-crazed, blood-drinking rituals. Samantha shook off the visions as she felt Killian's hand on her shoulder.

"We should see if she is here," Killian suggested, unaware of Samantha's unnaturally keen night vision.

As they proceeded deeper into the room, she realized most of the dozen or so inhabitants were engaged in various levels of pre-fornication. Aroused by the ambiance, and expecting Samantha to be feeling the cocktail's effects, Killian placed his arm around Samantha's waist. It was at that precise moment she realized what had transpired—they had been drugged.

Nathan began groping Gabrielle as Carthan began pulling her skirt up from behind. She forcefully smacked their hands away. Dougan and Robert seized Tori, just as Carthan wrapped one arm around Gabrielle and with the other covered her mouth.

Suddenly, Killian screamed. Samantha had grabbed his arm and snapped his wrist like a twig. Gabrielle whirled, tossing her assaulters aside. Tori looked astonished as the two men went flying across the room. *My turn,* she thought. She grabbed the two men groping her and smashed their heads together. They collapsed, blood oozing from their skulls.

Samantha grabbed Tori's hand, then Gabrielle's. "Let's go girls," she said.

"Can you believe those jackasses? They tried to drug us," Samantha said as they rushed to exit.

"You two were amazing," Tori exclaimed. "I had no idea we were that strong."

"Honey, that had nothing to do with vampire strength," Gabrielle gloated. "That was forty years of us being married to two of the biggest badasses on the planet."

"I am sorry I did not act sooner. I did not want to make a mistake," Tori explained.

"You did fine," Gabrielle replied. "Unless your life is in danger, it is far more important to do little or nothing rather than risk exposing our race."

"You said they drugged us. Why do I not feel strange?"

"It is like drinking alcohol, sweetie," Gabrielle began. "You must consume a large quantity to feel any affects."

Samantha stared at the bar on the corner of St. Louis and Bourbon. Even in the cold of December, the balcony party was in full gear. "Speaking of which, after that ordeal, I'm ready for a drink."

Gabrielle followed Samantha's gaze and smiled. "I know that bar. Didn't you tell me some fool jumped off of the balcony once, just to impress you."

Samantha looked at Tori. "She's referring to Nicholas," she explained, the memory forcing a minute smile. "The very first night we met he jumped off that balcony, in some misguided attempt to win my heart."

"It appears to have worked."

"For a vampire, that leap is nothing," Gabrielle quipped. "But back then, Nicholas was somewhat mortal, and quite foolish." The three stared at the balcony; each recreating the scene in their minds when suddenly Gabrielle grabbed their hands. "My Jarhead does not like to dance, but I do. We will have a drink *and* a dance before we continue our search."

"After what just happened, maybe two," Samantha moaned.

CHAPTER SEVENTEEN

THE HOUSE IN Kingston was little more than a shack, with a rusted iron bed, a couple of fifty-year-old recliners, a rickety table, and a mismatched chair set. With no plumbing or electricity, its most valuable amenity was darkness.

Ştefan rested in the beige recliner and studied the pulsating heap of mummified flesh. It was breathing, or at least making attempts to do so. Wrestling with his conscience, one part begged to decapitate the creature, the other to feed its cravings. He studied the beast as the hours of darkness waned.

As dusk approached, he sighed heavily and opened the cooler that rested on the dusty floor. Daniel had insisted *this thing,* Èdouard Barousse, had some pivotal role to play in Ştefan's plans for conquest. But how did Daniel know? He couldn't have known. *Had Daniel's claims been intentionally vague, much like the many charlatan fortune-tellers of Jackson Square? Had he actually mentioned Ştefan's rebellion?* Those questions had plagued and paralyzed Ştefan ever since fleeing Louisiana with Barousse.

Ştefan drew up a small quantity of blood from the vile with a large syringe and worked it gently into the creature's mouth. Slowly rationing the dosage over several hours, the creature began taking on human form. By three in the morning, darkened orbs appeared where one would expect to find its eyes.

As sunrise neared, the creature's hands feebly reached for Ştefan, tugging at his leg, its eyes pleading for one last feed before dawn. As the beast lay calmly, Ştefan drifted off.

Ştefan slept in restless fits. In his dreams, great winged demons soared over a scorched valley. What once had been vast evergreen forests were now laid to charred waste. Rivers ran dry, and the few that remained, flowed with streams of lava. Chained to the ruins of what once was Poenari, helplessly he watched as hordes of demons raped and sodomized his family. And he wailed in shame.

"What is it you fear?" a strange voice queried weakly.

And in the presence of their master's voice, the demons fled. And in his dream, as with reality, Ştefan replied, "Evil."

"As do I," the voice replied calmly.

Ştefan opened his eyes to find the eyes of the creature locked in his gaze.

"It must have been a terrible dream," the creature observed. "I know these dreams; for years uncounted, they were the only companions I have known."

"You are Èdouard Barousse?"

"In a life long ago, that was my name. Tell me friend, what year is this?"

Ştefan pulled another syringe of blood, this time filling the tube. "Can you take this, or do you require my help?"

"I am afraid my arms don't have the strength to wipe my nose."

Ştefan dropped to a knee and guided the syringe into Barousse's mouth. "Don't worry, your strength will return. The year is two thousand fifty-two."

A broken expression filled Barousse's face as tears pooled. "Do you mean to tell me, sir, three centuries have passed, and yet I still live?"

"Do you know what you are, Èdouard?"

Barousse closed his eyes as if to hide from some bitter memory. "I became some creature, some ungodly animal. It was my penitence, I know. For you see, I was hard and cruel, and in the end, I must have lost my mind. I killed and drank the blood of my fellow man and my slaves." Barousse turned his head away, as if the vile confession shamed him terribly. "And as my sins overwhelmed me, even the golden light of the sun became my curse."

Ştefan returned to his seat. "Had you ever heard of a creature of the night, commonly known as a vampire?"

"No."

"Do you remember a woman, a very beautiful one? Her name was Monique."

Barousse turned back, his eyes deeply intense. "I could never forget Monique."

Ştefan looked down to discover that Barousse had already emptied the syringe. "Monique was a vampire, a creature from the old world. Vampires, you see, cannot exist in the light of day. If you were to go outside in the direct sunlight, even now, your body would incinerate. They gain their strength, their supernatural strength, by drinking the blood of men. In return, they are blessed and cursed with eternal life, until the day they are killed by intention."

Confusion blanketed Barousse's face as he looked at the red droplets remaining in the syringe.

"It was Monique, Èdouard, who turned you into a creature of the night. I know this, because like you, I am a vampire."

"If this is life eternal, then set my spirit free. For I would rather die than to live in this corpse of a body," Barousse pleaded.

Ştefan placed a reassuring hand on his arm. "Do not worry, my friend. This body you possess will heal. In short time, you will look and be as healthy as I."

"How did I get this way?"

"Once your affliction became evident to your slaves, they chained you in a casket and then buried you deep in the bayou. Only your slaves knew of your fate, and several withstood great torture and even death, rather than disclose the truth."

"And Monique, the woman you claim turned me, how is it she left me to live out eternity beneath the ground?"

"That, my friend, is a very long story. One for another night. Rest now. We need to travel at sunset. In order to accomplish that, I need you to drink more."

Barousse closed his eyes and inhaled deeply. His eyes popped open again, the orbs clear and black. As he studied Ştefan's features, he said, "I am most sorry, my friend, I have forgotten my manners. What is your name?"

Ştefan sat erect, as if revealing his identity was to be reckoned with honor. "Ştefan Tepes."

Barousse's hands extended out to Ştefan. "Might I trouble you for another?" As Ştefan began to draw another syringe, Barousse continued his inquiry. "And please tell me, Ştefan, how is it that you have come to my rescue?"

Ştefan laughed softly. "That is a rather bizarre story. It was prophesized to me that our fates were somehow intertwined. I was told if I could locate and then liberate you, that somehow you would assist me in my journey."

"I cannot begin to imagine what assistance I could offer."

Ştefan closed his eyes, pursed his lips, and exhaled sharply from his nose. "I am a Tepes. In the line of my family, the roots of my ancestors, the origin of all vampirism, was born. Seven hundred years ago, Vlad Tepes brought this curse upon his family, and that curse has transcended every generation since. The one that made you was afflicted by the very curse, which started with Vlad the Impaler. It is my intention that I will be the Tepes to bring the curse to an end."

"Do you mean to tell me that you plan to bring this *immortality* to an end?"

Uncertain of Barousse's beliefs or schemes, Ştefan had inadvertently strayed from the truth and was now forced to lie. "It is an unnatural curse, sir, brought about by the unholy consumption of blood. Do you know your Bible?"

"I know the book, although one might say, the book does not know me. Perhaps when my strength recovers, we shall go and have a priest explain this curse."

"No, you see, with this curse all things considered holy only bring us misery. But it's my belief that there may be a path to immortality beyond the curse. Where there have been others, only one remains uncursed."

Barousse attempted to shift his body to a sitting position, but failed. "Please explain. It appears that all that I am capable of still is to listen."

Ştefan injected another syringe into Èdouard's mouth, and this time Barousse's hands grasped the syringe with noticeable strength. "In this age, the world is full of great scientists. But my family chooses to keep our unique circumstances a matter of the utmost secrecy. I have made several attempts to convince them of their flawed intentions, but to no avail."

"I can understand why they would want to keep this a secret. Apparently, the fear of vampires leads to dreadful measures."

"That is archaic thinking. My grandfather rules Romania and has proven for over thirty-five years that our race can not only coexist, but can create great prosperity for all who seek it."

"But he chooses to hide in the shadows of his existence?"

"Yes, and he does not allow any of us the freedom to seek change."

Barousse stretched his legs. "Oh, look. It appears as if my legs have begun to work," he said with a gleam. He found Ştefan's eyes intently focused on his progress. "But you have a plan?"

"His forces are small. I have created a small militia of vampires loyal to my cause. We will travel to Romania and take control of the throne. As a Tepes, my birthright will not be questioned."

"If it is your birthright, then why the need for force?"

Ştefan sighed. The explanation remained a painful reality. "I have a half brother, and his bloodline is of royal descent. My mother is American, and therefore, my lineage is undesirable to my grandfather. But my brother would just as soon die as to succeed our grandfather. But as we are immortal, and time is our ally, my grandfather will wait until the day my brother would change his mind."

"I can see your predicament. But by your own admission, time is your ally. What is your hurry?"

Ştefan thought of Reese, and then thought of Gabrielle. "Love, sir. For as long as we live in the shadows, this affliction, this curse, it will not tolerate love born outside of our own race. It is the reason we fight our wars, it is the reason men kill, it is the reason men throw out all rational thinking and replace it with reckless abandon."

"So you will take what is your brother's by show of force if necessary? She must be exceptional."

"Love is, and it *is* my intention."

"I do not know what part you expect me to play, for I am no great warrior or military strategist." Barousse pushed against the floor, his ribs rising a few inches before falling. "Do you think you can help me to a chair. My body feels quite displeased, lying on its side for three hundred years."

Ştefan reached down and helped Barousse to his feet. With his body remaining grotesquely contracted, Barousse struggled for balance and then to straighten his torso. With Ştefan's assistance, Barousse groaned painfully, as his body conformed into an S-shaped curve. Each leg quivered wildly as he struggled to move in the direction of the unoccupied recliner. Once seated, the physical exertion seemed to drain what little strength Barousse had harvested. "May I have some more?"

As Ştefan emptied the second glass vial, he felt the rush of hunger.

Taking a vial for himself, he drank deeply of the burgundy nectar.

"I do not know what part you are to play, but the prophecy led me to you, to bring you here, and undoubtedly, before this story reaches its conclusion, your contribution will be revealed. Of this, I am certain."

"If this is the truth, then we should get on with it. My body seems to agree with your plans for resuscitation, so if you would kindly share another vial of that most delicious beverage."

"It is blood, Èdouard, human blood. Something you will drink much of, if we are to conquer my family."

For the first time, an expression of complexity shadowed Barousse's face. "Human blood. For some reason I feel that I shall not shed a tear for those who will serve my purpose."

Perhaps, a simple slip of the tongue, Ştefan thought. *After all, it is you, Èdouard, who is to serve my purpose.*

The girls returned home after their drinks and vaguely recounted their evening. They were truthful about what they did, but purposely omitted details. They knew that if Nicholas and Chuck had the full story they would destroy the bar and everyone in it.

Nicholas paced the library floors as Chuck, Gabrielle, Samantha, and Tori indulged in a late night snack in the kitchen. He had rechecked the history on his web browser and rummaged through the books and papers left on his desk, looking for any clues as to where Ştefan had gone or what he might have planned. Ignoring the clicking heels of Samantha's approach on the oak hardwood floors, he stared out the window.

"Why don't you join us, baby?" she asked, as she leaned against the doorframe, crossing her legs. Observing an uncharacteristic bout of stress, Samantha decided to attack her husband's Achilles' heel. Sliding her hands seductively over her thighs, she moaned ever so softly.

"Don't think I don't know what you are doing," Nicholas said, as he crossed the office and plopped in his desk chair. "Besides Ştefan and Isabelle, something is missing. I just don't know what it could be."

"Come have a glass with us, then we can go to bed." Samantha hiked her skirt up, exposing the satin and lace of her panties. "A little distraction will help clear your mind. We'll get it figured out tomorrow."

"Tomorrow, barring any change, I'm going to Canada. I've got to find Alex before he disappears again. You and Chuck can take care of business here for a day."

Samantha dropped her hemline as her disposition suddenly soured. "I may not have given birth to Alex," Samantha said, as she rounded the desk and crowded Nicholas's space, "but I raised him just the same as Ştefan. There's no way in hell you are going to Canada without me."

"It's my fault Alex, and now Ştefan, have—"

"*Our* fault," Samantha interrupted sharply. "Every decision made, we made together. I am equally responsible for this mess."

Nicholas sighed heavily in defeat. Sitting at his desk, Samantha's legs were directly in his line of sight. Placing a hand on her thigh, Nicholas relented. "I don't know what's more lethal, your logic, or these." His hand caressed her silky flesh as he devised his course of action. "I want to leave before sunrise, so we can get there before he has a chance to disappear again."

"I hate day flights. They're dangerous."

"Life is dangerous," Nicholas said, as he closed the tattered book on his desk. "Let's go have a drink so I can tell Chuck and Gabby the plan. Then we can go upstairs and you can explain your *distraction* concept."

Samantha pulled Nicholas's head to her waist and raked her hands through his hair. "Now, that's more like my naughty vampire."

CHAPTER EIGHTEEN

"IT WAS A beautiful sunset tonight," Sarah exclaimed, as she sat on the couch with her legs tucked underneath, wearing nothing but a very familiar sweater. The stars and moon painted the Bay of Fundy in abstract patterns of dazzling light and had mesmerized her for what seemed like hours.

Alex sat beside Sarah and wrapped his arm around her. "Before I came to darkness, I used to take our boat out into the bayou and watch the sun set. I'd stay out half the night, engrossed with the beauty of the heavens. And it wasn't until just now that I realized how much I miss it."

"Why now?"

"Because it's something that births a great passion in you. Watching the day expire, or be born anew, that is an experience we can never share. So I have found my first regret."

"I'm sure there will be other things we can't share."

"Like?"

"Periods, childbirth, bachelorette parties—very emotional times. Can't go there, can you?" Sarah rose from the couch and walked toward the window. "I think we can discover all sorts of things to replace the beauty of sunsets." Sarah slowly raised the sweater, revealing her flaming red lingerie. "What do you think?"

"I think you just cured me of regret," Alex said.

Sarah returned to the couch, but this time straddled Alex's lap and wrapped her arms around him. Her velvety lips began exploring his neck, forcing him to summon all of his resolve.

"Sarah, I need to ask you something."

Without pausing from her task, she uttered, "Yes?"

"I know I promised to have you back home in a few days."

Her hands were now tousling Alex's hair, as her lips and tongue entwined with his. "You did," she said breathing heavily.

"I don't want to take you back."

Reaching down, she tugged at the sweater until it was over her head and off her body. "Then don't," she huffed, as she began unfastening his pants.

And just like the sunset, Alex's resolve faded from view.

"In the nicer weather, I would suggest bicycles. But at twenty-one degrees, I think the car is a better decision."

"We could have stayed in. It looked like there was plenty of food," Sarah remarked. "What do you do when it snows a lot?"

"It depends. I can pretty much wait out an entire winter in my home, or I can still get out. I have a redneck monster truck that can pretty much drive through anything. With the snow coming, we would have taken it tonight, but my caretaker is doing a bit of maintenance on it."

Passing only an occasional lit house, Sarah strained to see in the pitch black of Route 774. "I have to admit, getting used to this much darkness will take some time."

"You do get used to it, to the point that when you go back to a city, the lights are almost annoying. I don't think our brains were actually designed to deal with the onslaught of illumination most cities offer." Alex downshifted hard into the nearly hairpin curve. In Welshpool, it was the closest thing to a bit of driving excitement he could find. "It's just another mile up the road."

"After a corner like that, I certainly hope so," Sarah complained, as she white-knuckled the door handle.

"Sorry, I've driven this road hundreds of times. I should have warned you. So, if you haven't figured it out already, this isn't a thriving metropolis, so the dining-out options are rather limited."

"I'll have to admit, I was rather put out that I haven't seen a McDonald's for days."

The glow of Sarah's smile was enough to thaw the frost off the night's bitter cut. As Alex wheeled into the Fireside Restaurant, they were greeted by a rather full parking lot. It was, after all, Saturday night, and the islanders were well accustomed to the weather. With a large storm on the horizon, everybody was taking the opportunity to eat and socialize before battening the hatches.

"Fireside? So I'm guessing we have a cozy, romantic table by the hearth?"

"That would be so cliché." He chuckled. "No, I have reserved us a table for two on the patio. You'll be able to really enjoy the stars from there."

"That would be an experience, freezing to death over dinner," Sarah replied, watching for a hint of truth in Alex's expression.

"Actually, only one of us would freeze to death. Technically speaking, in case you haven't read that chapter yet, I'm already considered dead."

Alex jumped out, opened Sarah's door, and the couple wasted not a second racing against the brutal northwest gale blowing off of Friar's Bay. Once inside, Sarah shook off her coat and looked over the log cabin motif. "Oh look, a fireplace, imagine that, and with a dead moose over it." Sarah couldn't help but notice that every table was taken, except for the one by the fireplace, which coincidentally had both a glass of wine and bourbon waiting. She turned to Alex and winked. "And look, drinks are already served. I'll bet I can guess which table is ours."

Alex waved to a nearby waitress as he ushered Sarah to the table. "The Coquilles St. Jacques is excellent, as is the Lobster Thermidor. But feel free to get whatever you want."

Sarah leaned close and whispered, "How can you tell?"

Alex pulled Sarah's chair out and seated her. "I *can* taste. Before I changed, I loved all sorts of food. Afterward, initially, food was very bland and undesirable." Alex sat, sniffed at the air, and made a curious expression before continuing to explain. "But over time, the senses return, smell and taste, and you find yourself eating just about everything. Not because you need to, but because it's pleasurable—except garlic dishes."

"Could you survive without it, food that is?" Sarah asked, as she took note of a couple arriving at the door.

"For the rest of my unnatural life, if the need arose." With his back to the door, Alex's smile dissipated instantly.

Alarmed by the change, Sarah asked, "What's wrong? Did I say something?"

"I thought I was ready for this, but on my terms." Alex downed his bourbon in a single swallow. "Hello Father, Mother," he said without turning to confirm their unexpected appearance.

Sarah's dumbfounded expression must have appeared somewhat comical to Nicholas and Samantha, as they suppressed their awkward smiles. Captivated by their beauty and grace, Sarah's admiration was so intense, her thoughts might as well have been broadcast with a megaphone.

Nicholas couldn't help but ease into a smile at her unspoken appreciation. "Hello," he said.

Alex's napkin hit the table with an angry snap of the wrist. "What are you doing here?"

Immediately taken with Sarah's radiant glow, Samantha instantly knew she remained a human. "You must be Sarah. I am Alex's stepmother, Samantha, but please call me Sam."

Alex stood, his chair noisily scraping the hardwood surface. "Father, can we have a word, in private?"

Temporarily ignoring his son's request, Nicholas introduced himself. "Hello, Sarah, I am Nick."

"It's an honor to meet the two of you. I've heard so much already," Sarah replied nervously.

"Sarah, Mother, please excuse us. I need to have a word with my father, in private," Alex insisted.

"Actually, if Sarah doesn't mind, we can pull up two chairs and talk here," Nicholas suggested.

"She minds," Alex snapped.

Feeling quite awkward, Sarah tried to play peacemaker. "Really, I don't mind if they sit."

Nicholas returned with two chairs and set them at the table. "There, isn't this nice?" Nicholas remarked.

Sarah nodded, and with a quaint smile rolled her eyes in the direction of Alex's chair, gesturing for him to sit.

"Ten years, son. I am surprised you are still angry."

"I was fine, until you showed up, *uninvited*."

"What, is this your private island?" Nicholas asked, donning a half-baked smile.

"Private enough, until now," Alex said.

"I apologize for the intrusion," Nicholas said to Sarah. "Now,

Alex, give me a chance to explain. I'll keep it short. We did not want to take the chance of you disappearing again, not until we had the opportunity to set things right. Son, I was wrong. We were *all* wrong, including your grandfather." Nicholas checked to ensure they hadn't drawn the attention of any nearby diners. Keeping a low voice, he continued, "We tried to shove his kingdom on you, to relieve *our* responsibility." Nicholas took Samantha's hand. "Neither one of *us* wanted it, and there you were, royal bloodlines, and mortal—at the time. We never should have allowed our expectations to interfere with your life."

Alex sat silent, contemplating a response.

Sarah broke the awkward silence. "Unfortunately, Alex has an issue with pride, which I gather runs in the family," she explained. "Although he would love to, this bull-headedness prohibits him from graciously accepting your apology. As his confidante and voice of reason, on his behalf, he thanks you and accepts your heartfelt apology."

Sarah's posture was almost regal, her nose aimed intentionally high, and her lips were pursed, leaving Alex no choice but to snicker at her antics.

"Actually, we were headed south in a few days," Alex explained. "Sarah forced me to realize it was past time to come home."

Samantha grabbed his face and planted a noisy smooch on his cheek. "We have missed you so badly."

"Yes, I have missed you guys too." The waitress retuned and set the bottles and glasses on the table. After pouring a round, Alex made a quick study of Sarah's disposition before continuing. "So, just to put my cards on the table, I am in love with Sarah, and I think she feels the same about me."

Samantha made a quick search for prying ears. "What about . . . you know."

"She knows everything."

"Everything?" Nicholas repeated.

"Yes, I do, Mister Tepes, or should I call you Count?" After her jest, Sarah appeared apprehensive.

Samantha patted her hand, reassuring Sarah her humor was well received. "Nick will be just fine, as long as he behaves."

"I love Alex," Sarah said. "Whatever his future holds, I will be there to share it with him. You understand that, don't you?"

"Historically, I would have stringently objected to this

relationship on many levels, followed by a heated debate," Nicholas said. "Had he the opportunity, my father would have never approved of Sam, for all of the wrong reasons. But it's obvious you two are in love. And as Sam has reminded me many times, in the end love is what really matters. And considering our beginning"—Nicholas winked at Samantha—"with all of the drama we have endured, I think the only statement I am qualified to make is, I wish the two of you all the happiness and love that Sam and I have shared, and if possible, even more."

"Thank you," Sarah replied timidly as Alex smiled uneasily.

Looking back to Sarah, Nicholas continued, "In our family history, love has taken an ass kicking unlike anything you can imagine, but it has always managed to persevere. It is true that our family's position concerning outsiders has been extreme, but you must understand the potential consequences of our family secret becoming public knowledge."

Great, Alex thought, *and here it comes.*

"Our family has remained a closed circle for nearly forty years, not a revolving door," Nicholas explained. "Being a part of this family is complicated, as I am sure Alex must have conveyed by now. It can also be very frustrating."

Samantha put her hand back on top of Sarah's. "What he's trying to say is, relationships are never easy, even more so in our family. But if you love our son, please know that we will do everything in our power to see that the two of you are happy." Samantha looked at Nicholas. "Does that sum it up?"

"Yup," Nicholas replied as he planted his lips behind the glass of bourbon.

Alex's defensive posture eased. In the ensuing silence, he refilled his glass and then his father's. "The last thing I ever thought I would say is, you are right. Trust me, this honestly hurts, because I've lived with a ration of shit for twenty odd years. But throughout my life, I've never found a love to compare with yours, until now. If I hadn't put up with all of your bullshit and gone into seclusion, I never would have met Sarah. So in a screwed up kind of way, the last tens years had a purpose, and I knew it from the moment I laid eyes on her."

"I'm not sure if we're supposed to say *you're welcome* for that," Samantha replied, treading carefully in the wake of the fragile reconciliation.

Alex refilled Sarah and Samantha's glasses. "A small part of me still wants to be pissed off at the two of you. After all, I've spent the last ten years hiding from everyone I love. But Sarah has convinced me to let *all* of it go, because if I cling to the past, I can never own my future, free and clear." He raised his glass. "So here's to an amazing woman, and our family, may this be a new beginning for us all."

After a few drinks, Sarah's inquisitive nature lit up like a crematory furnace. Sitting for what must have been close to two hours, Alex listened as his parents entertained Sarah with stories of their early days in New Orleans and his childhood.

Several of Alex's island acquaintances stopped by the table, curious as to his new companions. Due to their similar age appearance, he was forced to introduce his parents as cousins, while he simply announced Sarah as his friend. Once Alex's neighbors had moved on, Samantha barked, "Alex, shouldn't you be introducing Sarah as your girlfriend?"

"Mother, Sarah is not a girl, she's a woman," he teased.

"In France, you would introduce her as your lover. But on this island it might cause quite the scandal," Nicholas suggested.

"I'm not sure if I'm ready for the two of you boys to be together again," Samantha groaned. "Why don't you ask Sarah how she would like to be introduced?"

"I'm okay as his lover," Sarah replied with a mischievous twinkle, "or fiancé."

The notion of marriage had passed through Alex's mind, but only like a warm summer breeze, giving a brief wisp of comfort, and then quickly forsaken. Sarah's unforeseen admission overwhelmed him, and the shear emotional force caused a momentary hush across the restaurant.

"No," Alex said. "My lover? That will never do. I want you as a wife. Marry me, Sarah."

The wintery drive back was quieter than Alex expected. Sarah sat contemplative, staring out the car window into the icy darkness. He finally broke the silence.

"If you're scared or think this is all a mistake, it's alright." Alex leaned over and kissed Sarah softly. "But I have no second thoughts. I knew from the moment I laid eyes on you that this might happen. My greatest fear was that you would not feel the same. What you did back in town was lay my fear to rest. You were gracious and brilliant. You dazzled my parents—and me." Alex kissed Sarah again. "So now, it's just us. Sarah Phillips, if I promise to buy you a ring, will you marry me?"

Sitting in the Vultur, in front of the helicopter, with the headlights of Nicholas's rental car illuminating the pair from behind, Sarah kissed him briefly. "I don't need a ring. I only need you."

Sitting in their rental car, Nicholas said, "This is better than a drive-in movie."

Samantha backhanded her husband sharply. "Nicholas Tepes, mind your own business."

As the helicopter lifted off, Nicholas couldn't help but notice Samantha's death grip as the gust of wind tossed the helicopter off course. Patting her hand, he grinned. "Some things never change, do they?"

Samantha's terrified expression did not pass until the windswept helicopter ride ended and they touched down on the island. For Sarah's benefit, as the temperature had dropped another ten degrees, they hurried into the house. "Show me the wine," Samantha said to Sarah as she took her hand. "After that ride, I think we both need a glass."

Nicholas stood by the door, inspecting the layout. "What on earth possessed you to buy an island up here?" he asked as he shook off the snow.

"To avoid *unwanted* visitors," Alex replied. "Keeping nosy neighbors a healthy swim away affords me all of the privacy I want."

"This is very nice," Nicholas remarked. "It reminds me of my old place in Manhattan. It had a lot of windows as well, before, you know." Nicholas fashioned his fingers into fangs and smiled. "Where are the curtains?"

"Auto black glass."

"That cost a pretty penny," Nicholas remarked as he turned into the bedroom wing. Taking the lead on the tour, Alex followed quietly as his father repeatedly complimented him on the unique design and furnishings of his home. Returning to the living room, they found Sarah and Samantha nestled in on the couch.

"Hi, ladies, what on earth have you been chatting about?" Nicholas asked as he landed in the recliner just opposite the sofa.

Sarah looked to Alex, who stood beside his father, with her face glowing brightly. "Apparently, if it's okay with you, we are going to Romania."

"All of us, to meet the king and queen?" Nicholas surmised, with a strained expression.

"Yes," Samantha replied to Nicholas. "You know Angelique will want to see her son and meet Sarah, as soon as possible. It will be a nice distraction for your father." Samantha paused to sip her wine. "Before we drop the bomb."

Alex bent over, looking into his father's face. "Drop the bomb?"

"Tori," Samantha answered.

"Who is Tori?" Alex peered at his cringing father for an answer, but it was Samantha who explained.

"We met Tori in Paris. She reminded us both so much of Gabby." Samantha took an extended drink. "She was so young and dying from such an agonizing death. So we saved her."

"You made her a vampire?"

Silently, both his parents nodded.

Alex began to laugh. "Oh, this is classic. Grandfather is going to shit a bucket of garlic. I am not marrying a Romanian princess, and you guys made a vampire. Holy cow! Is this why you're so suddenly accepting of my life? Does Ştefan know about this?"

"Ştefan disappeared about two years ago. It just took him a little longer than you to get fed up with the family," Nicolas said. "It was all over some girl."

"Reese," Samantha added.

"Like you, he's been off the radar for almost two years. Then out of the blue, he showed up at home with Isabelle while we were in Paris. He and Izzy started digging into the history of a man named Èdouard Barousse. Barousse was a plantation owner and, most likely, became a vampire, courtesy of our favorite bitch, Monique. Buried alive by his slaves, sometime in the mid 1700s, it appears as if your brother found his grave and dug him up."

"Why?"

"That's the question that ended our vacation in Paris. We went home immediately, but by the time we returned, your brother, Isabelle, and Barousse's body were all gone. If Chuck hadn't found you, we'd still be with Chuck looking for your brother."

"Good old Uncle Chuck. I should have been more careful."

Nicholas spotted the bar and headed over. As he rummaged through the selection, he continued explaining. "He was rather pissed that you eluded him for so long."

"It was his own fault. He taught me everything he knew."

Pulling an unopened bottle of Macallan 50, he smiled in appreciation of his son's Scotch collection. "Apparently, Chuck has learned a few new tricks during your absence, which led us here. But you should have known better." Nicholas held the bottle up. "Is it alright to pour a couple of glasses, seeing as how this is a very special night?"

"Might as well, it was your bottle originally."

Alex stared at the blanket of snow covering the deck. "The weather is supposed to break tomorrow but only for a day before the next storm blows thorough. We should head home tomorrow night." The gleeful anticipation in Sarah's eyes expressed her desire. "I take it you'd like to tag along?"

"Of course."

"It will be Christmas in two days. Don't you want to spend it with your father?"

"I'll tell him I'm spending a couple days with your family. We can go see him before we go to Romania, if that's alright?"

"Then it's settled," Samantha chirped. "We're all going home."

Alex noted his father appearing to conceal some form of apprehension, but decided to not risk spoiling the evening. As the night grew long, Alex listened, smiled, and grimaced as Sarah and his parents talked of life, New Orleans, their travels, and Romania. As dawn neared, he showed his parents to the guest room, previously occupied by Sarah. Once alone and ready for bed, Sarah began removing her clothes, painstakingly slow and seductively.

"Oh no you don't," Alex whispered, as he backed Sarah into the bed. "Not with them right next door." Planting a kiss on her cheek, he tucked her in.

Alex grabbed a blanket and settled into the reclining love seat across the room. Ignoring her displeasure, he told her *good night* and turned out the light.

Two minutes had not passed before Sarah climbed into his lap. "I can be quiet," she whispered as she began kissing him. "Why don't you come to bed?"

"I am a terrible bed hog," Alex explained, as Sarah's efforts were already wreaking havoc.

"It's a big bed, and I don't need much space." Sarah pulled his hand from under the blanket and placed it on her naked breast.

"This is awkward," Alex complained softly.

"That seems to be a recurring theme these days." Sarah

giggled quietly.

"I've never had a sleep over," Alex confessed.

"Alex Tepes, are you saying you've never had a woman in your bed for the purpose of sleep?"

"Nope."

"Never nodded off after sex?"

"Nope."

"Are you afraid of some embarrassing behavior? Do you snore?"

"Not that I know of."

"Bed wetter?"

Although it was wasted in the darkness, Alex rolled his eyes. "If I climb in that bed with you, I can promise, those sheets will get wet."

Sarah covered her mouth as she giggled a little too loud. "You're not a night biter are you?"

"Is there any other time I should bite?"

"So you have sex with a woman and then what, just get up and leave?"

"Pretty much like that. I did lay in bed all night once. It was pretty damn awkward. Besides, sleep is when we are most vulnerable."

In the pitch black Sarah stood up, unaware of Alex's ogling admiration of her body. She fumbled for his hands. "You say you love me?" She pulled him to his feet. Without the benefit of any light, she groped her way to removing his clothes. "Sleep is nothing compared to the vulnerability of love." Sarah pulled him into the bed, and intertwining with his body, she whispered, "This isn't so bad, is it?"

A hushed, methodical rhythm of ecstasy filled the darkness, but it came from the guest room. Mortified by his parents' lack of discretion, Alex blushed in the darkness. Then came a quiver, followed by a tremble, and finally Sarah broke to snicker that vibrated their entire bed. Sensing Alex's lack of amusement, Sarah whispered, "Listen to them, the children of the night. What beautiful music they make."

Alex propped up and looked down on Sarah with a fixed expression of shock, which in the darkness did nothing to curb her amusement. "Did you just quote a line from Dracula?"

"Bite me." She chuckled rebelliously.

"And now you know the reason I ran away from them for ten years." Alex sighed as he pulled Sarah close. "I hope this makes you happy."

Sarah cozied herself into him. “Very.”

After a minute of silence, Alex said softly, “I believe, should the worst happen tonight while I sleep, it can be written, ‘Alex Tepes passed, in love with Sarah Phillips, and thus his life fulfilled.’”

Sarah pulled his arms around her tightly and sighed contently. “Yes, it would. Now go to sleep, my poet.”

CHAPTER NINETEEN

ÈDOUARD BAROUSSE STOOD statuesque on the stony cliff, the warm tropical air blowing his black hair off his shoulders. Ştefan stood by his side, observing his reaction to the majestic view. The serrated treetop mountains stretched as far as Barousse could see, the sound of the breezes filling his ears with a soothing song.

"So where is this army of yours?"

Ştefan pointed below. "Down there, in the lower cleft of the ravine."

"And so, it is time we should go to them?"

"Before we do, you should know my men are primarily Jamaicans."

"Many of my slaves were Jamaican. I do not have a problem with these people of the island."

Ştefan looked Barousse sternly in the eye. "I think it best if your former occupation be withheld," he warned.

"Do these savages not know their place?" Barousse asked innocently.

"Three hundred years have passed. Slavery does not exist, not as it did in your day. Any mention, or cavalier attitude, might cause trouble."

"Do these people not know their place?" Barousse's tone was more insistent.

Ştefan stopped Barousse's descent with a hand to the shoulder.

“That is exactly the attitude I’m talking about.”

“My dear Count Tepes, I was merely implying that *you* are their creator and leader. Black or white, as we prepare for battle, it is imperative they understand that there is no place for personal feelings in war. Anything less than absolute obedience will lead to defeat.”

“I know that, Èdouard, but all the same, please respect *all* of your brothers and treat them equally.”

“I should think that is a fair request,” Barousse said with confidence.

In the dimly lit room of the shotgun shack, the haggard old woman coughed as if to expel the contents of her life. Death was near. For two days now Isabelle sat by her side, holding her hand, knowing if she let go the gypsy would fail.

In the absence of an audience, Isabelle had confessed her deeds with Ştefan, praying she had not committed a grievous error. Stella had moaned and stirred, but never replied. One hundred and seventeen years old, Stella’s life had been full of fortunes, the occult, love, and friendships. Since her early thirties she had known Isabelle, and as her years faded, she bore witness to Isabelle’s eternal beauty.

Her eyes once so crystal blue, like the waters of the Caribbean, were now opaque and lifeless. Those same eyes witnessed ages of history, more than any other *mortal* in the Crescent City. All around her bed, statues in all sizes of the patron saints stood vigil. Faded, dusty pictures from a century of befriending so many of the artists of the Vieux Carré adorned the walls, validating Stella’s value to their creators. And her jewelry; blanketing the rickety mahogany dressing table, it awaited the day to be buried with its beloved owner.

Stella’s eyes parted, her words drowning in a pool of phlegm. “You muss bring ’im to me,” she labored to say through a coughing spasm.

Isabelle leaned in close and clutched the gypsy’s wrinkled hands.

“’E has returned. I muss see ’im.” Stella coughed harshly. “You bring ’im now.”

“Who, Stella?”

“Neecolas.”

Sarah dropped her bag upon entering the foyer. “Wow.” She turned and gave Alex a quick kiss. “This is amazing.”

"You kind of take it for granted when you grow up in it. But it does have its charm," Alex explained as he retrieved Sarah's bag. "Come on, I'll show you to our room so you can freshen up."

Chuck emerged from the library. "Gotcha, you little son of a bitch."

"Yeah, but it took you ten years, didn't it?" Alex said with a cocky smile.

"But I still got ya."

"Yes, you did. And thanks for not telling Father about my visit to New York, like we agreed . . . *remember*?"

Chuck cleared his throat. "I didn't mention your name one time. And if you had taken the time to check your car for trackers, I wouldn't have known, ergo I wouldn't have told your pops about locating a Vultur on Campobello Island. So technically, it's on you, Junior."

"If I thought for one minute . . . ," Alex said as he fingered Chuck in the chest. "Oh never mind. I'm glad he found me. It was time to put things right."

Chuck steered into Alex's side and elbowed him in the ribs. "So you gonna marry her?"

"Yes, that's the plan."

"I knew it. After seeing you two horn dogs together, I told Gabby so."

Alex looked back to Sarah, whose skin was not quite thick enough for the likes of Chuck just yet. "It's alright, Uncle Chuck's inappropriate banter is legendary. You've got to learn to kick him in the shin."

"Or someplace higher," Samantha interrupted as she smiled and winked at Chuck.

"Or someplace else," Alex continued, "if he offends you, which usually will be once or twice a day."

In an uncharacteristic moment of softness, Chuck approached Sarah. "I'm sorry. Alex has been like my own kid, and there's no way some hot little gold digger is going to latch her little claws into my boy without my approval."

"Chuck, before you just classified her as a gold digger, did you bother to run a background check?" Alex asked pointedly.

Chuck rolled his eyes. "Of course I did, dipstick, and I gotta tell you, when Daddy finds out baby girl is hooked up with Romania's most eligible vampire, he's gonna drop a nuclear bomb on the entire family." Chuck snickered as he headed back to the library. "Should've found some Transylvanian peasant girl or maybe a sheep," he said, halfway singing. Chuck was out of sight and in the library as he continued to ramble on. "When the old man finds out, he's liable to invade Romania."

Aware of Sarah's dismay, Samantha quickly moved to give her a hug. "Please try to ignore him, for now. Chuck is our devil's advocate. He has kept us safe for almost forty years. What he says is often over-reactive and insensitive, but when it comes to loving and protecting our family, there is no one better."

From inside the study, Chuck's laughter echoed. "That's right, Sarah Phillips. You need something, just call on good ol' Under-Chuck. Under fed, under paid, and definitely under laid."

"Chuck!" Samantha barked.

"Sorry, Sammy, just trying to live up to my reputation, that's all. Besides, growing up, I'm sure Sarah has heard much worse."

Sarah stuck her head inside the door of the library, and then said nervously, "Thanks for treating me like family."

Chuck glanced up from the computer screen. "You just take care of our boy, and I'll do the rest."

Nicholas arrived in the foyer just as Alex had joined Sarah in the study. "What are you two planning to do with the remainder of your night?"

Alex weighed his answer, remembering his parents' night on Campobello. He said, "We thought about heading up to bed to see how much noise we can make."

Just as his words ended, Sarah's backhand to his chest was silently delivered.

"I told you," Samantha moaned to her husband. If Nicholas Tepes thought after one hundred and five years of life his blushing days were over, he was mistaken. In Sarah's presence, his face glowed like a summer-ripened tomato.

Alex checked his watch; it was just after two. "Sarah's not a full-time night owl just yet. We'll probably just get settled in."

"I'm fine," Sarah said. "What would you like to do, Mister Tepes?"

"Please, Sarah, call me Nick," he reminded her for the third time. "I was going to take Alex and go look for Ştefan, or Isabelle. You are welcome to accompany us, if you would like."

From inside the library Chuck's gruff voice called out, "I've already got Gabby and Tori doing that, if anyone cared to ask the head of family security. But now that I am adequately staffed, I might choose to add a second crew."

Before Nicholas could reply, the front door swung open wildly. As Isabelle laid eyes on Nicholas she said, "She knew you were home."

"Who knew I was home?" Nicholas replied, as he stepped toward Isabelle.

"It is Stella." Isabelle's urgency was telegraphed across her face. "She needs to see you, now."

"Stella La Rue?" Nicholas asked, as Samantha joined his side.

"We must hurry. Her end is near."

"She was near death ten years ago. How is it that she still lives?"

"If you had taken the time to visit lately, you would know." Isabelle sneered as she grabbed Nicholas by the hand and pulled him toward the door.

"We're all coming," Samantha exclaimed.

Exiting the library first, Sarah drew a curious eye from Isabelle. When Alex followed, Isabelle appeared instantly dismayed. "Alex?"

"Hello, Isabelle."

Without reply, Isabelle turned and bolted out the door.

"That went well enough," Alex said as he took Sarah's hand. "We should go."

Out on the porch, watching Isabelle storm to the car, Sarah whispered, "Are they all that beautiful?"

"No, some are prettier." Alex winked at Sarah. "Are you sure you want to go?"

Sarah tugged at his hand, not intimidated by Isabelle's apparent anger.

The serenity of the empty neighborhood street was shattered by the sound of hurried feet scuttling across the wooden porch, the rattling of the glass panes as the door swung shut, and whispers of conversation.

"So, who is Stella?" Sarah asked as they climbed into the SUV.

Isabelle had already slid across the seat, pinned herself against the door, waiting with her eyes locked and loaded, and fuming.

"Stella La Rue is probably the only true fortune-teller we've ever known. She's gotta be over a hundred and ten," Alex explained, while his eyes begged Isabelle for leniency.

Aware of Isabelle's hostility toward Alex, Nicholas intervened. "Tell me, Isabelle, what was your interest in Èdouard Barousse?"

Surprised by his knowledge, Isabelle stammered, "Daniel came to me, and then Ştefan."

The SUV skidded to an abrupt halt as Nicholas twisted to face Isabelle. "Daniel?"

Remorsefully, Isabelle answered, "Yes, it was Daniel that led us to Barousse."

"Where is Ştefan now?" Nicholas demanded.

"I don't know, Nick." Isabelle shrank back into the seat. "After we found Barousse's body, Ştefan took me to my house, and that was the last I have seen of either of them."

"And Daniel?"

"I only saw him once and have not seen him since."

Nicholas punched the accelerator, and the Denali's tires smoked up the street. Racing down St. Charles, Samantha touched his shoulder. "Better slow down, baby. We don't need a ticket tonight."

Although Isabelle felt the weight of Alex's eyes, she refused to return the attention. Giving up, Alex broke the awkward silence. "I know I have a lot of explaining to do, and I know I hurt you."

"You hurt us all," Isabelle declared. "Especially your brother."

"When we get back I will explain it all, I promise. For now, just know I am so sorry for the pain I've caused everyone."

Isabelle turned her gaze to the passing buildings on Canal Street. Withholding any promise of forgiveness, the ride to Stella's home remained uncomfortably quiet. Mercifully, the traffic lights acknowledged the urgency of the journey and magically remained green. As Nicholas turned the Denali left onto Esplanade Avenue, Alex marveled at their improbable fortunes with the stoplights. How much had his life changed by the grace of one solitary red light beside some random coffee shop?

Five minutes later, they pulled up in front of Stella's home. Fearing they were too late, Gabrielle did not speak or wait but anxiously bolted for the front door.

The oddly shaped houses puzzled Sarah. "Why are all these houses so skinny?" she asked Alex.

"They're called shotgun houses. Originally, homes were taxed on their street frontage, so owners made them skinny but long. Later, they started taxing property owners on the number of rooms and hallways. So many, like Stella's, have only two or three rooms and no hallways. They say the name comes from the fact that if you fired a shotgun in the front door, the pellets would go right out the back of the house. But the name could simply be a misinterpretation of the African term *to-gun*, which means place of assembly."

"Well, that's certainly interesting, Professor Tepes."

"My father bought this place for Stella years ago. But apparently, he has not been in touch with her for some time."

As only four candles lit the entire house, the darkness held a distinctive eeriness. Flickering shadows danced upon the walls and floors, creating a foreboding atmosphere. Detecting the shift in Sarah's pheromones, Alex took her hand. As they entered the bedroom, they found the family congregated in the corner, surrounding Stella's bed.

"Is she . . .?" Alex asked.

"She has not left us, yet," Isabelle replied, gently holding Stella's frail hand in her own.

As the family stood in silent vigil, the back door began to creak ever so slowly. The first footfall of the intruder set Nicholas on full alert. One by one, the labored steps drew nearer. With no wind to carry their scent, Nicholas moved to get a line of sight on the trespasser.

"Nicholas Tepes, I believed our paths were never to cross again."

"Daniel?"

Stepping into the room, Daniel's gaunt features were barely visible through the scarce candlelight.

Daniel reached out, grasping Nicholas by the shoulders. "It is good to see you again, my friend."

"Daniel, please tell me what you have involved my son in."

Daniel moved to Stella's bedside and caressed the side of her face, causing Stella to moan faintly. "About a month ago, Father Jay came to give our dear Stella her last rites." Daniel's back snapped and popped as he struggled to stand erect.

"In some state of delirium, she claimed this man, Èdouard Barousse, haunted her dreams from beyond the grave. In her ranting, she claimed Barousse held the key to salvation of the accursed." Daniel took Stella's hand and kissed it. "Father Jay reported this to the bishop, and up the ladder it went, all the way to Rome. I was home in Tuscany, my duty served, when I received the call to return to America. At my age, can you imagine?"

Daniel wrapped his arm around Nicholas's shoulder. "After your return to New Orleans, thirty-two years ago, the diocese has maintained a distant, but watchful, eye for anything that might expose their role in the affair of the convent."

"Why not send somebody younger? You have served your time."

"There are so few remaining of the Faith and the Order. Who

else could they send to Stella, or to you?"

"But why did you involve Ştefan and Isabelle?"

Daniel looked back to Stella. "In her visions, the task was for Ştefan alone. Much as it was your task to bring freedom to Angelique and her companions, forty years ago. But just as you had assistance, I knew Ştefan would require greater wisdom."

Nicholas looked around Daniel to get a glimpse of Stella. "And she told you nothing else?"

"Only what I have told you."

Nicholas returned to Stella's side. "Stella, I have come as you asked. What is it you have to share with me?"

Unconscious, Stella barely moaned. Nicholas attempted to awake her.

"Wake, my precious soul, your journey awaits the eternal light. Through the darkness you will pass, until at peace, your mind shall rest." Again Nicholas repeated the words, this time in the tongue of his ancestors. "*Treziţi sufletul meu preţios, călătoria aşteaptă lumina eterna. Prin întunericul va trece, până la pace mintea ta se va odihni.*"

Stella appeared agitated as she moaned louder, her body fighting the incantation. Nicholas repeated the Romanian verses again. Stella's eyes bitterly rolled open, clear as the days of her youth. "Nee-ko-las."

"Yes, Stella."

Stella's eyes searched the unfamiliar faces that had surrounded her closely. "Sa-man-ta?"

"Yes, Stella," Samantha replied with a well of tears forming.

"An zo it is, as I 'ave seen." Stella gasped weakly. "Ba-rousse?" she struggled to articulate.

"Ştefan has found him, but why?" The dreadful tone of Nicholas's reply was also etched on his face.

Again, Stella wheezed then coughed, the painful effects all too obvious. "'E is da path to da light."

"But how, Stella?" Nicholas pleaded.

Stella raised a crooked finger to the ceiling and then toward Alex. "In your 'art, chu know dis already, Nee-ko-las. For a man to be reborn, da vampire 'ave to die. De only path is tru Him."

Stella's eyes closed, her head rolled to the side, and with her last breath a glow of serenity cleansed her face.

"Stella?" Isabelle cried.

Daniel stepped beside Stella's lifeless body and anointed her forehead. "Father, Son, and Holy Spirit. Your days of longing for the journey home, Stella La Rue, have now come to an end." Daniel looked back at his friends and managed a smile. "She walks beside the One who saves us all."

Across the room Kahlea, Stella's crystal ball, began to glow with the intensity of a blazing harvest moon. Pulsing like a heartbeat, with every thump it began to fade until all that remained was a lifeless globe of crystal.

CHAPTER TWENTY

ŞTEFAN KNELT ON the cave's floor and studied the maps one last time, just as he had done almost every night for a year. The time had come to mobilize his forces, and there would be no room for error. Over the final passing days, Ştefan had found no true purpose for Èdouard Barousse. In sharing his plans, Barousse offered no great insight, or knowledge, of battle strategy. *He's worthless,* Ştefan thought.

"So, it is tomorrow then?" Morgan asked as he entered the cave.

"Yes. The ship is scheduled to make way at eleven."

"The journey to Algiers will be long. Our people will be hungry."

"This is what we have trained for," Ştefan replied mundanely.

"And what if there is a problem? If the ship should not make port in a timely manner and miss the cargo planes?"

Ştefan put the map down with an irritated sigh. "We can go twice as long, longer if need be. And if all else fails, we have the crew."

Morgan looked at the map on the ground. "And from Algiers?"

"We sail to Constanta. Arrangements have already been made for our arrival. There is an abandoned monastery here"—Ştefan pointed to the location—"in the Carpathians, where we will set camp. I traveled there many times in my youth and know the area well. It's not far from Poenari."

"And you believe we are ready?"

Ştefan folded the map. "What's on your mind, Morgan?"

"It's Barousse. He's given me no reason, but I just don't trust him. He's with Apollo too much. I'm worried they have a hidden agenda."

Ştefan walked slowly to the opening of the cave and studied the groups of men. "I've seen no cause for alarm. After all, we all share a common goal."

"Are you sure? Should we honestly trust a man who enslaved and brutalized his fellow man? With an army and then a nation, it worries me what he might do with the power."

"It is my power, Morgan, and it will be my kingdom. And from our new nation, we will no longer live in caves or the shadows of night. The world will know of our race and they will understand they need not live in fear. We have forty years of peaceful existence as proof and only need a powerful global platform to make the world understand."

"And you believe that *all* of these men will abide by your laws, with the freedom Europe offers, once our true nature is revealed?"

"I believe that all who follow me are true to our cause. They have been trained from their rebirth to understand our laws and the consequences of dissention. In Romania, they will discover an abundance they have never known."

"Still, I hear whispers of discontent," Morgan said sharply.

"We all grow restless. This will pass once we arrive in Romania."

Morgan searched the various huddles of men until he found the pair of his concern. "It's just . . . those two." He nodded in the direction across the camp. "I have often doubted Apollo's allegiance, and now, it would appear that Barousse has become his confidant."

Ştefan smiled. "Apollo is a handful, I agree, but I will deal with him as needed. As for Barousse, he has been in the ground for three centuries. I will not hesitate to put him back in the ground if he so much as leans out of line."

In the distance, the silhouette of the trees flashed like jagged peaks against a massive streak of lightning. Thunder rumbled across the mountains, shaking the ground beneath their feet.

"You see that, Morgan? Even God knows a great storm is coming."

Unlike the previous stormy night, the sky was alive with starlit tranquility. Ştefan's mood was soured, this time by Barousse's inquisition.

"And remind me one last time, why aren't you traveling with us?"

"Èdouard, I have told you three times. I will meet the ship in Constanta," Ştefan replied impatiently, as the pair watched the last of Ştefan's militia load into the cargo containers. "You need to go, they will be here in ten minutes to load the containers."

"And exactly why shouldn't one of us be free to guard the containers from the outside?"

"Is there a problem?" Ştefan glared at Barousse.

"No, Ştefan, there isn't a problem. But I think I speak for everyone when I say, we would feel more secure knowing we were not completely at the mercy of the ship's crew."

"Morgan has raised no such concerns, or Apollo. Did they appoint you their spokesperson, Èdouard?"

"No. But we would all feel much better knowing you were traveling with us."

Ştefan sighed with great aggravation. "My entire plan rests on your safe passage. But as you are so insistent—I'll have you know that I have several crewmen I trust implicitly with your safety; they will journey by air and sea and be watching over you," Ştefan said, as he cut an imposing glare. "If there are no other pressing matters, you would please join your brothers so I can seal the containers before the transportation company arrives for the pick up."

Before locking the door on each container, he shared his final words of inspiration with each crew. "Tonight marks our new beginning. In the coming days, we will never live in the shadows again. Rest easy my brothers, knowing soon all the world will respect, admire, and, if necessary, *fear* the very ground we walk."

Ştefan waited on the dock until his two co-conspirators arrived for the containers. As Ştefan watched the last of the containers transported to the ship, he checked his watch. In a few short hours he would be back in New Orleans for one final visit as Ştefan Tepes, clandestine vampire. Upon his next return, the entire world would know his name.

After three nights of futile searching the French Quarter, Nicholas's restlessness was painfully evident. As soon as Stella was interred, Nicholas decided it was time to travel to Romania. Having been notified of his return, Levente and Angelique were most eager to see Alex.

Isabelle had taken to Sarah rather quickly after Alex's lengthy apology. Laced with groveling, he promised to never repeat the disappearing act ever again. It was then decided by the women that they should go to Frenchmen Street for one last night of revelry and bonding before the long trip to Romania.

With the women gone for the night, Nicholas, Alex, and Chuck used the opportunity to discuss potential strategies.

"I think it's a stupid idea," Chuck bellowed from the distressed leather love seat in the corner of the library. He poured another glass of bourbon as he continued. "Ştefan is gone. Me staying here is like having a twelve-inch dick in a lesbian bar—totally worthless. I'm in charge of security, and with all of you traveling to Romania, I should be going as well."

"Out of the question, Chuck," Nicholas demanded. "If Ştefan should return, I want you here to make damn sure he stays. And find Barousse while you're at it. The guy's three hundred years old, he's got no tech savvy, so find him."

"That fucker was off the grid before there was a grid. Without a cell or a credit card or any facial ID, it ain't gonna be easy," Chuck sneered. "This bourbon tastes like water. If there's one thing I miss about being human, this would be it."

Ignoring Chuck's customary ranting, Nicholas continued checking itineraries on his computer. "So, are you ready?" he asked Alex.

Alex squirmed in his seat, thinking his last-minute agenda change would drive his father nuts. "Actually, Sarah and I will meet you in New York for the flight over. We're going to Washington to see her father."

Without as much as a twitch, Nicholas replied, "That's a great idea."

Before Alex could grasp his father's new relaxed attitude, Chuck piped in, "You mean you're gonna go tell the old man that his baby girl is gonna marry a fang banger?" Chuck laughed. "I can't wait to hear how that goes. Better yet, wear a GoPro camera."

"What exactly does her father do in Washington?" Nicholas asked, continuing to ignore Chuck.

Chuck burst out with a laugh, nearly spitting his bourbon across the room. "Come on, Nick, you already know Snack Pack's daddy is on the joint chiefs of staff."

Alex looked at his father for an explanation.

"Oh, ain't this gonna be one hell of a party," Chuck said.

"Father, is there something I should know?"

"I got this one," Chuck said, as he jumped to his feet. "*Numero uno.* You have to know Romania's energy policies and military initiatives have created a certain level of consternation for our government. I am sure the good general has spent many a night planning military ops against Romania. Throw in some good ol' CIA infiltration bullshit, and you've got a recipe for a complete clusterfuck." Standing behind Alex, he patted his back. "The general, when he hears baby britches is gonna marry the future King of Romania or, better yet, when grandpa Levente finds out—*ho-lee shit.* You're gonna need me twenty-four seven, Junior, just to stay alive."

"I have taken that into consideration," Alex replied somberly.

"Oh yeah? Well check this *one* out, Junior. Say there, Nicky, here's a trivia question. In 2009, at the ripe young age of thirty-two, who was the rock star Marine that President Obama appointed to head up the CIA?"

Nicholas grimaced with his reply. "That would be Captain Stafford Phillips, United States Marine Corp."

Bewildered by his father's knowledge, Alex stared at his father.

Chuck was smiling like an alter boy at a call girl slumber party. "In 2012, who was head of the CIA when the order to terminate Brian Denman was given?"

Nicholas was silent as he looked away, the strife etched across his face told the answer. Recollecting his father's history, Alex quickly remembered it was 2012 when the CIA attempted, for the second time, to kill his father.

"And as a result of those orders, what happened to Samantha?"

"Okay, I get it Chuck," Alex urged.

"When General Phillips learns you're Brian Denman's son, he's probably going to suspect that you're on some mission of vengeance. You'll be damn lucky if the ol' fucker don't try to strangle you with his bare hands." The ensuing silence was short lived. Chuck was in the *zone.* "But he won't be able to kill you, 'cause you're a vampire. Sorry, General Phillips, your baby girl is marrying the vengeful, bloodsucking, future King of Romania. Are you okay with that?"

"Maybe Chuck's right, son. Maybe I should go with you."

"You?" Alex hissed. "I can't believe this. *He* ordered your assassination? I can't imagine how your presence would help me in any way."

"Just remember, son, you've got to be honest."

"Hell's bells, after Sarah comes home tonight and finds this out, we might just elope."

Sarah reached for Alex's hand and gripped it firmly as they walked up the stairs of the general's home. "Relax, it will be fine. I promise," Sarah insisted.

Alex had briefly considered omitting the new details of her father's role in Samantha's death. But he knew if the topic came up, blindsiding her with the details in front of her father could be disastrous. Sarah took the news of her father's duties as well as could be expected. "If your family can accept who my father is, then he's going to have to learn to deal with your family as well," she explained to Alex the previous night.

Just as Sarah opened the door to her home, the general was eagerly waiting for her arrival. Hugging his daughter joyfully, he cast suspicious eyes, inspecting the infidel thoroughly.

Sarah expelled a nervous sigh. "Daddy, this is Alex. Alex, my father."

"General Phillips, it's an honor to meet you, sir." The general's grip was substantially firmer, and Alex thought it best to reciprocate with slightly less pressure.

"Nice to meet you, Alex." The general's eyes studied Alex's intently, while Alex did his best to not look away. "So you're the reason my girl's homecoming was delayed?"

"That was my idea, Dad," Sarah replied, attempting to gauge her father's disposition.

"Come on in. Would you like a drink, Alex?"

"I'm fine, General, but if you'd like one, I'd be more than happy to join you." Alex's smile was cordial, even though he knew the first impression was a done deal.

"Sarah!"

"I know the drill, Dad, and I've already warned Alex. I'll go to the kitchen and finish whatever you have started for dinner. I'll see you when the interrogation is complete."

The general smiled at Sarah. "In here, son," he said as he guided Alex into his study.

"What's your pleasure?" the general asked, as he glanced back at Alex.

"Bourbon, neat, or whatever you're drinking."

"Good answer, my daughter has prepared you well." He poured a very generous glass from a Baccarat decanter. "What shall we drink to?"

"Sarah," Alex replied.

"It's not your first bourbon, I see."

"No, I've shared quite a few with my father," Alex said, as he gazed at the wall of books. "It appears that you and my father share a passion for reading."

"Education, it's the key to a successful life." The general took a long draw from his glass and sat it down. "Please, sit."

The general gestured to a pair of provincial wingback chairs with a mahogany round cocktail table in-between, positioned in front of a crackling fireplace.

"As my daughter has prepped you, I'm sure you already know, I don't mince words. Sarah's education is paramount to me. I don't know your intentions, but her well-being and career is of the utmost importance, and I will not tolerate any young Casanova screwing up all she has worked for."

"I appreciate your candor, sir. I can assure you, whatever path she chooses is equally important to me."

"What do you do, Alex?"

"I write, and I study international politics."

"That's a pretty vague bullshit answer, son. Let's cut to the chase."

"Okay then. My name is Alex Tepes. My grandfather is Levente Tepes, King of Romania. Sarah and I are very much in love, and I have come to ask you for her hand in marriage. Was that concise enough, sir?"

The general stared harshly and then scoffed. "I thought you looked familiar. If you don't mind, I will defer my judgment about you until after dinner."

"That's certainly a reasonable request, but before you start tabulating your opinions, I'd like to say that I've traveled the world, and my oats are well sowed. Sarah is the most outstanding young woman I have ever known. I will love her and honor her for the rest of our lives."

"That's a nice pitch, son. Well rehearsed."

"Thank you, sir. If it failed, I had another."

"Well, let's hear that one too."

"My father wanted you to know that you owe it to him to give me a chance."

"Son, I don't believe I have ever met your father. Your grandfather yes, but not your dad."

"Not directly, but you did know of him. During your command of the CIA, you had to be aware of the initiative to eliminate agents who had outlived their purpose. You knew my father by the name of Nick Gabriel, or perhaps his alias, Brian Denman."

"So you are telling me, Nick Gabriel, is the *son* of Levente Tepes? And you're Levente's grandson. Do you have any clue how utterly ludicrous that sounds?"

"I could do you one better, but I think that's enough for tonight. Sarah has met my father, and in a few days, we will travel to Romania where she will meet my grandfather. You are more than welcome to join us, if you still have your doubts, *sir*."

The general refilled Alex's drink, handed it back, and raised his glass.

"If your father *is* Nick Gabriel, he was the best I've ever seen—before New York. There is no way I will ever forget *that* debacle. It was the ugliest possible scenario. Dozens of witnesses, a civilian casualty, a dead agent, and two missing bodies, what a cluster fuck. All because your dad, who was supposed to have been terminated ten years prior, got careless and arrested in New Orleans. And what your father did to my agent."

"Your agent killed my father's fiancé."

The general shot his drink down and refilled his glass. "Hell, that almost ended my career." He took a long, slow draw as he relived the memory. "And that mess in Brooklyn, it had your fathers signature all over it. We never made the connection, or figured out why he chose to massacre that cult, but apparently he performed a great service to the people of New York. Then just like magic, every electronic file concerning him disappeared forever."

"Father was always good with computers," Alex proudly proclaimed.

"And your father, is he—?"

"He's alright, you might say."

"Alex, I find myself in unfamiliar territory. I have to admit, this is a bombshell I was not prepared for. You're nothing like the other boys my daughter has dragged home. At the risk of instigating an international incident and detaining you as a terrorist until I figure you out, I suggest we have dinner." The general took another hard swallow. "Nick Gabriel's kid, I'll be damned. You got balls, son, just like your father."

Alex reached in his pocket and handed over a diamond engagement ring. "A fair shake, sir, that's all I ask. After all, it's just an engagement."

The general inspected the ring briefly. "Are you certain you don't want to buy my girl an obnoxiously big diamond?"

"No, I think this one is perfect."

The general handed the ring back. "Alex, for the sake of argument, let's say I have a lapse in judgment and agree. If you are to ask my daughter for her hand, it will be done in this room, in front of me."

With a small victory at hand, Alex smiled. "General, sir, there's one more thing I need to say."

"Yes, go on."

"My Uncle Chuck, Chuck Reager, sends his love," Alex said.

"Chuck Reager is alive?"

"Very much so. Once he discovered who I was dating, let's just say he shared some interesting stories."

"I'll bet," the general grumbled. "Chuck's got to be at least my age. How's he doing?"

Alex couldn't help but smile thinking of the reunion that eventually would come. "He's still a ballbuster, but outside of that, shockingly better than one might believe."

"You run with a good crowd, son, for the most part. Can't say I care much for your grandfather, but who knows, maybe in time." Stopping short of the kitchen door, the general turned. "What the hell. It is only an engagement after all, but if you hurt my girl in any way, I'll bury you so deep the maggots won't even bother to shit on you."

"Understood, sir."

"And one final condition." The general's squint was meant to intimidate. "When you get back from Romania, you put Chuck and your father in my study for a detailed debriefing. Understood?"

"Yes, sir."

❧

Returning to the general's study after dinner, Alex and Sarah watched as the general rekindled the fire. Sarah sipped her glass of Chardonnay as her eyes were transfixed on the flames. The anticipation on the general's face was apparent, as they passed the time in light conversation.

As the evening grew late, it was becoming painstakingly obvious to Sarah her father was growing tired. Awaiting the judgmental hammer that had befallen her previous love interest—two had been put in a cab and sent to a nearby hotel, and Brad had been shown the couch and her father's gun—Sarah's anticipation grew.

Sensing her anxiety, Alex knew it was time "You know, we'll be leaving for Romania early in the morning?" he reminded Sarah and her father.

"Yes," Sarah replied. She looked at her father, whose eyes quickly diverted away.

"Your father and I agree it would be much more appropriate," Alex said as he dropped to his knee and retrieved the diamond ring from his pocket, "that you should be introduced as my fiancé."

Hearing his words, Sarah's face was aglow. "Alex? What are you doing?"

"Sarah Phillips, I am asking you to marry me."

Sarah cut a quick glance in the general's direction, who nodded as he smiled, and then directed her attention back to Alex. "Are you kidding, right here, right now?" Alex spoke not a word, but waited patiently for her reply. "Oh my," she chirped. "Yes, I will."

As Alex slid the ring on her finger, Sarah lunged from the chair, hugging him as though the moment would pass like a dream. Sarah glanced over Alex's shoulder at her father and thought she saw the trace of a tear. Nodding his head in approval, he rose from his chair.

"I'm an old man, and it is well past my curfew, especially considering the time you two are leaving in the morning. Sarah, I know you will show Alex where *everything* is." The general stopped, bent down on Alex's level, and smiled. "Well done, my boy."

"Good night, Daddy," Sarah said as she watched her father depart. Trading her attention between the ring and Alex, she asked, "It's a perfect fit, how did you know?"

"Are you kidding, with all of the scheming and conniving women in my life? You don't stand a chance."

Sarah laughed as she held on tightly. "How much did you tell him?"

"Almost everything. Everything, except my drinking problem."

CHAPTER TWENTY-ONE

SARAH STUDIED THE fading lights of Paris as the train glided down the tracks; the faint, rhythmic, metallic clanking of the wheels rolling down the track was quickly becoming a familiar, almost soothing sound.

She finally turned and stared at Alex, holding her engagement ring clearly in his peripheral line of sight and silently scrutinized every angle of it.

"Is something wrong with your ring, dear, or are you purposely trying to conquer my attention?" Alex asked, his nose remaining buried in Hemingway's *For Whom the Bell Tolls.*

"No. Am I disrupting your reading?" Sarah thrust her hand further into his line of sight.

"Do I need to make you take your clothes off right here and run around the train naked?" he asked, still focused on his book.

Sarah pulled the book down. "You do and you will suffer a slow, agonizing death."

"Fair enough, Sarah Phillips," Alex said as he folded the book. "What's on your mind?"

"Why don't you try reading it, and tell me what I'm thinking," she teased.

Her mood was so frisky; Alex could not help but play along. "Okay, you're very happy."

Sarah backhanded Alex's arm lightly. "Duh, the train porter could have told me that."

"You're very happy about spending New Year's in Paris, and about being engaged."

Alex was spot on, but Sarah was not about to concede the battle back to Hemingway. "Better do better. Any garden variety psychic would know that."

"That *is* what you're thinking." Alex gazed deeply into her playful eyes. "*Ten days.* You're wondering how all of this has happened in only ten days."

Sarah's expression changed, as she redirected her thoughts.

"Oh, I like the lingerie," Alex said grinning broadly. "But no, the castle doesn't have any hallways that look like that, and even if it did, the stone floor is too cold and way too uncomfortable for *that*."

Sarah pushed back, and her eyes popped wide. "You can actually see what I'm thinking?"

"I can do one better," Alex said, with a sinister smirk.

"Oh, stop that," Sarah pleaded as she blushed. "How can you just make me think that, or that? Oh my, you can stop now," Sarah insisted as she began to squirm in her seat. "If you don't stop now, we're going to have to find the sleeping car," she whispered.

Alex tried, but could not conceal his amusement.

"How long did you say the trip was?" Sarah asked as she slid her hand on his leg.

"About twenty hours."

"Hmm, that's too bad." Sarah hands returned to her lap. Looking forward, she tried to regain her composure. "What does your family do when the sun comes up?"

"This is a private car, so we hang *the do not disturb sign*, pull the shades, and sleep like we always do."

"So, will you tell me what's next on the agenda?"

"Once in Bucharest, we will be formally received at the Presidential Palace. It will be an evening reception. After a bunch of pomp and circumstance, basically a lot of ass kissing, my grandfather will publically announce a masquerade in honor of my return, to be held at Poenari. The invitations have already been sent. At the ball, he will introduce you as my fiancé. After that, you will suffer much ass kissing as well."

"Oh no, I can't do that," Sarah said, as she retreated against the train window.

"Can't do what, have your ass kissed? If memory serves me correctly, you rather enjoyed it."

"Stop it, Alex. You know what I mean." Sarah pouted, crossing her arms. "I wouldn't have a clue what to say. I'll come across like a complete idiot."

Alex leaned close and wrestled her hand free. "It's alright, baby. The queen will be at your side the entire evening. She'll have your back."

"The queen? Oh God, can we please just go back to Campobello? I never even thought about all of this."

"*If we decide* for me to succeed my grandfather, although technically he is considered president, the vast majority of Romanians consider him their king and would accept me as the heir. So if I do become king, guess what that will make you, baby?"

Terrorized by the sudden epiphany, Sarah's face turned white. "I feel really sick. I think I'm going to puke."

Alex closed his eyes and began to hum an ancient Romanian song. From deep in his chest, the melody's soothing chords filled Sarah's mind, instantly easing her anxieties.

"Are you doing that too?" she asked in a mellow voice, as her posture began to relax. "That song is pretty, what is it?"

"It's a song my Aunt Rena used to sing to me when I was little. And you don't worry. If there's one thing I'm sure of, it's your ability to deal with adversity." Alex pulled Sarah close. "Come here. It's been a long few days. Why don't you rest?" Humming the lullaby and caressing her head, within minutes, Sarah was sleeping soundly on Alex's shoulder.

A short while later, Nicholas stopped by for a visit. "She *is* quite beautiful, son."

Alex peeked up from his book and nodded. Placing his hand on Alex's shoulder, Nicholas whispered, "You know, if you don't want to do this, you don't have to. We can have a nice visit and then just go back to whatever life we choose. It's not like the time clock is ticking for any of us."

"Well, not all of us," Alex replied, as he tilted his head toward Sarah. "I know it wasn't your intention to make Sam a vampire, but do you have any regrets that she is?"

"Ask me that after we've been married for two hundred years," Nicholas said with a chuckle. "Regrets, no. But the decision was made for me. If I was in your position and able to choose, knowing what I know now, I probably would have done it myself. I'm pretty sure your grandfather will agree to whatever the two of you decide. The bigger hard sell will be Sarah's father, that is if you plan on telling him."

"That's going to be Sarah's call. But all of my life, I was made to believe this was all a curse. Besides a few missteps, I think we've all lived pretty good lives and done good things a lot of church-going people don't even do. I guess we won't know till we're dead if we were truly cursed. But if we are, I don't want that for her."

"And now you finally understand the dilemma first hand. Love fucks you up like that." Nicholas patted his son's shoulder. "Have faith, the answer will come."

"Sounding a little bit like Daniel there, Dad."

"There was a day, a few years ago, when I would have considered that an insult. But now, thank you."

"Did you sleep well?" Sarah asked, as she planted playful kisses on Alex's lips.

"Not as well as if I were back home, but well enough." Returning his seat to the upright position, he popped his head up and looked around. Throughout the darkened coach, it appeared as if they were the first to rise. "Is it dark yet?"

"It's not dark, but the sun has set. Is it alright if I open the shade?"

Alex's hands took familiar liberties as Sarah began to stretch across his body to retract the light-occluding shade. "You really don't want to start something you can't finish, do you?" Sarah twisted and leaned her body in, ensuring that her breasts made full contact, as she slid back into her seat. "Two can play that game," she said seductively, as her attention drifted to the passing landscape. "I sat in the other car for a few hours, watching the scenery. It was quite remarkable."

"It's why we prefer the train."

"How can you ever appreciate the true beauty in the darkness?"

"Trust me, we can see just fine at night. In fact, we prefer the night to a cloudy day. Even during a daytime storm, the glare is uncomfortable and tends to wash out colors."

With the failing light, as the contrast between trees, rock, and earth faded, distinguishing details became difficult. Sarah leaned over Alex again and focused her attention to faint objects along the tracks. "Are those wolves?"

Without looking, Alex already knew the answer. "Yes."

Sarah moved closer to the glass, again placing her body precariously close to Alex's wandering hands. Intrigued by the wolves, she paid little attention to his intentions. "It looks like they're just watching the train."

"They can sense our presence. There's some kind of bond between the wolves and my family, perhaps with all vampires. Legend has it, vampires can shape shift into bats, mist, and even wolves. But if that were true, that knowledge passed with my ancestors centuries ago."

"That's a shame. I'd love to have you as a pet wolf," Sarah said, as she jabbed Alex in the ribs.

"Don't be fooled by their complacent appearance," Samantha warned, as she arrived silently from behind. "If hungry or threatened, they can be quite deadly."

"Good evening, Mother," Alex said sardonically. "How nice of you to sneak by."

"I wasn't aware that I was sneaking. Perhaps you were just distracted by the wolves." Before Sarah could recover from her blush, Samantha sat in the seat in front of them.

"Good evening, Mrs. Tep—Sam."

Finding Sarah's awkwardness charming, Samantha smiled. "We will be in Bucharest in a few hours. Your father and I think it's best if Sarah comes with us. Although we have tried to keep our arrival a secret, undoubtedly, some paparazzi might have discovered Alex's homecoming. Even without media presence, Romania's most beloved grandson, who has been missing for ten years, might certainly be recognized."

"What about you and Nick?" Sarah asked.

"Nick has never been identified as the son of Levente or Alex's father. After the hullabaloo in New York forty years ago, we couldn't risk an ex-CIA agent, who was supposed to be dead, resurface as a prime suspect in the Brooklyn massacre and be linked to the King of Romania."

"That's too bad," Sarah said sadly.

"Not really. Nick and I love our life just as it is. So we don't mind using the palace back door."

"So have you and Dad discussed what's going to happen if and when Sarah's father lets the cat out the bag, or in our case, the bat out of the cave?"

"If there is an issue with Sarah's father, I know your grandfather will have a solution. We're not going to allow ancient history to get in the way of your lives together. Speaking of that, your father and I were discussing your concerns."

"Thanks, Mom. I think Tori is calling." Alex excused her with a head nod. As he watched his mother return to her seat, Sarah grabbed his shirt and jerked him around.

"What happened to everything out in the open? You have concerns about me, and you talked to your father about them?"

Alex sighed heavily. "We've had this discussion. My father and I talked about the possibility of you becoming . . . more like me."

"A vampire, like you?"

Alex shook his head. "He has a unique perspective, and he is the only one qualified to offer advice based on experience. So no, it's not some new secret. You and I have already had this conversation, more than once."

Sarah was ready. She had made her mind up on Campobello Island. "So there's no way you will change your mind and do it on the train?" Unbuttoning her second button on her blouse, Sarah tugged at her collar, enticing Alex with her flesh. "I am a virgin, you know."

"Oh, I know what you are. You're a comedian." Alex flipped her collar up, concealing her pulsating jugular vein. He peeked around the seat before popping the third button, exposing her white lace brassiere. "That's much better."

Sarah turned and looked back between the seats, satisfying her desire for privacy. She loosened another button and pulled Alex's hand inside her bra. "Does this change anything?"

Alex's hand ran up and pulled the strap off Sarah's shoulder. With her breast fully exposed he leaned down and breathed in her scent. Planting light kisses on and around her breasts, Sarah moaned ever so quietly as she tugged at his hair. Alex turned and spoke softly, "I must warn you, I bite."

"Oh God, please do."

The aroma of her arousal brought Alex to the brink of his restraint. As Sarah's heart pounded, the veins in her breasts swelled with blood, taunting her lover. Alex's mouth salivated for the delicate nectar of Sarah's blood.

"Please," she implored.

Unexpectedly, and surprisingly effortlessly, Alex kissed her breasts once more, before pulling her blouse together and fastening the buttons. Looking into Sarah's ravished eyes, he explained, "You know, if I were to take you now we could never have children; one of us must be mortal at conception."

Still breathless and disoriented, Sarah stared at Alex as she struggled to contemplate his explanation. It took a long minute, but finally she replied, "After seeing how you and your brother turned out, I'm not so sure that is a bad thing."

Ştefan stood on the porch of his bayou shack, knowing Reese's imprisonment was near an end. Conflicted by love and family, he stood silently, blowing billows of steam from his mouth. *She has to hate me*, he thought. Rightfully so, she was bitter. *Stockholm syndrome*—that was the only logical explanation for Reese having fucked him on his last visit. But what would happen if he took her now? Would he create an uncontrollable, bloodthirsty, and power-craving vampire such as Monique? But could he honestly afford to free her?

Again, he placed his hand on the lock and again he walked away. He loved Reese, that much was certain, even though he had fucked Isabelle the very next night after his last visit. The overpowering frustration was consuming Ştefan's thoughts and actions. *Loveless.* Reese's hollow fucking of him. *Loveless.* The truth of Isabelle's heart. *Anger*. His father and his grandfather were to blame for his misery. Love would never be his to possess.

Ştefan knew he should have obeyed the family rules and never told Reese of his true nature. None of this would have been necessary. But he was proud and arrogant, believing Reese would love him, as his mother had loved his father, even after Samantha had learned of his father's affliction. Ştefan's hand was back on the lock, as he deliberated. Jiggling the lock and twisting the key, Ştefan slowly opened the door. Appearing frightened, Reese cowered in the corner.

"What's wrong?" Ştefan asked.

"I want to go home."

"In a few short weeks, I'll return and take you home, or give you the world." As Ştefan moved closer, Reese withdrew further. Disheartened by her fear, Ştefan stopped and frowned. "You don't have to be scared. There was a time you loved me. Sadly, it wasn't strong enough to weather my secret, and I will regret that for the rest of my life." Ştefan began to return to the door. "I'll be back for you soon."

"Wait," Reese implored. "I know this is as much my fault as it is yours," Reese confessed, as she stepped from the corner. "Making love to you, it was so good. It made me realize that maybe I've been wrong. I do love you, Ştefan. I'm just scared."

Ştefan immediately approached Reese, his spirits lifted higher than they had been in years. As he extended his arms to embrace her, Reese swung a makeshift stake deep into the side of his skull. As Ştefan collapsed to the floor, Reese slashed at Ştefan's throat with a knife. As a pool of blood quickly spread across the dusty planks, Reese ran for the door.

"I'm sorry, Ştefan. I am so, so sorry." Reese pulled the door shut and locked it. Tonight, fortune was on her side as the light of the moon afforded enough illumination to see the boat's control panel. As the motor hummed to life, Reese wiped away a pool of tears. "I do love you, Ştefan," she cried, as she steered away from the dock, "and always will."

CHAPTER TWENTY-TWO

SARAH STOOD BEFORE the black iron fences of the Crețulescu Palace with her mouth agape.

"By Buckingham standards, it's a little small, but Levente would have no other palace for his residence," Samantha explained as she stood arm in arm with Sarah. "Initially, there were those opposed to the family taking over the landmark, but after a few years, all objections ceased. Levente is truly the champion of the Romanian people."

"I don't think I can do this." Sarah grimaced as she stared at the palace. "I'm not queen material."

"Very few are, dear. Very shortly, you will meet Alex's biological mother, and the queen, Angelique. You don't need to be nervous. She is very much like the rest of us. Over time, she will teach you, just as Levente will teach Alex. When the time comes, if you should decide to ascend, you will be more than ready to take your place."

Sarah studied the surrounding landscape. "There doesn't seem to be any security, at least not like the White House. Can anyone just walk in?"

"No. Trust me, my husband and Chuck took great pride in designing the most elaborate security system on the planet." Pointing around to the phantom security forces, Samantha explained, "*They* knew who we were from about six blocks away. And once inside the gates, the entirety of the grounds are electrified. And the snipers are all trained by Nick."

"Oh."

"The palace walls are steel reinforced by stone, and the windows are six-inch-thick Trivex. Missiles will bounce off that stuff. The first floor is mostly offices and security, and the second and third floors are family living spaces. I'm sure Nick will bore you with all of the details. He loves giving tours. But enough of the technical stuff, it's time to meet the rest of our family."

Two centurions stood guard at the main gate, each seeming impervious to two beautiful women that had been standing on the opposite side.

"President Tepes is expecting us," Samantha announced, as she handed over their passports.

The first guard snapped his heels and turned to Samantha. With a thick Slavic accent he ordered, "Hand on d' pad, eye in d' scanner, *vă rog.*

Samantha did as instructed and then prompted Sarah to do the same. The gates swung open and as they passed, Samantha replied, "*Mulțumesc.*"

"You speak Romanian?" Sarah asked.

"Yes, as you will also in time. There is a unique process of teaching it, where the language is learned through telepathic power of suggestion." Unceremoniously, the arching stained glass and wood door swung open as a tuxedoed butler silently nodded the guests to enter. "It's a shame you're not getting the royal treatment yet. It does tend to make one feel quite *special.*"

Just as Sarah began to speak, the great hall's splendor overwhelmed her. The ebony and bone checkerboard marble floors glistened like mirrors. Sarah recognized Monet, Picasso, and a Rembrandt, along with other great works of canvass and sculpture. Intricate marble ornamentations accented the moldings and railings throughout the grand entrance. The French provincial furniture was too busy and uncomfortable for Sarah's taste.

Samantha checked her watch. "Nick should be here soon. He did not want your introduction to be jaded by Tori's." Samantha took Sarah's hand and led her to the marble stairs. "You can gawk later. It's time to meet the king and queen."

As they climbed the steps, Sarah couldn't help but notice the crystal chandelier. It appeared to be a twin to the one in New

Orleans, only three times as large.

As they entered the sitting room, Levente and Angelique rose to meet them. Levente went straight to Sarah, took her hand and kissed it. In a business-like tone, he said, "I am Dracula. I bid you . . . velcome."

His pale skin contrasted sharply against his black sport coat and pants, but appeared to match his white crew-neck shirt perfectly. His wavy, jet-black hair was brushed back and tousled perfectly. Slowly, his perceptive, gray eyes rose to meet Sarah's.

Locked in a mesmerizing gaze, it was Angelique who ended the uncomfortable silence. "Levente! You're scaring the poor girl."

Sarah blushed. "No, I'm fine."

Levente began to laugh softly, causing Angelique to backhand him in the arm. *Apparently, this must be a ritual performed by the women of the Tepes family on their men*, Sarah thought.

"I can't believe you just did that," Angelique moaned.

Still amused with himself, Levente rubbed out the imaginary pain. "Do you know how long I have waited to use Bela's line? When Nicholas told me you had been reading vampire books, and watching movies, I couldn't resist the temptation."

Sarah's apprehension eased, as Angelique forced her husband aside. "Well, let us have a look at you." Taking a concise inventory of Sarah's attributes, Angelique smiled. "Sam, she is more beautiful than you described, or I imagined. Please, let's go relax by the fire."

Just like regular people, Sarah thought. Angelique, the queen; her beauty and grace was everything she had expected. *Three hundred years old, and Samantha, nearly seventy- five; how long would it be before the three would look the same age? How long before I am mistaken for their mother?*

The incredible warmth of the blazing logs rapidly thawed Sarah's chilled flesh. The glass of Chianti, poured from an antique decanter, quickly warmed Sarah's bones.

"So," Angelique began, "your trip was comfortable?"

Before Sarah could answer, Levente interrupted, "Oh, can we please dispense with the small talk and get right to brass tacks, before the boys return?"

The three women looked at Levente suspiciously.

"There will be sufficient time for trivial conversation later. Plans must be made, if there are plans to be made." Levente sat on the edge of the Queen Anne sofa, positioning himself as close as possible to Sarah, who was seated in the matching armchair. "Do you love my grandson?"

"Yes, I do," Sarah replied firmly, while finding it hard to maintain eye contact through the intensity of his eyes.

"And you would marry him, regardless of all this?" Levente swept his hand about the room.

"Honestly, at this very minute, *all of this*," Sarah said as she mimicked the hand gesture, "scares the hell out of me a lot more than vampires do."

Levente laughed. "You are wise beyond your years, Sarah Phillips."

Samantha and Angelique breathed a collective sigh of relief, as Levente's demeanor shifted. "I told you she was special," Samantha whispered to Angelique.

"Sarah," Levente continued, "*all of this*, royalty included, it is all insignificant if you are not happy. All of *this* is worthless, should your love fail. Love must always be your first priority."

Not quite the conversation she had expected upon their first encounter. Sarah smiled gently. "Yes, sir."

"Outside of love, my biggest concern is your father. As to the timing or method of how we explain our particular *lifestyle*, I have not seen a solution, as of yet. I believe several high-ranking dignitaries from your country will accompany him as well, so I feel this week may not be the appropriate time to make such a confession. But I do feel it needs to be done before your wedding."

"I agree, sir."

"Angelique, would you please pour the rest of us a glass of wine." Levente waited until the glasses had been passed around. "Sarah, you are family now. As such, the formalities are unnecessary in private. Please, call me Levente, or grandfather, grandpa . . . whatever you are comfortable with."

"Okay," Sarah replied.

"To Sarah and Alex." Levente raised his glass and watched as the women in his life followed his lead. After setting his glass down, he asked, "Now, where are my boys?"

"Alex," Samantha began explaining, "is out in the city, making sure he is spotted. It was Nick's idea to create a media event."

Levente considered the scenario. "Yes, a good idea, but he has to know Angelique is most anxious to see him. And I am surprised Nick would risk the attention of being seen with Alex."

"Oh," Samantha said nervously. "Nick's not with him. He'll be here shortly."

"Why did he not accompany you?" Angelique asked.

"He said too many people arriving simultaneously might draw attention."

Levente's expression brightened. "Too many people? Is Ştefan with him? Do I finally get to enjoy the company of both grandsons at one time, after so many years?"

"No," Samantha replied sadly. "Ştefan is still angry."

Levente's disappointment was genuinely obvious. With the exception of his insistence that Alex succeed his position, he had never shown one single instance of favoritism. "You mean he's angry with me, don't you?" Levente sighed.

"No, it was all of us, and that girl, Reese," Samantha explained.

"It seems my policies have been counterproductive to romance, wouldn't you agree?" Levente said, specifically to Sarah. Not waiting for her reply, he continued, "So who else is Nicholas bringing? Chuck and Gabrielle? I miss those two, especially Chuck."

Samantha hesitated, although she knew, all too well, Levente would instantly recognize Tori's vampire scent. "He should be here any minute."

"Why do you appear so uncomfortable, Samantha?" Levente asked, before suddenly redirecting his attention to the hallway. "Never mind, I sense my son has finally arrived." Levente sniffed at the air. "What is this?" With a look of ire, he cut his eyes to Samantha. "Who does Nicholas bring to our home?"

Levente rose and made his way to the door, meeting Nicholas as he turned the corner. Angelique followed immediately, as her husband's temperament had quickly changed.

Levente knew instantly the woman with Nicholas was a vampire. Levente measured his words carefully. "Nicholas, before I tell you how good it is to see you, apparently you have an introduction to make."

"Father, this is Victoria, but she goes by the name Tori."

"Tori, I am most delighted to meet you." Taking her hand, Levente kissed it lightly. "This is my wife, Angelique, and apparently, you already know Sarah and Samantha." Levente cut an imposing glare to his son before continuing. "Angelique, will you please offer Tori a glass of wine, by the fire. I believe Nicholas needs to see me in private."

Tori followed Angelique sheepishly to the fireplace. "You will have to excuse my husband. If there's one thing he truly detests it's surprises." Understanding the severity of the situation, Angelique's calm demeanor eased all three women's anxiety. "Now, Samantha, would you care to enlighten me as to the circumstances that has led Tori to our family before Levente returns."

Levente led Nicholas back to the first floor into a small office and closed the door. "Sit," he ordered. "This is certainly not how I expected our first meeting, in almost two years, to go."

With his hands in his lap, Nicholas looked at his father but remained silent.

"Who is responsible for *that*?" Levente pointed a finger towards the ceiling.

"I am."

"What in hell's damnation possessed you to create a vampire?" Levente's tone was stern, but not harsh. "Our regulations have been a sacred decree for nearly forty years. They are the foundation of our very survival."

"Your *laws* are the primary reason our family has imploded," Nicholas replied softly but defiantly.

"Imploded? If you are referring to Alex and Ştefan, their disappearing tantrums were the result of juvenile, hormone-driven lust. So, Alex was gone ten years. Now he is back. In the grand scheme of our life, that's nothing. But give the mortals a reason to hunt us down and we will all wind up buried in the mountain, or worse. Is that what you want?"

Nicholas turned his head away. He wanted to argue that the foundations were flawed, that Alex had returned way beyond the boundaries of the *regulations*, but he knew this was about the *other* regulation. "Of course not."

"Did you not stop to consider that making Tori one of us could lead to the death of Samantha, Chuck, Gabrielle—your sons?"

Nicholas stared into his father's eyes. "I did."

"You need to take care of your lapse in judgment." Levente's decision was resolute, just as it had been with the rise of his Romanian empire.

Nicholas had lived with, and around, his father's stubborn determination for forty years. No siege towers or battering rams had ever penetrated the fortress of his father's resolve. "You know, Father, for forty years I have abided by everything you have said and done."

"And you have prospered beyond your imagination," Levente reinforced, as he thumped his finger on the desk.

"This isn't about prospering, it's about something much bigger. It's about reclaiming our humanity, even if we aren't human. Sam and I, after much deliberation, chose to save that young girl's life. And she is worthy of *so* much more."

Nicholas eyed the bottle of Scotch behind his father, craving the comfort it offered in life long ago, he thought of another of Chuck's idioms, *Old habits never die; we just fucking hide 'em.* With greater conviction, Nicholas proclaimed, "Alex is going to marry the girl he loves. In reality, our secret may not survive the wedding. Haven't we lived in the shadows long enough?"

"Have you lived long enough, or your sons, or Samantha?"

"We did not take Tori without great deliberation. And I am prepared to put an end to her if it becomes apparent that a mistake has been made. But it is my firm belief that she has much to contribute to our family's future."

Levente propped his elbows on the desk and his chin against his knuckles. "I wish I could share your confidence, my son. But I have been sensing an impending storm in our family's future, and now you bring this young woman into our midst. I think perhaps you should take care if it now, rather than wait for something to happen."

"It? Her name is Tori. And even though Samantha made her, I know her soul. She is much like Gabrielle. Would you have ended her life as well?"

"Gabrielle was already a vampire," Levente said calmly.

Nicholas rose from his chair and slapped his hand against the desk. "So was Monique, and yet we know the difference between her and the rest of us."

Levente continued to stare into his son's eyes as a smile broached his face. "There it is! There is the passion you have contained for too long. Life is so meaningless without it. Your Tori may live, unless she gives cause to change my mind. But I pray your instincts have not been blinded by your wife's creation."

Samantha continuously fidgeted with her wine glass, swirling, then sipping, then checking the door. "They certainly have been gone long enough."

Angelique glanced to the empty hallway and smiled. "This is no small thing the two of you have done. I am certain Nicholas is getting an earful." Angelique looked at Tori sympathetically. "Do not despair, my child. My husband is accustomed to obedience. It is far beyond the time he understands change is necessary." She glanced at Samantha, and then at Sarah. "It took several nights of forceful persuasion to convince him that Alex's choices were his own and not his grandfather's."

Sarah leaned forward. "So, initially he was against me?"

"Darling, Levente is against everything not of his design. He is the architect of this nation's prosperity. Through all of his accomplishments there has always been dissention. Our precarious relationship with your country is just one simple example." Angelique directed her attention to Samantha. "He is struggling with the concept of compromise as he contemplates our future, and the transitions that must occur. Some things are going to be beyond his power to control."

"Excuse me if I'm speaking out of place, but why does he want to retire?" Tori asked softly.

"Never feel as if you do not have the right to ask these things. We are family." Angelique's demeanor was warm, quite the opposite of Levente's brief display a short while earlier. "I love my husband, but I am ready for life and freedom, much like Samantha's. Forty years of deception, secret departures, and obligations is enough. Directing her attention back to Sarah, she said, "You will discover in short order, if this is a life you desire. Our government is a democracy, and if you and Alex choose another path, they *will* elect a new leader. If the two of you choose to succeed Levente, by no means does it have to last as long as Levente's reign."

Sarah stared at her wine, then looked up only to discover all three were awaiting her reply. Suddenly, she was struck with the epiphany of how quickly her life had changed. *She* was in Romania, thousands of miles from home, sitting in a palace of vampires, discussing *her* becoming a queen or, perhaps, one of them. The overwhelming onslaught of emotion was painfully obvious.

Samantha sensed her sudden strife. "Maybe it's time we should tour the palace." Offering her hand to Sarah, Samantha put her arm around her. "Watching you, it brings back memories—this palace, obligations of royalty, or in your case, becoming one of us. It's enough to drive one to drinking."

CHAPTER TWENTY-THREE

ISABELLE WALKED PAST the vibrating phone before turning back in a huff and picking it up. Looking at the words texted, she dropped the phone. *Help me*. The cell had one purpose; it had been given to her by Ştefan. Isabelle frantically dialed the number. As it rang without answer, Isabelle's heart sank.

Isabelle ran through the doorway. "Chuck, help me, please."

Alarmed by Isabelle's tone, Chuck jumped up from his chair and dashed from the library, while Gabrielle came running from the kitchen. "What is it?"

"It's Ştefan. He needs my help." Isabelle's hands shook as she handed the phone to Chuck. "He sent this."

Gabrielle pulled Chuck's hand and read the message. "Have you called him?" she asked Isabelle.

"I did, but there was no answer."

Chuck pushed redial and waited. After the fifth ring, he hung up. "I need to locate his phone." Across the hall from the library was a locked door. Using the skeleton key from around his neck, Chuck unlocked the door and entered. Filled with electronic equipment, the room resembled a combat control room on a naval warship. Chuck typed in the number he had just dialed and waited. "What the hell? He's in middle of the bayou." Chuck grabbed two 9mms from the drawer. "Anyone want to tag along?"

Dressed in only a white T-shirt and a thong, Gabrielle turned for the stairs. "Don't you dare leave without me."

"We're going to the bayou, baby, no heels," Chuck shouted as she disappeared from view.

"Should you call Nick?" Isabelle asked.

"Are you kidding me? Nicky's got his hands full with the old man. He'll be damned lucky to not come home with his balls, and fangs, in a Chinese carry-out carton," Chuck scoffed. "We'll get out there and see what's going on first."

Levente nodded his head. "We have been absent too long. We should return to the others," he said while rising. "Just remember, she is your responsibility. Anything she does, you will be the one held accountable."

"I understood the responsibility before we made her." Nicholas remained seated as he thumped the desk. "There may be another problem," Nicholas warned with hesitation. Levente sat back down and cocked his head in silent anticipation. "Ştefan has returned to New Orleans, and was put to a dangerous task."

"By whom, may I ask?"

"Daniel. Most amazingly, he still lives. He sought out Ştefan and told him of a vampire, Èdouard Barousse, who was likely created by Monique. Around the time Angelique was imprisoned in the convent, his slaves buried him alive. We believe Ştefan has found Barousse's grave and recovered his body."

"Monique, to this very day her name continues to haunt me." Levente shook his head, as he stared at his son. "Why is this the first I am hearing of this?"

"We have been trying to locate Ştefan, and Barousse, but have been unable to do so. Chuck has remained behind to continue the search."

"You should have contacted me immediately. I would have sent my people." Levente's dire concern was easily detected by his tone. "I will dispatch them immediately."

"There is nothing they can do until Chuck locates them."

"They will be onsite and assist Chuck in his efforts," Levente insisted forcefully. "I fear our friend has lost some of his skills."

"Chuck has lost nothing," Nicholas protested.

"Alex eluded him for ten years," Levente said, as he thumped his index finger on the desk.

"And it was Chuck who trained Alex, and Ştefan." Nicholas leaned into the desk and returned a glare. "And don't tell me *your* people did not try to find him during those ten years either. I know better."

Levente sat back, pressed his back into the chair, and clenched his jaw. "One man may not be enough. Chuck should have reinforcements."

"I am not sure sending one, much less five, of your security forces to New Orleans is a good idea. I know how they operate. Any incident will only fuel the fire of tensions between our countries."

"And a vampire on the loose?"

"Who is not the responsibility of the Romanian government! You cannot send an unofficial hit squad to America. I agree Chuck may require assistance, which *we* will provide once he has located either Ştefan or Barousse." Nicholas's temperament eased, perceiving his father's ire has subsided.

"And what do you know of Barousse?"

"He was a Frenchman, forty-three years old, and owned a sizable indigo plantation. Like many savage plantation owners of the time, he beat, tortured, raped, and probably killed scores of slaves. We can only assume that his slaves eventually revolted and buried him alive. Outside of that, he was pretty much anonymous."

Levente rocked forward and placed both hands on the desk. "If Monique made him, Angelique should know something."

"She has already told me everything she knows," Nicholas replied, with trepidation.

"And exactly when did that occur?"

Nicholas forged the best defensive answer he could contrive, for Angelique's sake. "A week ago. But she knows nothing outside of the simple questions I asked concerning Barousse's history."

"We will discuss this further, but we *do* need to return to our guests," Levente instructed calmly.

Clouds had covered the brisk December night, and Chuck reminisced about the darkest nights in Colombia as he guided the Chris Craft through the glassy waters of the bayou. At times like this, he pined for the old days. Kill the bad guys and then get drunk. But the few remaining jarheads he knew complained of bad joints and eyesight and limp dicks. He looked back at Gabrielle and mused, *I guess this ain't so bad.*

According to the GPS on his phone, just beyond the upcoming bend in the river, a small branch broke off from Bayou Sorrel. If it was not navigable, Chuck knew they would have to go in on foot. "Holy hell," Chuck groaned, "we'll be damned lucky to make it out of this swamp by sunrise, much less make it back home."

"We can always stay in Baton Rouge if the need arises," Isabelle suggested.

"Izzy, are you sure you don't have a clue what Ştefan was doing out here?"

Isabelle steadied herself as she made her way back to Chuck. "No, Ştefan never talked about anything out here."

Chuck pointed to the branch in the river ahead. "Hang on, we're going in there." Without slowing, Chuck turned hard to starboard and motored past the small shack, vaguely illuminated by a light from within and the private property warning notification.

"Did you see that?" Gabrielle asked.

"I did."

"And you can read?" she continued.

"We don't have time to worry about hurting somebody's feelings. If Ştefan is out here, we're not going to have much time to get him out. Chuck eased back on the throttle, the sound of the boat's wake rushing up its stern replacing the hum of the motor. "No telling what kind of shit that boy's got himself into. It's better if they don't hear us coming."

"Not bull rushing in, guns blazing?" Gabrielle asked with a smile. "What about all of those stories?"

"If I knew for certain Ştefan were okay, we'd drive this boat right up their ass, baby. Be that as it may, the situation calls for stealth."

Gabrielle joined Chuck and Isabelle at the wheel. Gazing ahead, the dim light of another shack appeared out of the darkness. Chuck checked his GPS. "That's it." Chuck occasionally bumped the throttle, aiding the momentum of the boat toward the shack. A cypress stump rubbed the hull as a reminder to the precarious nature of the bayou. "Dammit, if I screw this boat up over all this. What the hell?"

"It looks like wolves," Gabrielle suggested.

Isabelle strained to see, but her vision could not compare to that of a vampire.

"Where?"

"On the porch," Gabrielle said.

Chuck pulled his 9mm from its holster and took aim. Gabrielle pulled his arm down. "Don't, not yet."

"Are you fucking kidding me? Do you see the size of those bitches? They look like the hounds of hell or something. Maybe Ştefan got his ass eaten by a couple of werewolves."

"If they are werewolves, then unless you have silver bullets we're screwed," Gabrielle explained. "Ease in, and try not to act aggressive."

As the boat drew to within ten feet, one of the wolves padded down the dock, teeth bared and snarling. "This don't look good," Chuck said as he prepared to throttle back.

"Let me handle this," Gabrielle suggested as she approached the bow. Saliva dripped from the wolf's mouth as it growled and snapped its teeth. The second wolf watched intently, its hackles rose as it guarded the door. Gabrielle began humming a song, one Chuck and Isabelle had never heard. As she hummed, she inched closer, slowly extending her hand. The beast snapped again in protest, its growl changing pitch.

"Gabby, I don't think this is a good idea," Isabelle warned quietly.

The wolf snarled and back peddled two steps. Gabrielle followed its footsteps, placing her first foot on the dock. Gabrielle stepped her other foot on the dock and dropped to her knees and continued the melodic lullaby. With her hand extended, the wolf began to creep forward, its ears remaining pinned back. First a growl, then a whimper, then its nose made contact with her hand. "I think you should stay in the boat while I see what's inside."

Isabelle stared at the wolf. "I have no problem with that."

Chuck, on the other hand, moved toward the front of the boat. "I don't know, baby, we don't know what's in there."

Chuck watched the wolf flinch as the shot rang out. Unaware of the source, it wasn't until the bullet struck his head that he was sure of the target. Into the bayou he fell, his head shattered by the projectile. As the wolves began to scramble into the trees, a second shot rang out. Just as she had begun to look for Chuck, the bullet impacted the back of Gabrielle's head. Fearful of the next shot, Isabelle dropped to the floor of the boat. From off in the bayou, she heard the bolt cocking and knew the next bullet would be hers. Chuck floated, face down, on the surface of the frigid waters, his blood intermixing with Gabrielle's, which dripped from the dock above. Isabelle cowered beside the seat, until she noticed Chuck's gun just above the wheel. Grasping the weapon, she ducked back down and inspected the pistol. Listening to the sound of crunching footsteps in the underbrush, Isabelle wished, more than ever, she had Gabrielle and Chuck's keen night vision.

As Isabelle listened to the faint growling of the wolves, she prayed that they would attack her assailant instead of her.

"Romi, Alex, away with you," the man ordered in a thick Creole accent. With no further words spoken, she listened as the wolves raced away. Having never fired a gun, Isabelle frantically inspected it, knowing it was her only salvation. From the dock, unable to lift her body or speak, Gabrielle groaned as the footsteps drew closer. Isabelle popped up, pointed the gun in the direction of the sounds, and squeezed the trigger. It didn't fire. "No bullets," she moaned. Isabelle tossed it onto the deck and made a mad dash for the cabin.

Pulling on the lock frantically, the sound of heavy boots landing on the porch caused her to panic. Looking to the forest, she knew the wolves would track her down. She turned, only to find a beast of a man approaching from behind.

"Looky wut I got here," the man boasted. "We don' git preddy lil things like you out here."

Fearing the rifle he clutched, Isabelle released the lock and backed away. "No, please don't!"

"Don't chu worry, Missy, ol' Lemar ain't gonna shoot you. He's gonna show you a good time." Grabbing her by the arm, he yanked her close. "Mmmm, you smells good, and I bets you be tight all over."

Reeking of liquor, Lemar growled as Isabelle slapped his face. "Don' go do that, or you be dead like dat girl." Lemar spit in the direction of Gabrielle's body before pushing Isabelle against the door and ripping her shirt open. "Dat's mo like it, Missy. Oowee, it gonna take two hans to git them britches off."

Against his weight and strength, Isabelle's efforts were wasted. As Lemar slammed her to the porch, her eyes were filled with the ghastly sight of Gabrielle's bloody and shattered skull.

The sound of water splashing onto the deck drew Lemar's attention. He turned back to find Chuck standing on the deck over Gabrielle's body. "Dam boy, you don' look so good. Did my bullet only nick you? Tell you wut, I git finished wit Missy here, and if you ain't dead yet, I'll share da leftovers. How'z dat?"

Chuck stared down at his wife's body, disbelieving she could survive such a cataclysmic trauma. Despite his own massive head injury, Chuck staggered forward, every step a labored effort.

Pinning Isabelle down, with his size fourteen boot around her throat, Lemar shook his head. "I'm tell'n you boy, you don' look good atall. Bedda hava sit down 'fore you die." Not remotely threatened by his wounded and barely able to walk victim, it never occurred to Lemar these were to be his last words. Standing face to face, Lemar fully expected Chuck to collapse dead when Chuck seized his head and twisted until it turned full circle. With his neck completely snapped, his head doubled over until it met his spine. Grabbing Lemar's shirt, Chuck slung the massive ragdoll corpse and watched as it bounced once on the pier before splashing into the water.

Isabelle pushed herself up and frantically hurried to Gabrielle's side. Lifting Gabrielle's head into her lap, she pleaded, "Gabby, Gabby, can you hear me?"

Gabrielle's eyes fluttered. "Ouch."

"Please, everyone sit," Levente requested, as he invited his family to the dining room table. "We will not wait on my grandson all night."

Amazed by the grandeur of the dining hall, Sarah turned in a full circle to take in its fine details. Two leaded crystal chandeliers illuminated the life-size portraits of people she did not recognize and the frescos on the ceilings, depicting heaven and Eden, and once again, furniture much too busy for her taste. The table would easily seat forty, but for tonight's purpose, the family was gathered at one end. Levente was seated at the head, with Angelique to his right, followed by Nicholas and Samantha. Sarah was seated to his left, next to an elderly gentleman she did not know, and then Tori.

"Sarah, allow me the pleasure of introducing you to Levente Tepes, The King of Romania." Levente gestured to the elderly man seated to her right, who then bowed his head. "Ştanis is his given name, but he has served as the face of Levente Tepes from the onset of my political career."

"I'm not sure I understand," Sarah replied.

"Of course, I should explain. The office of the president requires numerous appearances, many during the day. Additionally, everyone around us ages, yet we do not. Ştanis is the president the people need to see. He and I have partnered to run this country for thirty-seven years. But sadly, time dictates his need to retire."

As Sarah turned back to Ştanis, he smiled warmly. "It is a

pleasure to meet you," he said, as he kissed her hand.

"But how does that work? How do you know what to say all of the time?"

Ştanis looked to Levente, who nodded his approval. "Levente and I spent years together, discussing policy. It is like our minds are one. But on issues of grave measure . . . are you familiar with their powers of the mind?" Sarah nodded in affirmation. "Levente is nearby and shares his thoughts when needed."

Sarah absorbed the information. "Doesn't it bother you to make all of these grand accomplishments and have someone else in the spotlight?" Sarah asked Levente, before returning her attention to Ştanis. "Or have him tell you what to say and do?"

Levente smiled, delighted with Sarah's brash inquisitiveness. "Like my son, I have never aspired the prominence. My sole desire was to see my homeland prosper and know my people were taken care of."

"And I am living a life beyond any that I could have accomplished," Ştanis added. "I would have lived and died a peasant without Levente's leadership. And when the time comes to step down, I will have a choice."

"And the queen?" Sarah directed her attention to Angelique.

"You shall meet her tomorrow. She is quite an amazing woman. Much like you, in her younger days."

The kitchen door swung open and a host of waiters appeared, one for each guest. Laying the plates of sautéed pork, grilled potatoes, and mixed vegetables before each guest, they promptly disappeared back into the kitchen. "You probably are not aware of this, but before my grandson became a vampire," Levente said to Sarah, "he was never late for a meal."

CHAPTER TWENTY-FOUR

ALEX RUSHED INTO the dining room. "Sorry I'm late. Once a reporter showed up, any hopes of getting away at a decent hour were dashed. By tomorrow everyone should know I'm home."

"And what exactly did you tell them?" Levente asked, as he rose to greet his grandson. Angelique quickly jumped in front and embraced her son as if it would be their last hug.

"I am sorry for disappearing for so long," Alex said softly in her ear, "but I had to find my own way—and not the one chosen for me."

"I know," Angelique replied, as she pushed back and inspected his appearance. "Please, come sit. We can talk later."

Levente patted his grandson's back firmly. "It is good to see you, Alex."

Before Alex could sit, Sarah had come around the table to join the hugging. "I was beginning to worry," she said.

"I called a few old friends and told them I was back in town and wanted to have a drink. Just as I expected, one of them tipped off the press."

"And what happened next?" Angelique asked.

"Pictures and questions," Alex explained, as he placed his napkin in his lap. "I told the reporters I had been studying abroad, majoring in foreign relations, and was home for a big announcement."

"Which is?" Levente asked, as everyone leaned into the table and stared at Alex.

"After dinner, I will give Sarah a tour of the palace, alone, and we will have a discussion. If she has not changed her mind, then you will be announcing our engagement."

Levente showed only a glimmer of approval. "Is that all?"

"Sarah and I will return to America, after the holidays, to finish her degree. I will return to Romania and orchestrate a campaign, more so an inquiry, to decide if Romania and Sarah and I, are right for each other. *If* we decide, at that time, that a political career is the right choice, I will begin to take my place in the family hierarchy."

Nicholas set his utensils down and cleared his throat. "Son, I don't want to be the one to throw holy water in your hot tub, but have you considered how you will become a public figure? Before Ştefan made you what you are, this would have been a perfect plan. But tonight alone, your friends had to have taken notice of your youthful appearance."

Alex stood up and smiled cordially at his family. In doing so, his hair began to lengthen and gray, ever so slightly, as fine wrinkles appeared across his face.

"That is truly amazing," Tori exclaimed.

"Yes, it is," Levente concurred. "Tell me, Alex, how did you acquire this appearance- shifting ability? It has only been a whisper of a skill, once possessed by the ancient order."

Alex smiled. "I mastered the art of transformational meditation. It was through this skill that I learned to visualize myself as an older man, or a tanned beach bum, much like masking our scent, only a little more advanced."

"Indeed," Levente replied, casting a suspicious gaze at him.

At the conclusion of the meal, the family returned to the fireside. Levente had taken a particular interest in Tori, which left Nicholas and Samantha concerned as to his intent. As the evening wore on in lighthearted conversation, their suspicions were somewhat relieved. With the plans for the costume ball at Poenari becoming the central conversation for the women, the topic of the castle reminded Sarah of a lingering question. During a rare moment of silence, Sarah broached the only issue that remained a mystery to her.

"Alex has shared practically everything about his family. In piecing the stories together, there seems to be one subject that's avoided."

All eyes fell on Sarah. "Please, ask anything you will," Levente instructed.

"Alex has told me the circumstances of your entombment and how they found you. But nobody has explained how the family escaped."

Levente rose from his chair and momentarily faced the fireplace. "Poenari, over the centuries, has been an intrinsic part of our family history, specifically Elisabeta's death and my entombment. But the freedom that the few of us at this table obtained was won by the brutal bloodshed of noble, but very misguided, Romanians. It is not a tale I recount with pleasure or pride. But nonetheless, it is part of who we are, as a race."

Levente refilled Sarah's wine glass. "If you are truly to become family, you must learn we keep no secrets or share no lies, even through the darkest seasons. The night of our escape, we were responsible for the deaths of twenty-three soldiers, mostly Romanian, members of The Order of the Dragon. Their sole purpose was to protect the homeland against *this* very threat." Levente swept his arms about the room. "They falsely believed our family was nothing more than evil, dangerous vampires."

"I have no memory of the night I was rescued. It wasn't until the next night, as I fed from Chuck's blood, that I began to understand my circumstances." Levente took Angelique's hand, and they shared a smile. "The first thing I remembered was *this* beautiful face. And I was sure I had finally died, because in my heart, I knew she had perished years ago. As my consciousness improved, I became aware of my surroundings, at first the catacombs, the tomb that they had imprisoned me in, and then the chair, where my wife, Elisabeta, Nicholas's mother, was tortured and killed. Then I met my son, and the horror of the previous sixty-odd years melted away. He and the others had been busy, attempting to remove the stones from the castle stairs, in hopes they could dig their way to freedom.

"But what they did not know, Poenari's catacombs had many secret chambers. Not twenty meters from where they labored was the hidden entrance to the treasure vaults. It took all of the strength Nicholas and Chuck could muster to dislodge the secret stone door."

Defending his ego, Nicholas cleared his throat and injected, "Our strengths were failing from a lack of nutrition."

"Or in Chuck's case, being the nutrition," Samantha said, with a smile.

"Yes," Levente concurred. "But once the seal was broken, it moved rather easily. Inside the vault the wealth of treasures that had been hidden for so many centuries were largely ignored as we set out to reopen the old ventilation window. You see, the vault at one time was a prison cell with a single barred window looking out over the valley. If a prisoner were to somehow remove the bars, the fall to the river below would bring immediate death. Once the cell was converted to the treasure room, the portal was sealed with stone and mortar."

"Without tools, it took us almost two days to chisel the mortar and remove the bars," Nicholas explained.

Levente and Nicholas went on for a half an hour recounting how they reclaimed the throne and how the family's secret remained intact. Sarah and Tori listened, astonished as Levente recounted his decision to turn Chuck, to aid his son.

"And so it was, my son and Chuck defeated our enemies and saved our family."

"It was no easy task," Nicholas added solemnly, "traversing the wall and killing all of those men, who only believed as I once did. My penance for our victory is the weight of those souls I continue to bear."

"It was a dark hour, one that we rarely discuss," Samantha added.

Tori gazed at Nicholas with a new understanding. "Then my life, the very reason I still live, and all that your family has accomplished, it was decided by your victory, forty years ago."

"The potential exists for every word and action to alter history, for better or worse," Angelique answered. "The very fate of this nation has been decided infinite times by this family alone. Nick's blunder at the convent, his joining the CIA, the Communists killing his mother, Elisabeta . . . I could go on."

As the conversation waned, Alex and Sarah excused themselves. After their tour of the palace, Alex opened the ten-foot-high, white-and-gold-trimmed bedroom doors. Sarah's eye popped wide as she gawked at the lavish interior. As in practically every room, the French Provincial décor accented the artwork, chandelier, window treatments, and fireplace, which was stoked and burning brightly. The bed appeared almost twice the size of any she had ever seen.

"This is your room," Alex said.

Sarah stepped into the vastness of the chamber. "No, it's not."

"Is there a problem?"

"First of all, I am sure this palace must be haunted, so there's no way I'm sleeping alone. Secondly, all of this talk of murder and vampires and whatnot is going to give me nightmares. So, you're going to have to hold me, all night and day if need be."

"You know, after all you have learned, if you still want to marry me and play king and queen, we don't have to live *here*."

"That would be like the King and Queen of England not living in Buckingham Palace, you know." Sarah slipped her hand into Alex's shirt and raked her nails over his chest.

Alex pinned Sarah against the threshold and kissed her passionately. His left hand slid behind her head and his right hand under her dress. "You are a most amazing woman, Sarah Phillips."

"Please tell me," Sarah said, as she came up for air, "that your bedroom . . . was not decorated by Louis the Fourteenth."

"Please, tell me that is not sex that I am smelling," Samantha said from behind.

"Whoa," Alex nearly shouted as he and Sarah were startled to attention by Samantha's sudden appearance. "Mother," Alex scolded, "it's not polite to sneak up on people, again."

"I might say something similar about etiquette—and the location of your hand out in public." Samantha yanked Alex's hand from Sarah's leg and shoved it onto his stomach. "Make sure you wash that hand before you go to bed, lover boy," Samantha said, as she shoved him toward his room.

Alone with Sarah, she smiled warmly. "I just needed to tell you, you did amazingly well tonight, much better than I did on my first visit." She looked over Sarah's shoulder into the room. "I don't blame you one bit. I didn't want to stay alone in this room either." Samantha turned to leave, took three steps, and then turned back to Sarah and said with a mischievous smile, "And I didn't."

CHAPTER TWENTY-FIVE

CHUCK DROPPED TO his knees and studied Gabrielle's shattered skull, his own blood dripping down on her. "You're gonna be alright, baby. This shit happens to Nicky all the time."

"It hurts," Gabrielle groaned.

"Yeah it does, baby," Chuck said, as he surveyed the surrounding marshes. Placing his hand on his wound, he stood up and continued to look for additional shooters. "I can't believe Ștefan set us up like this," he said to Isabelle. "We've got to get Gabby in the boat and get the hell out of here," he said to Isabelle.

"Ștefan would not have done this," Isabelle snapped defensively. "Something is wrong."

"I can't think about all that right now. Fuck, this hurts!" Chuck groaned, as he pushed against his head. "Now I see what Nick was bitching about." Chuck scooped up Gabrielle and softly said, "It's gonna be alright, baby. Let's get you out of here."

"You should look inside," Isabelle suggested.

"And what, wait for those two beasts to come back, or another shooter? Fuck that. We're getting the hell out of here, right now. If Ștefan got himself in this mess, he can get himself out," Chuck said, as he laid Gabrielle across the seat.

Gabrielle put her hand against Chuck's face. "You need to look," she said weakly.

Chuck sighed heavily, knowing his wife would only force him to return. Looking back at the shack, he saw Isabelle tugging at the floating corpse, until she produced a crowded keychain. "Isabelle, are you crazy? There may be another shooter."

"We've got to look inside, Chuck."

"I'll come back tomorrow better prepared. I need to get the two of you out of here now, before his friends show up." Retrieving his gun off the deck, he hurried to the door. Isabelle was frantically trying keys when Chuck pulled her hand away. Racking back the 9mm, he put it in her hand. "Go watch Gabs. If anything comes near, shoot it." The sixth key slid into the lock with little effort. Removing the lock, Chuck tossed it over his shoulder, the splash echoing across the bayou. Chuck looked back to Isabelle. "I hope I don't regret this."

Chuck cracked the door and looked in. "Damn," he whispered, as the relatively plush interior took him by surprise. He quietly pulled the door back and returned to the boat. Reaching in his field jacket, he produced another handgun. "I feel better with this." Returning to the door, he kicked it forcefully and stormed in. Immediately, he spotted a pair of legs on the floor behind the breakfast bar. Moving cautiously, he discovered Ştefan's body, face down in a massive pool of blood, with a wooden spike stuck in his head. "Ştefan. Fuck," Chuck moaned. He holstered his gun, knelt down, and checked for a pulse. Either gone or just undetectable, Chuck feared the worst as he rolled Ştefan's body over.

Unable to speak, Ştefan's eyes weakly searched Chuck's face.

"What the hell did they do to you, boy?"

Isabelle entered the cabin and gasped as she beheld Ştefan's limp body. "Is he dead?"

"No, but he's got this stake in his head, and it looks like his throat's been slashed. "And he's gonna need blood, and so does Gabby. We've got to go."

"Can we make it back by sunrise?"

"I don't think we can even make Baton Rouge, to be honest," he sighed.

"Then we must stay here tonight," Isabelle said. "If they need blood, I'll give them what they need. Besides, you need to do something with that body out there."

Expended from his own injuries, Chuck trudged out the door. Returning with Gabrielle, he laid her on the bed. "Fuck, Tubby. If I'm lucky, the gators will drag him under for me." After inspecting Ştefan's injuries, Chuck decided his wound had sufficiently healed enough to attempt extracting the stake. "Izzy, bring me a towel, please."

"Are you sure that won't hurt him?" she asked with her back turned.

"I hope it hurts like hell." Once he had the makeshift bandage in place, Chuck twisted and pulled firmly, inching the stake back slowly. Ştefan screamed in agony as the wooden spear slurped as it was retracted. "Hold him, Izzy," Chuck hollered over Ştefan's screams. Pressing down, Isabelle could not look as blood and brain seeped from the wound.

With a final tug, the spike was free and Chuck quickly covered the hole with a towel. "You know, this is just like old times, Ştefan, except instead of saving your dad's ass, now I'm saving yours. Where would you people be without me?"

With his free hand, Chuck tapped Isabelle on the shoulder. "If you don't mind, Gabby needs blood. I'll hold the pressure here just a little longer, then I'm gonna bury Tubby before the sun comes up. After that, we need to wipe this place clean."

"What about you? Don't you need blood?"

"As disgusting as this might sound, Lard Ass ain't been dead long. It *almost* turns my stomach just thinking about it, but what the hell. Find me a pot, we're gonna need more blood than you've got if these two are going to have any chance to heal before we hit the road tomorrow night."

Isabelle gently tapped Chuck on the shoulder. Startled, he jumped from the recliner and scanned the room. "What is it, is something wrong?" he asked excitedly.

"No," Isabelle said calmly. "You fell asleep, and the sun has set."

Chuck looked at his wife. "Is she . . . ?"

"Gabby is still sleeping, as is Ştefan."

"That boy owes us big time. My head still hurts," Chuck said, as he splashed some water on his face and dried it with the hand towel. "Ştefan better wake up soon. He's got a lot of explaining to do."

"Maybe if you hadn't killed that guy, you could have questioned him."

"Last I remember, he was about to lay his pork chop in you, darlin. And you'll excuse me if I overreacted, but he did shoot me and Gabby."

Isabelle smiled. "I'm not saying you shouldn't have killed him, but sometimes that *shoot first* thing backfires."

Chuck stood proudly erect. "I'm a Jarhead, Izzy, that's how I roll."

"Well then don't complain about the consequences." Isabelle's tone was playful, considering the circumstances. "Besides, how many years has it been since you were a Marine?"

"How many years has it been since you were crowned Queen of the Ball Busters, Izzy," Chuck mimicked with a roll of his eyes. Standing beside the bed he looked at Gabrielle's head, which had made an impressive recovery. "Hey," he said softly, as he touched her shoulder.

"Hey," Gabrielle replied with a forced smile and her eyes still closed.

"That was some crazy shit last night, huh?"

Gabrielle rolled in the direction of Chuck's voice and opened her eyes. "I do not ever want to get shot again." She reached up and touched Chuck's wound.

"Or me," he replied. "Can you walk?"

Gabrielle raised herself with Chuck's assistance and propped on her elbow. "I think so."

Isabelle watched as Chuck kissed Gabrielle's forehead. Her heart sank as she looked at Ştefan, knowing if she had only allowed it, she could have known such love.

Chuck went over to the couch and shook Ştefan's shoulder. "Wake up, kid."

Unlike Gabrielle, Ştefan barely stirred.

"What's wrong with him," Isabelle asked in a panic.

"I'm guessing he lost a lot more blood than Gabby and me and was without it for longer." Kneeling beside the couch, Chuck shook him again. "Hey, kiddo."

Ştefan's eyes parted. "Can you understand me?" Chuck asked, as he moved closer. Ştefan nodded his head. "We need to leave, are you up to it?" Again, Ştefan nodded. "Can you walk?" Ştefan's eyes closed again. Chuck looked back to Isabelle. "This is how old man Tepes was when we found him."

Ştefan's hand moved slowly to Chuck's shoulder. Lacking the strength to pull himself up, Chuck slid his arm under Ştefan's back and brought him to a sitting position. "He needs more blood, Izzy."

"I can do that." Isabelle extended her arm. With his free hand,

Chuck punctured her wrist and brought it to Ştefan's mouth. In his weakness, Ştefan was barely able to drink the blood, the precious drops trailing down his chin. Chuck leaned Ştefan back slightly, making it easier for him to swallow. Watching Isabelle closely, he noticed her eyes begin to diminish. "Okay, that's gonna have to be enough."

Chuck looked back to Gabrielle who remained sitting on the bed. "Babe, are you ready?" Using her hands for support, with great effort Gabrielle rose, unsteadily, from the bed. "I'm gonna carry him out to the boat," Chuck said to Isabelle. "Help Gabby, and lock the door as you leave. We still don't know what this place is."

By the time they had returned to the Garden District, Ştefan had regained enough strength to walk with assistance from Chuck. Feeling quite diminished from his injuries and the lack of a good day's sleep, Chuck deposited Ştefan on the parlor sofa and sighed. "There you go, big guy." Once he was free of his burden, Chuck flopped down beside Ştefan.

"Everyone looks as if they need a drink," Isabelle observed as she left the room.

"None of that street bum shit tonight. You bring us Nick's secret stash," Chuck hollered to Isabelle.

Gabrielle dropped beside Chuck. "Forty years ago, when Nick nearly killed me in Miami, I thought nothing could feel worse."

"And?" Chuck asked, as he put an arm around her.

"I was wrong."

"That was a first for me. I've never been shot, ever. It sucked." With his head flopped against the back of the couch, Chuck rolled his head in Ştefan's direction. Ştefan stared blankly at a painting from the 1700s of the French Market.

"Is he going to be alright?" Gabrielle asked.

"I don't know, let's ask the dipshit. Yo, Ştefan, are you going to be okay?"

"Chuck!" Gabrielle scolded.

"Well, all of this was his fault," Chuck explained, as he continued to stare at Ştefan. "You know I'm right, don't you, boy?" Chuck insisted, as he lightly punched Ştefan's arm. "Wasn't I always there for you? But this time, not only did you run away, but you also used all the shit I taught you to hide from me. And look where that got us. Me and Gabby got our heads half blown off, and some big fat turd is dead in the bayou." Chuck turned back to Gabrielle. "So, in my book, he earned the title of dipshit."

Ştefan's head turned ever so slightly and a tear began to creep down his cheek.

"What's going on?" Isabelle asked, as she returned.

"I'm reaming Ştefan's ass. And maybe after we've all had a bottle or two, he can tell us what this was all about."

Isabelle handed Chuck and Gabrielle each a bottle. "I should call Nick and let him know we've found Ştefan."

"No," Chuck said in a raised tone, as he tore the lid off and guzzled half of its contents. "Not until we know what happened and where Barousse got off to."

"Drink this," Isabelle said, as she helped Ştefan drink.

"So what should we do now?" Gabrielle asked.

Chuck finished off his bottle and belched. "First, I'm gonna get us another bottle, then I'm gonna take a shower, and then he'd better be ready to talk.

An hour had passed before Chuck returned to the parlor with a fresh bottle of blood in hand. Isabelle caressed Ştefan's head as he leaned against her shoulder.

"He say anything?"

Isabelle took exception with Chuck's terse tone. "No, and maybe you should try not being such a hard ass."

"But, Izzy, that's what I do, darlin."

"I'm ready to talk," Ştefan said, his tone void of emotion.

"Welcome back to the land of the living. Living dead, that is. Boy, have I got a shit load of questions for you." The wingback chair screeched as Chuck dragged it across the wooden floor. Flopping down directly in front of Ştefan, Chuck began his interrogation. "First, what the hell were you doing in that shack?"

"It's mine."

Chuck sneered as he leaned forward. "Then who was that lard ass Cajun who shot me and Gabby?"

With a great deal of concern and effort, Ştefan sat up. "Lamar shot you?"

"He shot me and Gabby and was about to put the pork sword to Isabelle before I killed him." Chuck took a swig from his bottle, much like his old ways of drinking whiskey.

Ştefan looked at Isabelle, who confirmed with a nod, then back to Chuck. "He was my caretaker. He lived in the shack at the mouth of the tributary . . . and you *killed* him?

"Yep." Chuck took another swallow. "If he was your caretaker, then what the hell were you doing on the floor with a wooden spike stuck in your head and your throat slashed?"

Consumed with guilt, Ştefan looked away from Chuck and Isabelle. "I don't know what to say . . . it was a mistake." Ştefan covered his eyes briefly, before dragging his hands across his face, then pulling his hair. "It was Reese."

Isabelle pushed back. "Reese?"

"Two years ago I told her about me, about all of us."

"You did *what*?" Chuck asked sharply.

"I know, I know, but I wanted her to love me like I am, not what I pretended to be. She *had* to know the truth." Ştefan shook his head. "But she freaked out. I had no choice but to lock her in that cabin."

"What in the hell were you thinking?" Chuck bellowed.

"I don't know, but I couldn't undo it, and I couldn't tell father or you or anybody. So I kept her out there the last two years, promising I'd make it up to her."

"Oh, I can't wait to hear this one." Chuck crossed his arms and pressed back firmly in the chair. Gabrielle patted him on the shoulder, attempting to calm his temperament.

"How were *you* going to make it right, Ştefan?"

"I had to prove to her that there was no need to fear us. And the only way I figured to do that was if our lives were no longer secret."

Isabelle covered her mouth to conceal her dread as Gabrielle's fingernails dug into Chuck's shoulder. Clenching his bottle to the point of shattering, Chuck snarled, "What have you done, Ştefan?"

CHAPTER TWENTY-SIX

THE GONDOLA SWAYED gently in the brisk Carpathian winter winds. Sarah appeared uneasy with the rocking back and forth but said nothing. The darkness of the mountains was rarely interrupted, except for the flickering lights of the occasional home or village off in the distance.

"It's quite safe you know, the gondola. After you've used it a few times you get used to the motion. The only other way up is to hike it, which might be a little chilly tonight."

Gripping the bench she was seated on, Sarah was delighted by the flurries drifting by the window. Checking their progress toward the castle, she strained to see the forest far below. "Why didn't your grandfather build a road?"

Alex was standing, holding the support pole and allowing the motion to soothe him as he rocked back and forth. "He wanted it unspoiled, much the way it had remained for centuries. Once his intentions to rebuild the castle became known, land speculators tried to buy up the property on the mountain and in the valley. But he had the entire area declared a historic landmark, so it could not be developed. It's nice, the view from Poenari's watch towers, looking at those rugged mountains and not seeing a bunch of fast-food restaurants and hotels."

"It's kind of spooky," Sarah said with a strained smile.

Alex swung around on the pole, allowing his face to drop down just in front of hers. "Baby, I'm kind of spooky."

"Alex, you are a dork," Sarah said with a giggle.

"Then our children don't stand a chance, Miss Biology Nerd."

Sarah slid away from Alex's face and stared back out the window. "Children. I haven't even begun to think about that."

"It's alright, I only want about twelve." Alex plopped into the seat she had vacated. "Little Vlad, little Levente, little Nicky, but definitely can't do little Vazul, great grandpa was crazier than bat shit."

"Now you are really scaring me, Alex. Twelve?"

"Well, thirteen is unlucky, so even if we have fourteen, the thirteenth is going to be screwed. So we'll have to stop at twelve."

Sarah stared intensely at Alex. "I think you have altitude sickness."

"Oh, I do have a sickness, and later on, I'm going to get it all over you, lady."

Just as Sarah was about to reply, the gondola slowed as it pulled into the dock. The outside lights flickered on, and the door opened automatically. "*Velcome to Poenari,* Meeze Phillips, *vee 'ave been e-x-p-e-c-t-i-n-g* you," Alex said, in his most sinister Romanian accent.

"Had I known you were such a comedian . . . "

As they approached the castle, the doors slowly opened, the timbers and hinges creaking with the motion. Stepping into the dark grand foyer, Sarah looked around suspiciously. "Who is here?"

"It's just us," Alex replied, as the doors began to close slowly, the light of the dock fading.

"Alex," Sarah squealed.

"The darkness, I'm sorry. Repeat after me," Alex whispered in her ear, "*lumina.*"

"*Lumina,*" Sarah said meekly.

"A little louder, if you please."

"*Lumina*!" she called out. One by one, sconces and chandeliers flickered to life, their flames growing instantly bright. "Oh my, that is so cool."

"Want to see something even cooler? Blow them out."

Sarah puffed, and every light in the room was instantly doused into darkness.

"How cool is that?"

"*Lumina,*" Sarah commanded. The lights returned. "Okay, that's pretty impressive. What happens when you have a room full of people?"

"There is a *lock* command." By Sarah's wide-eyed expression, Alex knew she was excited. "So what do you want to see first?"

Sarah looked around mischievously. "Are we really the only ones here?"

"If you are thinking about running around the castle naked, or having sex on that rug over there," Alex said, pointing to an expansive, priceless Persian rug, "most rooms have surveillance."

"Can't you lock that out too?"

"If I did the phone would ring immediately. As the castle is uninhabited most of the time any movement, noise, or change in ambient temperature immediately triggers alarms."

"So, are they watching and listening now?"

"All bodies have specific signatures, body mass, heat, even scent. When you entered, the computers started collecting all of this data. I dare say that after you have showered, they will have a complete profile on your signature."

"After I've showered?"

"Yes, our personally selected, professional staff, well *most* are professional, there may be one or two perverts we missed in the screening process, they will study the video and key in all pertinent data."

"Like hell they will."

Sarah's shocked reaction made it impossible for Alex to continue the prank. Laughing lightly, he explained, "It started at the palace and continues here. There are heat sensors, laser scans, and scent detectors that compile detailed computerized information. The longer you're here, the more complete the profile. If you venture to a room where you don't belong, *they* will know. Go poking in the private fridge . . . you get the picture."

"I've never heard of any security system like this." Sarah stroked the coarse wool and cotton fabric as she began inspecting the tapestries that hung from the twenty-foot ceilings.

"There are technologies that exist that were not created for the capitalists of the world. My grandfather is a visionary, and part of that vision was superior education for every citizen of this country who wanted it. If you wanted to be a rocket scientist, you could be one. Even our farmers are educated to be technically superior to any others on the planet. And if you're a janitor and have an idea of how to build a better broom, your ideas have an accessible path to creation. My grandfather has turned us into a country of academics and inventors with a work ethic based on pay for productivity. It's why the car company he started builds the most sought after sports car on the planet. The question of how can we build it cheaper is never asked."

Alex took Sarah's hand and led her to the grand dining hall. "His key scientists understand, before a classified project ever begins, it is considered high treason to reveal even the smallest detail of the project. The men and women that apply for these jobs do so with the understanding that they will be compensated immensely, but the position is a *lifetime* appointment."

The passage was growing darker and Sarah could not wait to try her newly learned Romanian again. "*Ilumina.*" Once again a string of sconces sparked to life. "So your grandfather's energy policies, it's why our governments are not getting along?"

"America feels free, clean energy technology should be shared with the world. My grandfather believes it is a commodity to be sold at reasonable prices, unlike American energy corporations. It's why every time we hold an election, American companies and the government itself funds my grandfather's opponents, who are sympathetic to their cause."

"So, if I were to become one of your grandfather's key scientists and committed high treason, what would happen to me?"

Alex chuckled at the notion. "It would be my responsibility to personally punish you. *Ilumina,*" he said, as he swung open the dining hall double oak doors.

"Oh my, this is so amazing." Unlike the grand foyer, which was mostly stone, the dining hall was practically a forest of rose wood, mahogany, and ebony. Hand-carved panels and pillars lined the walls, intermixed with rich, green paisley wallpaper. Jars, urns, steins, and vases were methodically placed about the room. Just beyond the head of the table was a stone fireplace, large enough to park a small car in. On each side of the massive dining table hung six eight-foot high portraits, all renditions of family long perished. As they stood before the portrait of a beautiful, but mysterious, woman, Sarah appeared mesmerized.

"This is my great, great grandmother, Ilona Szilagy. Her original portrait was destroyed decades ago in an earthquake that decimated the castle. According to my grandfather, this is the original site of the dining hall, recreated from his memory."

"I love this room and, so far, the castle."

Alex snickered, knowing the tours next destination might change her opinion. "So, as you might imagine, castles are famous for their secret passages. Poenari is no different." To the right of Ilona's portrait was an ivory mantle, trimmed with molding and dental blocks. Alex pulled the fourth block and Ilona's portrait, and the wall above it began to slowly rise, revealing a narrow, steep stone stairwell leading down an extraordinarily dark passage. "The catacombs," Alex said, as he swung his arm out to usher her in front. "This passage and the catacombs are the only original amenities remaining."

"That's nice," Sarah replied timidly. "What's next?"

"The catacombs."

Sarah resisted Alex's nudging. "Aren't there caskets down there, and dead stuff?"

"Caskets, yes, but all of the unnatural remains have been removed. Even the ashes of my grandmother have been laid to a proper rest. Basically, all that remains is where the family sleeps."

"In caskets?"

"Yes, in caskets. It's like I told you earlier, the difference between a bed and a casket is substantial. If the time ever arrives for you, you will understand, completely."

"*If*? Don't you mean when?"

"We've got a lot of life to live between now and *that* decision. A year from now you might feel very differently, and as I can attest, there are no U-turns on this highway." Alex raised her arm and pulled it around his neck. "But until that day, you've got to get used to the dark and creepy places, because this isn't the only one."

Sarah smiled. "Can't my body double get used to the dark and scary places for me?"

"Who said we were going to have body doubles?" Sarah's bewildered expression begged for an explanation. "If, and it's a big if, we were to succeed my grandparents, I might be inclined to reveal the truth, or at least part of it. I'm tired of all this deception."

"If I get nightmares, Alex Tepes," Sarah warned as he tugged toward the steps.

"I'll be there to kiss them away," Alex promised. The dank passage spiraled down for what seemed like miles to Sarah. While she was not allowing her anxiety to be obvious, a strong fear emanated from her subconscious with each successive step.

"I certainly hope there is an elevator for the trip back up," Sarah quipped, as she pressed her hands against the cool stone to support her balance as they journeyed deeper into the mountain.

"Would you settle for a piggyback ride?" Before Sarah could answer, they had reached the bottom, and she became uncommonly silent. Choosing to clasp Alex's shirtsleeve for security, timidly she called out, "*Ilumina*." Even with such a soft pitch, the catacombs whispered her words back. As the torches lit, Sarah's expectations of a primitive, rugged cave were quashed. Although sparse, when compared to the castle, the floors were carpeted and the stone walls were painted with murals set amongst several Medieval tapestries. Depicting battles, royal families, unicorns, and, oddly enough, what appeared to be heaven, the images gave a warm character to an otherwise foreboding cavern.

Standing in front of the archway immediately to the left of the passage, Sarah studied the two caskets. Very simple in nature, the luster of cherry wood reflected Sarah's image. "Is this their—?"

Alex affirmed with a nod.

"I expected something more lavish."

"Well, they are pretty plush on the inside, Jacuzzi, wet bar, and workout room, but on the outside, just your basic box."

"Mock me again and you may find yourself sleeping in one," Sarah threatened, as she moved on to the next archway. The chamber was identical in size, but the walls were finished in a matte marble, and a black granite slab rested in the middle of the floor.

"My grandmother's grave," Alex reported solemnly. "If you go inside the room, to the far side you will find a cross engraved in the granite. For obvious reasons, it could not be facing outward. But make no mistake, cursed or not, my grandfather believes his wife does reside in heaven."

"That is so sad." Sarah's eyes glistened, as she reflected on Levente's recounting of his first wife's death. "His pain, it's almost as if I can feel it."

"Oh, it's very real. The love that perished that night, it will always remain in this place," Alex explained, as he took Sarah's hand.

"What about Angelique? Doesn't she mind?"

"Angelique is amazing. She understands life as it is, and as it was. You will find over time, Elisabeta's spirit will not abandon you to sorrow. There will come a day, as you make the trip down, the embodiment of love will fill your soul with such bliss that you will not want to leave. She gave her life for Levente, and my father.

Come down here enough and, in time, she will share the joy of love's mystery and power with you."

Sarah stared at the tomb, craving to experience more.

"Be patient, and she will come to you in time. Come, let me show you the tunnel." Alex pointed across the room to the far left corner. "It's behind that tapestry. It's not really hidden at all, from the inside, but it does have one hell of a security system."

As they headed toward the corner, Sarah took notice of the two remaining archways. "Are there coffins in there?"

Alex nodded his head. "Yes."

"Do you have one?" Sarah's tone was exceptionally nervous. Although she had not asked, while in Canada or New Orleans, Sarah suspected Alex had caskets in his other homes as well.

"The last two chambers are a little crowded. There are four caskets for my family in the room on the left, and Chuck, Gabby, and Sabine's are in the room on the right. If we all decided to sleep down here, which has never happened, we could." Wanting to change Sarah's focus, Alex nudged her shoulder away. "I forgot to mention, the room across from the treasure vault, at the base of the stairs, is a . . . *wine* cellar."

"Wine cellar, all the way down here?"

"Let's put it this way, they learned their lesson forty years ago. It would take years for us to starve to death down here."

With great trepidation, Sarah tugged Alex toward the first archway. "Can I see yours?"

Knowing this time would eventually arrive, Alex still felt awkward as he followed Sarah. As she stared at the four identical caskets, Alex fretted over her reaction. This harsh, grotesque reality could quite possibly supplant all of his love's best intentions.

Pointing to the third from the left, Sarah stated, "That one."

Sarah approached the casket and extended her hand until her fingertips made contact with the mahogany. One by one, each finger followed the first, until her whole hand rested on the cool, slick surface. Appearing to caress the wood, as if it were his flesh, Sarah walked the length of the box. Not sure of what to say, or if he should say anything, Alex waited silently for her reaction.

As she rounded the top of the casket, Sarah looked up at Alex with eyes that defied description. "You *are* a vampire."

Alex covered his mouth, not sure how to respond. In his mind, she already knew what he was, but in his heart, *this* made it real.

"I shouldn't have brought you down here, not yet." The intensity of Sarah's gaze stole his remaining words.

"It doesn't matter. One day I *will* join you." The determination in Sarah's voice revealed her will, or perhaps it simply was love.

"One would think, with all of the technology installed, your grandfather might have at least put one elevator in the castle. Between the stairs to the dungeon and now the tour, the only thing that's going to happen in bed, tonight, will be sleep."

"Oh, is that so? By the time that comes around, first night, all alone in the castle, you'll change your mind." As they reached the end of the spiral stairwell, Alex commanded, "*Deschis*," and the door lifted up and open. Sarah followed him out to the tower observatory.

"Oh my," Sarah cried out. "What a view." The snow-covered mountains and trees and random drifting clouds all glowed intensely against the nearly full moon. With the exception of a few scattered dwellings in the distance, the only sparkles to be seen were that of the stars. As a brisk gust of wind blew through the trees far below, Sarah shivered.

From behind, Alex wrapped his arms tightly around her. "You should see it with my eyes."

"One day, I will," she replied, as her body trembled.

Alex nuzzled his nose into Sarah's neck. "We should go back down. You're cold."

"Not yet."

Looking at the forest far below, he chuckled silently.

Sarah turned in his arms. "What's that for?"

"They are out there, watching us already." Alex pointed. "Over there."

"I don't see anything. Who is it?"

"The Order of the Dragon, my grandfather's imperial guard."

Sarah's shiver intensified. "Weren't they the ones trying to kill your grandfather?"

"Initially, they were created in the early 1400s to defend their particular views of Christianity, and just like the many divisions of the church, the order fragmented. Vlad Dracula controlled a sect, whose primary purpose was defeating the Ottomans. But as Vlad, and eventually Vazul, strayed from the path, the Order turned against them. Eventually, they looked to destroy my family for alleged crimes against Christianity—vampirism. But it was more the Communists influence, aided by a small group of Dragonist fanatics, who eventually led to my grandfather's imprisonment and my grandmother's murder."

"And now they guard your family?"

"Just like all religions, extremists exist. When my father and Chuck were forced to deal with the remnants of the Order, unknowingly, they killed off the last of the fanatics. Once my grandfather won control of Romania, he formed this new Order." Alex waved his hand in the direction of the mountainside. "Recruited in their youth and from Christian backgrounds, they are an elite unit. Their sole purpose is to protect the king."

"Okay, I can't wait to hear the logic behind this."

"Forming the Order from boys rooted in a Christian foundation certainly quelled most whispers of the *evil* Tepes family."

With another shiver, Sarah pecked Alex on the lips. "I think I'm ready to go in now." Peering at the seemingly endless spiral, Sarah clutched Alex's shirt as they headed down. After the last step was reached, Sarah sighed heavily. In the ensuing respite in conversation, Sarah meandered, looking curiously about her surroundings.

"So, is it just my imagination or have we seen every room in this castle, with the exception of our bedroom?"

Alex smiled devilishly. "Apparently, you have me all figured out."

"Somehow," Sarah replied, as she patted his cheek, "I seriously doubt that."

CHAPTER TWENTY-SEVEN

ŞTEFAN STARED AT the portrait of his grandfather that hung over the fireplace. He didn't know what he wanted to say. How much should he reveal, if anything? One thing was for certain; Reese had to be found. "We have to find her," he announced weakly.

"You know, Ştefan, there's so much shit wrapped up in this I don't know where to start. Any hopes of damage control may be useless." Chuck drank from his bottle like a wino hitting the sauce hard.

"I think it's time to call Nicholas," Isabelle suggested.

"And tell him what, Izzy? Until Ştefan tells us everything there's no need to involve him."

"We need to find Reese," Ştefan repeated.

"Shit, if she's gone to the police they could be on their way here with a warrant at any time," Chuck warned, as he began dialing a number on his cell. "Jackie, it's Chuck. NOPD got any kidnapping reports in the last twenty-four hours, or anything involving a Reese Davis? Yeah, I'll hold." Chuck muted his phone. "If they have anything, we're gonna have to haul ass to the safe house."

Gabrielle rose and stood by the archway. "Should I make preparations?"

"Go secure the stockpile and sleeping chambers, baby." Chuck glared at Ştefan. "You should have come to me before doing anything so fucking stupid. This could be devastating." Chuck paused to hear his friend's report. "No, thanks for checking. Please call me immediately should something pop."

"I need to know about Barousse, but first, I've gotta fix this," Chuck said. "Where would Reese have gone, Ştefan?"

"She lived with her brother, so she might be back at his place. You want me to go?"

"Fuck no! You are going to stay with Izzy; at this point you're a major liability. Izzy, take Gabby and Ştefan to your house and wait for me there."

"You might want her brother's address," Ştefan announced indignantly. "Wilson Davis, 709, St. Ann Street, third floor."

Chuck held up his phone and waved in leaving to signify he had things under control. As he passed Isabelle, he ordered in hushed tones, "Find out what he did with Barousse."

Chuck stared at the three-story, coral-colored building. The balconies were confined behind a twelve-foot block wall, with windows facing into the gated courtyard. The adjacent apartment's balcony fronted St. Ann, with stanchions that rose to the roof. Once the street was clear, with acrobatic agility, Chuck jumped up and grabbed the floor of the balcony, swung his body once, catapulted over the rail, and landed with barely a sound. He climbed the trellis and within seconds was on the roof. Jumping to the flat roof of Davis's apartment, he swung down from the roof and landed on the third floor balcony.

Chuck put his ear to the window and heard the sound of a television from inside. The shades were all drawn as he tiptoed window to window. He pulled his lock blade from his pocket and easily picked the old lock. The creaking door announced his arrival long before his foot ever entered.

Reese was there, sitting on the couch in a white cotton gown, her legs drawn to her stomach. In her right hand, she had a gun. "I didn't know who would come for me first, you or the police." Reese's hand shook, as she pointed the revolver at Chuck. "I had to do it, you know. Ştefan left me no choice."

Not wanting to wake the block with a gun blast, Chuck did not move. "Reese, how about lowering that gun, and we can talk this out."

Reese appeared to entertain his proposal, but declined. "I know what you do for the family. Are you here for revenge, or are the police on the way?"

"I am unarmed, Reese. I'm not here to hurt you. What you did in the bayou, he deserved . . . and he's not dead." Chuck waved his hand downward. "Please, just lower the gun. I don't want to get shot, again."

Reese pointed the gun at the floor but maintained a watchful eye. "How can that be? I stabbed his brain and cut his throat."

"Superficial wounds," Chuck said as he stepped one foot inside.

Reese raised the gun. "Don't you mean supernatural?"

Chuck knew if he had any hopes of salvaging the situation, he had to play ignorant. "Well, not really superficial. He may never talk again. The doctors are not sure what neuro damage has taken place. I just came here to find out what happened." Chuck took another step. "Can I sit, *please*?"

Reese sniffled as she waved the gun in the direction of the chair in the corner. "He told me, almost two years ago, he was a vampire, and that your entire family was also."

"Say *what*?" Chuck shouted.

"He locked me in a cabin, in the bayou, because he thought I would tell everyone. He kept me there, promising he was going to free me, promising he was going to make it right.

Chuck shook his head in disgust. "The boy has been off his meds for some time. We knew he was having these fantasies two years ago, but before his family could get him the help he needed, he disappeared, apparently with you."

"He showed me things—with a mirror, and fangs."

"Hollywood props. When he recovers, he'll likely be the one going to jail, or an institution," Chuck said. "How 'bout your family—they must be worried sick?"

"He had this man, Lamar. He would come every few days to bring me food and a laptop. I was allowed to email my family, as long as I went along with the pretense Ştefan and I had gone to South America for missionary work."

Chuck sighed. This was the situation he dreaded the most, death versus diplomacy. Instinctively, he knew what had to be done, but Reese did not deserve it. He had to decide quickly.

"Reese, I want to make you a proposition. I promise that you'll never have to see Ştefan again. For the time he kept you imprisoned, I will make sure that you are abundantly compensated. You'll never have to work a day in your life, if you choose. We will consider the stake in Ştefan's head and slashing his throat fair punishment for his actions, and as such, you will never have to legally answer for that. What's done can't be undone, for either of you. We can only move forward."

"It may not be that easy, Chuck."

"What else do you require, Reese?" Chuck asked, as he silently deliberated the simplicity and finality of option one.

"Chuck, I'm late."

Chuck checked his watch. "If you have to be somewhere we can hash out the details later. I'll have to have a legal agreement drafted up first anyhow."

"Not *that kind* of late, Chuck."

"*Oh* . . . damn. How'd that happen? Lamar?"

Reese fidgeted with the hem of her gown at her feet. "It was Ştefan."

Chuck's jaw practically dislodged. "How?"

"His last visit, about a month ago." Reese began to cry softly. "We did it . . . I have never been one day late, ever. Besides, I can feel something, inside of me. I know I am . . . I had sex with him, hoping he would let me go. When he returned a few days ago, I knew. And I knew if I didn't do something and he found out, I'd *never* be free, ever again."

"*If* you are pregnant, Ştefan will never know, unless you want him to. If you decide to keep the baby, the family will make sure you lack for nothing. For the immediate future, I want you to move to a better, cleaner place, affording more peace and privacy." Chuck watched as a palmetto bug scurried across the floor. "And less unwanted company."

Chuck sensed her mistrust. "Reese, you do know what I used to do. Please, trust me. If I had any doubts we wouldn't still be here talking. Let me do this for you. Let's get out of here, right now. Tomorrow, Gabby will come check in on you and see that you have everything you need. I promise you, the family will take care of you, no matter what."

Reese looked at Chuck for a long minute. "This is all I have to wear."

"See if your brother has something you can wear for the time being. I'll stop by the house and bring you some of Gabby's clothes."

Reese managed a smile. "You seem to have an answer for everything, Chuck."

Chuck managed to match Reese's smile. "Trust me, Reese, I'm making this up as fast as I can."

Chuck arrived at Isabelle's home just before three and found Gabrielle and Isabelle in the kitchen. With a couple of glasses poured before them, they appeared quite relaxed. The creaking of the old wooden floors announced his arrival.

"Well?" Gabrielle prompted.

"Where's Ştefan?"

"Upstairs sulking," Gabrielle answered in hushed tones.

Chuck stepped out of the kitchen and checked the hallway to ensure Ştefan was not around. "We've got a potential problem." Chuck looked to the women, as if he expected them to guess.

"And?" Gabrielle finally relented, fearing for Reese's wellbeing.

"I found her, and so far she hasn't told anyone, but that could change at any moment."

"So you left her there, alive?"

"I moved her to Bienville House, temporarily."

"Why on earth did you put her there?" Gabrielle asked.

"Because you're going there to sit with her, Gabby. She's gonna need food, money, and some clothes. I told her you'd help her with all of that."

"Me? Why do I need to sit with her?"

Chuck sipped from his wife's glass. "Are you ready for the punch line? It's a dandy. Reese thinks she's pregnant with Ştefan's child. She says she did it with him, like four weeks ago, and now her period didn't start. And now she claims she can *feel* something."

"Oh no," Isabelle groaned, as she covered her mouth.

"Which is why she's at Bienville House and why I need the two of you to watch her. This ain't my call no more. The old man would have my head if I dropped the woman carrying his great grandchild, especially if it might be another day-walker."

"We should call Nick," Gabby implored.

"No," Chuck commanded. "Let them have their little festivities, because it won't change a thing here." Chuck touched Gabrielle on the shoulder. "I need you to go sit with Reese while I sit on dipshit and think this thing through."

"What do you think Nick will do when he finds out Reese is pregnant?" Isabelle asked.

"Reese is pregnant?" Ştefan asked from outside of the kitchen. Stepping into the room, he stared at the trio intently awaiting an answer. Lacking any reply, his tone sharpened. "Where is she?"

"Ştefan," Chuck began.

"Don't you mean *dipshit*?"

"If the shoe fits," Chuck replied. "I have her somewhere safe. We don't know for a fact she is pregnant, and if she is, it's a damn good possibility your buffoon did it."

"I want to see her," Ştefan insisted.

"You ain't getting nowhere near Reese," Chuck replied forcefully. As the tension escalated, Gabrielle and Isabelle looked at each other with concern.

"You have no right to keep me from her, Chuck."

"Oh, I disagree, Junior. My wife and I were both shot thanks to your bullshit antics, and we are damn lucky the police are not breathing down our backs for aiding a kidnapper. Reese has no desire to see you after being imprisoned for two years by your psychotic ass, and I promised her I would make sure she never has to, just to keep her from going to the police. So no, I have every right to keep you from her," Chuck thundered as he encroached on Ştefan's personal space.

"If it wasn't for *the fucking family secret* none of this would have happened," Ştefan retorted. "I've really had enough of this shit."

"If it wasn't for the family secret, you'd be dead," Chuck admonished.

Ştefan pushed back at Chuck. "Fuck this. Fuck all of this! In a few days none of it will matter anymore!" he roared as he turned and stormed away.

CHAPTER TWENTY-EIGHT

SARAH STOOD IN the center of the ballroom. For the first time in hours it was quiet; the calm before the storm. The caterers and maids had been scurrying around for hours, like frantic rats. The preparations for the grand announcement, for now, were complete. Sarah gazed at her watch; the musicians would be arriving in a few hours to begin setting up for the night.

She wished Alex was awake to calm her, as only he could. With the sun still up, all of the family rested, leaving her alone for the first time since arriving. They needn't shun the daylight hours; the castle's many windows were designed with automatic sun sensing shades to ensure they could move about at any hour, should the need arise.

In her room, her gown was laid out across the bed—a beautiful crimson dress, with sequins and lace. With her hair curled and pinned, she was sure to resemble her favorite damsel, Scarlett O'Hara. She had spent the better part of the morning with a stylist, who would be returning soon to finish her preparations. Nails, makeup, and hair all had to be perfect for tonight's introduction and announcement.

Her father and the small US delegation spent the night at the palace in Bucharest. They, along with many other dignitaries, would be arriving at eight o'clock. In the meantime, Sarah and her butterflies pretty much had the run of the castle. Absorbed with the intricate carvings of the marble buffet, Sarah did not hear the approach from behind.

"The artistry is quite amazing."

Startled, Sarah turned to the voice. The face was quite handsome. He had blond hair, and his physique was cut very much like Alex's, well-defined cheekbones and warm chestnut eyes.

"Is this your first ball?"

"Yes," Sarah replied timidly.

"It's been a few years since they've hosted such an event. I missed the last one, but once you've been to a couple, it's no big deal. Are you with the caterer?"

Not knowing how much information to divulge to the stranger, Sarah kept her answers short. "No."

"A guest?" His smile was inviting, and he appeared to enjoy making a game of Sarah's vagueness.

"I think so."

The stranger chuckled. "A beautiful woman who guards her identity? Your English is good." The stranger looked up at the ceiling, collecting his thoughts and then raised his index finger skyward. "But of course, you are Secret Service?"

The thought made Sarah laugh. "No, definitely *not* Secret Service."

"Reporter, photographer . . . paparazzi?" Sarah shook her head. "By process of elimination, and those granted access to roam the castle, then you must be Sarah Phillips, daughter of General Phillips, soon-to-be wife of Alex Tepes, and one day"—the stranger swept his hand about the room—"queen of all of this, and of Romania."

"I suppose," Sarah replied with trepidation.

The stranger touched her gently on her arm. "You say that as if you're not so sure."

Sarah chuckled tensely as she looked at his hand on her arm. "Two weeks ago I was simply a college senior, four months from graduation. This is a bit overwhelming. It's such a big change."

"Indeed," the stranger remarked as he stepped away and gazed upon the ballroom. "It will be splendid, the formality of the masquerade, tuxedos and gowns, violins and cellos, music and laughter, all joyously playing across these walls—and lots of whispers. It is quite the spectacle to behold. First come the greetings and introductions, and then there will be the anticipation of tonight's purpose, and then the announcement. After that, *you* will be the center of all eyes. Speculation will run rampant, jealous lies will be told, gossip, and what about Alex? Is he ready to succeed the king?" Amused by the thought, the stranger chuckled again as he swept his arms about the ballroom. "Tonight will be unlike any other event these castle walls have witnessed."

Minutes passed, and believing her nerves could not have been any more ravaged, Sarah swallowed hard as a massive lump scaled her throat. "Who are you?"

"Oh, how rude of me." He took Sarah's hand and kissed it. Assessing her uncomfortable reaction, he apologized. "Forgive me, a habit learned from my father. *I* am your future brother-in-law, Ştefan Tepes."

Sarah's jaw practically unhinged. "Oh my, you're . . . Ştefan? Does Alex know you're here?"

"Not yet. I was planning on *surprising* him tonight," Ştefan said with an unsettling smile. He gazed about the ballroom. "It won't be long now. I'm sure you have much to do to prepare. Until tonight." Ştefan took a bow and backed away, leaving Sarah standing alone.

Sarah sat in the darkened room, fidgeting with her hair, watching Alex sleep. She couldn't help but wonder if she were not here, would he be in his casket? Visions of fleeing the castle, leaving Alex, Romania, and all of this unfathomable nonsense far behind ran rampant through her mind. She was not cut out for any of this. She *had* to leave.

But in the midst of her turmoil, the heart of the truth lay before her, sleeping peacefully. If she left, she would forsake love for the rest of her life. She knew the loss of Alex's love would leave a scar that would never heal.

Sarah's torrent of emotions flowed like a storm-tossed sea, stirring Alex. Sensing her presence, with his eyes remaining shut, he asked, "How long have you been watching me?"

"An hour, maybe," Sarah's voiced called softly from the padded window seat.

Alex opened his eyes and rolled in the direction of her voice. "Have you been up long?"

"Most of the day."

The darkness of the room could not conceal her anguish. "What's wrong?"

Sarah waited a long minute to reply. "I'm terrified."

Alex rolled to the edge of the bed and sat up. "You want to leave?"

"I almost did." Sarah walked slowly to the bed and sat beside him. Laying her head against his shoulder, Alex pulled her close. "I'm not sophisticated enough for this. But I love you so much. I know I have to do it."

"I'm not either, but things will fall into place over time. And if they don't, we'll find a new secret hideaway together. But for tonight, just be the woman I fell in love with."

In the comfort of Alex's arms, Sarah's anxiety relaxed, affording her the opportunity to remember the unexpected bombshell.

"I met your brother."

Alex sprang to his feet. "When?"

"An hour ago. He found me in the ballroom."

Alex paced the floor, his eyes darting about. "Where is he now?"

"I don't know. He didn't tell me where he was going."

Grabbing a T-shirt and jeans, Alex kissed Sarah on the cheek. "I'll be right back." Racing barefoot from the room he ran to Nicholas's bedroom. Rapidly knocking, but with no response, he finally barged in. Fortunately, his parents were practically dressed.

"What is it?" Nicholas asked.

"Did you know Ștefan is here?"

"Where?" Samantha said.

"Sarah saw him, about an hour ago, in the ballroom."

"I don't see how," Nicholas insisted. "Ștefan is in Louisiana." He reached for the phone and dialed. "Is Ștefan Tepes in the castle?" He listened while the guard on the other end checked the security logs. "Thank you . . . Sarah must have been mistaken. There is no trace of Ștefan here in the computer logs."

"Just because security can't find him, doesn't make it so. We've always made a game out of beating the system," Alex said. "I would call them back and tell them he *was* in the ballroom with Sarah, about an hour ago."

Sarah appeared at the bedroom door.

"Come in, my dear," Samantha said. "Alex tells us you saw Ștefan. What did he say?"

"Not too much, he just said he didn't want to miss the big event and that he'd see Alex tonight."

Nicholas dialed the phone again instructing security to search the premise and computer files for a possible imposter. He then dialed his most trusted confidant.

"Chuck, is there any reason you can think of that Ştefan should be here?"

"Ştefan was with me, but now, I don't know. But I've got to tell you, Nick, we have one big cluster fuck here . . ." Chuck apprised Nicholas of the situation with Reese and the attack. Nicholas listened, barely breathing and stunned. He hung up and turned to his wife, son, and Sarah.

"Apparently, things back in New Orleans have gotten quite out of hand," he said with a grimace. "I'm not even sure where to start."

"What is it?" Samantha asked.

"In addition to this Barousse business, according to Chuck, Ştefan kidnapped that girl he was mixed up with two years ago and has been keeping her under lock and key in the bayou. A few days ago, she escaped by stabbing, and nearly decapitating, our son. When Chuck and Gabby went to rescue him, some backwater Cajun shot both of them. After Chuck recovered, he was able to find Reese before she went to the police and now has Gabby sitting on her."

"Oh no," Sarah exclaimed.

Covering her mouth, Samantha stared speechless.

"Ştefan has recovered from his injuries, but Chuck has lost him, again. Chuck also informs me it is quite possible that while in captivity, Ştefan got the girl pregnant."

"Oh no," Samantha bemoaned. "And now he's here, but hiding from us? Why?"

Without an answer, Nicholas shook his head. "But worse yet, the likelihood exists that Ştefan successfully revived Èdouard Barousse, and now we have a rogue vampire somewhere out there."

"I don't believe my brother would endanger us any more than I would," Alex explained. "Besides, if reviving Barousse was Daniel's idea, I'm quite certain there is some higher purpose in all of this."

"Higher purpose?" Nicholas scoffed. "Do I need to remind you of the havoc that followed the last time he had a vision?"

"And as a result you have Sam and two sons. Your father was freed, and look what he's accomplished. Nobody ever said good things come without a price."

Nicholas contemplated his son's logic as he studied Samantha's face, waiting for her customary words of wisdom. "I just worry the price to be paid may be too costly, this time."

Dressed in his favorite black tuxedo, Alex watched in nervous anticipation as the first gondola arrived filled with festive guests. A few hardy, traditionalist Romanians chose to climb the steps to the castle, preferring to arrive in the manner of their ancestors centuries before.

Levente had taken a position in the greeting line, posing as a staff member. For nearly three decades he had stood in the shadows as his human stand-in, Ştanis, basked in the glory. But tonight he would personally greet the guests, just for the opportunity to participate in such a monumental event.

Festive banners and flags of visiting nations had been hung throughout the castle, greeting the dignitaries arriving in droves. In the ballroom, a string quartet echoed classical Romanian tunes through the lower reaches of the castle as the guests feasted on hors d'oeuvres and cocktails awaiting the arrival of the faux king.

Alex's ten-year absence had been billed as a self-induced sabbatical, intertwined with study and soul searching, abroad. Tonight's ball was to be a celebration of his return. The room was filled with dignitaries, or their proxies. Among them was the US delegation, led by his future father-in-law.

The general greeted Alex and introduced Ryan O'Connor, the US vice president.

"So, we finally get to meet the mysterious Alex Tepes," O'Connor said.

"Mister Vice President, I am honored by your presence."

As they shook hands, O'Connor replied, "Please, call me Ryan."

"As long as you promise to keep the general out of trouble."

As they shared a laugh, O'Connor gazed about the ballroom. "It looks to be one hell of a party." O'Connor leaned into Alex's ear. "It is my understanding that we are going to have some opportunities to become better acquainted."

"Yes, I believe that will be true," Alex answered with a sly smile.

"Excellent. I look forward to a long and healthy friendship. Now, may I introduce Secretary of State Louise Taylor?"

"Madame Secretary," Alex said, greeting her with the more traditional kiss on the hand.

"Please, call me Louise," she requested.

"Of course, Louise."

"I understand," O'Connor began, "that very few people know

the true purpose of this soirée."

Alex glanced at his watch. "For another twenty minutes, or thereabout."

"Then allow me, on behalf of the president, to congratulate you. Rest assured, if invited, President Davis would not miss the opportunity to attend such an event."

"I find it quite amazing," Louise Taylor began, "with the media's fascination concerning your reckless youth and sudden disappearance, that you were able to elude not only the press but the international agencies searching for you as well for almost ten years. Our own government had written you off as dead. The world's ability to locate terrorists could benefit immensely from your knowledge and experience."

"I believe the world's ability to deal with terrorism could benefit by the policies my grandfather has implemented during his term as president. But I am sure there will come a time, in the future, when we have the opportunity to discuss such matters."

Although the general did not agree with many of Levente Tepes's foreign policies, he had to smile at Alex's ability to handle Louise Taylor.

"Alex is right, Louise. Tonight is not the time to discuss such matters," the general suggested, rather forcefully.

Taylor feigned a smile in the general's direction before continuing, "I hear you and Sarah met in a coffee shop in Virginia?"

Alex could not help but smile at the happy memory. "Quite the chance meeting. If it hadn't been for one stoplight, I would have been in South Carolina the next morning. One traffic light, and here we are."

"Yes, quite remarkable. The twist of fate," the general remarked. "Speaking of being here, will your father be attending tonight? I would very much like to meet the legend."

Not expecting Alex's father to become a topic of conversation tonight, O'Connor cleared his throat, intending to thwart the general's intentions.

"My father has a great many reservations when it comes to making public appearances, considering the nature of his former employer's retirement package."

"The general briefed the president a few days ago, and it is on the president's behalf that I wish to offer a full apology," O'Connor began. "And while we all understand the covert nature of the agency's policies, we can never know the full extent of their actions. But I can promise you, the agency has been ordered to stand down in your father's affairs."

"Thank you. My father has continued to guard the secrets entrusted to him, despite the agency's efforts, and promises to play nice." The cordial smiles offered by Alex's guests were out of courtesy and not genuine pleasure in regards to his allegations. "But please, tell President Davis, despite the agency's past indiscretions, if I should succeed my grandfather, I hope to usher in a new era of American-Romanian relations. After all, I am a citizen and have lived in America most of my life."

O'Connor's politician's smile returned. "And I would consider it an honor to personally assist you in any way I could."

"At the risk of sounding ungrateful, Ryan, the best support you can offer is to remain clear of our affairs. Any premature collusion between our countries could be perceived, by our mutual enemies, as an excuse to turn their attention to Romania's borders."

"So, you admit we have mutual enemies?" Taylor asked.

Alex smiled at the trio, particularly at Taylor, who was slyly fishing for the commitment his grandfather never would offer. "That will have to be a conversation for another day, Madame Secretary." Turning his attention to the general, he asked, "General Phillips, would you like a little private time with your daughter before she comes down?"

"I believe I would."

"Ryan, Louise, if you will please excuse us, and by all means, make yourself at home," Alex said, as he led the general away.

Trekking across the castle, Alex filled the general's head with trivia about the reconstruction of Poenari. Upon reaching the seclusion of the second floor, the general placed his hand on Alex's shoulder, halting their progress.

"Alex," he began in stern hushed tones. "You and Sarah left so early the other day, I didn't get the chance to talk with you in private again." The general looked to the left and then to the right. "I know what you are."

Alex shuddered. This was probably the only topic he was not prepared to discuss, tonight. "General?"

"Your little visit, asking for my daughters hand, you put me on the spot. So, instead of sleeping that night, I did some research, and after you left, I did more. My daughter loves you, there's no debating that. I saw it in her eyes. But just know this, if you ever hurt her—I don't give a shit about any of this, you, your family—I will make sure you suffer for any harm that befalls her. Are we clear?"

Alex was anything but clear. "I'm sorry, sir, but have I done something to warrant your threats?"

"No, not yet. But before you disappeared, you and your brother were quite the players. Wild parties all over the globe, women, booze, and drugs . . . I could go on. You are still very young, and my daughter is not going to be the fodder of tabloid news while you whoop it up with mistresses all over the planet. Do I make myself clear?"

"That's my past, and it's part of the reason I disappeared. Trust me, if I still desired that life, I *would* be living it. I love Sarah. She has captivated my heart, and I would die to protect her. I hope that's enough."

The general looked over Alex's shoulder, down the hallway of the castle and all of its elaborate appointments, and sighed. "That's all I can ask for."

"Let's go find your daughter. She's eager to see you." Leading the general down the hall and breathing relief, Alex mused, *Perhaps we'll broach the vampire thing another day, like after you're dead.*

CHAPTER TWENTY-NINE

LEVENTE DISCRETELY POSITIONED himself in the middle of the audience. He listened to the conjectural whispers as to the future of Romania, while the guests eagerly awaited the faux king's arrival. A hush instantly fell upon the crowd at the screeching sound of the iron latch and seldom-used door as it swept open.

Lacking the usual pomp, Ştanis led Alex to the stage as a deathly silence swept the room. "My honored friends and guests," Ştanis announced into the microphone, "the anticipation of this night has long been desired; I have dreamt of it for years." Ştanis wrapped his arm around Alex and pulled him close. "As many of you already know, my eldest grandson, Alex, after an *excessively long* sabbatical, has returned home." As applause began to fill the hall, Ştanis hushed the crowd before continuing. "During his time abroad, he has studied international affairs and politics. Upon his return, we have discussed his place within the family and Romanian leadership. Over the course of the ensuing months, we will determine if my grandson will enter the political arena as a potential candidate to succeed me. But, my friends, that is a story for another day. Tonight, we are not here for the monotonous banter of politics; we are here to celebrate. It is with great honor that I announce my grandson is to be married."

The hall filled with a deafening roar of applause as Ştanis

gestured to the ballroom entrance. “My friends and honored guests, please allow me to introduce my future granddaughter, and countess, Sarah Michelle Phillips.” The Royal Honor Guard, decked out in their dress military attire, began parting the ballroom floor, leading the way for Sarah, who was escorted by her father.

At her father’s side, Sarah appeared as if she were floating up the processional. Framed by her spiraling, dark-sienna locks, her face blushed shyly as she smiled nervously to the flashing of hundreds of cameras.

Once the general presented her, Alex took her hand and acknowledged the enthusiastic applause. Not being one for pomp and circumstance, Alex raised his hand to calm the gathering. “Thank you all for coming tonight. I understand the logistical nightmare getting here on such short notice poses. When my grandfather told me he wanted to announce the engagement, I thought he would simply send out an email or two, or maybe place an announcement in the paper.” The laughter helped to calm Alex’s rattled nerves. “As this party is quite the event, I will be very brief. As far as our plans, Miss Phillips and I have not set a date, and at this junction, we have not decided exactly where our future together lies. Please, enjoy the night. We look forward to meeting as many of you as possible.”

After nearly two hours of schmoozing, Alex eventually escaped the spotlight. Making light conversation with a bartender, he finally relaxed while watching his many guests *whoop* it up on the dance floor. Occasionally spotting Sarah through the crowd, Alex marveled at her adaptability. Perhaps she was truly meant for this life. Checking his watch, he decided two hours, no more than three, would suffice before they would be free to excuse themselves.

“She is quite beautiful,” a familiar voice whispered in his ear. “Congratulations are in order, my brother.”

“Ştefan,” Alex exclaimed. Turning quickly, he discovered his costumed brother directly behind him.

“Surprised to see me?”

“I’m not entirely sure *surprised* is the proper adjective.”

“I could not miss my big brother’s grand affair. Not that I remember getting an invitation, or if anybody really gave a damn about where I was.”

“That’s bullshit, Ştefan. We all cared. You chose to disappear.

We all tried to find you. But just like me, Chuck trained you well."

"Yes, good ol' Chuck," Ştefan sneered, his anger still an open sore.

Alex scanned the crowded ballroom. "Have you seen father yet?"

"Do you think I would be wearing this ridiculous costume if I wanted to be seen?"

"They want to see you."

"Is that so? Just two years ago I was right here, ready to be what you would not. I had a woman, a damn good woman, that I loved. But none of that was good enough . . . I was not good enough, my brother."

"It's not like that, Ştefan."

"It is exactly like that." Ştefan jabbed his finger into Alex's arm. "You are the first born, and your blood is pure Romanian. My mother is a lowly American, and divorced for God's sake. And it will always be like that, as long as grandfather rules."

Alex gauged the undeniable anger in his brother's eyes. "You need to speak with father."

Ştefan gazed about the ballroom, looking for any signs of family. "Not to worry, my brother. I will do so, very soon," he replied in curt tones.

An unfamiliar trait in his tone and expression alarmed Alex. "I get it, Ştefan. I really do. But there's something else . . . something you're not telling me. What is it?"

"This. It's all bullshit. Why is it that everyone else is allowed to love who they will, except me. Sarah is beautiful and perfect and she loves you. And they all approve of her, but nobody gives a damn about me and what I want. I'm through with this. I will no longer bow down to the demands of this family. I will make my path, and everyone else can go to hell."

"Ştefan," Alex implored. "You know it has to be—"

"Listen to you, my brother. You have become just like them. You and your happiness can burn in hell, as well." Ştefan turned and hastily exited.

A King's Guard had been watching from nearby and arrived just as Ştefan departed. "Sir, is everything alright? You appeared upset."

"That man, the one who just left by the north passage, have security monitor his whereabouts immediately. Do not let him leave the castle. Then summon my father and grandfather, along with the captain of the guard, to my grandfather's private office. Tell them it is a matter of great urgency that we meet immediately."

Alex waited in Levente's private office, admiring the volumes of books that filled the mahogany bookcases. Levente was often heard to claim that everything one needed to know to be a superior world leader was contained behind the heavy oak and iron office door. There were no windows and only one door. The office afforded Levente hours, if not days, of seclusion when needed.

Lying beside his full leather chair, Alex spied what he believed to be the only work of fiction in the room. Just as he began inspecting the first edition of Stoker's *Dracula*, Nicholas, Levente, and Rojert Belogeise, captain of the Royal Guard, entered.

Levente closed the door, as all attention turned to Alex. "What is wrong?"

"Ştefan *is* here," Alex reported with a sense of urgency. Cutting his attention to Rojert, he said, "We talked for a few minutes, and then he exited the ballroom via the north passage. You need to find him, now." Alex turned his attention to his father. "What has happened to Ştefan? I fear he is up to some great evil."

Nicholas looked at his father, casting an air of blame, before turning his attention back to Alex. "You already know of Èdouard Barousse. We have no idea of his whereabouts, or what Ştefan's plans for him entail. But what we do know is Ştefan had fallen in love and then shared our secret with the girl. She did not receive the news well, and so your brother held her hostage for almost two years. A few days ago she escaped, almost killing Ştefan in the process."

"When were you going to share this?" Levente barked angrily.

"Tomorrow, after the ball was finished." Nicholas sighed heavily. "But according to Chuck, Ştefan became irrational when he overheard that the girl might be pregnant with his child."

"Oh shit," Alex moaned. "This is not good. Ştefan's attitude, it makes sense now. I think he is planning something to force us out in the open."

Levente rubbed the back of his neck as he gritted his teeth. "As soon as the guests are gone, I will call in more security to help locate Ştefan. Once he's found, we will hold council to determine our course of action." Levente gazed intently at Alex. "Ştefan is your brother, and Romania will one day soon be your kingdom. The future of our race may be in your hands to determine, much sooner than expected. You must be prepared to assert your authority in this matter."

"I am going to find Sam and begin searching for him now," Nicholas explained. "It's not like anyone will miss us."

"Alex, please continue as if nothing is wrong," Levente insisted. "The party will begin winding down soon; the last of the guests should be gone in an hour or so."

Levente took the book from Alex's hand. "I had never read this until Samantha told me Sarah was reading it. Should Ştefan cause some calamity, the greater tragedy will be, just as in this book, our race will continue to be portrayed as villains."

Levente swept out of the room with Nicholas directly behind. Left alone with his thoughts, Alex wondered how he would have reacted had his family rejected Sarah. He would have to consider the scenario before passing judgment on his brother.

Returning to the ballroom, Alex discovered Adelina and Angelique continuing to escort Sarah amongst the sea of guests. With only a smattering of guests departed, Alex knew it would be several hours before he could join the hunt for Ştefan.

As the night grew long and the final guests had departed, Alex bid his exhausted fiancé goodnight and returned for a meeting in Levente's office. Seated in a rather rigid armchair sipping bourbon, he wondered why in the hell he ever left Campobello Island. There was absolutely no desire to claim this room, or the castle, as his own. *Count, president, king,* he still had no aspirations to claim any of these titles. He held no sense of obligation, or right, to this ascension of power.

Swirling the glass of bourbon, Alex heard the approaching footsteps across the stone floors, announcing the end of his solitude. Nicholas arrived alone, and his eyes immediately targeted the glass in Alex's hand. "Got another glass?"

"For what it's worth."

"Damn straight. Nights like this I do miss a good stiff drink." He sighed. Out of frustration, he fired back the glass and thumped it hard onto the antique desk.

"You know that was about a four hundred dollar shot. You might want to try to enjoy it, just a wee bit," Alex said.

"Don't worry. I can afford it," Levente said as he breezed into the room. "You and your brother are quite the pair. First, you vanish for ten years, and now your brother has hacked into the most sophisticated security system on the planet and found a way to stroll about the castle without being detected," Levente said. "First with Sarah this afternoon, in the ballroom, and then two hours ago. He is not on either of the videos. It's like he is a ghost."

"I'm no ghost," Ştefan said as he entered the room, his footsteps utterly silent.

"Ştefan!" Nicholas bellowed.

"Yes, Ştefan indeed. Let's not waste time with an endless barrage of "why's" and "how's." I'm here to announce a long overdue regime change."

"Ştefan," Levente roared. "What are you doing?"

"Only what you should have done two years ago. Monday morning you will announce, actually your pawn Ştanis will announce, that he is stepping down in six months and will hold a special election at that time. He will then proceed to endorse me for his succession. I will take care of the rest."

"What in the hell are you talking about?" Levente roared. "What sort of incredulous joke is this?"

Alex looked into his brother's eyes; an unfamiliar phantom inhabited his blackened orbs. "Ştefan, what is going on?"

"What is going on, brother, is a plan I set in motion two years ago. I will no longer be the lowly, bastard grandson." Ştefan glared angrily at Levente and Nicholas. "My life is no longer a pawn on your chessboard. My army surrounds Poenari, and as long as everyone complies, there will be no need for violence."

"*Your* army?" Nicholas cried.

"Yes, father, *my* army, loyal to *my* cause."

"Ştefan, stop this madness," Nicholas demanded as he raised a fist in anger. "We all know where this will lead."

"Your logic is flawed. We are the leaders of the most powerful European nation, a feat accomplished by a vampire. It's time the world learns the truth and learns to deal with it."

Alex studied his brother's peculiar, aggressive expression and tone. "Ştefan, where is Barousse?"

Ştefan's eyes became ablaze with anger. "Where he is, is no concern of yours! What should concern you more is the whereabouts of your fiancé."

Alex's heart skipped a beat as the sum of Ştefan's words struck fear. "Keep him here," Alex demanded as he sprinted from the room. From the office, malicious laughter chased each and every stride of

Alex's flight. The adrenaline rush pushed him dangerously close to supernatural speeds in the castle. Shoving the bedroom door open, Alex found Sarah's gown placed neatly on the untouched bed. After checking the bath he dashed to his father's bedroom. Alarmed by Alex's frantic appearance, Samantha and Angelique rose from their seats by the fireplace.

"What's wrong," Samantha asked.

"It's Ştefan. We've got him in grandfather's office. He's done something with Sarah." Alex flew back to the office and plowed into Ştefan, driving him deeply into the bookcase.

With Alex's hands around his throat, Ştefan made no attempt to defend himself but instead struggled to laugh at his rage. "Brother," he gurgled.

"Where is she?" Alex growled.

Submitting to his brother's grasp, Ştefan wheezed, "She is safe—for now."

Nicholas and Levente crowded in just as Samantha and Angelique arrived.

"Ştefan, what in hell's name are you doing?" Nicholas shouted.

"Alex, what are you doing?" Samantha called.

"It's alright, Mother," Ştefan snorted, his smile rather sinister. "His rage is quite justified. We have taken Sarah to ensure the family will comply."

Samantha's shock took several seconds to register. "What? Why?"

"I have come to claim the throne that my brother declined. And, quite frankly, I am finished with that pure lineage bullshit and being forced to live my life to please all of you."

"Ştefan, Romania is a democracy. I can no more name you president than I could your brother," Levente reasoned.

"Monday, you will announce to the nation that your health has turned for the worse, and that I will be assisting you in all your endeavors. I will have won the people's confidence and will be duly elected when the elections are finally held."

Levente's anger was evident as he snarled, "What makes you think I will acquiesce to any of this foolishness?"

"My army surrounds this castle with an iron grip. You and Angelique will remain here until I have successfully ascended to the presidency. Ştanis will perish in time, as all humans do, leaving my rein uncontested."

"We are to be your prisoners?" Angelique cried.

"The accommodations will be much better, and the internment much shorter, than Grandfather's last confinement, I promise," Ştefan sneered as he finally pushed back against Alex. "Now," Ştefan began, as he straightened his shirt, "for dear Sarah's sake, I must insist you all return to your rooms and find whatever rest you may. Tomorrow night I will lay my plans down in great detail. Do as I command, and in time, you will find our family's name immortalized for all eternity."

"Ştefan," Nicholas pleaded.

"Not tonight, Father . . . or ever again."

CHAPTER THIRTY

IT WAS NEARLY dawn when Alex entered his father's room. "Clearly, my brother has suffered some lapse in sanity."

Samantha's consternation was evident, as she glared at Alex. "They will know you're in here."

"I'm certain they would be disappointed if we merely laid down quietly. I'm assuming they are controlling castle security remotely, which means they have eyes and ears in every room." Alex looked at Samantha sympathetically, and then hugged her. "Ştefan will be fine." He turned his attention to his father and hugged him. "Follow my instructions implicitly," Alex whispered to Nicholas. Alex dragged his hands over his father's shoulders and dropped a note inside his shirt. "We'll get through this," Alex said as he left.

"The sun will be up shortly, and we are going to need all of our strength. But I fear one of us needs to stand watch, in case they try something," Nicholas said.

"They?" Samantha appeared wounded by her husband's insinuation. "You mean our son, don't you?"

"Yes, the one who has now kidnapped two women and rebelled against his own family. *That son.*" Nicholas turned toward the hidden passage that would lead to the catacombs. "Keep a sharp ear; wake me if you hear anything. I do not want to find myself locked in my coffin for the next five hundred years."

Standing in the catacombs beside his casket, Nicholas reached inside his shirt and pulled the tightly folded note from inside.

These words should be from a book of fiction, not this deadly reality we face. Tonight I attempt to find Sarah. At seven o'clock I need you to disable their ability to monitor our actions. In my room you will find a laptop. It is imperative you plug in the power cord before you execute the program that is hidden in my cache of video files, marked Amusement Parks. You will find an embedded file within. The program will instantly disable their surveillance capabilities and allow you to regain control. Once I have secured Sarah and moved her to safety, I will return to assist the family in ending this uprising. Until I have succeeded, there can be no attempt to intercede in any form.

In Ştefan's eyes I see a stranger, not the brother I have loved for thirty-seven years. I honestly believe Èdouard Barousse has somehow corrupted my brother's mind, and I will take necessary action to free him from these bonds. Know that my actions are out of necessity and not anger or hate. When you find Ştefan, guard his mind, as Barousse will attempt to reclaim his body.

Alex

Nicholas knew the peril his sons faced. If Alex was right and Ştefan was under Barousse's power, he could be driven to kill the entire family. And Alex was no trained mercenary. Hell, as far as vampires go, he was still an infant. Standing beside his casket, he knew any to attempt sleep would be in vain. Climbing the steps, Nicholas lamented over forty years of parental choices. Apparently, some were downright wrong.

"I will not be able to rest, so you must," Nicholas announced, as he returned to his bedroom.

One look at her husband's troubled expression and Samantha nearly broke. "And you think I can?"

Nicholas kissed his wife tenderly, and then whispered, "Tonight, when Alex rises, I have to go with him. Have Father take you, Tori, Angelique, and whatever staff remains to the secret chamber, and stay there until I come for you."

Samantha began to object but Nicholas put a finger to her lips. "You already died once for me. I will not let it happen a second time." Kissing her softly, he hoped this would not be the last.

As the sun began to set over the rugged peaks of the Carpathians, Nicholas listened intently for his son's departure. There was no mistaking the screeching of the heavy metal door latch as it began to open. Nicholas sprung to the hallway, eager to intercept his son.

Alex turned, moving to halt to his father's intentions. "Not yet."

"I'm going with you," he whispered.

"If you do not execute your instructions there will be no going anywhere. Please, Father," Alex insisted in hushed tones.

Nicholas stared long and hard into his son's determined eyes. "Wait for me."

"Once Barousse is offline and the castle is secure, you can join me. But do not allow Grandfather to call in the Royal Guard, at least until Sarah is safe."

Nicholas nodded. "Thanks to the doors there's not much hope for surprise. Ştefan's got to know we are up."

"I certainly hope so. It will keep me from having to find him. Now please, go back to your room until it is time."

"I hope you know what you are doing, son."

"That would make two of us," Alex said as he quickly headed towards the stairs. As the castle was remarkably quiet, he assumed his grandfather had sequestered the staff. Determined to draw his brother out, Alex's steps were deliberately pronounced against the marble floors. Once inside the library, it wasn't long before Ştefan appeared.

"Alex, perhaps my instructions were not clear enough?"

"Ştefan, do you honestly think you can succeed in this madness?"

Ştefan sneered, "Madness? After tomorrow the world will know my name. The people of Romania will come to embrace me as their heir." Ştefan pointed angrily toward the portrait of his grandfather. "And then as their president. In time, the world will learn, and then bow down before, Ştefan Tepes, King of the Vampires. The only people that will truly give a fuck, is him and your mother. We will truly be free, my brother."

Searching Ştefan's eyes, Alex suspicions were confirmed. "If that were the extent of your scheme I could walk away. But what happens if you're wrong and the world turns on us?"

"Turn on us? Turn on a world without disease and the immortality we offer? Who would turn on this?"

"I don't know, maybe the trillion dollar industry that caters to disease, religious fanatics, perhaps the mortals left behind that we would feed on, just to name a few."

"Oh, my brother." Ştefan laughed. "Most of these people would kill to receive our gift. We offer what drugs and religion can't. Immortality. By the time the remaining minority rebels it will be too late for them."

Ştefan's cock-sure smile was all the instigation Alex needed. He launched into Ştefan, pinning him against the bookcase with his hands wrapped tightly around Ştefan's throat. "I would ask you where Sarah is, but I know it would be pointless."

"My brother, are we back to this again?" Ştefan's arrogance vanished as Alex constricted his grip. Intensifying his efforts, a sickening doom eroded Ştefan's confidence as he realized he was helpless against his brother's unexpected strength.

"Where is Sarah," Alex demanded, his grip tightening.

"She is mine," Ştefan defied in a voice that was not his own.

The light of the library flickered, signaling his father had executed the power surge. Knowing the insurgents were now blind to his actions within the castle, Alex peered deeply into the stranger's eyes residing within his brother.

"No, Èdouard, she is not yours to take." Sinking his teeth deep into Ştefan's neck, Alex drank relentlessly until Ştefan's body collapsed. Laying his body gently on the floor, he turned at the sound of his father's approach.

"Alex, what have you done?"

"No less than what you did with Gabrielle."

Nicholas bent down and studied his son's body and shallow breaths, so near the brink of death he was incapable of writhing from the excruciating pain. Reflecting back, over forty years ago, he envisioned Gabrielle lying in his lap, contorted in the thralls of death of his own making.

"You've gone too far. I never took Gabrielle this close."

"Gabrielle was not as Ştefan is. Èdouard Barousse has taken Ştefan's mind. This is the only way. If you must, give him only the smallest increments of blood. Do not allow him to regain his mental faculties, or he will be lost to Barousse again. I pray this, combined with Barousse's pending death, will free my brother."

Nicholas could hardly turn his eyes from the specter of the veşteji negru, *the black wither*. "Samantha and my father will have to look after Ştefan. I need to go with you," he said solemnly.

Alex placed a consolatory hand on his father's shoulder. "You must remain here and secure the castle and protect our family. What I am about to do, you cannot."

A spattering of footsteps and conversation from the stairs snapped Nicholas from his amazement-induced shock.

"This would not be the first time in history that family has committed such vile acts against its own," Levente explained as they drew near. "The Bible is full of this type of anarchy. I cannot think of any other course of action."

"But you will put Sarah's life in jeopardy," Samantha argued as they turned the corner. One by one, Samantha, Angelique, and Victoria all gasped at their horrific discovery. As Nicholas rose from the floor, Samantha cried out, "Is Ştefan dead?" The women rushed to Ştefan's body while looking to Nicholas for an explanation.

"No, he is alive, barely. Alex believes Èdouard Barousse has seized our son's mind, and this was his only solution to completely purge Barousse from Ştefan's body."

"How about killing Barousse?" Samantha replied indignantly.

"We do not know where Barousse is hiding," Nicholas sighed. "But if he kills Barousse while he controls Ştefan, our son might never be entirely free of that bastard."

"Where is Alex now?" Victoria asked.

"He—*disappeared*. I believe he has gone to find Barousse." Nicholas's angst was apparent, knowing the unforeseen dangers Alex faced.

"Then we must go with him," Levente ordered.

"No, Father, we can't. He has already left the castle."

"It is not too late. If none of Ştefan's accomplices have breached the castle we will fix our security system and then have Wilhelm track Alex's movements." Levente began to pick up the desktop phone when Nicholas placed his hand on his father's.

"No, we can't. Apparently, my son has learned to shape-shift. He became a mist, right before my eyes."

"How can this be?" Angelique asked, as she and Tori turned their attention from Ştefan.

Levente released the phone and turned to his family. "The legend of shape-shifting dates back to the ancient Egyptians, but only in fiction." Levente looked over to his books, as if he might find the answer tucked away on the shelf. "I have no answer to this phenomenon."

"Gabrielle showed me how to change our physical appearance, is this so different?" Victoria asked.

"Changing one's facial features, skin color, or hair is in itself no simple task. To change bone structure into an animal, or a mist, it is something altogether different," Levente explained.

Victoria mulled over Levente's wisdom briefly before asking, "Like moving so fast that humans cannot detect it?"

Levente stepped up to the inquisitive, fledgling vampire. "That too, is a myth. It is true that we are three times faster than our human counterparts, and our ability to perceive their thoughts makes our reactions appear unfathomably fast, but movement of this nature is quite impossible . . . is there something I do not know?"

"Actually, *that* is quite possible," Samantha replied, as she wiped away her tears and rose from Ştefan's side. "The night I became a vampire, Nicholas attacked the assassin so quickly all of the witnesses swore he simply disappeared. It wasn't until the police reviewed the surveillance files, and watched them in slow motion, that they were able to see him."

Levente eyed Nicholas scornfully. "I have heard the tale of this night many times. Why now am I just learning of this?"

"I don't know how it happened, and I have not been able to summon that power since that day." Nicholas returned to Ştefan's side, knelt down, and sliced his flesh with his fingernail. Spreading his son's lips, he allowed a trace of blood to fall into his mouth.

As Ştefan showed no response, Samantha beseeched, "He needs more."

"No, we cannot allow him to regain any strength. Not until we know Barousse is dead," Nicholas warned.

"We know nothing of Barousse," Angelique objected. "We do not know his strength, capabilities, or the size of his following. There could be a hundred or maybe a thousand of his soldiers. You can't send Alex out there alone."

"I didn't send him," Nicholas barked. "He bloody vaporized all on his own and made it quite clear he did not want any help. So unless anyone can suggest how we can follow him undetected, I am afraid we are stuck here until he returns."

"You said it yourself, my grandson is no warrior," Levente said forcefully. "I must prepare the Royal Guard for an assault."

"No!" Nicholas insisted, as he rose to his feet. "Until we know Sarah is safe, we take no action against Barousse."

Levente cut his eyes sharply at his son. "I am more concerned with Alex's welfare than the young lady's. Allowing him to attempt this rescue, unassisted, may prove the death of them both. If we intercede we can at least ensure Alex's safety."

"If something should happen to that girl, Levente, it will create an international incident," Samantha warned.

"I'm facing a potential coupe with global ramifications. I cannot be concerned with the Americans, or the life of one woman."

Samantha moved in front of Levente. "Yet, if she were to die, perhaps Alex might find a new wife, perhaps even a nice young *Romanian* girl."

"That's absurd, Samantha. Alex's life is very much in danger as well." Faced with an obvious, but rare, questioning of his judgment, Levente paused to consider his position. "We do not have enough security to guarantee the safety of this castle. Regardless of Alex's success or failure, if we do not fortify the castle, our entire family may be at risk from Barousse. We must prepare."

Samantha's anger was apparent, directed first to Levente, and then to Nicholas, whose lack of assertive support was infuriating. Turning to Angelique, she pleaded, "We've both raised Alex. Please, don't let them do this."

Angelique looked to her husband. Never had she questioned his wisdom in the affairs of security. Reluctantly, she sided with Samantha. "Surely, there is some other way. Sacrificing Alex and Sarah cannot be an option."

"Even if they found out the Royal Guard had deployed, they'd be fools to kill their only leverage," Nicholas said.

Levente nodded. "I agree."

Victoria cleared her throat timidly. "May I suggest a plan?" All eyes turned to her sheepish voice.

"If the Royal Guard is prepared to deploy, they could be here in less than two hours. Yes?" Levente nodded. "And you control the castle now?" Again Levente nodded. "And you will know in advance if Barousse attacks?" Levente rolled his eyes, but nodded again. "Why not give Alex time? If Barousse attacks, you can lock down the castle and then call in your Royal Guard, yes?"

"The doors and windows will not withstand an assault from an army of vampires," Levente explained.

"I was told there are passages, that remain secret, to escape the castle. If we are attacked, would there not be enough time for us to make our escape?" Victoria said.

"Retreat and surrender the castle? No, never," Levente said.

"Actually, Father," Nicholas interrupted, pausing briefly to compose his plan, "I think Tori might be on to something. It would be a catastrophe if you attack them in the open forest at night. But wait until Barousse attacks, and no doubt he will use the greater strength of his forces to strike. When he reaches the castle, call in the guard but have them hold at *Căpăţânenii Ungureni*. We only need to hold Poenari for two or three hours, more than enough time for Alex to rescue Sarah. Then we bait Barousse into seizing the castle, but we will escape through the tunnels. By dawn, in the confines of Poenari, without any hostages, your soldiers should be able to finish them off.

Levente didn't take long to deliberate. "I am not sure it is the best plan, but I believe it is the best we can come up with under our current circumstances. I will have security seal the castle, except for the main entrance, until we are under siege." Levente studied his unconscious grandson on the floor. Directing his attention to Nicholas, he said, "Go to Wilhelm and apprise them of our plans. I will take my grandson where he will be safe. Everyone else, quickly as possible, prepare to leave. We have to assume the assault may be imminent."

Levente effortlessly scooped Ştefan from the floor as Samantha and the rest watched with bated curiosity. Aware of the suspicious eyes upon him and perhaps the silent doubts of his intentions, Levente ordered softly, "Go now, I will take good care of Ştefan."

Just as Nicholas prepared to follow the women out, Wilhelm Kurtz, chief of security, entered. He studied Ştefan's limp body in Levente's arms.

"I had hoped to avoid this," Levente murmured to his son.

"Mister President," Wilhelm called eagerly, unable to disconnect from the sight of what he believed might be Ştefan's dead body.

"Ştefan is fine, Wilhelm. I'm afraid my grandson has been up to mischief and as a result it has become necessary to sedate him. Nicholas will brief you on a substantial threat that requires your immediate attention."

Wilhelm glanced to Nicholas, then to Ştefan, and finally back to Levente. "Sir, there has been a new development. General Phillips was to return to America tonight, but as he was unable to establish contact with his daughter throughout the day, he is in route to the castle to personally inquire of his daughter's status."

Levente rolled his eyes. "How soon?"

"Maybe forty-five minutes."

Levente took a step backwards, his consternation evident. "Where is Ştanis?"

"He returned to the palace last night."

Levente looked down at his grandson, then to Nicholas. "We have to turn General Phillips around. I cannot afford him interrupting Barousse's siege of Poenari." Levente paced the room, turned, and paced again. "It may be necessary to wake Ştefan, to some degree, as to ascertain information about Barousse and his forces." Levente turned his attention to Wilhelm. "Call the general back, and let him know we have spoken. Tell him Alex and Sarah drove out into the Carpathians today with intentions of returning to the palace tonight. Tell him that only security remains at the castle, and that the trip will be a waste of time."

"We move on the castle, *now*," Barousse proclaimed without hesitation.

Morgan stared at the blank computer screen, knowing his options were limited. "Shouldn't we give Ştefan a little more time?"

"It is obvious—they have gone on the offensive." Barousse looked to Apollo. "Ready our forces."

"But Ştefan," Morgan objected.

"Ştefan is no longer your commander, I am," Barousse barked. "I have seen his demise, at his own brother's hands no less. He underestimated Alex Tepes, and now I fear he is dead."

"How can you be sure?"

Barousse leaned uncomfortably close and peered into Morgan's eyes with his all-seeing gaze. "You saw it yourself on the monitor," he stated angrily. "If Ştefan were alive, they could not have seized our ability to control the castle security. How long before the Royal Guard arrives? Our forces were not designed to do battle with skilled soldiers. We must capture the Tepes family before that happens."

Morgan looked at the dank, moss-covered walls of the monastery. "I think you underestimate Ştefan's abilities."

"Seven demons of hell, Morgan! Did Ştefan underestimate your intelligence? This monastery is vulnerable, and with Ştefan gone, unless you wish us all to join him, we must strike now."

Knowing Ştefan had devised an alternate strategy should he

be killed, Morgan sighed heavily. "Ştefan trusted you; that much I know. I'll prepare my garrison."

"No," Barousse replied. "I will take your garrison and leave you twenty men to guard the girl. If we should fail to win the castle, she may be our only leverage. Can you still monitor the castle perimeter, or have we lost that ability as well?"

Morgan punched two keys on his computer and the heat signature grid illuminated on the topography map. "If anyone escapes the castle, or approaches any of our positions, be they vampire or human, I will know it."

Barousse studied the computer. Their vampire sentries had relieved their human mercenary counterparts at sunset and now surrounded a wide perimeter around the castle. Barousse thumped the track pad as he studied the positions of the vampire's blue heat signature, as opposed to the red indicators of the humans. "I told Ştefan we needed more men. We are stretched too thin, and I worry the humans are not rested enough."

Believing in Ştefan's tactics, Morgan's confidence was unshaken. "By the time our forces capture the castle, the humans will have had more than enough rest. The Royal Guard is ill prepared to deal with our army in the dark of the forest. If they should arrive in the night, they will be slaughtered. The castle will fall before sunrise."

Barousse reflected on Morgan's wisdom as he stepped away from the computer. Staring at the altar where a mighty crucifix once stood before their human army had stripped away all traces of Christian symbolism, Barousse caressed the jagged slab. "Did Ştefan ever tell you why he brought me here?"

Morgan moved alongside Barousse and stared ahead. "Ştefan shared many things, but never the nature of your purpose."

Barousse inhaled deeply, taking in the musty aroma of the surrounding stone walls. "It was for this very purpose. He never wanted to rule a nation. He only wanted freedom from this life of shadows and his family's domination. He resurrected me to rule this nation under his guidance."

Morgan turned a suspicious eye to Barousse. "Then it is your good fortune he is no longer here to dispute it. I have been with Ştefan from the onset, but I have no aspirations to rule anything." Morgan looked back to Apollo, who stood near the door. "He, on the other hand, might be an issue," he said in hushed tones.

Barousse turned squarely to Morgan. "Ştefan shared his concerns.

He was troubled by what he considered a distinct possibility of having to deal with Apollo's defiant ways. I, too, believe we will be forced to make hard choices, perhaps sooner rather than later."

Morgan silently reviewed his options. He wholeheartedly believed in Ştefan's plans for a new world order with vampires at the top of the food chain. He had no desire to lead a battle, much less a nation. He did not care for Barousse's ascension in rank, but he cared for Apollo even less. Ştefan *had* held Barousse in close confidence since his arrival from New Orleans. The choice had to be made; retreat was not an option. "I find myself in an uncomfortable situation. Our soldier's loyalty and trust may not easily be changed. If Ştefan is dead, and I remain here, there is little guarantee they will follow you—if the attack goes badly."

Barousse's smile was more concerning than reassuring. "That is why you must announce you have chosen me as your general when you give charge to our warriors. Once we control the Tepes family, and begin to implement Ştefan's plans, together we can choose a puppet to rule our kingdom."

"And what of Apollo? I do not believe he will willingly follow either of us, for long."

"Ştefan's plans for Apollo were clear; he will lead the charge into the castle. Should he survive, he will be dealt with accordingly."

Morgan nodded his head while looking toward the passage to the underground crypts. "And what of the girl?"

"Once the Tepes family has been dealt with use her to your delight, and then kill her. She knows too much."

Morgan cleared his throat. "If you're looking to draw the ire of the Americans . . . "

"She is a general's daughter, not the president's. Her death, along with the Tepes family, will be blamed on this insurrection, which we will distance ourselves from. Additionally, our new government's position on technology sharing will delight the Americans. They will shed no tears over the tragic death of one little girl."

Several miles southwest of Poenari, a heavy mist descended in the forest, flowing in and through the snow-covered evergreens. A driving, frigid wind had driven the plume into a dense area of evergreens and undergrowth.

The mist drew to the forest floor, amidst the brush, as if drawn by a magnet. As thin layers collected, the cloud became dense. Initially resembling a Rorschach test, it then evolved to Picasso, and finally pooled together into the shape of a massive, fleshy wolf. Hair began sprouting from the muscular haunches, broad shoulders, and thick neck. As the nose extended, snarling white teeth snapped at the air.

As the transformation finished, Alex let loose a blood-curdling howl, which echoed from the ravine across the neighboring mountains. With his wolf senses intensifying, he sniffed the air and gathered his bearings. Unable to conquer the powerful northeast winds as a mist, he was blown off his intended course in the completely wrong direction. Choosing the shape of a great grey wolf, Alex knew it would be much better suited for the climate and rocky, wooded terrain and provide a natural disguise from his enemies.

Discovering a small contingency of Barousse's forces positioned sparsely around the castle, the wolf restrained his pace. He could not afford to alert Barousse's sentries to his impending approach, or his unnatural speed. From the far side of the castle, it would take almost three hours to reach the monastery.

In the tranquil silence of the dense forest, the wolf listened to the showers of snow falling in hushed spatters. As the wind stiffened it caressed the trees, ferrying the scent of the wolf's prey. Steam bellowed from the wolf's snout as the snow gathered on his thick coarse fur. Howling the intent of revenge, the wolf broke into a gallop in the bleak, frigid night.

CHAPTER THIRTY-ONE

THE ONCE FORMIDABLE walls of the monastery were mostly obscured with vines and brush from a century of abandonment. Sinking in the frozen powder, nearly halfway up his snow-caked fur haunches, the wolf searched until it unearthed a thick branch. Gnawing intently, the wolf tore at the timber until its tip resembled a crude spear. With only the scent of evergreens and the stillness of snowfall, the wolf began its transformation.

Once back in human form, Alex needed clothing. The temperature had dropped to five below zero and his feet were well submerged beneath the fine white powder. Undead or not, it was savagely cold, and he was brutally naked. Utilizing the trees, he traced his wolf tracks back in the direction of the first sentry he had encountered. The vampire's silhouette appeared suddenly through the snow and darkness.

Had the guard been mortal, he would not have perceived Alex's attack. But as a vampire, the instant Alex broke from the cover of the trees he turned and met Alex head on. Ill prepared for an assault by his own kind, the guard's tactical blade was of no use as Alex's six-foot spear rammed into the vampire's chest. His eyes rolled backward, as he grasped at the bark-covered shaft only to feel the jagged wood slip through his hands. As Alex's momentum forced the spear clean through his body, they briefly stood face to face before Alex pushed his lifeless body to the ground.

To date, Alex's expertise killing rogue vampires had come vicariously through his father's tales. A sudden, and unexpected, weakness reverberated through his entire body, both physically and emotionally. He shuddered as the soul of his victim passed through him.

Dropping to his knees, Alex searched the dead vampire and found a duffle bag containing a two-way radio, a half a dozen stakes, a 9mm, and a long knife. Alex used the knife to decapitate the vampire and then hurriedly stripped the sentry's corpse and dressed himself. Grimacing at shoes that were two sizes too small, he stuffed the contents of the duffel bag. Barefoot in the face of the icy blast, Alex reclaimed his spear and wished he was still in the fur of a wolf.

At the edge of the tree line, Alex spied a small group of vampires guarding the great wooden monastery doors. Carelessly approaching too close, he was spotted by one of the sentries. Thinking he recognized the hooded jacket of their comrade, one called out in a Jamaican accent, "Markel, why have you abandoned your post?"

With the snow falling heavily and his hood pulled low, Alex was relatively confident of his anonymity. Replicating the accent, Alex replied, "I've had enough out there. It's too fucking cold."

Using the spear as a walking stick, Alex approached slowly, trying to conceal the blood of his first victim that covered the jacket. Just as the vampire recognized the scent of fresh blood, Alex angled his attack to drive the spear through two of the guards. As the third reached for Alex, he wielded the nine-inch blade and nearly decapitated him. With a second pass of the knife, the vampire's head was completely severed. In the death of three, Alex collapsed to his knees.

Stained with blood, the virgin January snow would not conceal the ghastly fate of his brother's fledgling Jamaican forces; there was no need to hide the bodies. Struggling to rise to his feet, Alex knew with every passing second, Sarah's life was in jeopardy.

As a teenager, Alex had explored the abandoned monastery countless times. Much like Poenari, he believed his brother would have hidden Sarah deep in the catacombs. Unfortunately, the secret tunnels exiting the monastery would be too time consuming to reach and virtually impossible to find in the snow. Chuck had always claimed simplicity was the best offense, so Alex decided to bull rush his way through the gauntlet of adversaries. Although it had been more than twenty years, he believed he could escape through one of two tunnels—tunnels Alex believed his brother had never discovered. In the narrow passages, no matter how many pursued, Alex could easily defend their rear.

Tucking the blade in his waistband, Alex pulled the stakes from the bag. Apprehensive of his failing strength, he looked at the 9mm and spare magazines. He suddenly remembered the tales of his father and the paralytic effects of a bullet to a vampire's head. With supreme confidence in his marksmanship, and three spare fifteen round magazines, he could potentially buy enough time to rescue Sarah and waltz right back out the front door.

Alex checked the magazine in the gun, huffed out a final billow of steam, and stormed through the doors. Six guards crumbled to the floor before the shots finished echoing out. It took Alex two shots to drop the last. For safe measure, he put an extra bullet in each vampire's head, before reloading. Sprinting for the stairway to the catacombs, Alex raced down the jagged stone stairwell until he stood just before the threshold of the ossuary. Bursting through the heavy wooden door, he flashed into the room, hitting two more targets in the blink of an eye. Discovering Sarah's limp body on a granite slab before him, Alex froze in his steps.

With the one remaining vampire positioned behind her, pressing a steel spike to her temple, Alex stepped cautiously forward. The clock was ticking. "Step away from Sarah, and you can leave here with your life. Harm her and you will suffer a fate worse than death, for all eternity."

Morgan pressed the spike until it pricked Sarah's flesh. "Her blood is rich. It will be such a shame to waste it."

"Your rebellion is over. The Royal Guard is sweeping down on Barousse as we speak. If you desire life, release her now," Alex warned firmly, as his demeanor remained calm.

"I can't think of any reason to trust the word of a man who would kill his own brother."

"Ştefan lives but is no longer under Barousse's control." Sensing his foe was far less confident, Alex pressed on. "This entire rebellion was Barousse's scheme. My brother never would have attacked his own family," Alex said, as he took two steps closer to Sarah's captor.

Morgan pressed the spike harder, the piercing of Sarah's flesh now obvious as the trickle of blood intensified. "You lie. Èdouard has seen Ştefan's death—by your hands."

"Èdouard lies. It is his perversion that brought you here, and it will be the doom of you and all of your companions. Release her, and I will take you to my brother."

"Morgan!" a voice called from above.

Alex turned his head to the voice above, and then looked back to his foe. "Our time is running out, *Morgan*. Look in my eyes and you will know beyond all truth, before Barousse can lay a hand on Sarah, I *will* kill us all."

As Morgan deliberated, Alex's patience ended abruptly and he fired. As Morgan collapsed, his shiny metal spike rattled and clanged as it hit the floor.

"Morgan," the voice bellowed urgently.

Alex's foot compressed the stone scrollwork at the base of the slab on which Sarah laid. Shoving firmly, the head of the slab pivoted from its base, revealing a dark passage below. He quickly scooped Sarah's cold, limp body from the slab and made his way through the cobwebs that lined the narrow passage. Once he reached the bottom, he pulled the rusted chain firmly, returning the slab to its original position. Entombed in absolute darkness, even Alex struggled to see in the abyss. Each footstep and breath was the only remaining sound. Cradled in Alex's arms and grazing the frozen stone, Sarah groaned.

"Don't wake yet, baby, I don't think you'd like this place," Alex said.

Apollo traced the steps of the assailant, screaming as he saw his guards sprawled on the ground and bleeding from their heads. "Morgan," he shouted, as he hurried down, only to find their prisoner gone and Morgan on the floor. Rolling the unconscious vampire to his back, Apollo's eyes filled with rage.

Unable to speak, Morgan's eyes rolled aimlessly around their bloody sockets. "Dammit," Apollo scoffed in frustration. As he rose from his knee, the freshly created scuffs in the floor caught his attention. Immediately, but to no avail, he began shoving at the slab.

"Dere mus be a hidden lever," Apollo growled.

Morgan groaned, beginning to recover from his injury. Apollo returned to his side and lifted his head from the floor. "Ar you feelin' betta?"

Morgan raised his hand to his wound and began groping about his fractured skull. "I'm—" Morgan's words abruptly ended, as Apollo's blade dissected his throat from behind.

With Morgan's blood gushing into his hands, Apollo gloated, "You 'ave always been weak, an' now your incompetence 'as 'urt our position. Ştefan is dead, an' I 'ave no plans to follow you." Unfazed by his sudden lightheadedness, brought on by the passing of Morgan's soul, Apollo began licking his hands, cleansing the evidence of his crime.

As two of his soldiers entered the chamber, Apollo stood, raising Morgan's head by the hair. "Look! Look wut dat bastard did to our Morgan! We will find 'im and feed 'im da flesh of 'is woman!"

The abysmal journey through the mountain was painstakingly long, dark, and cold, even for a vampire. The sounds of granite smashing down on granite had echoed for what seemed like an hour before subsiding. Knowing it was highly unlikely they had given up, Alex assumed they had broken through the slab, and the hunt was now on. In the darkness, the passages were unfamiliar, most ending abruptly. If he had mistakenly taken any one of those trails, his worst fear might become reality. Trapped by his adversaries, he would most likely be killed, abandoning Sarah to die in this place never to be found, or a fate even worse.

His one glimmer of hope was a small tunnel in the roof of the passage hidden by an overhanging rock formation. This was the one path he had discovered in his youth, which led to an opening on the far side of the mountain, miles from Barousse's forces. He had explored these caves more than a dozen times as a youngster before finding the hidden alcove. To the best of his knowledge, Ştefan never had. With any luck, if he could find it, the pack in pursuit wouldn't. Even so, this cave had a myriad of false exits, which could take days to sort through.

After several desperate hours in the dark, Alex thought he had found a mark he left two decades ago. Much to his chagrin, he could not decipher whether it was the stone's natural grain or the carved indicator from his youth. As Sarah continued to stir, Alex prayed upon all hope her sedated condition was induced by the consumption of vampire blood, rather than her having been fed on.

Cradling her in his arms, Alex pricked his lip, dabbed his finger, parted Sarah's lips, and guided his finger over her tongue. Repeating the process several times, he paused as her eyes began to open. Seized by fear and disoriented from sensory deprivation, her eyes begged for vision.

"Shh," Alex offered softly. "I have you now, baby."

"Why can't I see?" she whispered.

"We are in the heart of the mountain, and there is no light," Alex explained in tones just above a whisper. "It won't be much longer and we will be out of here."

Sarah began to tremble as her body's senses awoke to the extreme conditions. "I'm cold."

"Next time you get abducted, you might want to dress a little less risqué." Sarah's white, silk negligee did little to cover any parts of her body.

"Are we going to be alright? What's happening?"

"We'll be fine." Alex pulled Sarah tightly, wrapping his field coat around her. "Apparently, my brother, with some telepathic influence from Èdouard Barousse, has been plotting to take over the family empire for quite some time. He has an army, which is in the process of laying siege to Poenari as we speak. But now that you are safe, their leverage has ended. As soon as I can make contact, my grandfather will call in the Royal Guard to end this rebellion.

"Are we going to make it out?"

Alex sighed. "I wish I could tell you yes, but nothing is for certain." One thing that was certain; sunrise would be coming soon, and any hope of contacting, or returning to, the castle was fading fast.

Beyond Alex's sight and sense, a strong shift in the wind along the mountains blew a faint gust into the tunnel. Catching the fresh scent of snow and evergreens, Alex discovered the hidden tunnel. With Sarah securely in his arms, he stood to his feet. "It's time we were moving."

As they neared the mouth of the cave, the bitter winds howled, driving the snow down its throat. As the snow whipped about the jagged opening, the predawn glow outlined the blanketed forest perimeter. In the brief respite from the gusting winds, the sound of leaden snowflakes kissed the earth, filling the passing darkness with a false serenity. Alex knew Sarah could not survive the journey alone.

"The sun will be rising soon. There is no lightless refuge within safe traveling distance for me. I'm afraid we will have to wait out the day and strike out just after sunset tonight."

Sarah's face was nuzzled close to Alex's ear. Speaking weakly, she said, "I'm terribly cold."

Alex sensed Sarah's strength waning, as were his options. Unsure if they would remain hidden before the sun had set again, he stared at the flesh of her neck, her life and salvation in his arms. Constricting his resolve, fear whispered in Alex's ear, *Take her.* Removing his overcoat, Alex denied the demon. "Curl up tightly," he instructed Sarah. After she complied, he wrapped his jacket around her body.

"You need your jacket," she objected.

Alex tucked the jacket under her feet and then wrapped his arms around her, pulling her tightly. Harnessing all of his conscious thoughts, he began to elevate his body temperature. "I might be a little cold, but when the moon rises, we'll still be alive."

Trembling in his arms, Sarah felt a growing warmth envelope her body. As her shivering subsided, she strained to make out just a glimpse of her future husband. "I never told you when I fell in love with you. Did I?"

"The coffee shop?"

"Don't flatter yourself, Prince. You were not *that* charming."

As Alex smiled, his eyes illuminated an effervescent blue, allowing Sarah a glimpse of his face. "How'd you do that?"

"There're many things I can do, but they all require a great deal of concentration, some more than others. If I talk much longer, I will not be able to maintain my body heat."

Sarah became quiet, but only briefly. "It was the next day, in the hotel." Sarah waited for a reply, which did not come. "Do you realize that you have not written a single bit of poetry since that day?"

Alex did not immediately afford Sarah the satisfaction of an answer. As his body heat generated to Sarah, the creeping frost gnawed at his back. In a voice unfamiliar to her he spoke:

In the heart of the darkest season
where hope is a brittle memory
Love taunts those who seek refuge
within her gates,
with bleak eyes of sorrow
where no refuge is offered
and callous barbed arms
await the fools blinded by the promise of spring.

And yet here in the shadows
the fool sojourns on.
Heedless of the suffering
with outstretched arms
he beseeches the siren,
"Have your way with me.
For I shall withstand infinite heartbreak,
to bind up all that she is,
and live just one day
in the light of hearts so pure,
that neither time nor death
will erode our love."

As life's eternal tide
turns all that remains
to dust.

CHAPTER THIRTY-TWO

"WE WERE LUCKY to have survived the assault," Nicholas exclaimed. Samantha touched his shoulders gently, trying to soothe his rattled nerves. Acknowledging her gesture, he continued, "Only the imminent threat of daylight saved us, but now that Barousse has discovered our weakness, he will exploit it when they return."

Levente propped his hands upon the desk and sighed. "If I summon the Royal Guard, in all likelihood, Barousse will kill Sarah, and if they have him, Alex as well."

"There is still time," Samantha pleaded. "Until we know about Alex and Sarah, or Barousse actually enters the castle."

"There is less than an hour before sunrise. If Alex does not return . . . " Levente's attention drifted to the bookcase across the room. Pulling a map book from the shelf, he thumbed through the pages. "My men are reinforcing the tower door, but if Barousse focuses his invasion on the tower, we will not be able to withstand the assault." Levente unfolded the map and sprawled it across his desk. "Judging by the direction of their retreat, and the hour at which they pulled back, I feel certain their camp must be here." Levente's finger pointed to the abandoned monastery. "Judging by the hour of his attack tonight, we can assume the next attack will occur about the same time. I will have our special forces prepared for a rescue mission at the monastery, once the castle falls."

"Ştefan may be able to provide you with answers," Samantha added.

Levente understood her logic, but more critically, knew her emotional motives. "No, Samantha, we dare not risk rousing Ştefan until Barousse is dead."

Samantha turned her head away sharply. Outside of directly disobeying Levente's orders, she sought any angle that would release her son from the excruciating pain of the *veșteji negru.* Years ago, Gabrielle had recounted her own personal experience of the *black wither* to Samantha. The psychological scar left behind from sharing the experience never healed. And yet now, her very flesh and blood laid deep within the bowels of the castle writhing in agony, and she was helpless to abate his suffering.

"How many of Barousse's forces were killed?" Angelique inquired, in an effort to break the awkward silence.

"Six," Nicholas replied. "It would be nice to know just how many soldiers are in *this* army. Isn't it possible to reconfigure the Doppler to search for the heat signature of vampires?"

"It is, but then we will no longer see the humans," Levente explained.

"We already know there are thirty, and it would appear their only task is to maintain the perimeter. I really don't think Barousse would allow a band of humans to steal his glory."

Levente considered his son's logic briefly before picking up the phone. "Recalibrate the Doppler to fifty-seven degrees Celsius and expand the range out to sixteen kilometers. Call me with the results immediately."

Gauging Samantha's consternation, Angelique wrapped her arms around her tightly. "We *will* get our sons back."

Samantha leaned her shoulder into Angelique and feigned a smile. "I wish I could pray for that, but those days ended years ago.

Infuriated by the failure of his army to breech the castle and capture the Tepes family, forced to retreat in fear of the rising sun, and livid over Alex Tepes's escape, Barousse swiped his arm across the altar, sending candles, goblets of blood, and maps flying across the room. "What do you mean you cannot find them?" His enraged words echoed throughout the monastery.

Barousse's eyes filled with malice; he grabbed Apollo by the shirt and pulled him close. "Take all of these men, if you must. No one rests or comes out of that tunnel until Alex Tepes and that little bitch are back in my possession."

Demonstrating the necessary restraint Ştefan had preached, Apollo allowed Barousse's rant while every molecule within him restrained from striking Barousse down. Not knowing where the allegiance of the troops would fall, Apollo would bide his time until the guilt of Barousse's death could befall a deserving scapegoat. And that time would come . . . soon. "I will find them myself—to avenge Morgan's death. The men need rest if they are to march on the castle again."

"March they will, and tomorrow night, we will toast our victory with Tepes blood," Barousse proclaimed boldly. "The castle will fall tonight, and I will have no need for prisoners." Barousse released Apollo, realizing his authoritative aggression might alarm or displease him. "The end of the Tepes lineage is in your hands. If it pleases you, Apollo, impale their heads as a trophy to bear witness of your great accomplishment."

"Ştefan brought me to dis life. He an' Morgan were my brothers." Apollo paused to gaze at Morgan's headless body. Drawing his machete from its sheath, he hoisted it high. "I will cut da limbs from 'is livin body, then violate 'is woman before 'is eyes. I take her head an fill 'is mouth wit her flesh. I will open 'im and pierce 'is 'art, leaving 'im to bleed slowly to deat."

Barousse smiled as his mind was filled with the vivid, savage images. Part of him yearned to witness the event, while a greater part yearned to taste the flesh of Sarah Phillips. He knew he could not yield to the great temptation of the flesh ever again. It was, after all, this weakness for Monique that led to his two hundred years of entombment. Barousse considered a similar fate for Samantha Tepes to avenge Monique's murder by the hands of Nicholas Tepes.

Monique, so sensuous . . . beautiful . . . erotic . . . mesmerizing, captured his fancy like no living woman. Barousse freely offered his life to her; the thought of ageless years of passion with this sultry vixen was enticing beyond all dreams. Then wrenched away and imprisoned, each suffered unbearably for two hundred years. And in her brief freedom, she was savagely murdered at the hands of the cold-hearted mercenary. Nicholas Tepes, this usurper had to suffer an excruciatingly painful death.

Apollo could have Alex and Sarah to do with as he pleased. It was, after all, Nicholas Tepes that Barousse prized above all the others. The black wither, yes. Bleed Tepes to the point of death and force him to watch as Barousse performed every imaginable vile act he could conceive on Samantha. And yes, as Apollo had suggested, then feed him his wife's flesh.

"Go, find the children. Do all the evil you desire, and then join us at the castle. By then, Romania will be ours."

Apollo affirmed with a nod and a confident smile. With Ştefan, Morgan, and eventually the Tepes family dead, Barousse would be the only obstacle left to deal with. He could not have scripted a better plan. He scampered into the tunnel and disappeared from sight.

Dusk was within his grasp. The storm had ended three hours ago, and now patches of sunlight streamed through the snow laden trees. Alex need wait only about fifteen more minutes before he could race down the mountain with Sarah in his arms. There along the mountain pass he could requisition a car to speed them back to Poenari.

Just as he was about to wake Sarah, the faint footfalls of an approaching intruder elevated his alertness. Shaking Sarah gently, he covered her mouth. "Someone is coming. We've got to go."

Carrying her to the mouth of the cave, he set her down, her feet covered with makeshift shoes cut from his field jacket. "The sun has not set, so I cannot go with you. You must run straight, as best as you can, down this mountain. You will find a road in about twenty minutes. Go left when you get there, and you will find some cabins where you can seek help." Alex looked over his shoulder in the direction of the advancing enemy. "They are coming for us. You must go now."

"I'm not leaving you," Sarah objected, tears forming in her eyes. "I will die here with you."

"You don't understand. Death would be welcomed compared to what I fear they will do." Alex held Sarah's face gently. "I cannot fight them off if I also have to defend you." Sarah's expression did not convey an accord. "If you stay, we will die. You must leave, now." Alex ushered Sarah out into the snow, wrapped his field jacket tightly around her, and gave her a kiss. "Your feet will get cold, but don't stop. Head straight down the mountain as fast as you can. I'll catch up soon."

"I love you," Sarah said softly, not letting go.

"Then go quickly." Alex forced her from his arms and watched as she disappeared through the trees. Ten minutes, plus whatever amount of time he could stall before the pack would be hard on her trail. He turned slowly and awaited his unseen enemies. The wind through the tunnel remained brisk enough to usher his scent towards the closing threat.

Whatever relief Alex felt after discovering but one opponent, quickly dissipated as he summed up Apollo's massive physique. Were he mortal, there would be no concern whatsoever of his Herculean adversary, but he was a *vampire,* and a colossal one at that.

"Where's da girl?" Apollo barked.

"I sent her down the mountain at sunrise. By now, she should be back in Bucharest."

Apollo sneered; his barbaric plans of a brutal execution lay wasted. He quickly summed up his barefoot and shirtless foe. "Ready to die, Alex Tepes?" Instantly Apollo lunged at his foe, swinging the machete wildly. The blade found its mark, slicing deeply into Alex's side, cutting him nearly in half. Bleeding profusely, lunging and falling, Alex staggered deeper into the cave before he collapsed to the ground.

Standing at the mouth of the cave, Apollo looked at the fresh tracks in the snow. "Deez tracks don' look so old." Sniffing the air, a sinister smile crossed his face. "She is near." Apollo towered over Alex, reliving his initial intentions, while gazing on his mortally wounded opponent. Forcing Alex to his back with his foot, he lunged the machete through his left chest, piercing the lung and driving the blade deeply into the cave floor. Blood gushed from Alex's chest and mouth. Dropping to his knees, Apollo got in Alex's face. "In tree hours, Barousse will take da castle and kill your familee. I wish I coud be der, but"—Apollo looked outside at the fading light—"I tink I can now fine anoder way to 'ave fun. I be right back, don' go nowherez."

"Where is President Tepes," General Phillips growled, as he stood in the door of Levente's office.

"Please, come in. Let me pour you a drink," Levente offered, as he rose from his desk.

"Under the circumstances, I'd rather not." The scowl on the general's face warned Levente there would be no compromise. "My daughter is missing, and somehow an overturned fuel truck closed the highway here for nearly a day. I don't believe for one minute that both of those kids are traveling without phones. So unless you can produce some line of communication with my daughter in the next five minutes, I will have no other choice but to notify our State Department, and the president, as to my daughter's disappearance."

"General, please, come sit by the fire." Levente ushered the general to the fireside couches.

"Cut the hospitality horseshit," the general barked. "Where's my daughter, and where is President Tepes?"

Levente's eyes darkened. "I must insist, General, please sit down."

General Phillips had never experienced such an overwhelming necessity to comply with an undesirable request. Unaware of Levente's true identity, or powers, he blindly took a seat on the sofa. "I believe you know my son, Nicholas, or as you once knew him, Brian Denman."

"Your son?" The general's neck snapped sideways toward the sound of Nicholas's arrival. Jumping back to his feet, he nearly choked as he gazed upon what had to be some kind of sick joke. "What's the meaning of this? This cannot be Brian Denman!"

Nicholas glided into the room, void of speech or emotion. He stood in front of the general and peered into his eyes. "Just like seeing a ghost, General?"

Shocked by Nicholas's ageless appearance, the general swallowed hard. "I don't know what kind of bullshit nonsense is going on here. If this has something to do with my tenure at the agency, you will not use my daughter as a pawn for whatever retribution you are seeking."

Nicholas sighed heavily and turned to his father. "Shall I?"

Levente poured himself a scotch and looked at the general. "I will pour you a glass. Perhaps in a few minutes you will be ready for it, or maybe, should I say, need it." Levente poured two extra glasses and sat them on the mahogany table.

"Sit," Nicholas commanded, and the general begrudgingly complied.

"Before I explain all of this," Nicholas said, waving his arm about the room, "including my appearance, I'll advise you of our awkward crisis. We are in the middle of a small rebellion, which unexpectedly began last night. The rebels have kidnapped your daughter, and while I cannot confirm any operational progress, by now, our forces should have reclaimed Sarah and moved her to safety. Needless to say, any communications might give away our strategy, or her current location, and further prolong this uprising. As Alex is leading the effort, you should take comfort in knowing he will do nothing to jeopardize her life."

"I'll take that drink now," General Phillips said gruffly.

Levente extended his hand with the drink. "We will get her back, I promise."

The general nodded his head, took the glass, and shot the whiskey down. Levente offered a refill and the general extended his glass. "This rebellion, just how extensive is it?"

Levente set down the decanter and took a seat across from the general. "Small, maybe one hundred fifty soldiers, leadership included. We have already killed a small number of their troops and captured one of their leaders. After tonight, it should be all but finished."

"What is this all about? We were not aware of any terrorist chatter," the general reported. "Where is President Tepes?"

Nicholas looked at his father who nodded his approval. "General, there is a reason I look exactly as you remember. But before you rush to any snap judgment of my mental competency, you should know, I can prove every word I'm about to tell you." Gauging the general's skeptical expression, Nicholas knew this was going to be an uphill battle. "I would have much preferred you hearing this from Sarah, but due to current circumstances, I will have to suffice."

"Get on with it," General Phillips prompted, after taking another drink.

"The man you and the world believes to be President Tepes is a charlatan." Nicholas extended his drink in the direction of his father. "This *is* Levente Tepes, and I am his son Nicholas, or as you last knew me, Brian Denman. Our family does not suffer the human frailty of aging or disease, therefore, you see me as you remember. We are Nosferatu, or as you would more commonly refer to our race, vampires."

Outraged by the incredulous nonsense, the general stood up. "Just how stupid do you think I am?"

Nicholas waved his hand and the general's speech and body seized. Standing calmly before him, Nicholas continued, "Before you waste precious seconds trying to justify your limited knowledge of life's realities, let me say, I can recite every detail of each and every mission I performed for the CIA. Or maybe you'd like to hear the graphic details of the night you sanctioned an assassin to terminate my life. Perhaps, I could just show you these." Nicholas opened his mouth and flaunted his glossy fangs. "Or we can stand before a mirror, but I promise, my reflection does not exist."

The general's muscles twitched as he futilely struggled against Nicholas's dominating will. "Yes, you are beginning to understand. Before I release you, know this, our family has peacefully existed for hundreds of years without the need to take human life. My son Alex has not, and will not ever, harm your daughter for all of her natural life. He loves her, and at great risk to his own life, has gone to secure her freedom." Nicholas gently motioned his hand, releasing the repressive force he held over General Phillips.

"Any further discussion of what we are, or your daughter's relationship with my son, needs to be tabled until Sarah is safe and this unexpected rebellion is crushed."

Winded from his brief struggle, the general breathed heavily as he stared at Levente. "And you are truly Levente Tepes?"

Levente nodded. "Under different circumstances, Sarah and Alex were planning on returning to America and explaining our peculiar *circumstances* to you. As that conversation has been delayed, I must ask for your word that the nature of my family be held in the strictest of secrecy. You do understand the pandemonium that would ensue should the world learn of our existence . . . of our immortality."

Stupefied, General Phillips flopped back down, and with his mouth unevenly cracked, he silently stared at the flames. If not for the crackling of the logs, the room would have been void of all sound. Even though it remained half filled, General Phillips held out his snifter for a refill. "My daughter, is she one of you?"

"When they took her from the castle, she was not a vampire. It is our most sincere hope that she return the same."

General Phillips looked back to Nicholas. "You and I, we need to have a conversation—one day."

"Under better circumstances, we will, one day soon."

Apollo dragged Sarah back into the cave. "Look what I 'ave found, lit'l man." Half screaming, Sarah cried out for Alex, as Apollo flung her to the floor. Ripping open her jacket, he gawked at her scantily covered body. "I will enjoy dis lit'l morsel."

Apollo turned his attention to where Alex had lain, to find only Alex's impaled clothing remained. "Wut is dis, some trick of sorcery?" Apollo dragged Sarah to the pool of virtually frozen blood and then swept his foot through the gritty stone mix. Tugging forcefully against the blade, after several attempts it snapped in half.

Without a trace of Alex's whereabouts, there was nothing for Apollo to follow. "Maybe dis will bring your boy back." Kneeling down beside Sarah, he ripped open her negligée. "Come back, coward, an' watch me tear dis up."

Just out of Apollo's sight, a pink vapor pooled to the floor. Assimilating rapidly, the mass began to form a large torso with four stumps. As the thick neck took shape, the legs elongated and fur erupted over the entire body. Transforming last was the head, as ears and jaws lined with razor shape teeth, sprouted from the core. Intense black eyes, rabid with fury, set their sight on the tunnel ahead. Blood dripped from the wolf's belly as it arched its back, leaned onto its haunches, and then catapulted to the sound of Sarah's screams.

Straddled over her body, Apollo held his broken blade in his left hand while he wrestled to undo his pants with the right. Constantly fighting off Sarah's defensive punches, his attention strayed from the approaching danger. "Yeah, baby, dat's it, fight me."

The massive shadow came too fast. Even with his vampire perception, Apollo had no time to defend himself. With the wolf's mouth agape, its bear-trap jaws clamped down on Apollo's neck and drove him from atop Sarah. Almost twice Apollo's size, the wolf was impervious to Apollo's hacking at its ribs with the remnants of the machete. Thrashing side to side, the wolf flailed Apollo about until, with a bone crunching snap, he severed the vampire's head.

Propped on her elbows, bearing witness in absolute terror, Sarah crab crawled on her back toward the wall of the cave. As the wolf turned his attention to Sarah, she whimpered, "No."

The wolf padded forward, his gray fur saturated in Apollo's blood. Sarah recoiled into a fetal position. Weeping, nearly in shock, and expecting to be ravaged, she stared down the eyes of her destiny. With Apollo's blood dripping from its mouth, the wolf grimaced as its body began to contort before dissolving into a pink mist. It wasn't until Alex stood before her, completely naked, that she realized what had transpired.

Alex touched his hand to her lacerated temple. "You're hurt."

Sarah rose to her knees to inspect Alex's injury. With blood still trailing from his chest, Sarah touched his slowly healing scar. "I think you're hurt worse."

Alex pulled the oversized field jacket around her tightly before retrieving his own clothes. "I'll explain this later, but for now we need to get back to Poenari before it's too late."

"You should leave me here. I'll only slow you down."

Alex looked down at his body, and then smiled back to Sarah. "If you think I went through all of *this,* just to abandon you . . . " Sweeping Sarah back into his arms, he kissed her before pulling her close.

Through all of the traumatic events, Sarah's adoration held steadfast in her gaze. "You never told me, what was it that you think I took from you at the coffee shop."

Alex beamed as set his sights on the trees below. "My heart. But it doesn't matter now. It's yours to keep."

CHAPTER THIRTY-THREE

ALEX FOUND A château within a kilometer of the first road they crossed, less than a half hour after they began their descent. A man answered Alex's knock, believing him to be victim of some horrific auto accident. Once he had identified himself, and the urgency of his need to return to Poenari, the man gave Alex some clothes and a blanket for Sarah and blindly handed over his car keys, merely asking Alex to kindly return his SUV when done.

Sarah remained silent as Alex flew through the snow-covered mountain passes. Urged by his grandfather to return to Bucharest, he knew his brother's only hope was Barousse's death. Without bait, Barousse would likely flee in the face of the Royal Guard.

At the bottom of the southern approach to the castle, Alex stopped the car, got out, and sniffed at the air. "Where are you, Èdouard?" Sweeping Sarah into his arms, he ascended the ancient stairs to the castle. At the top, he studied the perimeter of the castle grounds, searching the forest for anything amiss. "I'm here," he said softly into the borrowed cellphone, his words forming a frozen mist.

The centuries-old steel bolts and reinforced teakwood doors screeched, broadcasting the labor of its task. Any hopes of a stealthy return were now laid to waste. Alex looked about impatiently, as he waited for the doors to swing open. Once the light from within the castle became apparent, with Sarah clinging tightly, Alex dashed across the footbridge to the welcome safety of Poenari's walls. He was long down the hall before the heavy thud and subsequent clank of the bolt afforded him relief.

Greeted by his family, and the general, in the great hall, Alex was quick to dispense with the congratulations and immediately began instructing his family of his intentions.

"Tori, take Sarah to her room. She needs warm clothes. The rest of you, especially the two of you"—Alex cut a glare to his father and grandfather—"prepare to evacuate the castle."

"But . . ." Nicholas began.

"No buts, Father. I am going to draw Barousse out and kill him. Unless anyone else can shape-shift, then you can't go the road I travel. By the time they take the castle, and realize we've abandoned it, we will all be safe. The Guard can finish them off after sunrise."

"I can help," Nicholas insisted.

"Barousse is a coward. If we are both there, in all likelihood, he will have his soldiers kill us both."

"Then let me draw him out. I killed Monique. I'm the one *he* really wants."

"They're too many; they will kill you, and nothing will be resolved."

Angelique rubbed her forehead. "The stubborn Tepes pride. Haven't we seen this before?" Directing her attention to Levente, she explained, "As dangerous as it sounds, I think Alex is right. If Barousse is not destroyed, we may never get Ştefan back in whole. If Alex's scenario does not present the opportunity to kill Barousse, his abilities to escape greatly exceed our own."

"My mother is right!" Alex proclaimed, as he collectively gauged his family's reactions.

It had been over an hour since Sarah had spoken. She stepped away from her father's arms and took Alex's hands. "Please don't go."

"I'll be safe."

Samantha had heard *that* promise before. "No," she objected loudly, recalling Nicholas's deadly confrontation with Monique and, years later, with Vincent. "I've heard that promise *too* many times before."

Nicholas stared at Alex, knowing if he failed he could lose both sons tonight. With great consternation, he replied, "We have to let him try."

"You promise me, Alex Tepes, if you cannot safely kill Barousse, you will get the hell out of there," Samantha pleaded.

Alex looked at Sarah's tear-filled eyes and haunted face, knowing Barousse's blood poisoned her as well. "I promise."

General Phillips stepped in front of Alex. "My daughter loves you, that's a fact. And you executed one hell of a rescue mission as well. But what you're proposing sounds more like a suicide mission. There's over a hundred hostiles approaching the castle, and I don't think they are going to allow you anywhere near this Barousse. So if that's the extent of your great plan, I say we *all* abandon the castle and let your grandfather's people take out Barousse and run clean ops."

"I can handle this," Alex said calmly.

"Son, your old man was a hell of an operative in his day, the best ever." The general peeked at Nicholas out of the corner of his eye. "But from what I know of you, you've never had one single day of military training. If anybody else wanted to volunteer, I'd say have at it. But Sarah loves you, for God's sake. Don't do this to her when you know there's a damn good chance you won't return. None of us need to die tonight. Call the Guard in, and let's all get the hell out of here together. We can rendezvous with the Guard in the morning."

"General Phillips, perhaps you forget our limitations," Levente injected.

"Oh damn, that's right. Sunlight."

As they all exchanged glances, awaiting another suggestion, Alex turned to Sarah. "Go with Tori and get some warmer clothes on. We'll all meet in my grandfather's office." Turning to the rest of his family, he sighed. "Alright, you win. Let's go."

"I have evacuated the remaining staff through the catacombs with instructions to remain there until dawn, unless they are discovered before," Levente reported to his family and the general.

"Why are we not with them?" Samantha asked, as Tori and Sarah arrived in the office.

"The southern tunnel may not be the safest escape. Although few people know of its existence, enough do. Ştefan knew of the tunnel, so our enemy may be waiting as well. That is why I've instructed the staff to wait in the catacombs until sunrise, when the Guard arrives."

"Why is the staff not going with us?" Samantha inquired.

Levente walked softly to the stone bookcase on the far wall of his office. Pulling two dusty books from the lowest shelf, he blindly felt for the latch. "Let's hope this works. This passage has never been used; its very existence is known only to three stone masons. No one else must ever know of it, else its secrecy will no longer remain."

The stone wall groaned as it begrudgingly cracked open. Even with all his vampire strength, Levente struggled to swing the bookcase open wide enough to allow their passage. A brief rush of musty air filled the office. On the rough granite, just inside the passage, hung a rack with lanterns.

Levente warned, "The way is treacherous, it is narrow and steep, with many twists and turns. At times you will have to watch your head. Lead them down with caution," he instructed Nicholas. "Alex and I will secure the passage and follow you down."

Alex kissed Sarah. "He needs my help to secure the door," he said, as he released her hands. "I'll be down right behind you." Sarah's expression revealed her apprehension and weakness, her eyes were pale and distraught, her feigned smile, a mere courtesy. "As soon as this is done, whatever you want, it will be yours," he promised.

Sarah's eyes offered only infinite weariness, as if their future was shrouded in doom. She kissed Alex softly on the lips. "It's only you."

He watched as Samantha, Angelique, and Tori began the descent behind his father. The general took his daughter's hand and led her down just four steep steps before they turned right and disappeared.

"I'll get the door, Grandfather," Alex said, as Levente replaced the books on the shelf.

"On these steps, without proper leverage, it may take both of us to pull it shut," Levente said as he stepped into the passage.

"No," Alex said, as he shoved his grandfather in, causing him to stumble. "Only one." Alex put all of his weight and strength into the bookcase and shoved until the thud and clank proclaimed the door was bolted shut.

As Alex moved through the office, the eerie silence that befell the deserted castle caused him to pause and listen for any evidence of life. Moving through the grand foyer, he began unbolting the main doors. Little wonder Barousse had abandoned his attempts to break the doors down. Without the aid of a hydraulic battering ram, the doors were impregnable. The thickly covered wood interior and exterior concealed armored steel plates built to withstand grenade launchers and light artillery shells.

The industrial hinges and bolt mechanisms were stainless steel constructed to withstand time, the forces of nature, and human assault. Had the tower access been made of the same design, outside of a nuclear bomb, the castle would have been unassailable. But a small sortie by Barousse's troops had scaled the stone tower, discovered the weakness and, after hours of effort, breached the tower. In the confines of the narrow stairwell, Levente's security team had managed to kill the small group of raiders. As the threat of dawn forced a full retreat, the Tepes family survived the initial assault.

But tonight, Barousse would launch the entirety of his strength at the newly discovered weakness. Overwhelming the scant resistance reported from their initial attack, the castle would fall quickly unless Barousse could be baited into another course of action.

With the assistance of its mechanized motor, the castle's main doors swung wide open. As a blast of cold air and a shower of snow blew deep into the hall, the tapestries slapped against the walls. The threat of renewed bloodshed cast the darkest gloom imaginable on the field of virgin-white powder.

Slushing beyond the reach of the foyer light, Alex trekked into the field of shin-deep snow. With the windows tightly secured and Poenari's spotlights doused, Alex's silhouette faded from sight against the surrounding forest.

"Èdouard Barousse," he bellowed against the rustling of the wind-tossed, snow-laden evergreens. "Èdouard Barousse, I am waiting for you."

"He's gone," Levente called out, as he rushed down the stairs to catch Nicholas.

"What do you mean?" Angelique asked.

"He pushed me inside the passage and sealed the door. He means to face Barousse, alone."

"Alex?" Sarah stammered.

"We have to go back," Samantha insisted.

"It's no use," Levente said, as he turned and stared into the darkness above. "The door is impenetrable from this side. The only way out is down."

"Then we have to go, Father," Nicholas implored. "Angelique and the general can take everyone to Bucharest." Nicholas turned to Angelique. "You know how to find the auto depot from here?" Angelique affirmed with a nod. Nicholas directed his attention back to his father. "We must help Alex."

Levente grabbed his son's shoulder. "If they are not guarding it, we can re-enter the castle from the catacomb's tunnel. It's only a kilometer from here."

Levente turned to the general. "General Phillips, I leave my family in your hands. They are all that matter to me."

"I will keep them safe," the general promised. "Go get our boy."

Levente and Nicholas pushed open the passage door, checked the surrounding forest for insurgents, and then disappeared in the flash of an eye.

Alone with a small battalion of women, the general shook his head as he knew what his daughter had in mind. One glance at the remaining women, and he knew they already agreed with Sarah's mindset. "We should go with them," Sarah implored.

"As my husband has reminded me on several occasions, we are no match for an army of the undead," Angelique replied. "But armed we could at least slow them down. At the last landing we passed on the way down there is a small armory."

"No," General Phillips insisted. "I promised your husband to take you to safety."

"No, you promised to keep us safe, Dad," Sarah objected. "So I guess you're going with us to keep us safe."

The armory contained an assortment of guns, antique swords, and crossbows— everything they would need to battle with humans. As the general rummaged through the boxes, he grimaced. "I don't suppose we'll find any holy water or crosses in here."

Samantha inspected a box of vintage, Italian-made Beretta 9mms. Pulling a magazine from the dry storage locker, she shoved it in the gun, aimed at a stack of old tarps, and fired. Inspecting the bullet hole, she said, "This will do. Everybody grab two guns and as many magazines as you get in your pockets. We can at least slow Barousse's men until Alex is safe again." Samantha turned to the general. "General, please take Sarah to the palace at Bucharest. You will be safe there."

Sarah took a gun from the crate, smacked a magazine in, racked it back, and fired into the tarp. Ejecting the magazine, she cleared the chamber and handed the gun to Samantha for inspection. "I know how to shoot. I will not leave without Alex."

"You will only slow us down, Sarah. We must go without you," Samantha replied sympathetically.

"No!" Sarah barked defiantly. "All of you are willing to risk your life for Alex, as he did for me. I might not be a vampire, but with your permission or not, I will not abandon him or run while the rest of you fight my battle. Before this night is over, I will see Èdouard Barousse's blood on the snow."

General Phillips took his daughter's hand, determined to take her to safety. But the tears in her eyes and her obstinate expression convinced him otherwise. Conflicted by his love for his daughter versus his training as a Marine, he submitted. "Soldiers never abandon their brothers, regardless of the risk, and neither should family. You go ahead, and we will follow your tracks. My daughter is a fine shot."

Pleased with her future family's resolve, Angelique allowed herself a glimmer of a smile. "General, take a sword. If you should encounter a vampire, shoot it and then remove its head, please. If you come across any that have already been shot, please show them the same courtesy as well. I will have my chief of security, Tursik, waiting to lead you through the catacombs."

"Be safe," Tori said to Sarah before she and then Angelique and Samantha exchanged brief hugs and disappeared below.

"Shooting people is nothing like target practice. Are you sure you're up for this?" the general asked as he searched deeply into his daughters eyes.

"They are trying to kill the man I love, and if you'd seen the things I've seen them do, you wouldn't even ask." As Sarah headed down, she turned abruptly. "Besides, the entire world is counting on us."

As the general chased his daughter into the darkness, Sarah's words reinforced his resolve. Not only was it the fate of the world but the very existence of their entire race, resting in the ensuing battle.

"Èdouard Barousse," Alex bellowed into the night, the name expelled in a frosty plume of frozen breath.

Through the pitch black, snow showers, and trees he felt his adversaries' approach. The first silhouette to breach the forest perimeter was none other than Barousse. One by one, the thickness of evergreen sentinels yielded to a host of vampires. As Barousse continued toward Alex, he held his hand high, bringing his army's march to a halt.

His dark, shoulder-length hair waved in the stiff breeze, as did the tails of his long coat. Bearing a staff nearly as long as Barousse was tall, the slender vampire's deep-set eyes locked onto Alex's.

"I see you have eluded Apollo," Barousse said, as he measured each step forward.

"I've spent the better part of my life eluding people, Èdouard. It is a lesson that would have served you well. Attacking my family demonstrates a lack of civility and, to be perfectly honest, intelligence. I would have expected more of you."

Barousse snarled as he clutched his staff tightly. "Can I assume that you claim superiority with those attributes?"

"No, actually, I don't." Alex gauged the distance between Barousse and his forces as he spoke. "But I am here to put an end to this. My family is safely on the road to Bucharest as we speak. In the morning my grandfather's Royal Guard will be cleansing these mountains of you and your insignificant rebellion."

"They have abandoned the castle?" Barousse's sinister laugh echoed deeply into the woods. "You are right, Alex Tepes, perhaps you are not so smart. Defended by my soldiers, Poenari will be impregnable. We will break your grandfather's feeble human army and feast upon them. They will become my soldiers, and together we will march on Bucharest, where I will extinguish the Tepes lineage. And then I will make Sarah Phillips my blood whore."

Alex's confidence staggered at the notion. But his resolve and self-induced predicament left no other options. "Èdouard, you were a vile and evil man in life, as you are in death." Alex's words rang out clearly to all of Barousse's army, which remained gathered at the tree line. Riding a distant wind, a rumble of thunder rattled the core of the mountain. "You are the source of evil that curses this entire planet."

Barousse clutched his staff tighter and stepped slowly towards Alex. "It will take more than a rumble of snow thunder to save you now, boy."

Alex rolled his head to the heavens, and with the snow kissing his face, he cried out, "*Tată, mă adăpost de rău. Aruncat cei care păcătuit, şi deşi credinţa mea ma eliberat.*" Rumbling angrily, as if responding to Alex's calling, the thunder shook the ground violently.

"Nor do I fear your meaningless incantations." Barousse swept his staff quickly, its honed tip driving into Alex's chest and bursting out his back. Impaled through the heart, Alex clutched the staff and crumbled to his knees. As he fell backward, the tip of the spear propped his body in a grotesque deathly pose. Barousse laughed madly, amidst the roar of the encroaching storm.

A piercing cry erupted from the castle. "*No!*" Arriving to witness that fatal moment, Nicholas Tepes screamed in rage as he beheld his son's fate.

"Nicholas, we can't," Levente implored, as he yanked his son back inside the door. "We must bar the doors, or we shall all perish."

Locking in stares of animosity, Levente and Barousse exchanged their silent lethal intentions. "Old man, you are next," Barousse bellowed, as a bolt of lightning struck deep in the forest. "Let us finish this tonight, like men."

Resolved to save his son, Levente turned away and shoved Nicholas back inside to clear the door. "He will pay for this outrage. But we must go now if we are to avenge Alex." Lightning streaked the sky, blinding eyes against the frozen field of white. Just before the door slammed shut, Levente looked upon his dead grandson one final second, with Barousse gloating above his prized trophy.

Screaming of his conquest above the raging storm, Barousse proclaimed, "Poenari and Romania are mine. Let tonight mark the dominion of our race." Sweeping his arm at the castle, he ordered his troops, "Take the castle, seal the catacombs, but leave Nicholas Tepes for me. Kill everyone else."

A large drop of rain fell upon Barousse's face. Turning his eyes to the heavens, he laughingly bellowed, "Not even Your rain will beset the reign of Èdouard Barousse."

CHAPTER THIRTY-FOUR

LEVENTE AND NICHOLAS returned to the catacombs and were met by Angelique, Samantha, and Tori all armed for combat. "What are you doing here?" Levente barked in agitated tones.

"We came to help," Angelique replied. "Why are you here? Where's my son?"

Nicholas took Angelique by the arm as Levente stood silently behind. "We were too late. Alex is gone."

Tears streamed down Angelique's face. "What do you mean?"

"Barousse killed Alex," Nicholas explained, the confession crushing his spirit into tears. "It happened just as we arrived. There was nothing we could do. With his army surrounding him, I could not even retrieve our son's body."

Levente touched his wife on the shoulder. "Barousse knows of the tunnel to the catacombs. We cannot avenge Alex if we are dead; we must go immediately."

Sobbing in Nicholas's arms, Angelique gazed at her husband and nodded.

Surrounded by the remaining staff of Poenari, all human, Levente barked out their options. "Barousse will seize our home shortly. Regretfully, there are but two options. You may choose to remain here and fight them off with the weapons you have. You only need hold out until dawn when the Royal Guard will arrive. If you choose to leave with us, it is three kilometers to the auxiliary transportation depot, through the snow and dark and the enemy. Either option will be perilous."

Levente's personal chef Wilhelm stepped forward, waiving a butcher's knife. "We will hold the catacombs, sir. Not one of those cowardly bastards shall pass this way."

"Wilhelm, you are a true and brave friend," Levente said while shaking the gruff Romanian's bear-sized hand. "We must go without delay." Levente suddenly noticed Sarah and her father were not amongst them. Turning to Samantha, he asked, "Where is the general and his daughter?"

In the face of Levente's ire, Samantha explained boldly, "They followed us. There was nothing we could do to stop them."

Could this possibly get any worse? Levente thought before huffing loudly. "I only hope this disobedience will not prove to be a lethal mistake." Levente lightly touched Angelique's cheek. "We must go with all haste."

As the group sped their way through the tunnel, they were met head on by Tursik. "Sir, Barousse's forces have reached the tunnel. I have sealed it, but I fear it will not hold long."

In despair, Levente turned back to his family. "If I cannot reach my office there will be no way to notify the Guard."

"We will go together," Nicholas insisted. "You may need my help getting there."

"These might help," Samantha said as she handed Nicholas her guns and ammunition.

"Sir, there is more," Tursik warned. "The general and Miss Sarah, they were coming through the forest to the tunnel but were captured."

Levente wanted to lash out at his wife and Samantha for their disobedience but refrained. The heartbreak of their loss was a colossal burden already. Choosing Tori as the unwitting and undeserving target of his irate glare, he fumed, "This is why you people need to listen to me. I am the president, after all."

As Levente and Nicholas reached the top of the passage, the hidden door in the great dining hall noisily creaked open. Listening intently, Levente slowly pushed the passage-concealing portrait of his grandmother upward. "It's clear," he whispered to his son. Moving quickly, he checked the hall before continuing. "They must not have breached the tower yet. If we should meet resistance, I will run interference. Lock yourself in the office door and call in the Guard. Then take the office passage back into the tunnel. You must remain there until you are sure it is safe. With Alex gone, now more than ever, it is imperative for you to survive me."

As Levente began to make his move, Nicholas grabbed his shoulder. "I will run interference. I have had the training. This is your country and your people. Only you can set things right."

"If we hurry, perhaps we both can make it." Levente quickly mulled over his plans. "After we've made the call, we can take the tunnel and circle back, and possibly take out Barousse's garrison at the catacomb entrance. Undoubtedly, they have taken Sarah and her father to Barousse. But if we are successful, the staff and our wives can still escape. Then you and I can see if any hope remains for the Americans. I owe my grandson that much."

"First things first," Nicholas said as he stepped in front of his father, "let's make that call."

The shuffling of their shoes was the only sound to be heard throughout the castle. Finding his office empty, Levente headed to the phone on his desk. "It is too quiet. Something is wrong."

Nicholas stood by the door, prepared to slam it shut at the first sight of invaders. As Levente brought the phone to his ear, a muffled thumping interrupted the eerie calm. Levente set the receiver down and walked back to the door. "What is that?"

"It appears to be coming from the castle's main doors," Nicholas suggested. "Make the call, and I will investigate."

Levente watched as his son cautiously made his way past the row of armored knights, moving with cat-like stealth, to the source. Nicholas looked back over his shoulder and lipped, *Make the call*, to his father. Through the thick timbers encasing the armored plates of Poenari's grand entrance, somebody was pounding from the other side.

Nicholas looked back once more; the marble arched stairwell to the second floor remained empty and quiet. Through the impenetrable stone walls, Nicholas was unable to fix his thoughts on the source. Removing a sword from the nearest armored knight, Nicholas returned to the door and propped it against the wall. If it were Barousse, he would at least kill his foe before a word could be uttered. Taking a Beretta in each hand, he keyed the entry code. The locking mechanisms swung into motion, as the metallic clanging of gears and bolts broke the still of the castle. Nicholas raised his hand, indicating for his father to hold his position. As the door groaned open, Nicholas was overwhelmed by the spectacle before him.

General Phillips stood in the doorway, grief and awe residing within the wrinkles of his face and the steely blue of his eyes. Over his shoulder, the bodies of countless corpses were strewn cross the lawn as a smoldering mist rose from their ruin. And in the center, Sarah had collapsed on her knees, holding Alex's lifeless body. Speechless, Nicholas stared at the carnage.

Sensing his son's dismay, Levente called out. "What is it, Nick?" Without a reply, he eased his way toward the door, forgetting about the call. As he joined his son, his eyes cast out bewilderment. "*What* happened here?"

"They captured us and brought us here to Barousse. Just as he was about to kill me the snow turned to rain, and it was like acid. He screamed—they *all* screamed as the water seared the flesh from their bodies. It was unlike anything I've ever witnessed."

"How could this be?" Nicholas asked. As he stepped to the threshold, Levente grabbed him by the arm. "I need to go to my son!" Nicholas implored.

"You cannot go out there. Whatever killed them might kill you as well. Touching Alex could be just as deadly," Levente warned.

Levente reached out and lightly touched the general's damp jacket. Recoiling his hand quickly, amidst a small plume of smoke and an instant acute pain, he winced. "It is holy water."

Nicholas looked to the snow-filled sky. "But how? Did Alex somehow arrange for the Forestry Service to deploy their firefighting aircraft and have them drop holy water on Barousse's army?"

The general looked back at his daughter, still cradling Alex's lifeless body. "If he did, it was nothing short of a brilliant strategy."

The trio all stared at the heartbreak transpiring before their eyes. Once more, the snow began to fall heavily, blanketing Sarah and Alex's corpse.

Levente's eyes sharpened on Alex's body. "Where is the cursed staff that impaled my grandson?"

"You promised." With all of her emotions completely exhausted, Sarah's tears no longer fell freely over Alex's body. Three times her father and the Poenari staff had tried to bring her and Alex's body inside the castle walls. Resigned to allow Sarah whatever time she needed, the family stood vigil in the doorway of the castle, watching for hours while reflecting on their love for Alex. Samantha had returned from the catacombs, with Ştefan following weakly. Devastated by the death of his brother, he sat alone on the floor, crouched in a tight ball.

"Sarah," General Phillips began, as he brushed away the thick coat of snow from the blanket draping the pair. "It's almost dawn, and you're nearly frozen. It's time to come inside, baby."

"The dawn will no longer harm him, you'll see," Sarah replied in broken tones. "Just a little bit longer, Daddy."

"The Royal Guard will be here soon, so not too much longer, dear." General Phillips looked back to Alex's family and raised his hands in surrender. Levente nodded his head, agreeing to allow Sarah to remain. As he approached the castle exasperated, he sighed. "I don't know what to do with her."

"I should go talk with her," Tori offered.

"No, Tori. I am afraid whatever holy water remains may still cause injury," Levente insisted. "When she is ready, her father and my staff will bring them back."

As the light from dawn turned the sky from black to gray, the Tepes family retreated deeper into the great hall, avoiding the discomfort that the light of day created. The snow had eased to flurries, and as the sun climbed higher, an occasional ray would break through the trees and the cloud's waning armor to find rest on the field of white.

Sarah lifted her head for the first time and surveyed the morbid field; Barousse's soldiers were little more than mounds of snow. Alex's blood had been purified white by the cleansing forces of the virgin powder. As a golden ray of light highlighted his body, Sarah marveled at his serenity.

Raising Alex's head, her lips met his for one final kiss. "I will always love you." Lowering his head back to the earth, she attempted to rise against her aching joints. A new reserve of tears began to flow as she pushed away from her love. "I will stay, if you just ask," she beseeched. With no reply and unable to feel her legs, unsteadily she pushed herself up. Looking back to her father, who remained standing patiently at the castle door, she nodded.

"*Staaaaaaay.*" The sound was soft and low, like whispering trees, the frigid breeze caressing their branches. Fearing to look,

Sarah solemnly took her first step away.

"*Staaay.*" Hushed, but more distinct, even though her goodbyes were completed, Sarah had no choice but to turn her attention to the source.

"At least long enough to help me up. I appear to be frozen to the ground." Although weak, but mirthfully mischievous, Alex's gaze filled Sarah's soul with instant jubilation. She lunged herself back into Alex, raised his face to hers, and kissed him, as if her life hung in the balance.

Witnessing his daughter's sudden collapse, and unaware of the reason, the general sighed. Turning his attention to Levente, he shook his head. "I think it's time we bring your grandson in, or my daughter is likely to freeze to death."

Levente silently motioned to his staff to carry out the unpleasant task. General Phillips turned back to the frigid lawn and grunted as he stepped back out into the cold. Squinting, he shielded his eyes from the sudden jailbreak of sunlight. "Sarah," he called gently. The sound of Levente's men trudging through the snow behind him drew his attention to their progress.

"Daddy, he's alive."

The general's head whipped around so quickly he nearly lost his balance. "Baby, there's no way." As he reached to touch Sarah's shoulder his eyes bulged from their sockets.

Alex's gaze met his, and with a weak smile across his face, Alex said, "Sir."

"You were dead. What happened . . .?" General Phillips surveyed the immediate area, looking for the staff that had impaled Alex only hours earlier. "Where's that confounded spear that killed you?"

"It melted, Daddy, in the rain," Sarah said gleefully.

"Can you help me up? I really am freezing," Alex stuttered.

General Phillips extended his hand, as Sarah guided Alex's head and shoulders up. Alex winced sharply as the general tugged. "Damn my chest hurts like hell."

Levente's staff halted immediately, witnessing the amazing resurrection of Levente's grandson. In the calm of the bitter January morning, the joyous proclamations of the miracle fell silent in the overwhelming presence of great faith and love.

As the clouds parted and sunlight barreled down on the assembly, Tursik was quick to warn, "Sir, the sunlight!"

Alex turned his face fully toward the glowing orb. “Oh God, I had forgotten just how good that feels.”

“Alex?” Sarah shrieked.

“It is faith,” Alex affirmed gratefully, basking in the golden glow, “that has defeated our enemies. Faith has broken the bonds of my curse and set me free.”

CPSIA information can be obtained
at www.ICGtesting.com
Printed in the USA
FSHW012301140521
81465FS

9 781633 933989